PRAISE FOR
THE INHERITOR

"Vivid, terrifying, and all too possible,
Tom Wither's novel sets a high bar in the
darkest speculative corner of the political thriller niche."
—Larry Brooks,
USA Today bestselling author of *Darkness Bound*

"*The Inheritor* is a spectacularly good thriller—
banging with action, filled with absolutely fascinating
and authentic details from the world of military
intelligence—fans of Tom Clancy will love it!"
—Max Byrd,
author of *The Paris Deadline*

THE INHERITOR

THE INHERITOR

Tom Wither

TURNER

Turner Publishing Company
424 Church Street • Suite 2240 • Nashville, Tennessee 37219
445 Park Avenue • 9th Floor • New York, New York 10022
www.turnerpublishing.com

THE INHERITOR

Cover design: Maxwell Roth
Book design: Kym Whitley

Library of Congress Catalog-in-Publishing Data

Wither, Tom.
 The inheritor / Tom Wither.
   pages cm
  ISBN 978-1-62045-495-4 (paperback)
1. Special forces (Military science)--Fiction. 2. Terrorism--United States--Fiction. I. Title.
 PS3623.I8647I55 2014
 811'.6--dc23

                              2014008606

Printed in the United States of America
14 15 16 17 18 19 0 9 8 7 6 5 4 3 2 1

Mom & Dad—Words just can't say enough.

To the men and women of the armed forces, intelligence community, federal and local law enforcement, and first responders throughout the United States and all their families—your service and sacrifices reflect the best of our nation's ideals and principles.
Thank you.

ACKNOWLEDGMENTS

Charlie, Ed, Elizabeth, Renee, Steve, and Warren for making sure I
didn't step over the line, Ellen for the eagle eyes, and Roger, my agent,
for appreciating my storytelling.

PROLOGUE

DAWN WAS HOURS AWAY A few nights before the new moon, the last sliver of the waning crescent almost gone, stars predominately hidden by thickening cloud cover. A pervasive silence hung over the farmland district of Abbottabad, broken briefly by the sounds of a stray dog foraging in the grass for rodents and other small animals for his midnight snack.

The houses in the northeastern section of Abbottabad belonged to lower-middle- or middle-class Pakistanis. Overall, they were clean and well-kept but modest structures usually separated by swaths of tilled and untilled land for the more well-to-do citizens, and houses backed up to one another on smaller plots for those less well-to-do.

Most of the houses in the farmlands were dark, save one. It sat in the center of the base portion of a large, triangular-shaped property, much larger than those nearby. The property's northern base leg was more than one hundred meters long, while its angled borders were more than seventy meters long each.

All along the compound perimeter stood a privacy wall whose western portion was ten feet tall, growing taller and then shorter as it stretched toward the eastern portion of the compound. As the wall flowed around the compound's southern border, it rose to eighteen feet to prevent a direct view of the main house, and then returned to ten feet in the northeast corner. The interior of the compound was designed to make any assault difficult. A short driveway running roughly north to south between two ten-foot-high inner walls with gates at either end divided the compound down the center into two major segments, eastern and western. The main three-story house stood in the eastern segment, abutting the northern base leg, its west wall a few meters from the inner wall protecting it from the driveway.

The compound had been built not quite six years ago, when it became apparent that a comfortable and safe hideaway was needed for the holy warrior sheik, his youngest wife, his two most trusted couriers, their families, and a few trusted fighters. The main house's roof was just beginning to weather from the strong winter storms that lashed northern Pakistan, its whitewashed concrete walls showing the first signs of minor cracking. The holy warrior sheik Osama Bin Laden and his youngest wife and some of his young children lived on the third floor, his two most trusted couriers and their families split between the first and second floors.

There was also a smaller, narrow one-story house running east-west along the southern portion of the inner wall protecting the main house. Immediately to the south was the apex of the compound's triangular perimeter. A few meters to the west were the inner vehicle gate and a pedestrian door in the inner wall that led to the inner courtyard and main house. A few single male jihadis occupied the smaller house and acted as a very rudimentary guard force, hardly worth the title. The compound was intended to be as unobtrusive as possible, but little things betrayed it if one looked closely enough: the barbed wire that topped the protective walls, the expensive satellite dishes for receiving European and Middle Eastern news broadcasts, and the fact that the small number of women who lived in the compound did not socialize with the other women in the small Abbottabad suburb of Bilal Town.

The thin, nineteen-year-old man with the broad shoulders and dark hair moved slowly up the steps in the main house to the third floor. The holy warrior sheik, the man he thought of as his surrogate father, had sent word to the small house for the young man to come see him. After passing through the small door in the inner wall surrounding the main house, he had crossed the short expanse of bare ground to the main house and been allowed to enter by the guards at the door. Another guard, who stood at the top of the steps before the door to the holy warrior and his young wife's quarters, lowered his AK-74 and tapped on the door behind him.

The door opened, and Bin Laden's wife beckoned him inside. The interior was illuminated by three small freestanding lights scattered around the rooms, the smell of cooked lamb and curried rice in the air from the evening meal. Electricity, television, and running water were the only modern conveniences. Internet and telephone lines would never enter this house or the smaller one.

The small set of rooms Bin Laden shared with his wife were functional, cluttered, and sparsely furnished in a largely open floor plan. A queen-sized mattress sat on a roughly hewn, darkly stained wooden frame next to a smaller twin bed with only a thin foam mattress. As was proper, Bin Laden slept on the larger bed, his wife in the smaller, less comfortable one, when she did not remain in the area reserved for the women in the rear of the first floor.

Some clothes, a few cushions, a cabinet for clothes, and old shopping bags were strewn about the common area. One small alcove held a desktop computer untouched by the Internet, a few laptops, several CD-ROMs, and USB memory sticks. Two prayer rugs lay on the floor before the beds, facing a little south of west toward Mecca. A cardboard barrel for trash dominated the common room, its contents taken outside and burned periodically to avoid the local trash collectors from compromising Bin Laden's location. A lone, inexpensive television sat on a wooden table against the eastern wall near the windows.

The house and the living conditions would never be considered opulent by Western eyes, but for the small middle-class suburb of Bilal, it was very comfortable.

Aziz spied his surrogate father kneeling on the prayer rug near his bed.

"Come in," called Bin Laden in Arabic.

Obediently, the young man moved to the older man and sat on the bare floor before him. It would not be proper to have knelt on the other prayer rug beside him unless bidden.

"Yes, Father," he replied, waiting patiently.

Aziz carefully watched the older man shift his weight on the prayer rug to a more comfortable position before he began to speak. He was in his late fifties; his long beard had turned nearly solid silver from the combination of age and the added stress from the infidel's hunt for him. His brown eyes held life, but not very well. The thick lips beneath the angular nose marked a tanned face and thin brows, his face instantly recognizable by nearly anyone in Southwest Asia, or the world for that matter. When he left the compound, he often dressed as a woman, both to hide his features and conceal the AK-47 he always carried. When his men drove him to meeting places, he sat in the back of the car as was proper for a woman, and therefore was paid no heed by others.

"Aziz, my son, you are strong. In time, you will grow stronger still. I have watched you carefully these past few years and you are mindful of the needs of our jihad. When Alem became ill and could no longer serve us here, you did what needed to be done, and now Alem is in Paradise."

As always, the older man referring to him as his son warmed Aziz. There was no bond of blood between them, but Aziz had always thought of him as his father. His own father had abandoned him and his mother when he was six for an infidel female. Fortunately, as he grew into a man, he came to hear the words of the holy warrior sheik and know the truth in them. After spending time as a child courier in Afghanistan's mountains for the holy cause, he had fought in his first battle when he was fifteen. Then, with Allah's guidance, he had come to join the holy warrior himself during his movement into the tribal lands to this protected location.

Aziz began to reply but the older man silenced him with a touch upon his knee and a warm smile. His hand felt cool to Aziz, betraying his medical condition.

"For now, listen, my son. I want you to hold this for me."

The older man held out an old and very-well-cared-for copy of the Qur'an. Aziz took it reverently, marveling at Bin Laden's generosity.

"My son, this is the Qur'an of my father. But it is not just the book of our faith that is dear to me. It is the key to our everlasting victory over the infidel. Open it to the last page."

Aziz did so and saw, written in Arabic on the inside cover in a firm hand, a series of telephone numbers.

"The numbers you see are not what they appear. The first six digits are the account numbers that hold the money the faithful have given to us to aid our holy cause. The last four numbers are the access codes needed to add or remove funds."

"But Father, why give this to me? There are others more—"

"No. You are the one to hold it. You are strong and Allah is with you. I entrust you with this knowledge because of the strength of your faith in Allah and our cause. No one knows of this but you and me."

"Yes, Father. Thank you."

"There is one other thing you must do for me."

"I shall do whatever you ask, Father."

Bin Laden smiled and continued, "That Holy Qur'an is more important than I am. You must protect it at all costs. Guard it with your life. I will have your promise before Allah on this."

"I swear before Allah I shall treasure and preserve this Holy Qur'an for as long I live."

Bin Laden smiled again. "I know you shall. Allah is great and merciful and I thank him every day for bringing you to me to serve the jihad against the Great Satan. Return to your quarters and sleep now. You will have duties to perform in a few hours."

Aziz rose and looked down on Bin Laden, silently begging for Allah's aid and mercy that he might keep his surrogate father strong and cure him of his afflictions. Clutching the Qur'an to his chest, he left his mentor's quarters and passed back through the guards, exiting the main house.

Aziz returned to the small house and entered, being as quiet as he could to avoid waking the three men sleeping on the floor in their sleeping bags. Crossing to his sleeping pallet, he picked up his small bag of possessions from the ground and took out his own Qur'an. He lovingly wrapped it in a silk cloth, cherishing it from the moment his mother gave it to him when he was seven.

Thinking carefully for a few minutes, he considered both copies of the holy book. He could not keep two; the others might ask why he had them. Deciding irrevocably, he unwrapped his mother's Qur'an from the silk cloth and wrapped up his father's, placing it carefully in the bag. He would give his mother's Qur'an to one of the other guards who had lost his, a charitable act that would be pleasing in Allah's sight and easily explained. If asked, he would tell the man that he had purchased a new one in one of the shops in town.

Aziz began to get up but quickly froze at the steady beating sound of a helicopter's rotor blades. It was a heavy, throbbing pulse made only by heavy-duty military-grade engines. A moment later, the sound multiplied. Helicopters this close, at this time of night, meant only one thing: the Americans had found them.

He dropped his mother's Qur'an onto his empty sleeping pallet, closed his bag of possessions, and slung the bag's strap over his head and shoulder. He had just begun to reach for his AK-47 when a sustained burst of machine-gun fire ripped through the stillness of the night. Aziz grabbed the weapon and ran out the door. He looked to the west and saw an unholy sight.

Two Boeing CH-47 Chinook helicopters, led by two Sikorsky MH-60 Black Hawks, were bearing down on the compound. They were dark, spectral outlines, their navigation and anticollision lights off. One of the Black Hawk's door gunners had opened fire on the compound. The sustained barrage of .30 caliber fire was chewing up the door to the main house. The other gunners were holding their fire and looking for targets.

Aziz stood frozen in his tracks. *How did they find us?* The two jihadis who had been sleeping emerged from the barracks behind him and took cover behind the gate in the wall that led to the driveway.

"Aziz!" shouted one of the men, "take cover by the wall!"

Aziz did not hear him. He was frozen in stunned horror as one of the Black Hawks came in hard and fast, the pilot using the power of the copter's two engines to halt its forward momentum quickly and hover over the center of the western area of the compound, a bare patch of ground where they burned the garbage.

Allah *was* with them. Something had gone wrong. Instead of hovering, the helicopter struggled to remain in the air for a moment, and then dropped to the ground hard, landing nose first, crushing its sturdy landing gear and nearly allowing the whirling rotor blades to chew into the protective inner wall.

With shouts of *"Allahu Akbar!"* the two jihadis leaned out from the cover positions behind the wall and began firing at the three remaining helicopters. The second Black Hawk began to orbit the compound, drawing the guard's fire, while its door gunners attempted to lay suppressing fire on the jihadis' positions, covering the two Chinooks as they approached.

Rounds chewed into the ground at Aziz's feet. He scrambled toward the inner wall, doing what he had been taught in the mountains: seek cover and assess the enemy first.

Aziz watched wide-eyed as the two massive Chinook troop transports settled into a hover forty feet above the western segment, their dual rotors creating a maelstrom of grit-laced wind.

Aziz's stunned horror quickly gave way to crushing despair as he saw two thick ropes drop from the center and rear sections of the Chinooks to the ground. Man after man began to slide down the ropes into the compound, first six, then twelve, then twenty-four, then forty. The two jihadis attempted to shoot at the descending men, but the Black Hawk's continuing fire pushed them back into cover.

Aziz wanted to wail aloud. He knew instinctively he and his father's people could not win against the Americans. They would capture or kill his beloved mentor in minutes. The Americans had brought overwhelming force to a compound with only six men inside the walls. He could do nothing but try to escape and preserve his mentor's legacy.

Thinking quickly, he dropped his AK and ran through the inner door next to the vehicle gate. He turned right to run east past the house, reaching the inner wall between the house and the eastern corner of the compound. He knew he had only moments before the assault unit regrouped after their deployment from the Chinooks and began fighting their way into the main house. He could hear the Black Hawk circling behind the house toward the west again. It would return in seconds. Perhaps the pilot and gunners would be too preoccupied covering the assault team's movement to notice him, and if they did, he hoped their Western ethics would prohibit them from shooting an unarmed man.

Adrenaline raced through his veins as he climbed the seven-foot-high inner wall and vaulted over it to the women's area where laundry hung to dry. He raced between laundry poles to the corner, where he ripped open the heavy bolts securing the door in the wall and then flung it open, hoping that the Americans did not have a supporting ground team surrounding the property.

Quickly scanning the grassy fields to the north, he saw nothing in the darkness save the line of eucalyptus trees less than one hundred meters away. Could he make it? He took a deep breath and ran as hard as he could across the packed-down dirt road, his feet hammering into the dry ground. The expected hail of gunfire did not come as he ran into the field, his bag of meager possessions slapping against his lower back. As the line of trees grew closer, he heard the distinctive sound of AK-47s firing, followed by gunfire he could not identify. It must be the Americans firing back. He ran even harder, hoping Allah would protect his naked back as he came closer to his shelter.

When he reached the stand of trees, he dropped prone, slid next to the trunk of a shorter tree, and turned around to look back the way he came. There was no sign of pursuit, and the remaining Black Hawk was still slowly orbiting the main house, the door gunners holding their fire.

Looking more closely at the compound, Aziz could just see the top edge of the spinning main rotor disk of the Black Hawk that had hard-landed, as well as most of its tail rotor rising above the level of the western wall. The Chinooks and Black Hawk had pulled back, climbing to a hundred feet and orbiting to the south of the compound.

The gunfire continued for a few minutes. Then the AK fire gradually diminished, followed by a brief silence and then the sound of distant, solid thumps. Aziz guessed the noises were probably small explosive charges to breach the door to the house, or possibly flash-bangs to disorient the occupants. May Allah curse them for harming the women and children!

A few moments more and Aziz heard muffled gunfire accompanied by brief flashes of light behind the first- and second-floor windows, and the sound of a woman screaming. Then two more flashes from behind the third-floor windows and muffled shots.

All was quiet for a few minutes. Then Aziz heard a woman's high-pitched wailing but could not make out the words.

The woman's wails were soon drowned out by the return of the Chinooks and remaining airborne Black Hawk. The Black Hawk hovered over the eastern end of the compound, and one Chinook hovered over the south end, both helicopters broadside to the compound, giving their gunners clear fields of fire. The second Chinook maneuvered west and then turned sharply east and descended toward the western end of the compound, flaring smartly and landing next to the stranded Black Hawk.

Aziz laid his face in the dirt and prayed that Allah would welcome his father into Paradise. The transport helicopter landing had signaled that it was over, the Americans must have killed everyone—Bin Laden had promised he would be a martyr before he would be an American prisoner.

After a few minutes, he heard the Chinook's power come back up. He raised his head and scanned the compound. The Chinook was slowly rising over the wall, skidding farther away to the south to clear the landing zone as its twin hovered nearby and lined up for landing. The now fully loaded Chinook hovered over the southwestern wall to cover the compound as its sister craft set down.

A few more minutes went by before the second Chinook lifted off, pivoted left, and headed northwest immediately, followed closely behind by the second Black Hawk. After the second Black Hawk had passed the compound, the remaining Chinook turned northwest and raced to join the formation. The helicopters stayed below a hundred feet, and when in formation, began to race toward the Pakistan-Afghanistan border at 140 knots. A few seconds later, the grounded Black Hawk exploded in a giant fireball, sending flames forty feet in the air.

Aziz stood. There was no point in hiding now. The infidel Americans had left, may Allah consign them to hellfire. His mentor was dead.

Aziz walked northeast, passing a few curious Pakistanis who had heard the commotion and were cautiously working their way down the road, some with cell phones to their ears, no doubt calling the local police or fire department. Avoiding as many people as he could, he walked among the houses until he saw a rusted red bike leaning against a shop's outer wall.

He mounted the bike and began to ride northeast toward the city of Kakul. Looking over his shoulder several times for the first mile, he began to assure himself that no one was taking any notice of him. Only then did he finally begin to relax and think. The Americans had found them. How? It did not matter now.

Bin Laden was dead, and the organization he built would soon die with him. The infidels had chased them throughout Afghanistan, before, during, and after their cowardly invasion of that once safe haven. He had traveled with his surrogate father and his brave fighters into Pakistan, where good men of Allah in Abbottabad helped them and hid them for many years. Now this had happened.

Aziz's eyes began to water and he allowed silent tears to drip for his mentor, his revered friend. Several miles later, when the dawn finally broke before him, Aziz had dried his tears and decided that his mentor's struggle was not over. He would carry it on, but not just yet. There was much to do first.

THE INHERITOR

CHAPTER 1

AN EARLY MORNING AT THE National Security Agency is like a morning at any other large corporation. Thousands of employees come to work in the same condition as the people who go to work at IBM or Intel: some drive in only half-awake, others are revved-up and ready to go, singing along with the radio or listening to the morning news. Emily was one of the latter, listening to the local all-news station, while she sat, along with the other commuters, in the thick traffic. *At least today is sunny and cool,* she thought. Rain or sleet on a fall morning made the commute an ordeal.

The only real difference between the NSA workers and those at other companies is how they get to their offices. She and every other NSA employee or military assignee must pass more than one security checkpoint once on the campus. Even after arriving at their cubicles, they have to unlock their desks, despite the fact that anything classified is always stored in a safe before they go home at night. Only after all the security checks and the removal of materials and files from secure storage can work finally begin.

"ARE YOU KIDDING ME?" Emily asked aloud to no one in particular. She was reading a report the CIA had sent over last night while she was home reading Mother Goose stories to her two-year-old.

Air Force Technical Sergeant Emily Thompson was in her midtwenties, eager, and as sharp as her uniform's creases. As a newly assigned analyst in NSA counterterrorism shop, or CTS as the insiders called it, she received all reports from the various government intelligence and law enforcement agencies that had anything to do with terrorists. Like all the other members of the combined military and civilian watch team, she had to read a variety of intelligence reporting that served as background knowledge for her post in CTS. The daily flow of intelligence reporting helped everyone in CTS when it came time to provide tactical intelligence support to military or law enforcement operations. This report, *Terrorist Organizations: Ethnic Makeup & Initial Formation,* was a 150-page discussion of the potential of new terrorist organizations to form based on the ratios of different ethnic populations in a given country.

"Mr. Cain, have you read this?"

David Cain was Chief of the CTS and a twenty-year veteran employee of the NSA. Cain was of medium height and build, with a habit of not wearing a tie despite his senior position. He looked down into the operations area, about six feet below his desk, where Thompson was sitting.

He reproached her mildly, "Emily, how many times have I told you not to call me Mr. Cain? My name is David. I don't expect anybody on our team to call me Mr. Cain unless the president or DIRNSA is in here," he said, using the official acronym for NSA Director. Smiling, he continued, "I don't see either of them on my calendar today, so you can call me David."

The rest of the CTS employees were also grinning. Having transferred in two weeks ago, Technical Sergeant Thompson still was not used to such an informal atmosphere in the mixed civilian and military assignment.

She brushed a few stray strands of blond hair behind her right ear before getting up from her desk. She walked up the steps to the raised platform where the desks of the CTS chief and his deputy rested.

From that vantage point, she could see the two widescreen projection televisions above the heads and in front of the six other watch standers in CTS. Each screen was twelve feet wide and seven feet high and illuminated by two projectors hanging from the ceiling. The screens could display all manner of graphic information, from real-time satellite imagery to the CTS office seal. When people without the correct security clearances entered CTS to repair equipment or shampoo the carpet, the screens displayed only the CTS seal.

The watch standers, their caffeine from their drinks starting to take effect, were at their desks reading the morning intelligence summaries from the sixteen intelligence and law enforcement agencies that made up the U.S. intelligence community. Their desks were arranged in a semicircle around the screens with signs hanging from the ceiling that designated what each person's operational function was. At the extreme left was the CIA desk, currently filled by Technical Sergeant Thompson; then moving clockwise, the NSA desk, the Communications Officer, the DIA desk, the DHS desk, and the FBI desk.

"Sorry, David, you know I'm still getting used to this."

"It's OK, Emily. Remember, we try to stay relaxed because when we're called to provide support, it can get very tense in here. I don't want my people worrying about protocol; I want them focused on their work. So, tell me what's wrong with the report."

Emily dropped it on his desk and said in an exasperated tone, "Is this what we are paying CIA for? Pie-in-the-sky notions about if there are too many of such and such ethnic group in a certain country, they will form a terrorist cell?"

Leaning back in his chair, David replied, "No. But we do tend to get one of those 'What-if' scenario reports about twice a year. It's always nice to have an out-of-the-box idea come across your desk once in a while for a laugh. Don't sweat it. Our job is to have every possible scrap of information or potential scenario at our fingertips if somebody hunting terrorists needs it. You're getting read into the CTS compartment today, aren't you?"

"Yes," she replied. She'd learned in training that all intelligence and operational activities within the Department of Defense, including the NSA, were held within classified "compartments," each identified by a specific codeword. In order to have access to a particular source of intelligence or operational activity, she—and any other employee—had to have passed an in-depth background check, have a "need-to-know," and sign a stack of paperwork.

"Good. Then we can turn off the damn red light in here and let you get ready to support the next exercise coming up. It'll be good training for you." Emily nodded, understanding that by custom, a colored flashing light was turned on to signal that an uncleared person was in the security compartment area, forcing everyone to put any real work away in desks or safes until that person left.

"Why don't you head off to the security office so they can read you in and we'll see you in about an hour?" Dave turned back to his work and Emily went back to her desk, dropped the CIA report on it, and headed out the door with a smile.

Finally, she thought, *I'm going to help these guys get some terrorists.* Like most people in uniform, Technical Sergeant Emily Thompson thought that the only good terrorist was a dead one.

"AND NOW IT BEGINS." HE recited the words silently as a prayer. Nearly six feet tall, dark-skinned, and bearded, the man's face was still young, in spite of approaching the middle of his third decade, yet his dark eyes were devoid of any youthful innocence. They were intelligent, and, if one looked closely enough, very cool and dispassionate.

There had been many years of silence, both on his part and on the part of the organizations he had built. All the work he had done: the planning, building, recruiting, and refining for a series of events that would fulfill a promise made many years ago. Now it was time to start. There would be no brave but anonymous statements to the press, no public rallies and speeches, no truculent fools wearing black masks, with simulated explosives strapped to their bodies, quick-marching through the streets of some poor neighborhood in the Middle East. Instead, a quiet and intent beginning, with educated, dedicated people recruited slowly over the years.

As with everything, it started with faith. His faith in Allah and his teachings, interpreted correctly as his old friend had taught him. Then time spent sharing that interpretation with a selected few, one at a time, each not knowing about the others.

After that came the training, not in desert camps where the enemy had come to expect it, but in facilities throughout the world, built with the money donated by the faithful. These facilities were sometimes located right under the noses of the enemy, places where no more than four or five trained at any one time. There they honed their skills with weapons and explosives. They also sharpened their minds by interpreting the Qur'an in the way he showed them. Preparation was extensive. The men studied maps and satellite imagery. Manuals and instructions for equipment were consulted to the point of memorization. Mastery of the plan and objectives was the goal. If they did not feel they knew their target intimately enough, the research continued. In all of this, the Internet proved an invaluable tool, but it would also serve one other purpose when the time came.

"We are prepared, are we not?" The question, stated in a tone that expected an affirmative response and no other, echoed off the walls of this chamber. Built specifically to be the control center for this operation, this would be the last time he would ever set foot within it. Soon it would be the solitary domain of the only other person in the room.

A great deal of information came into this room, all of it brought in by fiber-optic cable: news broadcasts, financial reports, all provided by the Internet. No satellite receivers or radio antennas sat on its roof to betray its location. It was, in fact, buried within a structure so innocuous as to escape notice. Those who built it were half a world away on several dozen disparate projects in different cities. Stocked with food for many days, it also had an escape route and, if needed, could be destroyed quickly.

"Yes, we are," said the other man in the room. He was the expert. Slightly over six feet tall, he was nearing fifty, his hair black but edged with a dirty gray fringe at the temples. He stood erect, feet shoulder width apart, calm, controlled, and confident. He could move from country to country in any number of identities and had spent the past three years preparing what was to come. He had monitored the training of all the faithful who had rallied to the cause. He had given them what they lacked, what they desperately needed. He taught them the skills of the professional spy, saboteur, and killer. He helped them handle the duality that comes from serving a great cause and having a life outside the cause. He had done well and he knew it. His gray eyes shifted to his benefactor.

"*Da.* We are prepared. When shall we begin?"

"Soon," replied the bearded man. "They will not expect this. They think they are prepared and protected. We know otherwise. We shall attack them and they will be unable to stop us. They have always had a blind spot, and we have always been stupid."

"Stupid?" asked the second man.

"Yes, my friend. We always claimed victory before it was ours to claim. We paraded ourselves before them in the media and made ourselves targets for their counterattacks. It will not be so this time. We shall be as meek as the Holy Qur'an demands of us. We shall take credit when the victory is achieved, not before."

The second man considered this perspective. *He is probably right. These extremists always announced their actions and intent, hoping to stir up the faithful. Now, when the authorities hunt them, they will not know who to hunt and that will make their task a difficult one. Good. If nothing else,* the professional in him offered up, *it would be more difficult for them to find* me. In the end, his concern was not the other man's cause; his only concerns were payment and survival.

"It shall be as you wish."

"TECHNICAL SERGEANT THOMPSON?" ASKED THE woman as Emily closed the door.

"Yes, ma'am," she replied.

"You're here to be briefed into the CTS compartment today?"

"Yes, ma'am," she answered.

"Then follow me, please." The middle-aged woman led Emily past her desk and down a short, narrow corridor where the last door on the left was ajar. It led into a spartanly furnished conference room, with an almond-colored decor and two plasma-screen monitors on one wall at the end of the conference table. Gesturing for Emily to sit across from her, the woman took a seat in front of a computer near the end of the table closest to the two plasma screens.

"Your ID, please," she asked. Emily handed her the special ID badge she had to wear inside the NSA complex, and the woman waived it over a proximity reader next to the computer.

The computer read her name from the badge, reached into its secure database, and began displaying Emily's information. Looking it over, the woman seemed satisfied and began typing on the keyboard. A few moments later, a printer in the corner started printing out forms. The woman retrieved the forms from the printer and returned to her seat. Taking Emily's ID badge and the forms, she passed them across to Emily.

"As you know, you are being read into the CTS security compartment today. I've verified your identity using your ID badge, and confirmed that your last background investigation and polygraph exam are recent enough to permit you access. Because you've been through this before, I'm sure you are familiar with the process, but I'll cover it briefly because the law and policy require it." Emily nodded and the woman continued.

"The first form is the standard nondisclosure agreement. It is the legally binding document acknowledging that you will not discuss, except with appropriately cleared persons having a need to know, the information protected within the CTS security compartment. The next form is the briefing acknowledgment form. It serves as the official documentation that I briefed you into the compartment today. When you are eventually debriefed from the compartment, you'll sign the 'debriefed' section of the form again. Do you have any questions?"

"No," replied Emily, "this is pretty routine so far."

"Good. Go ahead and read then sign the nondisclosure form. Take all the time you need to read it; if you have any questions about anything in it, just ask."

Emily pulled the form toward her and started to scan it, just to see if it had changed from the last seven or eight she had had to sign already. It was the usual legal language obligating her to hold the information in confidence, followed by the language about going to jail for at least twenty-five years and/or being fined $250,000 if she did not. Last was the "briefed" space at the end for her signature and the day's date, indicating her solemn promise not to violate that confidence.

"One question, are there any travel restrictions with this clearance?" she asked. Depending on what clearances she held, the government might require that she avoid traveling to certain countries, or that she at least notify the security office if she intended to travel to them.

"No more than the usual ones," replied the woman, "but always check with security before you go overseas for the latest threat information and advisory notices."

"OK, then. I'm ready if you are."

"All right," replied the woman, "if you'll look at the video screens, I'll start the briefing." The woman tapped a control imbedded in the table and the lights dimmed and then started the slide show.

"You are being read into the CTS compartment today. This briefing is classified TOP SECRET – CAPTIVE DRAGON. CAPTIVE DRAGON is the classified codeword for this compartment and covers the activities of the CTS in direct support to ongoing military operations against known terrorists, terrorist cells, terrorist organizations, and nation-states or elements of nation-states, as directed by the president. Members of the appropriate congressional committees are briefed into the CAPTIVE DRAGON compartment, and are kept properly informed in their oversight role by the directors of the intelligence community agencies. All CAPTIVE DRAGON activities are governed under the appropriate U.S. laws, to include U.S.C. Title 10 (Armed Forces), and U.S.C. Title 50 (War and National Defense). Intelligence support to U.S. law enforcement agencies is governed under U.S.C. Title 18 (Crimes and Criminal Procedure)."

As the woman began to drone on about proper marking of documents and other things she had heard and memorized over her young career in intelligence, Emily experienced a little thrill that came every time she was exposed to something like this. In part, the thrill came from being allowed into a world that very few of her fellow citizens would ever know about. It was also the flush of achievement in the official recognition that the government—made up of other good people like herself—had evaluated her background, tested her sincerity, and chosen to extend to her the nation's trust.

In doing so, they welcomed her into their community as an equal. In making her part of a smaller community within that community, they made her unique. It wasn't anything to compare with becoming a mother, but in terms of professional accomplishment, each new access would draw her further and further inside that circle of trust, and abusing that trust would be the equivalent of cutting off a limb, as far as she was concerned.

As the woman completed her briefing, Emily signed the second form, thanked the woman, and headed out the door back to CTS, her smile just a little wider than it was when she had walked in.

"DAMN!" *SPILLING HOT COFFEE ON yourself on the way to work is not a good way to start the day,* Johnson thought. *Why is it that you always spill it on your white shirt, instead of on black slacks where the stain wouldn't be noticeable?*

FBI Special Agent Dave Johnson's day was not going to get better. He returned home to change, reaffirming his intention to get that spill-proof travel mug he saw in the Bureau gift shop. The stain initially generated a disapproving look from his wife that had changed to a slight smile as he was heading out the door for work again. He received another disapproving look from the Special Agent in Charge of the FBI's Counterterrorism Office when he showed up late for the morning briefing.

As he walked into the meeting, the briefer paused when the door opened, which gave everyone an opportunity to take note of the truant agent. To make matters worse, the *Questions?* slide came up on the projection screen, which meant the briefing was over.

"SAIC French, do you have any questions?" the briefer intoned.

"No. Thank you." Steven French was a thirty-four-year veteran of the FBI. He had started out in the Bureau investigating crimes in the Detroit field division that warranted the federal government's interest. He had handled cases from bank holdups to kidnappings, with a little organized crime thrown in for good measure. After twelve years in various field offices, he took over the San Francisco office as Deputy SAIC. Soon after he had started, he successfully closed a case of industrial espionage against three of Silicon Valley's largest computer component makers, resulting in the prosecution of the company's senior executives—and bringing him to the attention of the FBI leadership. Shortly thereafter, he transferred to his own field division as SAIC San Antonio. Reassigned to the D.C. headquarters of the FBI a few years after September 11, 2001, he became the head of the Counterterrorism division of the FBI nine years later.

"All right, everyone. Thanks for your time. Agent Johnson, would you remain for a moment?" It was an order, not a request.

Everyone else filed out the doors, some with the obvious *I'm-glad-I'm-not-you* look that masked the humor they saw in the situation.

"I was unavoidably detained, sir."

The SAIC took a moment to look at the young agent. A little harried from running late, he was nonetheless standard FBI issue. He wore a dark charcoal suit and pewter tie with a fresh white shirt. Agent Johnson was still a baby agent, only two years out of Quantico, with eagerness in his brown eyes and the easy confidence in his five-foot-ten frame that came with being a member of one of the world's premier law enforcement agencies.

"Forget it. I'm not worried about that. I'm sure you would have been here on time if you could. Just don't let it become a habit." SAIC French was one of those people who had learned early on how to lead people, and he accepted that even with the best intentions, reality rarely cooperates with best-laid plans.

French paused a beat to let his admonition to the young agent sink in, and then moved on to business. "I want you to start looking at everything we have on al-Qaeda."

Great, thought Johnson. Researching an organization that was no longer a threat seemed like a dead end for his budding career. "With respect, sir, core al-Qaeda is dead and gone. After the SEALs killed Bin Laden in Pakistan, the central command structure of al-Qaeda coordinating attacks against the West was effectively dismantled either by drone strike or capture operations. We still have some of the core al-Qaeda members in Guantanamo. Hell, even our allies and countries that couldn't admit openly to being our allies turned all the al-Qaeda–connected people they had over to us. As you know, the only organizations left out there are the two dozen or so al-Qaeda offshoot organizations that are claiming to be the 'new' al-Qaeda, or vying for supremacy, none of which are capable of conducting a serious attack here."

French's look was that of a tolerant parent who needed to make it understood that some things had to be done whether they were exciting and career-enhancing or not, especially if the parent said so.

"I know that, Agent Johnson. I'm concerned about what we don't know about the core elements of al-Qaeda. We have a closed-session hearing with the Senate Homeland Security Committee in a few months and I want to be able to tell them that we've reviewed all our al-Qaeda materials and found nothing to concern us. Talk to whatever agency you need to, go to Guantanamo and interview the people we are still holding if you have to, but be thorough. I want you to dig, and be sure the well is still dry. Al-Qaeda is the only terrorist organization that ever seriously struck our country and we need to be sure it's dead."

"Yes, sir." *Well,* Johnson thought, *a little attention from the Counterterrorism division head wouldn't hurt my career. I just need to make sure I do a good job.*

SAIC French rose to leave. "Agent Johnson, that's all."

As Johnson headed out the door of the conference room and down the hall, he thought about the possibility of a promotion from this new assignment. His wife had been talking about starting a family. He was sure they would be good parents, and it wouldn't hurt to have a bigger income with a new baby or two in the house. So it would be worth it to be thorough and dig up what he could—first, because it was his sworn duty, and second, because his wife really liked to decorate.

CHAPTER 2

DUTY SHIFTS LIKE THIS REMINDED Emily of her months of long training in intelligence analysis. Doing this kind of work was an art more than a science. Of course, she knew that there were always scientific constants that apply to the information about any technical subject an analyst reviews. She also knew that, more often than not, it was a question of taking what an intelligence source had provided about an event or activity, tempering it with the knowledge of subjects ranging from typical cornfield crop yields to basic nuclear weapon production methodology, and using some common sense and deductive reasoning to reach a reasonable conclusion. Emily always enjoyed solving puzzles, but when the puzzle was solved or at least its general shape was known, she often struggled with what came next. The conclusions had to be compiled as written intelligence reports and sent to civilian and military leaders, sometimes just minutes after the information was acquired from a source. Then it was out of her hands, and the leaders, assuming they had read and fully understood the import of the information, used the reports to make informed judgments on foreign policy or military operations.

As an analyst, Emily was primarily a generalist, who spent the majority of her on-duty time constantly reviewing the available signals, human, or imagery intelligence, known as SIGINT, HUMINT, or IMINT in the acronym-filled military she had joined, to stay aware of everything going on in her assigned portfolio. From all this information, she could distill out what national policymakers and military commanders needed the most—accurate information that would help set national policy to avoid a war, or, when needed, win a war.

Emily kept reminding herself of her professional commitment as she waded through the thick stack of printed reports on her desk. *Nobody thinks a lone analyst sitting at a desk reading, occasionally taking a note or making a comment in the margin of a report written by a case officer handling a HUMINT or SIGINT source, is sexy enough for the movies,* she pondered. *They would rather see Daniel Craig portraying a sexy super-spy in a hair-raising car chase in Europe than watch an analyst actually identify and then locate someone who thinks killing innocent people for their political beliefs is acceptable.*

Emily accepted that the work was time consuming and tiring, but never mind-numbing. Wrapping her mind around a mystery that only she knew existed from the clues in front of her could be one of the most absorbing activities, from her perspective. *If we're lucky,* she thought, *the mystery has already been partially described by another analyst, or, if we aren't so lucky, by the eternally clueless media*—what was officially referred to as Open Source Intelligence, or OSINT. Then at least they would have a starting point. She knew, of course, the validity of that starting point may or may not be very good, *especially* if it came from the media, but at least it would be a start. It could take days, weeks, maybe even months, gathering every scrap of data produced by all the sources and sifting through it to build a coherent view of what the adversary, or potential adversary, was doing.

Emily got up and headed out of the office to the candy machine for a chocolate bar. Walking down the hall on autopilot, she kept going over what she had learned so far, as she cemented it and looked for what she had missed or not considered.

It was only an exercise, but Mr. Cain had told her that each exercise had to be treated like the real thing. A terrorist organization was planning to do *something*. The *something* was what she was supposed to figure out. They had given her two days to come up with the answer. She could ask the exercise controller for additional information, in the same fashion that she would query the various intelligence agencies in a real-world situation. Before she did that, she had to have some good questions to ask. Mr. Cain had told her that the two days was just that: forty-eight hours, not two eight-hour workdays. She could go home and spend time with her family, or sleep if she wanted, but within two days she needed to have some idea of what they were going to do. She had put in twelve hours yesterday and had done six hours so far today.

The Orange Terrorist Organization, the name of the fictitious organization for this and every other exercise, apparently had been sending money and people to Panama. The people they had sent included one person, probably a planner, and six to eight suspected operations types. The CIA who apparently had a HUMINT source in the Panamanian Immigration Service reported their movement into Panama. The money they had sent along was not really very much. NSA had reported that each of seven people suspected of being associated with the Orange Terrorists had each carried 3,000 U.S. dollars into an unspecified Central American country. OK. Taken together, that meant that at least seven *probable* Orange Terrorists were *probably* in Panama with *at least* 18,000 U.S. dollars.

Her training mandated the repeated use of the word *probable* in her current assessment. Intelligence analysts had to express their confidence in the information they present by including one of three qualifiers: *tenuously, possibly,* and *probably.* Using *tenuously* meant that she had only one piece of intelligence and was using 90 percent guesswork and previous target knowledge to draw a conclusion. Using *possibly* meant that she had two pieces of intelligence and the rest was guesswork and target knowledge. Using *probably* meant that she had three or more pieces of intelligence to confirm what she believed was about to happen based on her target knowledge. The only thing better than *probably* was a clear statement of what was going on, and she knew an analyst rarely, if ever, stated anything that way. Not from fear of being wrong, but from the need to state clearly what was known or inferred from the available intelligence—and most of the time, intelligence was fragmented and incomplete. In spite of that ever-present uncertainty, Emily had been taught that government policymakers and military commanders make decisions based on available intelligence, and that intelligence must be timely and clearly stated. Although she knew it was often not the case, Emily fervently hoped that the senior military leaders and the politicians would read the information as carefully as she wrote it.

Her mind drifted back to the problem at hand, and she recalled that there were also no reports of the Orange Terrorist Organization shipping any material resources, like explosives or guns, to Panama.

That thought brought Emily up short just as she was about to put her dollar bill into the candy machine. *No shipments of guns or explosives.* She would have to query the exercise controller, who would play the part of the intelligence community agencies, and make sure that there hadn't been any weapons or explosives smuggled into Panama in the last two or three years. If the answer was negative, then Emily needed to determine what local supplies of these there might be in Panama and find out if the Orange Terrorists were staying near any of them.

Emily pulled out her candy bar and made a mental note to run an extra half mile for the indulgence. Then she headed back to her desk to draft the simulated e-mail to the exercise controller.

THE SECOND MAN WAS READY now. The leader had given his permission and now it was time to begin. Fortunately, his means of communication were virtually undetectable.

He logged into the computer and connected to the Internet. It gave him access to all manner of information, posted, in some cases, stupidly by the computer geeks working for government departments across the world. Today, however, his job was not to glean information that these fools posted; he could amuse himself with that later.

Instead, he went to the website "Collectables for You," an online collectable items "market" run by a couple in Chicago. He accessed the portion of the site that listed the items collectors were interested in buying. Twelve buyers listed interest in American Civil War figurines dating from 1884 or earlier. He posted a message on the website stating that he expected some of these figurines to come into his possession soon, and wanted to know how soon the buyers could purchase.

With a click of the mouse, he left that site behind with a satisfied smile. After his "buyers" replied, he could decide when to begin. To pass the time, he would visit those government computer geek web pages and save anything that might be useful in the future.

SPECIAL AGENT JOHNSON'S DAY WAS still not getting any better. He had gone to his computer to pull up the records the Bureau had on al-Qaeda only to find that there were none. It took three calls to the computer systems division for him to get the name of someone he could ask about the FBI's records of al-Qaeda.

After speaking to the systems archivist, he learned that all the al-Qaeda–related records were no longer on the FBI's active computer system. He groaned aloud. When he told the archivist that he would inform the head of the Counterterrorism division that the records were lost, the faceless voice told him, "Oh, no. You don't understand, sir. They aren't lost. We saved them off to tape to save space in the computers."

Following a break for a sandwich and a soda, he made another phone call. Again it took three tries before he spoke to someone who knew the number to the contact who actually archived the records off the system.

The new faceless voice said, "I'm sorry, Agent Johnson, we are not allowed to load archived materials onto the main network. Federal regulations prohibit archived official FBI records from being loaded onto the primary network."

Incredulous, Johnson asked, "How can I view these records? I have a task from the head of the CT division and I need to access them as part of an official investigation!"

"I understand your concern, but the best we can do without violating the regulations is arrange to have the records you want loaded on a separate detachable hard drive. You can temporarily connect this to your computer."

Finally, he thought, *some progress.* As he was about to express his appreciation, the voice continued, "Unfortunately, getting you the drive will take two business days."

Realizing the futility of the situation, he sighed into the phone. "The detachable hard drive will do. Please bring it along as soon as you can."

He finally decided that as a workday, things had gone as badly as possible. It would be better to leave for the night and come back fresh tomorrow. He grabbed his suit jacket and headed for the elevator in the Hoover Building, hoping that a quiet dinner with his wife and a "practice session" at starting a family would help balance out the day.

CHAPTER 3

· ·

NAVY LIEUTENANT SHANE MATHEWS WAS sweating. Something had gone horribly wrong with this mission. His captain told him that he was being sent into an area of the Syrian Desert to take the place of SEAL Team Six's commanding officer who had been medevacked earlier in the day with acute appendicitis. He was to parachute in and the remainder of the team would locate him after he landed. They would then proceed to the suspected Syrian chemical weapons storage facility in the area and observe it for a few days.

Mathews thought that, on its face, the mission seemed straightforward. As he left the initial briefing, considering the newest challenge before him, he let his mind range over the nearly year and a half of training that qualified him as a member of the U.S. Special Forces community.

Joining the navy right out of college, his first exposure to the "lifestyle" of a SEAL, as his instructors referred to it, was the twenty-five-week BUD/S course at Naval Amphibious Base Coronado, where officers and enlisted men trained to gain initial entry to the SEAL community. Classes of eighty men were put through three phases of training, not including indoctrination, to find out who was mentally and physically capable of shouldering the burden of being a Tier 1 operator.

During Phase I, eight weeks of physical conditioning and group exercises to foster a team mentality shook him out of any romantic notions he had of being a SEAL. The seemingly endless repetitions of strenuous exercises, interspersed with trips to the surf zone, arms linked with his fellow trainees, to immerse himself in the 45- to 50-degree ocean water up to his chest for minutes at a time, bordered on torture. The unrelenting cold of the ocean seeped into his bones, leeched the heat from his body, and made him shake like sapling in a stiff breeze. He had managed to tolerate the first couple of trips, but after the sixth he started to wonder if he really wanted it badly enough.

Surf passage helped change his mind. He remembered the instructors laughing during the first couple of attempts as his boat crew failed to listen to the instructors and was thrown from the black rubber raft not fifty yards out into the ocean swells. Mathews remembered at that point that his mind seemed to go "click" and realized that he was in command, responsible for the crew, and started issuing orders. In short order his boat crew mastered paddling in rhythm with the waves, learned to keep the rubber boats properly balanced by distributing the weight of the eight-man crew, and worked more as a team to bring the boat out to the turnaround point and then back ashore safely.

From that point on, although Phase I remained challenging, he knew his boat crew would get through it. No matter what he and his boat crew did—surf passage, drag races with the heavy rubber boats, or log PT— he looked after his crew, encouraging them to stick together and work as a team to complete the training. The 200-pound telephone poles did not seem quite as heavy when they worked together, even when the instructors ordered them to race up and down the berms with them. Even running on the beach in combat boots for four miles passed quickly.

He was always impressed with the attention to detail his boat crew members gave even when physically exhausted by the training. Not paying attention to an instructor's directions, or being last to complete any task, always resulted in punishment. Punishment at the hands of a SEAL instructor always meant additional exercise. More push-ups in more difficult positions, more log PT with heavier logs, with endless crunches and leg raises thrown in to spread the pain and exhaustion throughout the body. To an outsider, the resulting punishment might have seemed excessive, but Mathews understood that if the enemy caught you on a real mission, you could be imprisoned, used to embarrass your country, killed, or, worst of all in the mind of a SEAL, fail to accomplish the assigned mission.

After the initial problems with surf passage, no one on his crew ever came in last during a race, or misunderstood an instructor's orders. By the end of the week, he had spoken to each man in his boat crew, and he knew they had looked inside themselves and decided to accept the level of commitment the SEALs demand.

Many others in the class did not. They "dropped on request" and left the course. A quarter of Mathews' class DOR'd by the end of the first week.

He endured the second week of BUD/S as the instructors continued to set a hard pace for the trainees. Instead of conditioning runs, Mathews and his boat crew had to take five-mile swims in ocean water temperatures between 45 to 50 degrees once a day and had to listen to the SEAL instructors following in small boats encouraging those who kept falling behind to DOR.

By the time the dreaded "Hell Week" started two weeks into training, Mathews knew he would graduate. For seven straight days, Mathews took everything the rotating shifts of instructors could dish out: log PT, runs, five-mile swims, races in the ocean with the rubber boats, the base tour to simulate a SEAL team humping their gear to an extraction point. All on a combined total of eight hours of sleep. Mathews smiled, remembering how totally out of it he was near the end, a zombie in damp BDUs, covered in sand, standing along the beach in the light of early morning, watching another class, farther along in BUD/S training, run by in the midst of a twenty-six-mile run. He grasped the instructor's meaning— Hell Week was only the beginning of training. When Hell Week was over, there were only twenty-six trainees left of the original eighty, and he was the senior officer in the class.

Mathews enjoyed dive training during Phase II. The procedures and education in dive physics were a breeze, primarily because he was already a certified diver. He even enjoyed the land warfare portion in Phase III, primarily because the instructors treated him and his class more like men, and a little less like raw trainees, as they handled live weapons and explosives.

Leading his class during the live-fire night exercise was the most thrilling moment of his young military career. Under the watchful eyes of his instructors, he planned and executed an assault on a simulated enemy site, secured it, searched it for available intelligence, and then placed explosive charges on critical equipment before exfiltrating the area.

Standing before the admiral on graduation day, he was honored to stand among the eighteen men left in his class. Four weeks of parachute training, and fifteen additional weeks of SEAL qualification training later, he proudly accepted his orders to Team Three and his "Budweiser" badge.

Mathews had been commanding one of SEAL Team Three's platoons of sixteen men for nearly a year now. In his late twenties, with sandy, close-cropped hair, blue eyes, and a build like an NFL running back, his career was off to a great start, and, more important, his reputation within the team as a capable operator was growing. The midlevel NCOs sought him out for advice now, and he had been selected by the team leadership to manage the training platoon.

He had been through many special missions, doing things that he had only dreamed of before becoming a SEAL. He had thought it a little odd that the navy wanted him to parachute in to replace the medevacked officer. SEAL teams were filled with overachievers in every sense of the word, and the next ranking officer or NCO on Team Six should have been able to handle the mission.

Regardless, the mission was a relatively simple one. Move toward a suspected Syrian chemical weapons manufacturing site, remain undetected, and observe the site for six days before moving to the extraction point for a helicopter pickup on the night of day seven.

He carried the usual equipment load-out. His personal weapons—a Heckler & Koch MP-10 submachine gun and silencer, a 9mm Beretta pistol, a short-range radio for team communications, night vision goggles, a Global Positioning System unit, 450 rounds of ammunition, eight quarts of water, and nine MREs. In total, this gave him the usual sixty-five pounds of gear to haul around in addition to his Kevlar flak vest, helmet, and desert goggles.

Unfortunately, Team Six had not found him when he landed. He moved to a shallow ditch—called a *wadi* in this part of the world—and began to wait. He had made two very short radio transmissions trying to raise Team Six, but there was no response. He did not want to call again in case a Syrian listening post might hear the radio call and send troops out to investigate. He briefly considered calling for extraction, but that was useless, because Team Six had the satellite radio with them. His only course of action was to complete the mission and move to the extraction point. Hopefully, he would come across Team Six along the way.

Nervous, but not about to panic, Mathews pulled out his GPS unit to determine his position only to find out that the damned thing did not work. He checked the batteries and determined they were good, and then inspected the case for damage. It looked all right, but he assumed it was damaged during his parachute drop. He looked up, but the high-altitude cloud cover he had parachuted through blanked out the stars.

Pulling out his map, he checked the area of the drop zone described in his briefing and looked for terrain features that might help him determine his position. After a few minutes, he was able to figure out where he was and that the chemical plant he was supposed to watch was to the north.

Choosing a spot on the map that seemed to provide good cover, he donned his night vision goggles, held his weapon in the ready position, and began to hike toward his newly selected observation point.

IN THE DARKNESS ON A ridgeline a mile away, two figures dressed in desert camouflage lay facedown in the talcum powder–like sand. They observed through starlight scopes the distant figure of a man moving north through the desert. After Mathews had moved almost to the edge of their vision, the two crawled down the sloping face of the ridge. When they were sure they were unseen, they rose to their feet and moved north.

TWO HOURS LATER, MATHEWS STOPPED and knelt on the ground. Using his goggles he carefully scanned the ground ahead looking for signs of human habitation or enemy troops. He was in a flat area of a large wadi with a steep ridgeline to his left and open desert to his right. The lower level of the center of the wadi kept him below the floor of the desert proper, shielding him from being seen. Soon the sun would rise and he was only two miles from his observation point. It would not do him any good to hurry and wander unknowingly into an ambush or unsuspecting group of Syrian troops on patrol. He had checked his back trail several times during his march. In every instance, he saw nothing, but he could not shake the feeling of nervousness from not making contact with the rest of Team Six.

Realizing again that he could do nothing but continue the mission and hope to contact Team Six near the objective, he checked his weapon to ensure the safety was off, and began to move north again.

FARTHER BACK IN THE WADI, around a 90-degree bend, the two men shadowing Mathews waited calmly. Neither had a weapon in his hand although both carried 9mm Beretta pistols with attached silencers in what looked like old-fashioned gunslinger holsters. The holsters were actually strapped to their thighs along with the usual belt-type attachment so that the weapon's grip would be positioned at the wearer's hand when standing, allowing him to rapidly draw and fire if a primary weapon jammed. Yet neither man was carrying a rifle or submachine gun.

They did, however, carry radios. One of the men checked the frequency his radio was set to and keyed the transmit button, "Rodeo-25, this is Ghost One, status please."

"Ghost One, Rodeo-25, the target is proceeding north again. Same pace. Appears to be heading for the prebriefed objective."

"Rodeo-25, Ghost One copies."

THE KIOWA RECONNAISSANCE HELICOPTER KNOWN as Rodeo-25 for this mission held its hover 1,700 feet above the desert floor on the other side of the ridge to the left of the wadi. The only part of the helicopter visible above the ridgeline was its ball-shaped battlefield observation and targeting pod, attached to a mast that stuck up from the center of the drive shaft from the main rotor.

Within the two-man crew compartment, the pilot concentrated on holding the helicopter steady in the nightly desert downdraft, while the reconnaissance systems officer worked the controls for the observation and targeting pod.

On one of the view screens in the helicopter, a miniature image of Lt. Mathews in darker and lighter shades of green from the night vision mode of the camera continued to walk toward his observation point.

"I'm going to back off the camera a little so we can see them all." Matching spoken word with action, the reconnaissance systems officer spun a dial, and the camera view widened until both Lt. Mathews and the other two men were in view.

"Make sure you can see him clearly enough to warn them when he stops again. I don't feel like having to explain ourselves to the general if we blow this."

The reconnaissance systems officer gave the pilot a withering look that went unappreciated due to the blacked-out cockpit and the pilot's attention to the proximity of the ridge. "I will, you just make sure we don't fly into that little hill over there."

MATHEWS HAD REACHED HIS OBSERVATION point. He left the wadi and began to climb the ridgeline to his left until he was about forty feet from the top.

Once there he began to dig a shelf out of the side about three feet high, four feet deep, and six feet long. *Prisoners in U.S. jails get more living space,* he thought, *but such is the life of a member of U.S. Special Forces.*

Covered in sweat from his rapid digging, with the sky beginning to lighten in the east, he took out a twenty-five-foot square section of desert camouflage netting and began to anchor it across the L-shaped shelf, concealing it from view while leaving one corner unattached.

Using his camouflage scarf as a broom to obliterate his footprints, he backed into it and affixed the last corner of the netting into position.

Under normal circumstances, he thought, *a person might expect a hearty meal and a good night's sleep after a busy day. Not so for me.* He took out his binoculars and tucked them under the bottom edge of the netting on top of the lower edge of the shelf, lay down in the dirt, and began observing the suspected chemical weapons storage building below.

It was a relatively nondescript structure, made of what appeared to be corrugated sheet metal painted a shade of brown much like the surrounding desert. The building had two large loading doors that looked like overgrown garage doors. Each had a single person-sized door built into it at ground level. The building had one barbed-wire fence around the perimeter and a guardpost at the only gap in the fence line. The gap permitted the only road in the area to enter the perimeter. The road went off into the southwest, toward the Jordanian border.

The two soldiers at the guardpost were dressed in Syrian army fatigues and appeared unimpressed with their duty assignment for the day. One sat inside the guardpost, his helmet off, talking to the other, who stood leaning up against the doorframe, facing into the guardpost, not looking outward for any threat. Both men had the dark features common in this part of the world. The seated one had a mustache, the other was cleanly shaven.

"My God," Mathews breathed with a slight smile on his face, "I could take the two of them out now and walk around in the building."

Not that he would do any such thing. He continued to watch the area, carrying out his orders. Occasionally, his thoughts would stray to the mystery of where Team Six was. When that happened, he would scan the desert around the facility looking for any sign that they had gone to ground somewhere nearby. With no sign of them, he continued on his mission.

BACK IN THE WADI, JUST short of the end of the ridge and out of sight of Mathews, Ghost One checked his radio's frequency setting again, "Ghost One to Ghost Two, do you have him?"

"Two to One, affirm. We've got him. You're relieved."

ON TOP OF THE BUILDING, concealed within what appeared to be an air-conditioning unit, Ghost Two put down his radio and put his eyes to the binoculars in the fixed mount. He had locked them in on Mathews' position while he was digging it and could clearly see the camouflaged position through the false grate in the side of the mock air conditioner.

There was a noise from below as the trap door within the false air conditioner opened and a second man entered the prop.

"How's he doing?"

"Living up to his billing so far," the other man whispered. "He finished his approach to a well-selected observation point before dawn, managed to camouflage it before sun up, and aside from the two transmissions after he landed, he's stayed off his radio. Full marks so far."

"Good. We'll see if he does as well during phase two. How long do we let him wait for it?"

"About three days."

"I'll be back to relieve you in a couple of hours." With that said, the second man opened the trap door again and left.

SECRET – ORANGE SUNRISE – EXERCISE

FROM: CTS INTELLIGENCE WATCH
TO: TBD

The Orange Terrorist group appears to be preparing to conduct an operation against the Panama Canal. At least seven members of the organization are currently in Panama. One of these members is a known Orange Terrorist Group Planner; the remaining members are operations personnel. They are carrying at least $18,000 in U.S. currency. As yet, no intelligence information has revealed where they are staying in Panama or what other resources they may have at their disposal.

The planning officer's background is in heavy construction. He was educated at the Bonn University and graduated with a bachelor's degree in Structural Engineering. Given this information, it is highly likely that the group will be targeting significant structures within Panama. One of the most obvious targets, from both a political and military standpoint, would be the Panama Canal. Other potential targets may include Panamanian government buildings and U.S. military bases in Panama.

Given the economic situation in Panama, and the relative ease with which explosives and arms can be obtained, it is extremely likely that the group in Panama will obtain any explosives or weapons required locally.

Recommend that all U.S. military, Panamanian government offices, and Canal Zone security personnel maintain an increased alert posture and that local security forces maintain surveillance of known arms dealers in the Central and South American regions.

SECRET – ORANGE SUNRISE – EXERCISE

"WHAT DO YOU THINK, DAVID?" Emily's question was born of impatience and lack of sleep. She sat next to Cain's desk in the CTS in a rumpled uniform, eyes bleary and hair slightly mussed, while Cain, with his freshly shaven face, sipped his morning coffee.

"Not bad, Emily. Not bad at all. I expect this didn't take you all night to write, so why were you here?"

"I was hoping the exercise controller would have some more information for me before the deadline, so I waited. My husband was home with our son, so it wasn't a problem."

"What's your recommended distribution for this message?"

"At the minimum, I suggest U.S. Southern Command in Panama, the State Department so they can pass it to the Panamanians and other Central and South American governments, and the usual folks in the intelligence community."

"Good, you only left out one thing. This message definitely needs to be sent out to those addressees, but we also need to publish it on our web page so it can be pulled by anyone interested."

For decades, the intelligence community used a single mode of thought when it came to providing intelligence to the government. Trained operators and analysts collected, processed, and analyzed information from various sources for usable intelligence. They then drafted and transmitted tactical and formal reports to the people and organizations that requested information about topics of interest. For instance, if the Pentagon said to the U.S. intelligence agencies, "Tell me about all tank movements in Country X," all the intelligence agencies would gather intelligence about where the tanks were in Country X, and then send a report about that to the Pentagon.

After the advent of the Internet, something similar began to take hold in the intelligence community: INTELINK, the Internet of the intelligence community, a completely private version of the Internet correctly referred to, in tech-speak, as a secure Intranet protected by multiple layers of encryption. Working at NSA, Emily would be able to gain access to it within the CTS watch center, inside the secure government facility, as it could not be accessed via the Internet. Like her, each intelligence provider could simply make all the information they currently had available on INTELINK. Then each agency or commander could simply retrieve exactly what they needed, when needed. Of course, certain high-priority items were still transmitted directly: critical reports, notices of war breaking out, and terrorism alerts, similar to the report Emily just drafted. Such things could not wait for an agency or user to realize they were available—plus, it always took the government forever to get rid of old systems and methods of doing things.

"Oh," said Emily, which resulted in a yawn. "I'd forgotten about that, sorry."

"Forget it. You've done pretty well so far. I will tell you this, though: losing sleep is also the purpose of this exercise. I don't want you just honing your analytical skills during these exercises. Learn the rhythm of working this kind of a problem. A tired mind makes mistakes and exercises poor judgment. While you waited last night, you should have gotten a catnap or two in. Instead, you stayed awake and ended up forgetting something important. If you do that when this is for real, you run the risk of contributing to a mission failure. That will mean one of two things: a terrorist gets away or manages to accomplish his mission." Cain's voice hardened a little. "The latter option will mean innocent civilians or your fellow men and women in uniform die."

Upon hearing that, Emily became wide-awake. "I'll remember, Mr. Cain." It was not David now.

"I'm sure you will," he replied. "Now go home and get some sleep, your next training exercise will be providing live support to a special operations team."

As Emily left, Cain smiled to himself. *Her analytical skills and drive are good, and she's a fast learner. The real test will be how well she handles the stress of combat support.* At that thought, his smile faded.

He had seen many people come into this office and then go out just as quickly. He hoped Emily would not be one of them. She was just too sharp to lose.

CHAPTER 4

· ·

MATHEWS WAS AWAKE NOW. HE had nodded off again and was beginning to get frustrated with himself. It was not just the normal level of stress that came with combat operations; it was being alone. Team Six was still nowhere to be found, and he had been at his observation point for nearly four days.

The blind he had constructed for himself was holding up pretty well, but it was confining. His muscles were stiff from remaining in one position for too long, but to move meant that the guards nearby might detect him, and detection meant death or imprisonment in Syria. The embarrassment to his country and the expectation that his captors would not exactly put him up in the local Hilton Hotel motivated him to remain still.

The temperature was a relatively comfortable 80 degrees, more so in the direct sunshine for the guards, which explained why they were goofing off again inside the shack by the road.

Suddenly, the far left garage door began to rattle open. The guards quickly gathered themselves and resumed their proper posts along each side of the entrance road with an eye toward the opening door.

From the shadowed interior came the distant sound of indistinct shouting. Mathews focused his binoculars on the entrance but couldn't see much beyond the door, except for the edge of the concrete floor.

The next thing he saw made his blood chill. A man stumbled through the opening into the sunlight. His hands were tied behind his back, and his ankles were tied together but left loose enough to harm his dignity. He fell onto the beaten sand that led to the door, and Mathews could see that he was hardly in the best of shape. The man, with blond hair and pale skin, was obviously not a Syrian. He was wearing desert camouflaged fatigue pants, no boots, and a torn brown T-shirt covered with blood. His face was battered, bruised, and bloody.

As Mathews watched, two more guards walked from the building to the man and pulled him to his feet. The guards dragged him halfway between the door and the fence line and began to beat and kick him while they shouted at him in Arabic.

After several minutes of this, another man emerged from the building. He was a Syrian officer. The differences in his uniform were plain to see, as was the arrogance in his walk. It proclaimed his authority despite the fact that his authority extended no farther than the fence perimeter. He shouted a command to the guards. They stopped beating the blond man and held him up between them.

The officer wasted no words as he drew close to the prisoner; he simply drew his pistol and fired eight shots into his chest. Blood sprayed out and the body went instantly limp before the two Syrian soldiers dropped him to the sand.

Mathews' hands gripped the binoculars hard enough to crack the case. What was going on? That had to be a member of Team Six. He was surely dead now. How did the team get captured? It was very likely that the rest of the team was in that building and would soon suffer the same fate.

While this ran through his mind, the Syrian soldiers dragged the inert body of the dead SEAL back into the building.

As the door began to close behind them, Mathews decided that he would obey the cardinal rule of the teams, "Never leave anyone behind."

"WELL, I'M SURE THAT GOT his attention," said the man wearing the stars of a general officer.

"Yes, sir," was the reply from the current Ghost Two. "His discipline is excellent. He didn't try to rush the compound, and he didn't attempt a long-distance shot at the 'officer.' This guy is really doing well."

"When do you think he'll come in?" asked the general.

"Tonight," said Ghost Two with a grim smile on his face. "He just watched one of his own die. He'll be in tonight at least to verify if we're holding the rest of the team, if not try to get them out. We'll even make it look a little more inviting, just to be sure."

THE TWO GUARDS ON THE gate were gone. Darkness had fallen, and just before twilight reached this part of the world, the Syrian officer had called out to the two guards and beckoned them into the building. They had run into the building, the door had shut behind them, and that was the last he had seen of them.

Mathews decided at that moment to leave his blind and head into the compound. Over the past three days, he had watched the building and its perimeter. There were no cameras or other electronic devices, just the guards, and now they had been gone for thirty minutes.

He left his perch and moved slowly down the ridgeline to a spot about 200 feet from the opening in the fence. After studying the building again, he donned his night vision equipment and began walking across the intervening distance with his H&K MP-10 at the ready, the selector set to three-round burst.

Someone less well trained might have run across the distance, he thought, *but running makes more noise than walking quickly. Fast walking also provides better weapon control than running.*

Fortunately, there were no lights on the building. This left the entire surrounding area as dark as the night. Mathews moved quickly toward the left garage door, holding his body at an angle and covering both doors with his weapon as he moved.

Standing next to the doorframe, he stood still and listened. There were no sounds coming from within the building and because he had no explosives or lock-picking equipment to breach the door, he had to hope that luck was with him.

Reaching out slowly to turn the knob set within the garage door, he waited for the inevitable disappointment that would come with discovering it was locked. But luck was with him. The knob turned and he gently twisted until it stopped. Slowly opening the door a crack, he listened and peeked into the interior. It was dark inside, but his night vision equipment revealed an empty garage with a concrete loading dock in the rear.

He opened the door and entered, moving immediately to his left and keeping his back to the wall. Pausing for a moment, he kept his eyes and his weapon on the large loading doors directly across from the garage entry doors. There was a set of five concrete steps along the left wall leading up to the loading dock level. Just beyond the steps was a door to what was probably an office, with a large window to its right that overlooked the dock area.

Mathews climbed the steps slowly, alert for any sound or movement, and approached the office door. Leaning out to look through the window, he could see that the office was dark and empty, with a door in its far wall.

He opened the office door and slowly approached the door within it. He listened for a moment. Then he heard the sharp smack of a hand against flesh.

"Talk, you American pig!"

The voice was speaking heavily accented English. There was a pause, then another crack of flesh striking flesh.

"Tell me how many more of you are out there, or you will die like your friend!"

There was silence, then another crack, this time followed by the sounds of heavy breathing and a two-word answer. "Fuck you."

"American pig!" the man screamed in reply, followed by the sounds of a new beating. Not just the open-handed slaps as before, but a thicker, heavier sound of fists striking face and body.

Mathews had had enough. He reached out and began to turn the handle of the door to see if it was locked. As he did so, his vision flared into white pain as bright lights suddenly illuminated the office. As he tore the night vision gear from his head, a voice thundered, "Lt. Mathews, this is General Crane! This is an exercise! Stand down immediately and safe your weapon."

Blinking to clear his eyes from the bright spots induced by the sudden flare of light amplified by the goggles, Mathews looked around and saw a single officer in desert BDUs staring down at him from a catwalk above the office.

"Lieutenant Mathews, you are in Saudi Arabia, not Syria, and you have been undergoing an evaluation of your abilities for the past several days. Stand down, and safe that weapon."

Mathews was beyond bewildered and continued to stare at the general for a moment before slowly lowering his weapon to point toward a spot about six feet below the general.

"Sir, you'll excuse me if I find that a little hard to believe."

"I understand, Lieutenant. The door is going to open behind you and an officer is going to come out slowly. I suspect you'll recognize him. Captain Mallory, step out here slowly."

Behind Mathews, the door opened and as he swiveled to bring his weapon into line with the doorway, the blond American who had been "killed" earlier in the day stepped into the room, his hands empty and in the open.

As Mathews stared at him, his look changed from bewilderment to total disbelief. Putting his weapon on safe, Mathews turned to look up at the general.

"With all respect, sir, what the hell is going on?"

Smiling at the familiar look he was getting from the confused, soon-to-be former SEAL, he said, "Come with me and I'll explain."

With that, Mallory gestured toward the office door leading to the loading bay, opened it, and walked onto the loading dock. Mathews followed him and noticed some changes inside. Six armed men dressed in black Nomex with suppressed MP-10s were standing near the door. Their weapons pointed at the floor, but Mathews expected that they were prepared to enter the office if he had threatened the general's life in any way. He couldn't read their faces, because each man's features were hidden behind black baklavas under their Kevlar helmets. The eyes that followed him showed mirth, however, and the determination of men that probably would have wounded or killed him if they needed to.

Mallory opened the garage door and led the way out to an unmarked helicopter that was just landing. Its anticollision lights were off, and Mathews could see the pilots from the red glow of the instruments. The helicopter was unusually quiet and painted flat black. It was a NOTAR, or No Tail Rotor, design variant on the Hughes 500D. The NOTAR design reduced noise by removing the tail rotor and by ducting the air stream generated by the main rotor into the fuselage toward where the tail rotor usually went. The air controlled by a series of vents near the tail kept the helicopter stable. Without the tail rotor's noise, the helicopter became much quieter to operate, which explained why Mathews hadn't heard its approach.

The general, Captain Mallory, and Mathews boarded the helicopter and it took off at once, moving south toward Riyadh.

THE SYSTEMS GUYS HAD FINALLY installed the separate hard drive containing the information he had asked for four days ago.

Agent Johnson was sipping his morning coffee and wondered how the promised two days had turned into four before he reproached himself for the futility of even wondering. Pursuing the matter with the systems guys was pointless; it would only piss him off more and waste time he could better spend doing what he was ordered to do.

In the intervening days, he had gathered maps of Afghanistan, Pakistan, and Iran from the National Imagery and Mapping Agency. NIMA made maps of everything for the U.S. government. If it existed on the surface of the earth, NIMA created a map of it.

The maps were nicely appointed, with any population center greater than 1,000 people marked by a blue circle, along with the political boundaries and major geographic features indicated.

Johnson had also spent time in the FBI archives, going over the records that had not yet been put in a computer database, pulling a list of all the known members of al-Qaeda and determining their current status. Some were in prison in various countries; others were confirmed dead according to DNA samples and eyewitness accounts provided by U.S. service members. A few were missing, presumed dead. These and any others he could find would be the focus of his efforts.

Before he started, he needed to make one other query. He, like many others in the intelligence community, often had more than one phone on their desks. Johnson had three.

One was the in-house FBI secure phone system that had no connectivity to external public phone lines, used to discuss ongoing cases. The second was the outside phone line on the public system with a

Secure Terminal Equipment, or STE, handset that would protect his calls to a degree sufficient to protect information classified TOP SECRET and below, so long as he called someone with another STE-equipped phone line.

The third phone was the "grey phone." More of an off-white, and very special, it was part of the secure DOD-wide phone system with limited connectivity to other government agencies. The system ran over a series of secure telephone switches that connected all the government intelligence agencies and the military. The calls made on that phone were totally secure and invulnerable to eavesdroppers. There were very few of these phones at the FBI, and Johnson was fortunate to have one.

Finding the grey line number he wanted in the INTELINK online phone directory, he dialed while taking one last sip of his morning coffee.

"4572, Cain," was the response after the ringing stopped.

"Mr. Cain, this is Special Agent Johnson of the FBI."

"What can I do for you, Agent Johnson?"

"I've been asked by the Agent in Charge of the Counterterrorism division to take a look at everything we have on al-Qaeda. I wanted to ask you to give me a point-of-contact in your organization I can work with on this."

"No problem. You can work with our FBI liaison Fred Simpson. You can reach him at 4575. In fact, I'm surprised you didn't know who he was."

"I do know he's there, but I was reluctant to talk to him without informing you first. You are his boss while he's assigned to CTS and I wanted your approval before contacting him."

"Well, I appreciate the consideration, Agent Johnson. Feel free to contact him with whatever questions you have. I'll see to it that he expects your information requests."

"Thanks, Mr. Cain."

"Please call me David; we're pretty informal over here."

"Sure thing, David, thanks again."

"Good-bye."

Now that the easy part of the morning was over, it was time to dig into those hard drive files. The first queries would be for all the transcripts of the interrogations conducted of captured al-Qaeda members still held at Guantanamo; the next would be all information related to the people on the list of al-Qaeda members who were missing-presumed dead.

The search strategy would be simple and very broad. Entering terms like "transcript," "suspect," "al-Qaeda," "members," and logically AND-ing them together so the computer would find only files with all four terms, he executed the first search. While the computer began his initial search, he went to the break room to make another cup of coffee.

IN THE PORT OF BALTIMORE, the MV *Spring Tide* was approaching pier number 32, her crew standing near the starboard rails, ready to throw the messenger lines.

MV *Spring Tide* was a container ship, operated by Mediterranean Seaways, Inc. She had just finished making her fortieth journey across the Atlantic from the French port of Brest. She was a sun-faded green, and her hull was rusting near the anchor ports. She was filled to capacity with brown, orange, and green steel shipping containers, each as large as a school bus, all sealed with customs inspection tags and padlocks. The containers were stacked as high as the container ship's bridge. A tug was helping her nestle close to the pier.

Spring Tide's seamen threw the messenger lines over the rails into the waiting arms of the pier workers, who attached them to the heavy hawsers that would secure the ship to the shore for unloading. The sailors pulled the thick hawsers back on board the ship and tied them off. As each pair of seamen completed their task, they signaled to the ship's bridge with a wave.

When the ship was secure, the captain signaled the engine room, "Finished with Engines," and directed the first mate to oversee the unloading.

On board the ship, workers removed the tie-down chains and holding pins from the containers, and giant cranes perched on blue pedestals on the pier began to lift the containers off the ship.

Each crane's mast towered above the level of the ship, its cables reaching down toward the next container ready for unloading. The crew worked as quickly as safety permitted, moving along the tops of the containers with ease, jumping from the one they had just attached to the crane's cables to the next to be unloaded.

As the cable attachments were completed and after his shipmates moved to the next container, the crewmember working with the crane operator would make a radio call over his walkie-talkie. Then the crane would take up the slack and lift the container off the ship before placing it on the pier in a storage area for customs check. After the customs officials were satisfied, it would be loaded onto a tractor-trailer or train for the last part of its journey.

The crane lifted the next container in the sequence clear of the ship. As the crane rotated to move the container slowly across the ship to a point over the pier, the breeze picked up slightly and caused it to sway. The first mate called out for tag lines for the remaining containers, but it was too late for this one. The hardened steel coupling that held the four lines fast to the crane's main cable sheared off and the container dropped eighty feet to the concrete pier.

The inertia of the container's 6,000 kg mass came to a sudden halt on the solid concrete pier, making both ends bow outwards. This structural weakness caused the catastrophic failure of the doors at one end of the container, which flew open as if a giant fist had punched through them from the inside.

Spilling to the ground outside of the now-wrecked doors were several wooden crates labeled "Windmere Manufacturing." Some of the crates fared no better than the doors had. Those stacked near the top closest to the doors were thrown outward, shattering on impact, fanning their contents around them. Others, near the floor of the container, merely tumbled forward or had not moved, held in place by those above that were mostly unaffected.

Fortunately, no one was standing beneath the container when it fell, although the sound got everyone's attention and scattered a group of seagulls nearby.

Many of the men, including the on-duty customs inspector, ran over to the crate to make sure no one had been hurt. When they had satisfied themselves that everyone was accounted for and had all their limbs, they began to notice the contents of the destroyed crates.

"What the hell is this?" cried the inspector.

All around the front of the container were assault rifles and cellophane-wrapped blocks of what looked like modeling clay.

"Don't touch anything!" the inspector yelled. "Get away from this container and halt the unloading. That ship is impounded. Everyone on board is confined to the ship until I say otherwise."

The inspector's career had just taken an unexpected turn for the better, all because of a puff of wind and some bad practices on the part of the ship's crew. Unfortunately, it was also the first indication that something else unexpected, and unpleasant, was about to happen.

THE COMPUTER FINISHED ITS SEARCH of the al-Qaeda records and provided Agent Johnson a list of files to review. He wanted to have the hard copy to work with so he printed the records. He would need that printed copy because the guys would be back in another day or two to take the disk away.

After he sent the files to the printer, he regretted it: the computer told him there were more than 2,000 pages. He grabbed two reams of paper, loaded them into the printer's paper tray, and then decided it was time for a trip to the soda machine. By the time he returned, the first few of several hundred transcripts had printed.

Taking a sip of his soda, he began to read, looking for anomalies in the statements or indications that someone might have slipped through the net the U.S. and NATO military forces had spread throughout Afghanistan. Reading through the transcripts was long and laborious. Yawning, Johnson leaned back in his chair to stretch.

Three and a half hours later he hadn't found anything that jumped out at him. He pitched his now-empty soda can in the recycle bin and stood up for a quick walk around the office to clear his head a little. He still had more than 1,700 pages of transcripts to read. Most of the interrogations yielded a great deal of information that was intended to be misleading or was simply outrageous. Prisoners told of whole armies that were under the command of Bin Laden or giant fleets of planes or rockets that would decimate the United States. Others spoke of the power of Allah crushing the U.S. on their behalf. Johnson would not criticize anyone's religious beliefs, even a terrorist's, but he seriously doubted that Allah would crush the U.S. at the request of a bunch of murderers.

Ignoring his fatigue, he returned to his desk and started a new transcript. This one was from a man named Ali al-Mushaff who claimed to know someone who had received money to support the holy warriors in Afghanistan. He called the man who received the money "Sadig."

Wait a minute. Sadig al-Faisal was on the missing list. Johnson was sure of it. He pulled it out and checked. Sadig al-Faisal *was* there—listed as "missing-presumed dead" with no additional details. Another check, this time of the State Department's listing of Taliban officials. Al-Faisal was the Taliban finance minister and was last known to be in Afghanistan.

Returning to the Ali al-Mushaff transcript, Johnson read on. Al-Mushaff told his Army interrogators that he traveled with Sadig and "his brother Abdul" toward Pakistan after the U.S. airstrikes commenced in the early days of Operation Enduring Freedom. As they were about to cross the border to safety several weeks later, a U.S. Army patrol from Task Force Eagle came across them. Al-Mushaff's party opened fire. The patrol returned fire and called in supporting fire from a patrolling AC-130 gunship. The few survivors of the second pass from the AC-130 chose to surrender instead of dying on the mountainside. According to the addendum to the interrogation transcript, Task Force Eagle took al-Mushaff prisoner in the mountains on the Pakistani border. The addendum also said that al-Mushaff was still in custody at Guantanamo, but nowhere in the transcript was "Sadig" mentioned again.

Johnson made a note to call Guantanamo and arrange an interview with this man. He needed to follow up on Sadig's fate in order to close the book on him for the government.

Before that, he had more reading to do.

"DAVID!" CAME THE LOUD EXCLAMATION. Fred Simpson's tone was not alarmed, but it demanded immediate attention. Simpson was a soft-spoken, twelve-year FBI veteran, not prone to histrionics. Any loud comments from him were meant to carry within the CTS, gaining the attention of not only whoever he was calling but also the whole CTS staff.

"FBI reports an undeclared shipment of weapons and explosives found in a shipping container in the port of Baltimore. Customs just passed them the info. The Baltimore field office is sending a team to investigate. No further details at this time."

Cain moved from his desk down to the operations floor.

"All right, people, check your sources *now*. Look for any indications of known terrorist groups moving arms or explosives into or through the U.S. in the past month. I want to have our information ready to match with the FBI's. Fred, tell the Bureau we want a complete list of all the ports that ship has visited, the name of the port where that container was loaded, and a complete rundown on the crew as soon as they can provide it."

The CTS exploded into action. Everyone ran to their desks, grabbing phones and headsets. The headsets, slim with only one earpiece, permitted the CTS team to communicate without yelling in the room and were hardwired so that no transmission might escape the office. The phones were "ring-down" lines, a point-to-point connection between CTS and the watch centers in each of the agencies they liaised with. Each desk officer also had a grey phone, and a STE connected to the public phone system.

Cain continued to stand on the operations floor, relaxed and watching patiently as his people went to work. When they seemed off to a good start and had no immediate questions, he returned to his desk for the soft drink he'd opened earlier. He knew from long experience that there was little to do right now but wait. The FBI agents needed time to investigate, and his people needed time to gather and collate the available intelligence before taking any action.

The atmosphere in the CTS had changed over to what mission control in NASA looked like during the Apollo program moon missions. Quiet yet intense people worked at computer terminals, resulting in almost complete silence. The only sounds now were the muted conversations of the CTS staff talking over the headset links and the soft click of computer keys being pressed, broken only by the occasional click of a mouse selecting an icon within a graphical interface.

Lieutenant Osborn, the NSA operations liaison, looked up and broke the near silence first. "David, NSA doesn't have any information about an arms or explosive shipment destined for the U.S. They are standing by to run the ship name and port listing as soon as we can get it."

"Fred," Cain replied, "has the FBI given you that information yet?"

"No, I'm querying them now and relaying NSA's preliminary read."

Simpson spoke into his ring-down phone to the FBI watch center and waited a moment, then began typing at his computer. The overhead projector on the right cleared and the data Fred was typing began to come up.

SECRET – CAPTIVE DRAGON

SHIP NAME:	*MV* Spring Tide
HOMEPORT:	*Rotterdam, Netherlands*
OPERATOR:	*Mediterranean Seaways, Inc.*
PORTS VISITED:	*Unknown (FBI will provide)*
CONTRABAND:	*Unspecified number of AK-47s*
	Unspecified quantity of Composition 4
NOTES:	*Contraband located in one shipping container.*
	A search of all others will be conducted.

SECRET – CAPTIVE DRAGON

David spoke up again, "All right, folks, you know what to do, run the ship's name and see what we get. Don't search for the AKs or C-4 until we get the port listing. You'll end up with too much information that will be unrelated to this ship. Let's keep the information search focused."

After a few moments' work, one by one Cain's people turned to look at him, shaking their heads in the negative. Every time Cain saw another person shake his or her head, his expression moved farther and farther from calm impassivity to increasing wonderment. *Nothing?* It was simply impossible that nothing came back.

Somebody in the intelligence community had to have something on the ship. The community kept all manner of records on ships that transported all kinds of illicit cargos, especially cargos for terrorists. If none of them had any information, then that meant that no one had been keeping an eye on the *Spring Tide* and her movements. That did not bode well. Determining which terrorist or criminal group was associated with the *Spring Tide* had just gotten considerably harder.

They just had to wait and hope for more information from the FBI interviews of the crew, or information from some other intelligence source.

But it was information they would never get.

CHAPTER 5

THE GULFSTREAM G350 COMPLETED ITS approach to Runway 10 at 140 knots and began to flare out in preparation for landing. The jet was liveried in white and nothing else. Most unusual for an aircraft, it didn't even have a serial number on the fuselage to identify its country of origin, provide it with a radio call sign, or use to communicate with air traffic control.

The main gear of the G350 touched down gently at 125 knots. As soon as its nose wheel touched the pavement, the engines reversed their thrust while the wing flaps split to deform the airflow over the wings and add more braking power.

The airstrip was in a completely deserted area of the desert in the southwestern United States. There were no houses nearby; in fact, there was no sign at all of human habitation outside of the airstrip, its east-west oriented twin, the control tower, and one enormous hangar.

As soon as the G350 reduced speed to a rate fit for driving instead of flying, it turned left onto the taxiway designated "Charlie" and began to move toward the hangar. The hangar was at least 2,000 feet long and wide—large enough to allow eight 747s to enter wingtip to wingtip and still be swallowed whole. It looked deep enough to hold another eight 747s and must have rivaled the Boeing assembly plant in Seattle in interior floor space.

When it reached the hangar, the G350 stopped. From the outside, it looked like a small bird waiting for someone to open the door to the largest nest ever created.

After a moment, the center set of three monstrous doors guarding the contents of the hangar began to open. They stopped at ninety feet— no more than ten feet wider than the eighty-foot wingspan of the G350.

The pilot of the G350 increased his throttle slightly until the thrust of the engines overcame the aircraft's inertia and it began to roll forward into the opening. When the plane was moving, he reduced the throttle to idle. The aircraft continued to roll into the hangar where two men with lighted wands began to guide it toward its parking space along the right side of the hangar near the monstrous doors. After the G350 parked, the engines were shut down and the passenger door on the side of the aircraft swung open, followed by the extension of the stairwell from the interior of the fuselage, below the door.

Waiting near the door were two men and one dog. The men were uniformed in a variation on military battle dress uniform, except in this case the uniforms were black, not camouflage green or brown. Each man's uniform had only two adornments: the man's military rank insignia in subdued black, and a cloth nametape sewn over the left pocket. The dog was a ninety-seven pound German Shepherd named Zeus whose collar was adorned with tag in the form of the stripes of an Air Force master sergeant.

General Crane stepped from the aircraft and returned the greetings of his aide and the base commander, Air Force Colonel Aaron Simon.

"Welcome back, General," said Colonel Simon.

"Thanks, Aaron. Anything worth reporting?" replied the general.

"No, sir. It's been the usual routine. How did your recruiting mission go?"

Motioning to the airplane, General Crane said, "Meet Lieutenant Mathews."

Mathews was emerging from the plane and trying to take in the enormity of the hangar. The smell of lubricants and aviation fuel mixed with diesel exhaust permeated the air. There was a set of AH-64D Apache attack helicopters, four Boeing 747-400s, and two C-17 Globemaster III cargo aircraft along just one wall. Mathews was in awe.

The side of the hangar the G350 had parked on had a medium-sized

THE INHERITOR | 49

two-story office building in the rear corner with what looked like a spare parts bay containing engines and other large aircraft parts. There was also a 747-sized empty area with large yellow fire extinguishers placed at intervals that Mathews thought might be a parking spot for visiting aircraft.

Parked along the remaining part of the hangar wall were two KC-10 Extender refueling tankers; another G350, a virtual twin to the one he flew in on; and two longer-range G550s. Four F-22 Raptor fighters completed the set. Maintenance personnel were working on various aircraft, and, as he watched, one female Air Force mechanic towed a jet engine across the floor from the parts bay toward one of the C-17s whose left engine was missing from its pylon.

As Mathews' mind tried to grasp the kind of mission a unit would be given that would allow them to have a facility like this with several billion dollars of military and civilian hardware assigned to it, he noticed the three officers looking at him expectantly and with no small amusement. Since he had not met the colonel yet, and both men were indoors, military custom required a verbal greeting and not a salute.

"Hello, Colonel."

"Lieutenant Mathews," Colonel Simon replied, extending his hand to the younger officer.

Mathews then greeted the general's aide and took a quick look at the dog, which was already looking at him with interest but no overt signs of friendliness.

Noticing this, Colonel Simon said, "Don't mind Zeus, Lieutenant. He's well trained and very friendly. You'll be seeing him around."

Extending his hand to the dog for a sniff, and then a quick scratch along his neck, Mathews looked to the general in expectation of new orders. He wasn't disappointed.

"All right, Lieutenant," said the general, "for the next few days you are going to be undergoing a more thorough background check and filling out some forms. My aide will arrange for you to be escorted everywhere throughout this complex."

"Complex, sir?" Mathews asked in a puzzled voice. "There is nothing but the airfield and the hangar from what I can see."

With a smile, the general replied, "Come with us, Mathews."

The general led the small group toward the back of the hangar. Zeus kept pace with Colonel Simon as they approached the rear wall. There were two large areas offset to the right of the rear wall's centerline surrounded by large yellow stenciling on the hangar's floor. The stenciling formed two large yellow squares, one within another, outlining both sections of the floor. The portions of the hangar's floor within the two squares were composed of steel grating instead of reinforced concrete. Within the gap between the squares were the words, "WARNING – KEEP AREA CLEAR" in two-foot-high letters, repeated at intervals all the way around the perimeter of two rectangles. At each corner of the outer squares were red lights, embedded in the floor, that were currently dormant.

Mathews assumed that these were massive aircraft elevators of some kind. He'd seen similar layouts on aircraft carrier plane elevators. The major difference between the ones on the carrier and these was the size. Each looked as if it could easily allow one of the 747-400s with its more than 200-foot wingspan to park on it with room to spare.

The general led the way. He walked obliquely past the aircraft elevators and a pedestrian-sized freight elevator to what appeared to be a more conventional passenger elevator where two men in desert camouflage, body armor, and AR-15 rifles stood guard. This elevator was installed in a small box structure.

As the general and his party approached, the two guards came to attention and allowed them to enter the elevator. The elevator had a larger interior than normal, and looked as if it could hold twenty people or so. It was well lit and finished in burnished steel.

Colonel Simon removed an ID badge from his pocket and waived it near the elevator controls. A soft chime, accompanied by a green light on the panel, indicated the elevator was active, and the colonel pressed the button for Level 2.

As the elevator began to descend, the general spoke again. "Lieutenant, my aide will take you to the administration office on Level 2 to fill out your paperwork for your clearance, and then to your temporary quarters on the same level."

"Yes, sir."

"Unfortunately," the general continued, "until your security clearance has been granted, you will be confined to Level 2. Base personnel will deliver meals or snacks to your temporary quarters. You are not to go the hangar on Level 1 or attempt to leave Level 2 without an escort. Call my aide for an escort if you need some fresh air outside. Is that clear?"

"Yes, sir, it is," replied Mathews as the doors opened on Level 2 and the general's aide stepped out motioning Mathews to follow. "May I ask how long it will take?"

The colonel pressed another button on the elevator panel and the doors began to close. The general replied, "As long as it takes, Lieutenant."

IT HAD BEEN THREE DAYS since the MV *Spring Tide* had docked in Baltimore with the container of guns and explosives. In those three days, Cain thought as he read the summary report, the intelligence community knew little more than that.

Cain's eyes scanned rapidly down the page, pulling out the important details. The shipping container contained 150 AK-47s and almost 100 pounds of C-4 explosive. The FBI's forensic laboratory in Quantico had begun processing all the AKs and the C-4 to see what the scientists could learn from them.

The FBI's careful and detailed interrogation of the crew members and the Port of Baltimore customs officials and dockworkers had turned up nothing anomalous. What Cain thought was worse was that NSA, CIA, and DIA had nothing. *Nothing at all.* That was also the strangest thing, in Cain's opinion. He knew that normally the intelligence agencies (or at least one of them) get a whiff of something. A HUMINT source tells a field agent that he or she "heard something about guns and explosives being put on a ship," or a SIGINT source reports "a known terrorist or criminal overseas has bought the military equipment and wants to ship it to the States."

Even though Cain knew an individual piece of information gathered during intelligence activities by itself wasn't enough to take action on immediately, there was usually *something* to build on. Only in books and Hollywood could actionable information be developed and properly vetted in a matter of minutes or hours. In the real world, Cain understood through his long years of experience that developing intelligence sources, most of which he would never know about, took days, weeks, and more often months. Complicating the process was the pervasive oversight that carefully monitored U.S. intelligence community activities to ensure that the rights of U.S. citizens were protected. Even the use of intelligence information, unless a process was already established or a crisis was imminent, took days or weeks more. Otherwise, the lives of U.S. service members or intelligence officers might be risked in an unacceptable way or for no good reason.

Cain continued to go over and over it, looking for a thread he could direct his people to investigate. The CTS mandate was to uncover potential terrorist actions before they occurred and coordinate the response to them. That response could be a legal one in the form of warranted surveillance or arrest by the FBI on U.S. soil or a military one if the people involved were outside the U.S. It was within Cain's authority to recommend such actions to the FBI or the DoD, when he felt he could justify that recommendation based on the available intelligence.

The FBI was very good at warranted surveillance of everyone from suspected drug dealers to bank robbers, so long as sufficient evidence existed to convince a judge that a crime was being committed. In the case of military action overseas, Cain knew the options were watch, capture, or kill. Surveillance could lead to other terrorists, and, when performed in concert with friendly governments, was easy enough to do. The FBI coordinated it with the same efficiency it applied to U.S. domestic concerns.

Surveillance in countries less friendly to the U.S. was also possible, but added more risk, because the CIA or military would have to handle it in a manner that kept the host country ignorant of the action. They were not likely to approve of it anyway.

The FBI preferred capture, of course. A live terrorist could be interrogated and new information garnered; friendly governments facilitated this and usually did the capture operation themselves, potentially with some help from the U.S. military. Unfriendly governments might be told about it after the person was in U.S. custody, usually because the unfriendly government would tell the target of such an operation in time for them to flee capture. In either case, if a known terrorist became a threat to the team sent in to get him, or other innocent people in the vicinity, then that terrorist had chosen death, to be delivered at the hands of people who trained regularly at delivering it in the most conscientious manner.

IN HIS HIDDEN COMMAND POST, the man leaned back from his computer with a look of satisfaction. His "buyers" were ready. Each of the twelve had responded to his ad saying that they were ready to take delivery of the figurines within five days of his say-so.

The man rose, headed over to the industrial class refrigerator/freezer, and removed a filet mignon. He took it over to the worktable in the center of the kitchen area, took some paprika, garlic powder, salt, and black pepper, and sprinkled it on the steak. He lit one of the gas burners and set the oven to preheat. He added some olive oil to spun aluminum pan and then began to sear the steak, thinking about the destruction he was going to cause.

He would not be harming anyone directly, but, as the controller of this operation, he was setting events into motion that would certainly result in deaths. Innocent men, women, and almost certainly children would die because of the orders he would give. His previous employer had trained him that civilian casualties were to be avoided but were a fact of life. In this case, civilian casualties were the goal of his current employer. He disliked this, but the money his employer offered had far outpaced anything his other potential job opportunities had offered.

Turning the steak over to sear the other side, he thought about the seven-figure first installment of his payment spread across five different bank accounts in five different countries. That money alone made up for nearly twenty years of receiving a pittance from a government that had cast him aside after he had sweated and schemed his way to the rank of colonel in its service. Was that the fee being paid to an executioner or a merely a facilitator, and how much culpability is there in the deaths of others if you are only a facilitator? Certainly, in the eyes of American law, he would likely be a conspirator or perhaps an accessory. Either way he would be as guilty in the American criminal system of those who indirectly killed.

In the end, however, he would achieve his goal of financial independence, to gain the ability to go where he wished and to live how he wished.

He placed the steak in the preheated oven to finish cooking and took salad ingredients from the refrigerator. He had broken so many laws in so many different countries during his professional life that breaking U.S. laws was no problem unless he got arrested. For that to happen, the people he trained would need to describe him and, more important, know where to find him, and they did not have the latter piece of information, nor would they ever. While the American federal and state police forces were capable and well funded, a description alone would not enable his capture. It might make leaving the country more difficult, but he had plans for that. He would only be acting as the professional consultant and organizer for this man Aziz. It was hardly different from what he had already done for a government considerably less generous than his current employer was.

Removing his steak from the oven, plating it, and taking both it and the salad to the table, he began to eat while he continued to mull over this issue. It came down to loyalty. Previously, he had given his loyalty to his nation, more specifically to his nation's leaders, and they abused it. They did not return that loyalty with either a well-earned pension or advancement to a general's rank. Instead, they looked upon him distastefully, a necessary, but unwanted, element within their intelligence service.

Publicly at least, the Russian government did not want to continue the perception that its security organs would come kill or arrest someone in the night. In the initial stages of the so-called democratization of Russia, the more heavy-handed and typically direct forms of controlling the masses were seldom applied. It was at this point that he joined the Federal Security Service, previously known and feared under its former name as the *Komitet Gosudarstvennoy Bezopasnosti,* or KGB. When the more authoritarian rule of one of the former Directors of the Federal Security Service began, his rule as president, then prime minister with a puppet president, then president again returned things to a more normal state as far as he was concerned. He rose steadily but not quickly in rank during these years, volunteering for the more difficult and direct methods of dealing with whoever threatened the *Rodina.*

As fate would have it, more moderate leaders came to power soon after the hardline president's sudden heart attack later in his second term. In the new era of the "rule-of-law," the direct methods of control were considered abusive and potentially illegal. Evidence of assassinations by the FSB emerged, followed by court inquiries and public disavowal by the new government. His entire division, kept secret for so long, was summarily dissolved and the officers with his skill set hidden away in other divisions within the FSB or retired as quickly as the paperwork could be processed for those deemed to be potential liabilities. He had even heard rumors of a few declared psychologically unfit for other duties because they enjoyed killing too much suddenly dying in tragic "training accidents" rather than being given more mundane tasks they would not likely have adapted to.

He was eventually chosen for the path of retirement and jettisoned in a manner more consistent with a bag of trash. He was called into an unscheduled meeting one afternoon in a first-floor conference room, where three of his superior's security men waited. One frisked him for weapons before all three escorted him down the hall into his superior's office. The conversation was short.

"The Rodina thanks you for your service," said his balding supervisor, one of the new crop of law-and-order managers within the FSB, gesturing to a tan envelope on the desk.

He had not even moved toward it before one of the security men took the envelope, forced it into his jacket pocket, took his FSB credentials, and then the three of them hustled him out of the building. Standing outside in the headquarters in the snow falling on Lubyanka Square, he read the dismissal papers in the envelope, both bewildered and angered by the depth of their betrayal. Worse, the document admonished him that the revelation of any state secrets to the media or public would result in immediate criminal action and imprisonment.

After nearly two years of trying to find work with comparable pay, and his marriage heading irreconcilably to a divorce, he decided to become a paid consultant to others in the arts of espionage and paramilitary operations. He traded loyalty to a nation for loyalty to a paycheck, never to the person who signed the checks. He would not make that mistake again.

Compared to his current consulting efforts, his previous private employers never asked for anything this large scale before. A quiet surveillance of a person here or there, stealing a document or two from an office with no one the wiser were the usual flavor of the jobs. Occasionally, he might train a small team of men and sometimes women in small unit tactics or explosives handling, but never bothered to ask for too much information about what they would do with the knowledge. Then Aziz found him. The first thing Aziz told him was how much the job paid. He had agreed almost immediately, asking few questions. Only after he had begun training the people Aziz called "the faithful" did he realize what he had gotten himself involved in.

He snorted briefly as he finished his salad. His former FSB instructors were always warning him to see all the way to the end of the mission. Since he began selling his loyalty to the highest or most available bidder, he had fallen into a trap he knew he should have avoided.

Disposing of the remnants of his meal, he considered leaving now. If he did, the operation would be stillborn. All the procedures and communications links that would enable everything Aziz envisioned would be unavailable to him, and the initial phases of the operation would never happen. He could hide, but he suspected that Aziz would send people to kill him. Although he had numerous identities, Aziz just might find him again. There was also the matter of the remaining portion of his payment. Another $4 million would ensure he would never have to work again. He could walk away after this operation and start again somewhere in South America or in the Pacific. He could live a luxurious lifestyle and see any assassins coming from far away with the right payments to the proper government officials. As a wealthy man, he could develop the contacts in the local police force and other local citizens he would need in order to stay alive, finally becoming the arbiter of his own fate. In the end, to him, that was more important now.

Besides, people died every day in the world. He would not be the one killing these anyway. Let Aziz have his little war with the U.S. In the end, he would walk away wealthy, one way or another.

Returning to the computer, and exhibiting no unease, he logged in and responded to each of the buyers, telling them he would have the figurines in five days.

MATHEWS WAS ON THE PHONE with his mother, and his mother was asking too many questions.

"Mom, you know I can't answer that, so please don't ask," he said with no small exasperation. His mother was a great person, but her curiosity about her son's work, borne from pride though it was, sometimes made him uneasy. As a SEAL, he had told his mother several times that what he did was a secret and that he was not allowed to tell even family members. That created problems and questions from relatives, "Where's Shane now?" "Do you think he'll be home for the holidays?" "Where is Shane deployed to now?" Each time, his mom or dad had to answer with a version of "I don't know," because he could not tell them. It was part of the price of being a SEAL, and he expected that to get worse.

The pretty redhead at the counter helping him fill out the security forms had explained that the base's phone system was set up to make it look like it was calling from one random U.S. city after another. It might be Flagstaff, Arizona, one month, then Billings, Montana, the next, and then another random U.S. city, and so on, so that relatives or other outsiders would never figure out where the base was. Mathews mused silently that it must have made it difficult for the phone company to send the bill to the right place, but then he turned his mind back to the problem at hand.

"What's Dad's social security number?" he asked his mom.

"Dad isn't home now, and I don't have a head for those kinds of things," she replied.

Exasperated, he said, "Mom, when will Dad get home?"

"He'll be back in about an hour, Shaney. Why do you need his social security number anyway?"

"I told you, Mom, I have to fill out some forms on my background for the navy and they need to know."

"Doesn't the navy already know your father's social security number? I mean, the government already knows it, why don't you ask them?"

Mathews smiled, "It doesn't work that way, Mom. The social security administration guys aren't allowed to tell the navy the social security number of everyone in the country. That would violate the law. I have to ask him for it, and then he has to voluntarily provide it."

"But why do they need it at all?" she asked for the third time.

Becoming more frustrated by the second, he said, "Mom, they just do, that's how the process works. I have to ask him or you for it, I give it to them, and they verify that Dad is who he says he is, so that the security guys are sure I'm who I say I am."

"But—"

"Look, Mom, I'll call back and talk to Dad in an hour or so, OK?"

"All right, Shaney," she replied, "I still don't understand this. It seems so silly."

"I know, Mom," he answered. "I'll call back in an hour. Bye."

He heard the quick "bye" from his mother before he hung up and knew that his dad would get an earful from Mom when he got back. Dad would understand, he was a former navy man and would get Mom to understand.

"Sorry about that," he said to the girl behind the counter who was trying not to hear but couldn't help it, "Mom's terrific, but she just doesn't understand sometimes."

"It's OK," she replied with a smile. "You aren't the first person to go through this kind of a detailed background check."

He may not have been the first one to go through this, but this kind of scrutiny was new to him. He had to provide nearly everything there was to know about his identity and background; all that was left was giving a blood sample. He had filled in the forms with the schools he attended; every job he ever held, including working for the navy; his personal references; complete background information on his parents—names, birth dates and places, social security numbers; names and addresses of his aunts and uncles. They even wanted passport numbers for him and his parents.

Not having any of this information would likely cost him the opportunity to work here, wherever here was. He did not want to screw that up.

The look on his face must have betrayed his concern, because the girl said, "Don't worry about it too much. The security folks almost never get a complete package of information on someone. They would prefer it, but as long as they have a name and an address, they can usually confirm what they need to."

"Thanks," he replied. Gesturing to the nearby longue area he said, "I'll sit over here if it's all right until I can call my dad."

"Since you have the time, why don't you come with me and we'll get a Coke on the way to your psych eval?" she responded.

"Psych eval?" he repeated with a quizzical look.

"Yes," she said with another amused smile. "Everyone assigned here has to undergo one as part of the clearance process. It won't hurt a bit."

The smile lingered on her face as she gauged his reaction, and then she took his arm and led him down the hallway toward the snack area where a refrigerator was kept stocked with sodas and bottled water for the Level 2 staff. The SEAL, Ranger, and Recon Marine types always worried the most about the psych eval. They might face combat with as little concern as they would walking into a bathroom, but tell them a psychologist will evaluate them and they'll become instantly wary and nervous. Although it rarely happened, anyone who responded by panicking or getting agitated got immediately reassigned back to his or her original unit. If the reaction was very bad, they were usually discharged from the service.

For that reason, the procedure was for her to spring the psych eval requirement unexpectedly on the new recruits like Mathews in order to gauge their reactions. As the undercover member of the security staff, chosen as much for her good looks as her ability to use the .40 S&W automatic clipped under her desk, she had to write up a report as part of his security package.

CHAPTER 6

· ·

IT WAS 5:30 IN THE morning and 73 degrees in San Antonio, the low for the unusually warm fall day. The five men in the back of the van, however, were sweating profusely, even with the air conditioning set to maximum.

The driver was taking them to a twenty-four-hour self-storage facility. They had divested themselves of any identification or jewelry. They were also wearing dark nondescript clothes—either jeans and dark blue T-shirts or casual slacks and knit shirts. The men were all dark-skinned and cleanly shaven. Their skin color owed more to their Middle Eastern heritage than to exposure to the strong sun in the southern U.S., but it permitted each to pass for one of the numerous Mexican American citizens of San Antonio.

Most of the men had entered Texas by crossing the border illegally as part of small groups of migrant workers looking for better-paying jobs in the U.S. But, unlike the more than 600,000 law-abiding Mexican Americans in San Antonio, these men intended to kill as many people as they could before their "normal" workday began. Aziz and his followers would bring death to the infidel population of the Great Satan.

Each of the men spoke Spanish quite well after spending six months in their home countries learning the language using computer software. Aziz arranged to have someone friendly to the faith in the U.S. buy the software and ship them to the resident imam at a mosque in Lebanon;

he understood the faith properly and allowed the men to study there.

When their initial language training was complete, they had moved into Mexico, found modest accommodations, and spent another six months to a year speaking Spanish with native Mexicans. Living in Mexico allowed each man to spend time developing the personal contacts needed later for their trip across the border. They made friends in the local bars with men who wanted to come to the States. Each of Aziz's men, in fact, contributed the lion's share of the money needed for the group to cross the border and live for a short time in the U.S. until they could find work.

The actual border-crossing had proved to be ridiculously easy. Each man's small group paid another Mexican, known to insiders as a "burro," to drive them to a point near the Mexico-Texas border known to be under limited surveillance by the U.S. Border Patrol. When at their jump-off point, they simply walked across in broad daylight. One of the groups even crossed a small, waist-deep river to reach the border and never saw a single patrol agent during the six-hour walk.

After they were inside the United States, an American sympathetic to the plight of the poor immigrant Mexicans loaded them into his van and took them to a local church that provided food and shelter for the homeless. He did not even accept money for what he considered a charitable act pleasing to God. Like the local church, some of the other area churches even helped the immigrants look for work with construction or farming businesses, many of which were quick to welcome willing workers at a wage that a U.S. citizen would consider a pittance.

Once in the U.S., Aziz's terrorists would unobtrusively slip away from their lodgings to a prearranged pickup point. In the case of the San Antonio group, that was the small four-bedroom house the van driver had rented.

The driver was al-Qaeda's point man in San Antonio. He had seen the reply from the unknown man on the collectable figurines website telling him that today was the day to act. The five men had been in San Antonio for nearly three months, using the false documentation the driver had provided them to obtain entry-level jobs in local stores or construction companies.

In their off hours over the last several months, each man traveled separately to the storage facility the group was headed for now, using the time to prepare for today. As the van approached the key-card-controlled gate of the storage facility, the driver mentally reviewed what he would do with the van after today.

He had replaced the van's normal license plates with a set he had stolen three hours ago from a car parked on a side street; he would dump them down a sewer grate after he put the originals back on when the day's work was done.

The van was plain white and its tires were well worn. When the morning's activities were complete, he would have the tires replaced with new ones at a nearby garage. The van would also receive a thorough interior vacuuming and be run through a car wash twice to keep any forensic traces to a minimum. Then he would never use it again. In fact, it would be sold within the week to a small used-car dealer on the other side of the city.

The driver stopped at the entrance of the storage facility. He lowered the window and slid his card out to the key-card-reader slot and then punched in his four-digit code with his rubber-gloved finger. The electronically controlled gate slid open. He steered through the gate and proceeded slowly down the main access road. After seventy-five yards, he turned right toward one of the rows of storage cells. Each cell in the block was contained in a long, concrete building and was accessed through an orange roll-up door secured with a lock.

As the driver turned, each man put on an oversized hat and sunglasses and donned a pair of thin rubber gloves. Then each man drew a small keyring containing two keys from his pocket and waited.

The driver reached the first storage cell and halted the van. One of the men in the back immediately slid open the side door and stepped out. Moving toward the storage door, he bent to insert one of the keys into the lock as the van glided down the row to another cell, where the second of the five exited to unlock his storage cell. The first man's lock clicked and he pulled the door up, revealing an almond-colored 1979 Chevy Scottsdale K10 pickup truck with a white fiberglass cap on the bed.

He got into the truck, started it, and drove into the alley between the long storage cell buildings, where he stopped. Stepping out of the truck, he crossed to the open unit's door, reached up, pulled it closed, and then relocked it.

He got back into the truck and pulled its door closed, and then noticed the white van heading back up the road it came in on toward the gate.

Behind him, the other men had pulled their vehicles into the alley between the storage buildings. The last man was just returning to his brown 1983 Lincoln Town Car after locking his storage unit as the first man put his truck in gear and began to follow the van out of the gate. The other men followed.

After they left the storage area and its video surveillance coverage, the men removed their oversized hats and sunglasses and strictly obeyed the speed limits and traffic signals on the way to their destinations.

FORTY MINUTES LATER, THE FIRST man pulled the Chevy over on the side of the road on Crockett Street near San Antonio's famed River Walk in the downtown area. He slid open the partition window that led to the truck bed, reached through the narrow opening under the edge of a black tarp, and pulled a small device through the window, its black wires leading back into the truck bed area. Checking the settings on the device, he pressed a red button on it and then reached back through the window to set it down on the truck bed, its wires trailing back under the tarp-covered lump in the darkness of the bed.

Carrying his hat and glasses, he exited the truck, locked the doors, removed two quarters from his pocket, and crossed to the nearest parking meter. He put the quarters into the meter and watched the electronic display change from "Expired" to "2:00 Hours"—more than enough time.

Moving down Crockett Street, he discarded his hat and sunglasses in a trashbin and then removed his rubber gloves and dropped them in a different trashcan. The infidels were so helpful. He continued west and turned left onto Navarro Street before stopping next to a VIA bus stop. In a few minutes, he would board the bus and head across town to his regular job in the Big T grocery store. *Allahu Akbar!*

THE OTHER FOUR MEN COMPLETED the same task in other locations in San Antonio. The second man parked his 1988 Ford Bronco in the lot north of the Alamo just across East Houston Street, armed its cargo, walked across the lot to 3rd Street, and hailed a cab for the trip back to his apartment. He was not due at work in the nearby Radio Shack until noon.

The third man parked his 2006 Mercedes CLS along Dallas Street near the Baptist Medical Center within sight of the Emergency entrance. He hung a replica of the Medical Center's parking pass for doctors on the rearview mirror and exited the car. Locking it, he crossed to the VIA bus stop on Navarro Street, just as the purple and white bus was pulling up. Once on board, he noticed the first driver from his group sitting on the right side and took a seat six rows in front of him, but did not acknowledge him or approach him in any way. Looking out the window, he said a quiet prayer for success to Allah as the first bright rays of sunlight began to shine.

The fourth man parked his 1994 Dodge Grand Caravan minivan in the parking lot of a San Antonio Motor Lodge, then crossed Santa Rosa Avenue and hailed a cab to his job at a construction site in the southwestern part of the city.

The last of Aziz's men had the job that entailed more risk, but the driver of the white van would help. The fifth man drove his Lincoln south on the Southwest Freeway, officially known as I-10, until he reached the I-35 South junction, where both major highways merged. As he entered the junction, he turned on his emergency flashers and pulled off to the left side of the road into the V-shaped area formed by the joining roadways and stopped the car. Moving quickly without trying to rush too much, he exited the car, moved to the hood, and opened it. Feeling the heat rising from the big V-8, he reached inside the engine compartment, gripped some of the wiring that led to the car's computer module, and began pulling on it. The wiring was covered in grease, and he had trouble holding on to it. Finally, by twisting the wire into a loop around his hand, he yanked it free of the computer's housing, effectively disabling it.

Hearing the sound of a car pulling up behind him, he looked up to see the white van. Its emergency flashers were blinking, the headlights briefly blinding the Lincoln's driver as the van came to a stop.

The driver of the van got out and walked over to shake hands. For the benefit of the drivers passing by, he pretended to look inside the engine compartment. He removed a pair of wire cutters from his pants and cut the terminal connectors off the wires the driver had pulled out of the car's computer, allowing the connector ends to fall to the ground. The car would not move under its own power again.

After playacting a few more moments of animated conversation, both men walked over to the van and got in. The driver started it and accelerated to merge with the light morning traffic heading south on I-35. He would drop the man off at his apartment and then take the van in for its new tires after swapping the plates again. Allah was with them so far, he thought. The infidels would feel the crushing weight of Allah's justice this day.

The brown Lincoln remained undisturbed at the interstate junction, its yellow emergency flashers blinking once every two seconds, and its hood up in the universal sign of engine trouble.

BY 7 A.M., TRAFFIC ON THE highways in the San Antonio area was as thick as it ever got during a workweek. The cars slogged along, slowly crawling forward at irregular intervals but not stopping. Officer José Bravo was among them in his patrol car, heading south on I-10. As he approached the I-35 junction, he noticed an abandoned brown Lincoln with its hood up and flashers blinking. Radioing in his intention to check out the vehicle, he activated his light bar and pulled left out of traffic behind the vehicle. The passenger compartment appeared empty, and with the hood up, he assumed that whoever left it would be returning to have it towed. He keyed the Texas license plate number into his computer for a quick wants/warrants check. The vehicle didn't come back as stolen, so he decided he would give it a quick once-over and then put a warning sticker on it. If it was still here in two days, the city would tow it and the owner would have to pay a fine and the impound fee.

Officer Bravo got out of his cruiser with the sticker pad tucked in the small of his back, holding his flashlight with his left hand and resting his right hand lightly on the butt of his holstered sidearm. *You never know what you're walking into as you approach a vehicle, no matter how innocent the scene appears*, he thought, and so he always followed proper procedure.

He approached the vehicle slowly, the thick soles of his shoes crunching on the tiny pieces of loose gravel underfoot. His well-trained eyes never left the car, and he continued walking in the driver's blind spot, using as much of the car as possible for cover.

Once he could see inside the vehicle, a quick check with his flashlight verified that the passenger compartment was empty, as he suspected. Removing his sticker pad and placing it on the roof, he wrote the date and time on the top sticker. As he began to peel off the backing, he heard his cell phone chime.

He opened it up and saw that his wife had sent him a text message. "Bring home milk – we love you." Deciding to respond later, he smiled at the thought of his wife of ten years and their two children. The kids were always drinking milk. He and his wife would need to buy a cow soon to keep up with the demand.

Returning to work, he placed then red violation sticker on the driver's side window. Then the timer inside the car reached zero.

WHEN THE COMPOSITION C-4, COMMONLY just known as C-4, in the trunk of the Lincoln detonated, it chemically decomposed so quickly that the gases released expanded outward at a rate of 26,400 feet per second. The steel of the car's body in front of that expanding pressure wave fragmented into thousands of pieces. Right behind the pieces of the car's body, the twenty pounds of nails packed around the thirty, two-pound blocks of C-4 accelerated outward just as quickly.

Officer Bravo died first. The nails and the parts of the car body that surrendered to the laws of physics literally tore his body, ballistic vest, sidearm, and clothes into tiny pieces a few microseconds after the car had disintegrated. A man dedicated to helping others, Officer Bravo would have been appalled to know that bone fragments from his body and the shattered pieces of his equipment shot into people nearby, killing them instantly.

The expanding wall of debris from the car moved outward from the junction at a speed no human mind could possibly recognize and react to in time to avoid. Vehicles on both nearby highways immediately turned into burning wreckage, their occupants dead from overwhelming penetrating trauma.

Cars slammed into other vehicles blown in front of them by the explosion. Drivers farther away from the blast site slammed on their brakes in an attempt to avoid crashes and injury. Some were successful, others were not.

A big rig moving at seventy miles an hour became an out-of-control battering ram when its driver tried to push his brake pedal through the floor of the cab and swerved to avoid hitting anything. In spite of his heroic efforts, the 60,000 pounds of steel and cargo wouldn't stop. The rig immediately jackknifed and rolled over, slamming the driver's head into the cab's roof, breaking his neck and crushing his skull. The rig's momentum carried it toward the slowing cars approaching the junction and crushed several of them, finishing the work of the explosives by killing victims who might have otherwise survived. Fires broke out everywhere as hot metal and sparking electrical systems ignited gasoline from ruptured tanks.

The survivors on the edges of the explosion were the worst off. The nails around the C-4 punctured their bodies, destroying eyes, impaling organs, and piercing gas tanks with hot metal, which caused secondary explosions and fires.

As the minds of the wounded survivors began to catch up with the injuries to the bodies they lived in, the screaming began. One moment, there was peace and the morning commute, the next, there was carnage within a 300-foot radius of the blast.

EMERGENCY CALLS BEGAN TO FLOOD in to the San Antonio 911 Dispatch Center from the I-10/I-35 junction, and San Antonio's first responders moved into action. All area police cruisers immediately headed for the area. Those nearest heard the detonation through closed windows and saw the smoke, so without waiting for orders, they instantly activated their lights and sirens and accelerated toward the small mushroom cloud rising into the sky. Many of them used their radio microphones to alert the dispatchers of the disaster.

The continuing cascade of 911 calls into the dispatch center and the increasingly horrified voices of the people on the scene interspersed with the background screams of the wounded began to worry the dispatchers. They started to realize the number of wounded would be large, and they had no idea how many had died. Once the senior dispatchers made sense of the combined chaos of the 911 calls and the radio calls from the cruisers approaching the scene, they put out a general disaster alert to all fire and police forces in the area. The disaster alert, coupled with immediate on-scene coverage by the news media helicopters, caused the administrators of the area hospitals to implement their mass-casualty plans. The hospitals paged all off-duty doctors and nurses and asked that they should come to work immediately or remain near a phone and expect extended duty shifts.

FROM HIS OFFICE, THE MAYOR watched the scene of the explosion on TV with his chief of police, who had come up for a previously scheduled meeting. The mayor wondered what tanker truck had caused such a large explosion. He could see only the wreckage of one truck on the screen from the overhead shot provided by the orbiting news helicopter, but it was not a tanker truck. No matter. It was a horrible tragedy, but car accidents and the occasional explosion happened from time to time.

Once the chief of police and the fire chief gave him some answers, he would have to talk to the public. He asked his press secretary to tell the media that he would have a statement in an hour or so, and continued to watch the coverage on TV.

TEN MINUTES AFTER THE FIRST explosion, the timers in the Dodge van in the Motor Lodge parking lot and the Ford SUV across from the Alamo also went off.

The van's explosive load-out was the same as the brown Lincoln's. The nails and metal fragments from the van ripped through the thin walls of the nearby motel, killing dozens of men, women, and children sleeping in their beds, and shattering the glass doors in the entryway. Flying glass fragments sliced up the four people in the lobby and the two hotel desk clerks. They all bled profusely, but would survive.

The small groups of people walking across the hotel's parking lot getting an early start on the day were not as lucky. The blast threw them into the exterior walls of the building, and they were crushed to death by the pressure wave and the impact. Some were tossed into the middle of the parking lot, to lay bleeding from penetrating wounds from the flying debris and broken bones. One man was thrown into the path of an oncoming car on Santa Rosa Avenue and was mercifully unconscious when the car, having no time to stop, crushed his skull like a sledgehammer hitting a cantaloupe.

THE FORD SUV HAD BEEN loaded with ball bearings instead of nails. The ball bearings raced away at 23,000 feet per second from the remains of the SUV, tearing through exterior walls and embedding themselves in rooms of nearby buildings, most of which were unoccupied. They shattered huge sections of the exterior walls of the old mission famous for the heroic last stand against the Mexican Army under General Santa Anna.

The damage to this historic monument would be irreparable, but miraculously, no one died from the exploding SUV. The lights at the nearby intersections had been red when the counter in the SUV reached zero, creating an artificial buffer around the vehicle. The flying debris missed the few pedestrians inside the zone, and the Alamo was devoid of tourists this early in the morning.

"WHAT THE HELL IS GOING ON?" the mayor was starting to wonder. The newsies were reporting two other possible explosions in the city and showing overhead video from their helicopters of smoke clouds. One was rising in the vicinity of the Alamo, the other in a section of the city he did not immediately identify as having any significant landmark. The chief of police was on his feet now, staring at the TV, thinking to himself, *No, it couldn't be. Not here.*

THE SAN ANTONIO 911 CENTER had deteriorated from busy and tense into barely controlled chaos. Calls were now coming in about two other explosions and urgent requests for paramedics, ambulances, and the fire department. Dispatchers called area police and fire units and directed them to the sites of the newest detonations. In between radio calls, they looked at each other with sadness and horror as they did what they could to coordinate the response to these fatal disasters.

AT THE I-10/I-35 JUNCTION, traffic was backed up for miles to the north on both highways. Dozens of people north of the scene had rushed to the center of the carnage carrying small first-aid kits and fire extinguishers from their cars and trucks. Paramedics, firefighters, and ambulances were arriving every few minutes, heading through city streets and then up the southbound off-ramps to reach the scene. They began to search for survivors, finding fewer and fewer the closer they moved toward the center of the devastation. Most survivors were at the outer edges, suffering from horrendous wounds from flying glass and metal and in some cases, first- and second-degree burns. Firefighters began soaking the scene with retardant foam and water to put out the sporadic vehicle fires and dilute the gasoline puddles on the concrete.

News helicopters hovered over the area, and two police helicopters with onboard paramedics landed in the southbound lanes of the highway, ready to fly the most grievously wounded to the city's hospitals with level one trauma centers as soon as they could be safely moved.

As the ambulances were loaded with the less critically wounded, the drivers headed off the highway and called in to find out which hospitals were available to take their patients. The most seriously injured were taken to Christus Santa Rosa and Southwest General hospitals; the more moderate injuries were transported to Baptist Medical Center.

ON CROCKETT STREET NEAR THE River Walk, the detonator in the 1979 Chevy truck with the white cap reached zero.

Another people-killer packed with nails to increase the effectiveness of the shrapnel, it detonated with the same lethal force as the other car bombs. Forty-five people in the immediate area died as the shrapnel lanced into their vital organs, while eighty-two more suffered critical injuries. As more bystanders outside this blast zone ran to help where they could, the screams began in another area of the city.

AS THE VIDEO FEED FROM the news helicopter zoomed in near the River Walk where the latest cloud of smoke was rising, the chief of police looked at the mayor and said in as level a voice as twenty-three years of experience could give him, "Our city is under attack, sir. This is not coincidence or multiple accidents. We need to move you to the city emergency management center and, as of now, you and your family are under police protection twenty-four hours a day."

The chief grabbed the phone, dialed a number from memory, and began issuing orders. The mayor sat stunned in his leather chair, eyes glued to the TV, the chief's words not quite sinking in yet. He never expected this. This was not New York. Why would they hit his city? His thoughts became random as his unprepared mind tried to grapple with the horrific reality.

He had a meeting in an hour about the budget. Maybe he should call his wife and see if the kids were all right? What about the dinner tonight at the Kiwanis Club? He was supposed to get an award tonight. He would have to reschedule it.

As the chief rattled off orders, he looked at the mayor, saw the unfocused eyes and the pale face of a man in shock, and silently cursed him. Most politicians were about as useful in a crisis as baby wipes at a sewage spill. Like so many other politicians, they never learn that crisis management is part of the job once they take office. They never think it could happen *here.*

FOUR AMBULANCES WERE ALREADY IN the bays at the emergency entrance to the Baptist Medical Center, and the driver of the Northside Ambulance Company's Unit 5 would have to wait before he brought this load of wounded people in. The patients in the back were some of the walking wounded from the I-10/I-35 highway scene. The paramedic kept an eye on them for additional signs of shock, routinely checking for responsive pupils and any signs of tenderness or delirium. The driver pulled the ambulance onto Dallas Street and stopped next to a Mercedes CLS to wait for the ambulance bay to clear.

JUST MINUTES LATER, THE TIMER on the bomb in the CLS went off. Nails exploded everywhere, shredding the ambulance and the people within it without remorse or hesitation. The nails pierced the thin walls of the other ambulances in the bays and slashed through the Emergency Room proper, killing men, women, and children innocently waiting with colds, broken arms, and fevers. Some of the other survivors from the highway waiting in exam rooms and three of the ambulance crews heading back out to their rigs were also hit by nails and other flying debris, making their injuries worse—and killing even more.

BY NOW, IT WAS NATIONAL and international news. The cable networks had picked up the video feed from the San Antonio television stations and were broadcasting it continuously. A few moments later, it was international news. U.S. and foreign government agency watch centers and the command posts of various U.S. military installations were watching as well.

"David," asked Emily with some desperation, "what do we do?"

Cain's face revealed a mixture of grim acceptance and horrified resignation. "Everybody stand by. Get to your positions and wait for the phones to ring. The folks in San Antonio have their hands full at the moment, and we can't do much more than watch. Keep an eye on the information feeds from your agencies. Look out for world reaction and any claims of responsibility that seem credible. For now, that's all we can do."

Thinking for a moment, he then said, "Expect that we will be working some longer shifts for the next week or so. Call home if you need to and make the necessary arrangements."

HEADING EAST OVER THE ATLANTIC near the Azores, Aziz was sitting on a leather chair in his G550 traveling at Mach .85 at an altitude of

43,000 feet. He was enjoying a glass of freshly squeezed Florida orange juice and watching TV. The satellite dish in the aerodynamic fairing on the top of the G550's fuselage had cost him $20,000, but it was worth every penny. Capable of tracking any satellite even at the speeds the jet traveled at, it was currently locked on to Intelsat 25, allowing him to watch the BBC World News feed.

His eyes devoured the broadcasted scenes. All those dead bodies, the smoke, the fires, and the complete chaos he had brought to the infidels. This was truly the work of Allah. He had become Allah's flaming sword of vengeance.

He washed his face and hands, removed his personal prayer rug from one of the storage cabinets, and set it on the floor. He faced Mecca, which happened to be in the direction the jet was traveling, and began to pray. His smile did not falter as he continued his devotions.

OFF THE COAST OF SOUTH CAROLINA, a Marine Corps KC-130F cargo plane began to level off at 25,000 feet. The major in command glanced at his instruments and began trimming the aircraft to level flight. When he was satisfied, he engaged the autopilot. The aircraft was on a course south that the autopilot would adjust at least three more times under the watchful eyes of the major and his copilot before beginning the decent into Guantanamo.

Keeping one hand on the yoke, he looked behind him and down to the enlisted loadmaster standing at the base of the stairs leading to the cockpit. "Tell the civvy we should arrive in about five and a half hours."

"Yes, sir," the NCO replied loudly, so he could be heard over the drone of the transport's four Allison turboprop engines. He headed back toward the passenger seats that were installed between the cockpit and the cargo in the rear of the plane. If the plane landed hard or crashed and the cargo broke free, the pallets of fresh food, MREs, spare parts, and mail from the U.S. would be cushioned by the passengers' bodies as inertia would drive the pallets into the front bulkhead. Even worse, the passengers would watch it happen because they were facing the rear of the aircraft.

The loadmaster walked along the right side of the cargo hold to the seat row closest to the cargo pallets, where the only civilian on board sat alone by unspoken agreement among the Marine passengers. The Marines were not being intentionally rude; they just did not associate with civilians beyond the usual pleasantries. Of course, if the civilians were attractive females, then that was another matter. Special Agent Johnson did not meet that requirement.

The loadmaster leaned down to be heard over the engines, and said, practically in Johnson's ear, "Five and a half hours, sir." A Marine would refer to a tree as "sir" given the need to address one.

Johnson, like everyone else in the cargo area, was wearing bright yellow earplugs but heard the loadmaster clearly. The government could have a cargo plane built that could refuel in midair, deploy an M-1 tank from its cargo bay at 180 knots, refuel another aircraft, and perform rocket-assisted takeoffs from unimproved runways—but they wouldn't insulate the cargo area to protect the ears of its travelers or keep anyone warm. On board this aircraft, people were one step below cargo as far as its engineers were concerned.

Johnson wrapped himself in two blankets the loadmaster had provided before takeoff with a slightly superior grin. He nodded his thanks rather than shouting back and gave him a thumbs-up to show that he had understood before wrapping the blankets tighter around himself to ward off the chilly air in the cargo hold. The loadmaster, his superior grin back in place, turned and moved forward in the aircraft to talk to the other Marines on board. Doubtless, the loadmaster wanted to tell a few jokes about the "soft" civilian to his fellows.

JOHNSON GOT SETTLED COMFORTABLY IN the blankets, tried to ignore the strong smell of aviation fuel in the cargo hold, and closed his eyes to return to his musings about the man he would interrogate in Guantanamo.

Ali al-Mushaff was a former Taliban district head in the eastern part of Afghanistan, near the capital, Kabul. He spent his time ensuring the enforcers of Sharia law were well funded by taking teams of hired thugs out into the small shops that lined the marketplaces in Jalalabad and shaking down the shopkeepers for "donations" to the faith that would prove their devotion to Allah. Naturally, Ali always kept a small percentage as his rightful earnings from doing the work of Allah. Taliban finance minister Sadig al-Faisal received the rest.

Johnson knew from the transcripts of Ali's other interrogation sessions that Ali's work had brought him to Sadig's attention because of his continual ability to produce more wealth for the Taliban than the other district heads did. Sadig routinely asked him to Kabul to dine with his family. Ali even once attended a dinner with the Great Leader of the Jihad as the guest of honor.

Beyond that, the transcripts had produced little more than anecdotal information about the workings of the Taliban and his methods of gathering "donations." Ali was always careful to state that the shopkeepers voluntarily provided the money, but the interrogators noted that it was obvious that the assaults and intimidation of Ali's heavies were the primary reasons for the shopkeepers to part with their money.

Sadig was the person Johnson really wanted to know about. As the Taliban Finance Minister, Sadig managed the Taliban's finances, and the money certainly wasn't all kept in Afghanistan. The Taliban had only had seven years of total rule over a nation, but they had used that time well.

After gaining control, the Taliban leadership immediately plundered the country's limited treasury. The taxes paid in the name of Allah by the people were used to buy arms and equipment, establish comfortable residences for the leaders, and join forces with similar extremist organizations like al-Qaeda. While not a wealthy country, Afghanistan did have one very large and profitable cash crop in place when the Taliban took over: the poppy.

Although the Taliban took steps to eliminate all poppy growing within Afghanistan, some fields were "appropriated" and maintained by Taliban leaders to ensure a continuing positive cash flow. The remaining fields were slowly plowed under over a period of five years, but only after as much opium as possible had been harvested from them. This allowed the Taliban to claim to be outlawing and destroying a narcotic incompatible with their faith, but reap the monetary rewards quietly. As with many extremists, religious or not, hypocrisy was the order of the day.

After the opium resin had been gathered from the lacerated bulbs of the poppy flower, the Taliban sold it to drug dealers to convert into heroin. The amount of money raised from this was mildly embarrassing to the Taliban leaders, and it was certainly not used to improve the lives of the Afghan people. They were, after all, not nearly as pious as the Taliban leadership.

Sums of money in the tens or hundreds of millions of U.S. dollars or euros didn't do anyone any good just sitting in a bank in downtown Kabul. The Taliban then invested or transferred that money out of the country and stored it in safe banks elsewhere in the world under the names of trusted nominees. Some of that money was gifted to al-Qaeda. The question was, where did it go? Sadig would know, if he was still alive. Johnson would try to persuade Ali to tell him where to find Sadig.

The KC-130F shuddered briefly in the airflow and Johnson tried to shift in the narrow seat to a more comfortable position. His right buttock had fallen asleep and he needed to get the circulation restarted. He reached under his seat, got a bottle of water from his travel bag, and took a big swig from it.

Resettling himself, he looked at his watch and saw that he still had five hours to go. He decided he would sleep for the rest of the flight, so he closed his eyes and imagined his wife's smiling face. Thinking of her was the best way to let his mind relax and then drift. A few minutes later, he was sound asleep as the KC-130F continued to drone south toward Cuba.

CHAPTER 7

"LIEUTENANT MATHEWS?" ASKED COLONEL SIMON. The question startled Mathews awake. He had been dozing in a leather chair in front of the TV in the Level 2 lounge. The room was spartanly furnished with two brown leather couches, a wooden table in the corner, and four matching leather chairs on a white tile floor. A commercial for a toilet-bowl cleaner was flashing on the screen. Looking up to see Colonel Simon leaning over him, Mathews quickly got to his feet. Zeus, naturally accompanying his master, sat on the floor by the door.

"Sorry, sir," he responded, "I didn't notice you come in."

The colonel was all business. "How long have you been asleep?"

"A few minutes," Mathews answered. It was a little surprising to see a full-bird colonel pissed about a lowly lieutenant catching a few winks when he wasn't even on duty.

"Then I can safely assume you weren't watching the news," the colonel responded with a slightly mollified look.

"No, sir. I was watching the History Channel. They had a series on about—"

"Forget it. We've just been attacked. A series of car bombs were detonated in San Antonio. We don't know if they were suicide bombers or something else."

Mathews' face changed from freshly roused to surprised, to the look of a man trained to defend his nation, looking for an enemy to shoot at.

"How can I help, sir?" was his only question.

The colonel noted the change in the SEAL with satisfaction. This young man was going to be worth having on the team.

"The general has decided to authorize your access to our mission and as of now you are part of the team. He is shortcutting the standard process. If we've been attacked and we get assigned a mission in response, we'll use all the people we can get. Come with me and you'll get your security briefing and your new access badge."

Mathews followed the colonel down the hall to the conference room, with Zeus trotting after his master. Mathews sat in one of the steel-gray chairs along one side of the government-issued conference table that Simon motioned toward. Colonel Simon gestured toward the floor and Zeus promptly lay down near the door, eyes glued to his master. Simon touched a control mounted on the table and the lights dimmed in the room. He touched another and the first briefing slide illuminated the old-fashioned pull-down screen hanging from the wall at the end of the table.

The colonel began, "You are being read into the security compartment that protects our operations. As a member of this unit, your life and the lives of your fellow team members will be dependent upon you keeping everything that you do here a secret. You are familiar with these restrictions as a SEAL, and you are still subject to them. Do you understand?"

"Yes, sir," replied Mathews. This was old hat. He knew not to talk about what you do on missions, not even in your sleep. That was the first rule when you joined a SEAL team.

"All right then, before we start, it's time for you to sign some paperwork."

Paperwork? thought Mathews. That was new. Usually, being a SEAL and having his life on the line meant that no one expected him to blow a mission by talking about it. He'd never had to sign anything agreeing to keep his mouth shut.

The colonel slid two forms across the table to him and then dropped a pen on top of them. Seeing the look of confusion on the younger man's face, he said, "You sign, or you go back to your parent unit." It was a matter-of-fact tone of command that might have been used to tell the SEAL something as basic as "You drink water regularly or you die."

The steel behind those words was unmistakable. Sign or you go no further. Never one to back away from any challenge, Mathews took the pen, didn't so much as glance at the forms except to find the places his signature belonged, and signed them both.

Colonel Simon leaned across the table and gathered up the forms and the pen.

"Let's begin," he intoned and he looked toward the briefing screen. Mathews turned his attention to the screen as the colonel began to read from the slide projected on it.

"This briefing is classified, TOP SECRET – CAPTIVE DRAGON. CAPTIVE DRAGON is the classified codeword for the security compartment that protects our operations and their associated intelligence support. We conduct operations against known terrorists, terrorist cells, terrorist organizations, and nation-states or elements of nation-states, as directed by the president and the secretary of defense. Members of the appropriate congressional committees are briefed into the CAPTIVE DRAGON compartment and are kept properly informed of our actions by the secretary of defense. All CAPTIVE DRAGON operations are governed under the appropriate U.S. laws, to include U.S.C. Title 10 (Armed Forces), and U.S.C. Title 50 (War and National Defense). Intelligence support to U.S. law enforcement agencies is governed under U.S.C. Title 18 (Crimes and Criminal Procedure)."

The colonel paused and looked at Mathews. "Any questions so far?"

Smiling slightly, the lieutenant responded, "No, sir."

"Very well." The colonel continued, "Our operations can include covert surveillance of terrorists overseas, the capture of these terrorists in cooperation with a foreign government, and, on rare occasions, the elimination of a terrorist if they don't 'come along peacefully,' as they say in the old westerns."

Looking intently at Mathews again, he said, "I want this clearly understood—we are not assassins, Lieutenant. We are members of the U.S. military and act accordingly. If a bad guy chooses a firefight as opposed to surrender, then we defend ourselves as needed, but we don't shoot people in the head in the middle of the night and leave the bodies for the vultures, no matter what they've done. Is that clear?"

"Yes, sir," replied Mathews emphatically, nodding his head once.

"Good," responded the colonel, the edge creeping back into his voice, "because if you violate the rules of engagement we tell you to operate under, you will go to Fort Leavenworth Prison for the next thirty years, clear?"

An even more emphatic Mathews answered, "I understand you very clearly, sir."

"You'd better." Turning back to the briefing, he continued, "There is also an intelligence support component that is provided by the counter-terrorism folks based out of Fort Meade, referred to as CTS. We won't and will never know the sources they use to provide us the information they have, but when they provide it, we listen and treat it as gospel. That information is also classified within this security compartment and will bear the codewords CAPTIVE DRAGON. Additionally, whatever we learn while on a mission is fed back into them."

The colonel touched a control on the conference table and the lights came back up. "Do you have any questions?"

Turning from the screen to face Colonel Simon, Mathews thought a moment and said, "Yes, sir. What will I be doing?"

"Before I answer that," the colonel stood and Mathews followed suit, "let me welcome you to the 152nd Joint Special Missions Unit." The colonel reached out to shake Mathews' hand.

"We are administratively attached directly to the Joint Chiefs of Staff and take our orders directly from the chairman. Those orders will originate in either the SECDEFs office or the White House. Informally, we're known as the Wraiths."

"Thank you, sir," replied Mathews, his face lit up like a sixteen-year-old getting his own car on Christmas morning.

Smiling at the young man's enthusiasm, the colonel headed for the door. Zeus rose from the floor and trotted out into the hallway, and then looked back expectantly, waiting for his master. Zeus had been through this routine more times than the lieutenant had. Mathews followed Colonel Simon out into the hallway. Unlike the dog, he didn't know where they were heading next.

The colonel led Mathews back down the hall past the lounge toward the entry area and the passenger elevator Mathews had come in on. As they reached it, the colonel pulled an ID badge from his pocket and handed it to Mathews.

"That's yours," he said, "keep it with you at all times when you're here. Prior to missions, it will be surrendered at your jump-off point and returned when you return. Without it, you go nowhere on this base and are subject to immediate arrest by the guard force if you are asked for it and can't produce it."

Nodding, Mathews took the badge. His picture and an expiration date were on the front, but that was all. On the back was a black-and-white digitized photo of him in the upper right corner and a black magnetic stripe down the length of the left side.

"The badge has a chip in it that can be read by a scanner," said the colonel while Mathews inspected the new ID. "Don't ever swipe it in one of the readers. Always wave it over the blue square on the reader in the same swiping movement you would use if you did swipe it through. The magnetic stripe on the back is a fake. It's intended to catch anyone trying to use the badge to gain access to a secure area."

Simon continued, a friendly warning in his tone, "If you swipe it through a reader, security teams with drawn weapons show up and will make your day very unpleasant. Go ahead and check to see if it works."

Mathews waved the badge over the blue spot on the reader and the elevator doors opened. The colonel stepped in, Zeus hot on his heels, and then Mathews joined them.

The colonel motioned toward the elevator controls and the associated badge reader, "There are nine levels to this complex, not counting the hangar level you came in from. The complex itself is a refurbished nuclear weapons assembly, a storage and handling facility we took over from the Department of Energy after the last nuclear weapons reduction treaty took effect. It was built deep underground to limit radiation leakage or damage to the environment in the event of an accidental detonation. We expanded the surface facilities to accommodate our little Air Force and converted the original first two levels into a depot-level maintenance facility for the aircraft."

Waving his badge over the card reader, he pressed the button for Level 8.

"Level 1 is the main hangar beneath the surface. It serves as long-term aircraft and parts storage as well as a larger work area for depot-level maintenance on the aircraft. Level 2 is a 'showplace' administrative area. It also holds a small security detachment and some temporary quarters for visitors and people awaiting clearances."

The elevator began its descent and the colonel continued, "Level 3 is the main base security office, command post, and the security armory. Level 4 has the enlisted quarters, a small post exchange, and the third level of an indoor park. Level 5 has officer quarters, another small post exchange, and the second level of the indoor park. Level 6 provides housing for lieutenant colonels and above, another small post exchange, and the first level of the indoor park. Level 7 holds the main command post and operations planning areas."

The elevator chimed and came to a halt. The doors, however, didn't open. The colonel turned to Mathews.

"Levels 7, 8, and 9 require that at least one person present an ID badge to the reader before the doors open."

Demonstrating, the colonel waved his badge at the blue spot on the reader and the doors slid open to reveal two men in body armor holding AR-15 automatic rifles. They stood facing the door across the small hallway from the elevator behind four layered sheets of clear polycarbonate with spaces on each side. This would provide them solid cover to protect themselves from any gunfire from the elevator car.

As the colonel, trailed by Zeus and Mathews, left the elevator, each man came to attention and then tracked their rifle muzzles toward the group when they walked past.

The colonel followed the hall left in a 90-degree turn and then right through another 90-degree turn down a hallway roughly 200 feet long with heavily reinforced doors along its walls. Each door had a sign on it and a badge reader on the wall next to the handle. Keeping pace with the colonel and Zeus, Mathews tried to read some of the signs but only caught "Ops Plans" and "Team Areas" as they walked past, and "Security Post 8" on the last door on the left.

Drawing his attention back to their destination, he noticed that the doorway at the end of the hall was not just heavily reinforced but an actual machined steel vault door. Easily eight feet high and wide, it looked just like the vault door in the main branch of the Chemical Bank his father used to take him to as a boy to deposit his allowance money.

It must have been three feet thick, and the six-inch pins that secured it were hardened and tempered steel.

"The nuclear weapon triggers used to be stored here," Simon said. "We use it for secure storage of personal equipment."

The door was wide open, its edge touching the outer wall. Immediately inside it, Mathews saw the closed inner steel cage door and two men behind it carrying sidearms in shoulder holsters. Seeing the colonel approach, each man came to attention and greeted him.

"Good afternoon, gentlemen," said the colonel. "This is Lieutenant Mathews, a new member of the team. He needs to be outfitted with the usual gear."

Turning to Mathews he said, "After they've outfitted you, use your badge to access the 'Team Areas' door. When you're inside, ask for Captain Mallory. He's expecting you. He'll get you set up with a training schedule. You have a great deal to learn."

Mathews tried to look deeper into the vault as one of the men opened the inner cage door. "Yes, sir," he responded.

The colonel turned and headed back down the corridor with Zeus by his side. One of the men behind the cage door said with the slyest grin as he opened it, "Welcome to the Wraiths, Lieutenant. Please step into the cage and strip down to your undershorts."

CAIN WAS STARING AT THE screens in the CTS watch center. On the large screen to the left were the news feeds, split into four quadrants: three cable news networks—Fox, CNN, and MSNBC—and the Arab language news broadcast from Al Arabiya, transmitted from Dubai. On the screen at the right was a current list of the information the U.S. government had on what had happened. It was woefully uninformative.

SECRET – CAPTIVE DRAGON
Apparent Multiple VBIED Attacks – San Antonio, TX

CONFIRMED DEAD:	78 (Expected to Reach More Than 300)
INJURED:	200+ (Estimate)

VBIED PLATFORMS:	5
INDICATIONS & WARNING:	NONE
AVAILABLE INTELLIGENCE:	NONE
ACTIONS:	

> Homeland Security & FBI Investigation Teams En Route
> Homeland Security Raised Terror Threat Level to Imminent
> All State & Local Governments Notified

SECRET – CAPTIVE DRAGON

The only classified items were the last two. Anyone could get the other information by watching TV for five minutes.

Cain hated this facet of his profession. His nation had just been attacked and, as a member of one of the most capable and resourceful intelligence communities in the world, he had nothing to work with. No intelligence source had even hinted at this. None of the major agencies had any indication that a series of car bombs would be detonated in a major city.

He had taken a call from the Director of NSA's executive officer fifteen minutes ago. The DIRNSA would be there in a few moments to see what CTS had on the events, and Cain had precious little information to offer him.

Reaching into his sport coat's inner pocket, he withdrew a blue necktie and began to put it on, and then stuffed it back in his coat in annoyance. If the DIRNSA complained he was not wearing a tie in the middle of this, he probably did not need to be DIRNSA.

"Listen up, people. DIRNSA will be here in a few minutes. If he asks you a question, answer him candidly and completely."

They absorbed his announcement, and seeing that he had nothing more to add, returned to monitoring the information flow from the agencies.

As Cain looked his people over, he noticed Emily sitting at her position with a stony expression of near anger. He walked down the steps into the liaison area and touched her on the shoulder.

"What's wrong? You look like you want to take someone's head off!"

She turned toward him and shook her head in frustration, "Why don't we know who did this? CIA should have given us something by now."

"Emily," he replied in his best mentor voice, "This is a domestic attack that requires a domestic response first. You can be sure that every one of the intelligence agencies is hitting their sources for any information on what happened, but that takes time. We aren't in the business of developing sources and reporting intelligence. We are in the business of collating all the information that is relevant and providing it to decision makers and the military. That means we have to be patient and let the investigators and intelligence analysts do their jobs first."

Emily's expression softened, but only a little, so he continued, "Take a deep breath and let it out. Calm down a little and remember that the time to do our part will come. It's just not our time now."

She did as he instructed and her face relaxed a little more. "All right," she said, "I'll keep that in mind and wait for our turn."

Returning to his desk above the operations floor, he tried to take his own advice but failed miserably. Unlike Sergeant Thompson, he'd been doing this long enough to know that sometimes you never got enough actionable information to do anything. That was real frustration. Now was not the time for her to learn that lesson, though.

The door behind Cain swung open and the DIRNSA, Air Force General Terry Holland, walked up behind Cain to read the information on the right screen.

Holland was of medium height but had a stocky build from weight lifting. He was in his midforties, his short dark hair showing very little silver. He was an Air Force Academy graduate who, unlike most general officers in the Air Force, had never flown a plane in his life. His career as an intelligence officer started in Europe as a liaison with the Italian government, and then moved on to command various intelligence units. His last posting was as the Chief of Intelligence for the Joint Chiefs of Staff, back when he was only a lowly three-star general.

After a few moments' study, he said, "Bring me up to speed, David."

"We've got damn little of anything, sir."

"I noticed," said the general, equally grim faced. "I've spoken to our division leaders and told them to start their people on longer shifts to develop as many new sources as they can to find out who did this. Our focus will be limited to foreign sources as usual, but we can increase our efforts to ensure we don't miss something significant."

"General," said Cain as he turned to face him, "I don't suppose you'll be letting me in on any of those sources this time?" he asked with a wry smile.

"David," the general said in admonishment, "we don't change the rules or the law, no matter what the crisis. The people serving in CTS do not need to know sources and methods of information. You do need the information we develop that is relevant to your assigned mission. You don't need to know how we got it. You remember TRAVELING JUDAS, right?"

Letting a breath out, Cain replied, "Yes." TRAVELING JUDAS was the internal cover term given to the largest, most damaging leak in the history of U.S. intelligence. Terrorists and adversary nations around the world went to school on what one naive, ignorant, and massively egotistical government contractor did because he thought he knew better. His actions cost tens of millions of dollars and hundreds of thousands of man hours of effort to restore lost intelligence sources throughout the agencies. They also cost many innocent lives. From that point on, controls were tightened, and now, sources and methods information were provided only on a strict need-to-know basis.

Properly rebuked, Cain continued, "It's just frustration getting the better of me. All this," he gestured to the screen on the left, now showing four images of broken bodies lying on the concrete highway, "and we have no warning. That bothers me."

The general looked at the screen for a moment. "I know what you mean. Everything we do, the things we do catch and take action to stop, and even so, the bastards only have to get lucky once. We do what the law allows, we keep Congress and the president informed, and then we catch hell when we miss something like this. Hell from the press, from Congress, from the public. I can't even disclose our successes to offset it—then we would be limiting our effectiveness because the bad guys will learn how we do it and counter it. It's a lovely little trap, isn't it?"

The question was a rhetorical one for both men, and the trap was one that they had long since decided to step into as part of their professions. But Cain nodded in agreement anyway and smiled. "Well, in a hundred years or so, when the successes aren't classified anymore, we can tell all the stories we want, right, General?"

Smiling in return, the general clapped him on the shoulder and said, "Keep me informed as needed. I'm going to see what else I can do to get you what you need to kill the little bastards who did this."

Then he turned and headed out the door behind Cain's workspace. The general, like most military members, didn't think in terms of arrest or capture like the law enforcement types. He preferred his terrorists dead. Being a general officer, however, he understood that if the FBI or a foreign partner's law enforcement service could arrest, try, and convict them, then that would have to be good enough.

Cain turned his attention away from the door and the smile faded from his face. Looking at the screen on the right, he'd noticed it had changed, and not for the better.

SECRET – CAPTIVE DRAGON
Apparent Multiple VBIED Attacks – San Antonio, TX

CONFIRMED DEAD:	125 (Expected to Reach More Than 300)
INJURED:	200+ (Estimate)
VBIED PLATFORMS:	5
INDICATIONS & WARNING:	NONE
AVAILABLE INTELLIGENCE:	NONE

ACTIONS:
> Homeland Security & FBI Investigation Teams En Route
> ETA 6 Hours – 2300Z
> Homeland Security Raised Terror Threat Level to Imminent
> All State & Local Governments Notified

WORLDWIDE REACTION:
> UK/Australia/France/Spain/Italy – Sympathies & Offers of Assistance
> Iran – Government statement approving actions of valiant jihadis against the Great Satan

SECRET – CAPTIVE DRAGON

Damn Iranians, Cain thought. The count of the dead had increased by 47. Watching the deaths of Americans always seemed to make the Iranian government's day.

Cain wasn't naive enough to think that the entire country of Iran hated America. He'd read enough studies both from the government and academia to know that the average Iranian was pretty much like the average American. They wanted to raise their children in peace, become educated, and own a little land. It was not their fault that a group of ultraconservative religious leaders had appropriated the Iranian government.

In the name of their religion, those leaders had decided that America was the Great Satan, opposed to the rightful place of Islam as the only religion in the world. And so America was the cause of all of Iran's problems. It was more complex than that of course, and Cain thought that although America had made mistakes in how it dealt with some of the Arab nations, it never wanted to force a particular religious belief on anyone or any nation. And it didn't want to keep other people from practicing their religion.

In the end, that's the major difference, and the major reason America is a better nation than most, thought Cain. America welcomed and encouraged its people to worship as they chose. In fact, the First Amendment to the U.S. Constitution guaranteed that right to anyone standing on U.S. soil, whether a U.S. citizen or not. In Iran, if you were anything other than a Shiite Muslim, you needed to practice your faith as unobtrusively as possible, lest you incur the wrath of the government and the religious authorities.

Someday, he thought, if the Iranian people could vote without the government's influence involved, there might be a more representative government where religious leaders would not hold so much sway. He remembered when they had tried it once a number of years back, and the Iranian Supreme Leadership, backed by the military and police, had ended up having more influence over the election's outcome than the Iranian people had. For now, that government would cheer the deaths of the innocent, and Cain could do nothing more than read about it and feel frustrated.

CHAPTER 8

"GEAR DOWN AND LOCKED," INTONED the copilot, his eyes on the three indicator lights that had just turned green on the instrument panel.

"Copy," replied the major, pushing the throttles forward a little to compensate for the increased drag of the landing gear protruding from the KC-130F's underside.

"Flaps to 40, call it out," he said, continuing the litany of the approach procedure.

The copilot pulled down on the lever controlling the flaps, and they moved obediently to the 40-degree down position. "Airspeed 150," he said responding to the second part of the major's instruction.

The major kept his eyes locked on the end of the only runway at Guantanamo Bay Naval Station as he pulled the throttles back a little, keeping the aircraft pointed at the touchdown point a hundred feet in front of the white hash marks at the eastern end of Runway 28. The breeze from the ocean to the south was light today, so the major couldn't feel the wind buffet his aircraft as he usually did.

"135," said the copilot, his eyes moving from the instruments to the cockpit windows, evaluating their approach. He realized he would probably lose the twenty bucks he had bet with the major, who thought they would touch down before the aircraft passed the second dashed white line down the runway's centerline. He'd banked on the wind being stronger today.

The major pulled back a little on the yoke and the four-engine transport flared out and kissed the 8,000-foot-long runway with its main landing gear just before the second dashed line had passed under the aircraft.

"Arm them, and pay up, young captain," the major ordered with a smile behind his sunglasses.

The copilot pulled the lever down that armed the speed brakes for deployment once the throttles had been moved to zero and once the pitch on the props reversed. "Armed, and see me on payday," he responded.

The major pulled the throttles back, altered the pitch of the propellers so that the engines would try to push the plane backwards, and then advanced the throttles again in one smooth motion to apply reverse thrust. As he did so, the airbrakes deployed and the Hercules transport began to slow.

The major decided to be lenient with the younger man's money, but not his flying. "I'll settle for a beer at the club during the layover, and you'll take a better look at the weather next time if you intend to fly with me again."

The mild edge in his voice got the point across. "Yes, sir."

After a brief conversation with ground control, the major turned the KC-130F right at the third taxiway and drove it toward the wide concrete parking area. The major saw a sailor in dungarees and a blue shirt with the usual orange wands directing them to a parking spot. He knew he could always count on the navy to show him where to park.

He guided his aircraft into their assigned spot, waited until the ground crew had chocked the wheels, and then he and the captain began the shutdown procedure.

In the rear of the Hercules, Special Agent Johnson had been jolted awake by the landing and had shrugged off his blankets, stretched, and began stuffing his water bottle back into his bag.

The loadmaster moved toward the tail of the aircraft and used the internal controls to open the huge clamshell cargo door. As the door moved up toward the top of the fuselage, the warm humid air of the Caribbean basin smothered the passengers. Johnson began sweating almost immediately and quickly decided against putting his suit coat on. He made sure his gold badge was clearly visible on his belt and his sidearm secured at his right hip.

After the Hercules came to a stop and the noise from the engines died, Johnson grabbed his belongings and then headed for the rear cargo door. When he reached it, the loadmaster grabbed his arm. He had that annoying smile on his face again.

"Earplugs," he said with a slightly raised voice.

Chagrined, Johnson pulled them from his ears. They had been there long enough to feel natural so he'd forgotten them. He thanked the man and headed off the aircraft through the cavernous door, happy to leave the still-smiling loadmaster behind him.

Reaching the bottom of the ramps that led from the KC-130F's cargo hold to the parking apron, Johnson got his first look at Cuba.

There wasn't much to see. Bare concrete reflected the sun's heat, adding to the ovenlike temperatures. The typical airfield buildings surrounded the apron, and the small strips of grass around the buildings were trimmed with the precision of a military haircut. There were one or two palm trees in the distance outside the airfield's perimeter.

The sailors on the ground crew were milling about, plugging electrical and fuel lines into the Hercules, most of them sweating as much as Johnson was. At least the air smelled good. As close to the sea as they were, the salt in the air and its incredible freshness, despite the high humidity, felt great in his lungs. He took a couple of deep breaths, dug his sunglasses out from his suit coat, and put them on.

With the glare from the sunlight now manageable, Johnson noticed the sailor with the orange wands approaching him.

"Special Agent Johnson?"

"That's correct," he said, looking down at her. She was cuter than he expected an airplane mechanic to be.

"Head over to the terminal building, sir. Someone is waiting for you," she said, gesturing toward the one-story building about fifty yards from the Hercules.

He thanked her and began walking toward the terminal. Once he was out from under the shadow of the transport, the sun really began to beat down on him. He could feel the sweat gathering under his arms and in the small of his back. He pulled open the old-fashioned aluminum-framed glass door and walked into the much cooler terminal building.

The terminal's interior was sparse. Several rows of hard plastic chairs in faded green and an ugly glowing orange dominated the room. On one side was a counter manned by two sailors who were part-time ticket agents and part-time baggage handlers. The paint was peeling in some places and a couple of the corners were a little moldy near the ceiling.

Johnson stood still for a moment inside the glass doors and just let the cool air soak into him. The combination of the cooler air and his sweat gave him the goose bumps.

"Agent Johnson," inquired the man to his left. He was of average height and had dark hair and eyes. He was dressed in a dark blue T-shirt with the FBI crest emblazoned on the upper left chest, tan cotton cargo pants, and black boots. His badge showed at his hip, but Johnson didn't see his sidearm.

"That's me," Johnson replied.

"I'm Eric Pittman, the FBI liaison to Camp Delta. Welcome to Cuba."

Taking the man's hand and shaking it firmly, Johnson said, "Nice to meet you. Is this the only cool place on this island?"

Grinning, Pittman took Johnson's bag. "No, but if you aren't into tropical weather, you may be out of luck. Follow me and I'll get you to your quarters for the next couple of days."

Pacing with Pittman as he headed toward the terminal exit, Johnson said, "Tropical weather I don't mind at all, but this humidity isn't exactly what I expected."

"It's only this bad because there's a low-pressure system stalled over the island until tomorrow. Once we get the sea breeze back, it'll be fine."

They got into Pittman's car, a desert-brown Marine Corps–issue Humvee, and took off. Pittman turned left out of the terminal parking lot and then right onto the road leading toward the Leeward Ferry terminal. The rough ride made Johnson wish for the Hercules and its thinly padded seats.

"I've been in on all of Ali's interrogations; you shouldn't have any trouble talking to him. He's pretty much resigned himself to staying here until we release him, and he's trying to get into our good graces. If you approach it from that standpoint, you won't have any trouble."

"OK," said Johnson, "I want grab a shower and something to eat and then take a stab at him in the morning. I want to go over the transcripts and see the prisoner log of his activities before I have a go at him."

"Sure," replied Pittman, "we keep the prisoners isolated from the news as much as possible, so the car bombings in San Antonio shouldn't affect your talk with him."

"Car bombs!" exclaimed Johnson. "What car bombs?"

THE NEWS REPORTS WERE GOOD. The man was pleased. Not over-joyed or feeling the need to pray to a beneficent god like his employer was probably doing, but pleased. The first mission had gone well. The carnage and uncertain statements from the mayor in San Antonio were just what he expected.

The American security establishment was undoubtedly moving into high gear. Investigators from the FBI and the ATF were moving into the San Antonio area as fast as airplanes and cars could move them. Extra personnel from hospitals in Austin and Dallas and Corpus Christi were heading to the San Antonio area under police escort. Their presence wouldn't save lives, but it would reduce the number of work hours the people in the city's medical centers would have to put in.

The mayor had declared the next three days to be days of mourning and reflection and had ordered people to remain clear of the major blast areas while the investigations got under way. Even members of the NTSB were coming to San Antonio to assist in reviewing the structural safety of bridges and the elevated portions of the I-10/I-35 highway junction.

The Department of Homeland Security had also issued an Imminent Threat Alert for the entire nation, warning people to pay close attention to vehicles of any kind parked in unusual places or containing strange payloads.

The president was rumored to be considering a national day of mourning, which would likely happen, and several congressional leaders had already made speeches decrying the "horrible events in the great city of San Antonio" and vowed to do "everything possible to help the people of Texas heal and move forward after the great tragedy." Three congressional representatives had said those exact same words within twenty minutes on three different cable news networks.

The man smiled at that. It was probably a fluke, but American politicians did like their sound bites. Aides for the other two congressional representatives probably liked the first representative's statement enough to copy the major parts so their bosses could get in front of the cameras quickly with a concerned look and kind words to demonstrate their sincerity.

The man was reasonably sure that all three were sincere, but having their concern packaged and delivered for TV made it less meaningful than it should have been. Instead, it came across as artificial, rather than something from the heart. No matter. They would have other things to demonstrate concern about soon enough.

Turning from his bank of televisions, he broke the screen lock on his computer and brought up his word processing application. He opened up one of the files and sent it to one of the four printers he had. It obediently burned off six copies of the document in six different fonts. He then opened another set of files on the computer, and then donned a pair of rubber gloves.

He removed the sheets from the printer and then began printing the newly opened files one at a time, inserting a single business-size envelope into the printer for each one. Each envelope emerged from the printer bearing an address in the same font as one of the previously printed documents.

Folding each document carefully with his gloved hands, he inserted them into their corresponding envelopes and then used a damp sponge to moisten the seals, running a gloved finger along the lips to ensure they were closed. He peeled self-sticking stamps off a roll and affixed one to each envelope.

He walked over to the printer, disconnected it from the network, extracted the ink cartridges and set them aside, wiped it down carefully with a damp rag, and then put it inside a heavy brown paper bag. He similarly wiped down the ink cartridges and then placed them in a smaller brown paper bag. He stapled each bag shut and placed them by the door.

The man pulled on a dark leather jacket and put a pair of leather gloves over the rubber gloves he already wore. He took the six letters from his desk, picked up the two brown paper bags, and headed out the door.

The man emerged into the midafternoon sun and began walking

down the street. A light breeze blew, cooling his exposed cheeks, the sun at his back. Four blocks later, he turned left into the driveway of a local pizzeria and headed into the lot in the back. The gravel crunched under his feet. As he reached the back of the small building, he saw that the lot was empty save for the green dumpster. The pizzeria's owner hadn't put a lock on it yet. Good.

Looking around to be sure he was alone, the man slid the side door of the dumpster open and was greeted by the putrid smell of rotting tomatoes and other garbage. Wrinkling his nose, he dropped both brown bags into the dumpster, slid the door closed, and walked back down the driveway toward the street.

After continuing another two blocks, he crossed the street and began walking back the way he came, the sunlight now in his face, feeling the cool wind at his back. He slowed a block later looking surreptitiously at the house to his immediate left. The owner's car was gone, and more important, the flag on the mailbox was up. The traffic coming toward him was light but steady and so he slowed his pace a little.

As a gap finally appeared in the oncoming traffic, he moved toward the curb, put his right foot up on the retaining wall just to the right of the mailbox, bent forward to retie his shoe, and used the bulk of his body to block the view of the mailbox from the drivers. He withdrew the envelopes from his right jacket pocket with his gloved left hand, quickly opened the mailbox, placed the six letters on the other mail already inside, and then closed it.

He used his now-free left hand to finish tying his right shoe, and then continued back up the street past his command post toward his next destination. As he did so, the little white mail truck passed him as it headed down the street, blinker lights flashing as the U.S. Postal Service completed this portion of its appointed rounds for the day.

A HALF HOUR LATER, THE man walked into a public library and turned immediately left in the entry alcove toward one of the only public phone booths he could find outside the international airport. It was, of course, deathly quiet in the building, but, given the time of day, relatively few patrons were in the library.

Reaching for the phone with his still gloved left hand, he used his right hand to extract a single prepaid calling card from his jacket. Consulting the back of the card, he dialed the code from the instructions and the number he wanted from memory. After a few seconds, he followed the voice promptings and entered the sixteen-digit card number. A thank-you message from the phone company played, and then the phone rang.

The ringing stopped, and he heard the recorded message of an answering machine. The voice was a man's speaking unaccented English, "Hello, you've reached 410-555-6867. Please leave your name, message, and a number I can reach you at and I'll return your call as soon as possible."

The second man wouldn't leave a name or number, but he would leave a message. "Hello, Mr. Davis. Your dry cleaning is ready. The bill will be $21.95. Please pick it up within one day, or there will be an extra charge."

Hanging the phone up, the second man bent the plastic card back and forth a few times until he could tear it in half and then threw one half into a trashcan near the library's entrance, and headed out the door for the walk back toward his command post. On his way, he discarded the second half into a public trashcan near a bus stop. Phase II would start sometime tomorrow.

IN SAN ANTONIO, THE SUN had finally set beyond the western horizon, slipping quickly below the hilly terrain. The fires were out now, the living moved to hospitals, and the locations of the dead marked and photographed.

Crews worked under the watchful eyes of professional crime scene investigators to remove each body. Many of the dead who were still encased in the twisted, smoldering wreckage of cars would take longer to remove from the scene for autopsy and identification. Like surgeons, the criminalists orchestrated the dissection of the vehicles that entombed the dead in order to preserve as much of the evidence as possible.

A team of six exhausted firemen spent two painstaking hours removing three children, still belted into their safety seats, and their mother from a burnt minivan surrounded by other ruined vehicles. When they had access to the passenger compartment, the dedicated first responders did their best to hold their emotions in check as they gently and respectfully carried the burned bodies of the children and their mother toward the waiting ambulances.

FBI, ATF, and NSTB investigators, all wearing their distinctive windbreakers, worked throughout the scene of the bombing, and more were coming. The FBI director offered the SAIC San Antonio every FBI agent in the southwestern United States for the asking, and the SAIC said yes without hesitation. Recognizing the magnitude of the disaster, the SAICs in the Dallas/Fort Worth and Phoenix field offices didn't wait for a request from the FBI director. They ordered all available agents to report to the SAIC San Antonio at the FBI command post at the Federal Building by the fastest means available.

While the NTSB investigators concentrated on assessing the structural integrity of the roadway, FBI and ATF agents working in tandem rapidly assessed the bombing site, determining the detonation's locus. The paired agents quickly sectioned off the area and began searching for any fragment that might have been a bomb component. Within hours, the first residual components of the bombs had been identified, photographed, bagged, and inventoried.

AS HORRIFIED AS ANYONE ELSE watching the images of the carnage, the Commander of the Air Force's Intelligence, Surveillance, and Reconnaissance Agency, headquartered in San Antonio, asked the SAIC San Antonio if his people could help. The SAIC said he could use anyone he could spare. After coordinating briefly with the mayor's office, the Air Force two-star sent airmen who would have otherwise spent their day mowing lawns and fixing military vehicles to augment a portion of the Lackland AFB security police force. The augmented force headed for the I-10/I-35 disaster site with body armor, weapons, and emergency medical supplies. They provided a security perimeter that no one but emergency personnel dared cross.

Not to be outdone in generosity, the Army two-star in command of Fort Sam Houston sent two companies of military police put together from the Army units in the area to provide perimeter security at the other bombing sites.

Anticipating the need to move material and equipment in and out of San Antonio quickly, the chairman of FedEx called the Director of Homeland Security and offered whatever cargo planes were needed—all he asked was that the U.S. government pay for the fuel. FedEx would cover the cost for the flight crews and the aircraft maintenance for the next month. The Director of the FBI immediately accepted his offer and relayed it to the SAIC San Antonio.

Thanks in part to all the manpower and assistance, the first pieces of evidence collected from the car bomb locations in San Antonio were winging their way to the FBI lab in Quantico, Virginia, before midnight. The Air Force security contingent provided a military convoy that carried the three plastic mil-spec containers and three FBI agents from the Dallas office as official custodians to San Antonio International Airport at ninety miles per hour, its lights flashing and sirens screaming.

When they arrived at the airport's cargo terminal, the freshly refueled FedEx 767 that would take them to Reagan National Airport was already turning over its starboard engine. The convoy entered the field and drove straight to the cargo aircraft–parking pad. As the two FBI agents, helped by two of the Air Force security policemen, carried the plastic containers up the steps into the aircraft, another FedEx 767 had landed on runway 12 Right, bringing in an NTSB mobile command post and 200 pints of blood from the Red Cross to replenish the supplies consumed in the past day.

Three and a half hours later, in the darkness of the new moon, the 767 landed at Reagan National Airport and taxied toward the general aviation parking area. Two black Chevy Suburban SUVs, red and blue lights flashing, were already waiting.

The agents escorting the evidence containers each carried one down the steps from the 767. At the base of the ramp were four more agents wearing their blue windbreakers with the large yellow "FBI" letters emblazoned on the back. The agents on the ground helped the escort agents secure the containers in the back of the lead SUV. Once loaded, the Suburbans roared out onto the George Washington Parkway.

All the agents boarded the SUVs and they roared away from the airport, sirens wailing. They headed north on the George Washington Memorial Parkway and merged onto I-395 heading west and then south to I-95 and across the Capital Beltway. The two-vehicle convoy headed south for another twenty minutes and then took the Fuller Road off-ramp toward Marine Corps Base Quantico. Twenty minutes later as they approached the entrance to Quantico Marine Base, both drivers killed the sirens, lit their interior lights, and slowed to a stop at the main gate. Each agent presented their credentials to the uniformed Marines on duty, already alerted to expect the SUVs. The Marines waved the agents through the gate and a Marine guard force Humvee that had been waiting for them lit off its red and blue flashing lights and led the way into the base. Ten minutes after crossing the base security perimeter, the small convoy pulled up outside of the cargo delivery entrance of the FBI Forensics Lab.

At the delivery entrance, two men in starched lab coats signed for the containers, placed them on a handcart, and pushed them into the building. The FBI agents, their jobs finished for the night, extinguished the flashing lights on their vehicles and drove back to FBI Headquarters in Washington, D.C. There they would complete the required paperwork, and, if they could find an unused couch somewhere, get some sleep.

IN THE FORENSICS LAB, THINGS moved more sedately, both for reasons of science, which can take time, and to follow proper procedure, which also takes time.

The two technicians had already resigned themselves to getting little sleep that night and had decided that, at the minimum, they would log in all the evidence first and then go home and get some sleep before beginning their work in earnest. Rolling the handcart into the lab, they removed the individually bagged items from the containers and began the mandatory inventory. By four in the morning, they had finished double-checking the inventory and had entered it into the lab's computer system. After placing each labeled bag back into one of the containers and putting the containers in the evidence locker and securing it, the techs turned out the lights and headed home.

A SOUND STARTLED EMILY AWAKE. She nearly fell out of her chair. The lights in the CTS watch center had been dimmed for the night shift and Emily had called home and told her husband, Jerry, she needed to stay at work tonight. *He's such a sweetheart,* she thought, considering his reaction. He knew she enjoyed her work, and, as long as it didn't take her away from their infant son for too long, he understood and never complained. Tonight he had even volunteered to bring in pizza for the crew on watch. When she went down to get it from him at the security perimeter, she spent a few minutes holding and talking to the baby. Then she kissed them both and started back inside, pizzas in hand and a change of clothes in a gym bag over her shoulder. When she turned back to look at them just once more, she saw her little guy waving bye-bye to her in his smiling father's arms.

"Emily, you don't have to stay." Cain had drawn her aside to the CTS entrance for a quiet conversation midway through the swing shift.

Emily looked out at the members of the swing team as she answered him. "I know, but I want to stay with this and I can provide some continuity from the day shift if they have questions."

Cain frowned, not really impressed with the defense of her decision. "I've already placed the day crew on telephone standby; they'll call if they need anything."

Emily looked back at him with a smile. "If I'm here, they won't have to. I've already talked to my husband. I don't mind, really." She gestured toward the conference room. "I'll catch some shut-eye in there if it stays quiet."

Now it was Cain's turn to let his eyes wander across the members of the swing-shift team while he considered her offer. He knew that she needed to feel she was doing *something* even though for now, there was little to do. He understood her need but also had the experience to know how to manage what the military referred to as "battle rhythm"—the method of managing rest and work periods to ensure everyone remained effective. Emily was still inexperienced enough that she would push herself when she should lay back just a little.

As with most lessons, Cain thought they should come from—and be reinforced by—personal experience.

"OK," he relented. "Stick around and help out where you can, but be sure to get some rest. I expect you ready to go for the day shift tomorrow."

Cain turned and headed out the door, and she acknowledged her victory with "Yes, Mr. Cain," to his retreating back.

TO KEEP HERSELF BUSY, SHE helped the swing-shift folks monitor the incoming intelligence and answered all their questions about what she had witnessed firsthand, but, by the time the midpoint of the shift rolled around, there really wasn't much left to do. She decided to sit with the swing-shift CIA liaison, Mr. Weber. He was kind enough to share some of his microwave popcorn while they alternated reading incoming reports and glancing up at the news broadcasts from the major networks, which the swing-shift leader had put up on the large displays. All the news outlets were still conducting live broadcasts from the bombing scenes with on-scene crews, while the network anchors would jump in from time to time to rerun the video from the bombings, ensuring the nation's collective psyche was scarred appropriately as witnesses to the historic, tragic events.

By 8 P.M., the swing team's leader decided enough was enough and reached for the master console that controlled the large displays. He moved the Fox News feed to his desktop monitor, where he alone could keep an eye on it in case there was a breaking news item, and then switched the main screens to BBC America for a family-friendly movie to provide everyone with some escape.

CHAPTER 9

· ·

MALLORY SAID THIS WOULD BE FUN, Mathews thought. *He must have meant fun for him.* Mathews would have closed his eyes and shook his head at the thought, but decided it would be better to keep his eyes open since he might get shot at soon.

Ten hours ago, after the two combat arms specialists had him remove his clothes, the senior of the two, a Marine Gunnery Sergeant, had taken a small device off a shelf and told him to raise his arms and hold still. As he said this, the second man, an Air Force master sergeant, headed off into the depths of the vault.

The Marine activated the device, which emitted a thin beam of red light, and began moving it up and down Mathews' body as he walked around him. Mathews turned to follow the man's movements, and was rewarded with a stern, "Hold still, sir," delivered in the same tone a parent would use if their kid was about to stick his finger in the power outlet for the second time.

Mathews did as he was told—arguing with this man about his tone was not likely to get him anywhere. This situation was bizarre enough already.

The Marine restarted his scan of the SEAL's body as the master sergeant returned carrying a rifle and a pistol.

"These are your new weapons, Lieutenant," he said, placing them on the table about five feet behind Mathews. The Marine was about halfway through his scan, and Mathews craned his neck to the left to get a better look at the rifle. It was a Heckler & Koch M8. He had only heard about them as part of the future weapons program. He didn't think any were actually being issued to anyone yet.

The Marine caught the look on his face. With an amused expression as he continued his scan, he told him, "We get all the new toys, Lieutenant. All your weapons and equipment will be things publicly advertised as 'on the drawing board' or still in testing. In reality, once the initial testing regimen is complete and the weapons deemed safe for use, we get the first shipments. It only costs a couple of million to outfit our unit with the latest and greatest, but getting Congress to authorize a couple of billion for a whole division to sport the new gear can take awhile. More important, the fact that we use the new stuff before anyone thinks it's been fielded gives us an edge. That's also why it's classified information, so forget I mentioned it."

Mathews hardly heard him. The weapon he knew as the XM8, apparently now the M8, was supposed to be the next best thing. The Gunny interrupted his thoughts and said, "Wait here, Lieutenant, and don't dress yet. I'll be right back," and walked past the table into the back of the equipment vault. As he passed from sight, the master sergeant returned with an equipment harness in his left hand, a box tucked under his right arm, and a vest hanging from his right hand.

"I peeked in your shoes when you took them off. Lucky you, we've got one set of nine-and-a-half boots left and they're yours now. Hope they fit." Noticing Mathews' look of avarice directed at the rifle on the table, he said, "Beauty, isn't she? We'll give you the rundown in a minute."

The Marine came back into the room, carrying four sealed pouches. He placed all four pouches on the table, reached behind his back, withdrew a knife from a concealed sheath in a smooth motion, and slit each bag open.

"All right, sir," he began, "we'll be issuing you your first set of combat gear. We're going to explain it to you and watch you put it on."

Puzzled, Mathews started to protest that he didn't need help getting dressed, but the Marine ignored him and just kept talking. "The first issue item you need to learn how to wear is the thermal-control suit and biosensors. The thermal-control suit is sized very specifically to cling to you to ensure it works properly. You wear nothing beneath it but shorts, understood?" he paused.

Mathews wasn't any more enlightened yet, but replied, "Understood, Gunny, but what is this stuff? What does it do?"

The Gunny smiled. "The thermal-control suit—or TCS—keeps you cool in the summer and warm in the winter. The imbedded biosensors will also tell your commanding officer or supporting medical person-nel if you are dehydrated, and what your heart rate, blood pressure, and respiration are any time they need to know them."

As the Gunny watched, Mathews put the two-piece garment on and then the Gunny showed him how to connect the two data harnesses together. While Mathews donned the TCS, the master sergeant slipped back into the rear of the vault and began hunting around on the shelves for something. *Now I know what a mummy feels like,* Mathews thought. *It might be what spandex feels like to a woman.* He felt every breath now as a conscious act. The suit even felt slick against his skin.

"How will it heat or cool me?" he asked the Gunny.

The Gunny pulled a small bundle of tubes and a connector harness from behind his right hip. "You connect these to a five-pound battlefield electronics package that hooks into your combat webbing. The package consists of the onboard computer, an encrypted radio, the heating and cooling system, and the battery pack. The onboard computer monitors your vital signs and transmits updates at regular intervals. It also moni-tors your body temperature and adjusts the heating and cooling system as needed. The battery pack can run for twelve hours or so. It's a spe-cial high-density lithium polymer battery with a built-in solar cell for recharging. The biosensors in the suit are the same kind you'd find in any hospital, they're just woven into the fabric. The tubes run through-out the suit and carry water. The heating and cooling system runs auto-matically based on your current body temperature and will circulate cool or warm water through the inner layers as needed."

"What kind of extremes is the unit rated for?" Mathews asked with arched eyebrows.

"You aren't going to be Superman in this, sir. It's designed to keep you from expending large amounts of energy to keep warm or cool, and keep you in the fight longer. It's not designed or intended to make you invincible, just more effective. Got it?"

With a mildly crestfallen look, Mathews asked, "What else do you have for me?"

"A few more things, sir," replied the master sergeant, returning from the rear of the vault. He brushed some dust off his pants with his right hand and carried a hard black plastic case by its handle. "Please put on the BDUs Gunny put on the table and your boots while I brief you on your weapons."

"No offense," replied Mathews wryly, "but why is the Air Force guy briefing the weapons, and the Marine is briefing me on the clothes?"

The Air Force Senior NCO smiled brightly. "Oh, that's easy, sir, the Gunny lost our last friendly competition on the small arms range. He who shoots better gets to do the weapons briefs for the newbies."

The Marine managed to look positively embarrassed and utterly grim at the same time. The Air Force puke had even beaten him during the hostage rescue portion of the competition, putting two rounds through the simulated bad guy's head before the Gunny even got off a shot. He had to admit the puke could shoot, but he was still taking shit about it from his fellow Marines on the base.

As Mathews pulled on his black BDU pants, the master sergeant continued, "Meet the Heckler & Koch M8, Lieutenant. Chambered for the 5.56mm NATO round, it comes with a semi-opaque thirty-round magazine, so you can check your remaining ammo visually. Our magazines have color-coded bases so you can identify the load-outs; green is standard 5.56mm NATO rounds, red is light-load 5.56mm NATO for use with a sound suppressor, and the dayglow yellow are blanks for practice use with an attachable laser rig on our computerized range.

"The M8 is a modular weapon and you can change its configuration in about three minutes, once you're proficient. The standard configuration for our teams includes the M320 20mm grenade launcher. You can replace the standard twelve-and-a-half-inch barrel with a nine-inch barrel and shorten the stock for a more concealable personal defense variant. You can also replace the standard barrel with a twenty-inch barrel and front support legs for sniper work. In every case except the personal defense variant, the integrated optical sight with a laser illuminator is standard."

Pausing for a second to catch his breath and to give Mathews a chance to absorb that, he continued, "The entire weapon weighs less than six pounds empty, eight pounds with a full magazine and a 20mm grenade chambered. It permits semiautomatic, three-round burst, and fully automatic rates of fire, and delivers rounds to target at 2,675 feet per second without the sound suppressor."

Beaming like a proud parent, the senior NCO picked up the M8, ensured it was cleared by engaging the safety, pulling the bolt open, and then looking in the chamber and down through the magazine receiver. He then offered it to the SEAL, muzzle pointed at the floor, and said, "Go ahead and feel the weight, sir."

Mathews, having donned his black BDU shirt and boots, reached out to grasp the M8. He also visually checked the chamber and magazine receiver to ensure the weapon was unloaded and safe, and then began looking it over. It was almost three feet long, and still smelled of oil and machined metal. Pulling the rifle up to his cheek, he looked through the sight, placing the red dot hovering dead center within the sight's optics on a point where the concrete wall met the concrete floor, his back to the two armorers. It felt good. The weight was very close to the M4 he was comfortable with, but the sights were better. Overall, it felt better engineered, more solid perhaps. He looked forward to putting some rounds through it to see how quickly he could master it.

"Not bad," Mathews breathed, his cheek still pressed against the butt of the M8. "What else do you have for me?"

The airman continued, "You'll use a standard issue M9 Beretta pistol with suppressor as a sidearm," gesturing to the pistol and its holster lying on the table. "The really neat part is the helmet."

Grinning again, the master sergeant opened the black plastic case he had brought to the table on his last trip back and withdrew a helmet. Shaped more like a motorcycle helmet, with a clear visor extending halfway down the face portion, it had a lower portion that would protect his jaw and lower face. In addition, on each side of the helmet, two small cylinders appeared molded into the body just above eye level. The airman crossed to a rack of equipment on one wall next to the table, pulled a cable off the shelf, and plugged one end into the helmet. The cable's other end was already connected to a console in the rack.

"Come here, Lieutenant," the senior NCO said, lifting the helmet up, "and put this on."

Curious, Mathews put the M8 on the table and walked over. He allowed him to slip the helmet on.

"Wow."

"As you can see," explained the master sergeant, "the helmet includes a virtual overlay of the world around you. You'll have to practice a little to get used to it, but you'll love it. When you train or are in the field everything will work fully. While I have you plugged into this diagnostic equipment, you'll only see test patterns and enhanced vision modes. In the upper right-hand corner, you'll see a map of the area around you. The map can be provided by the field command post supporting you based on available mapping data, remotely piloted drone data, and whatever other intelligence is available. At the top center, you'll see the narrow strip of a compass. It rotates as you move your head and is marked in 10-degree increments. Any questions so far?"

"No, I'm fine," replied Mathews. *This is better than any video game!* "Keep going."

The airman reached for the side of Mathews' head, under the helmet's rim, and pressed a recessed button.

"Oh, that's cool," said Mathews. The clear area of the visor, excluding the map and compass areas, had just become the ghostly black and white of an infrared image. Mathews felt the sergeant touch the other side of his head in the same way and the infrared image faded out, replaced with a light-amplified view of the room.

"The onboard computer will automatically switch back and forth from one view to another based on ambient light conditions, but, since nothing is foolproof, you can manually turn the cameras on and off as needed. When you're in bright sunlight, the computer puts both cameras in standby mode, but brightens the map and compass displays." Finishing his demonstration, the sergeant turned off the test equipment and helped Mathews remove the helmet.

"That's really sweet," Mathews said, his smile huge. "I take it that this isn't widely available yet either."

"No, it's not," replied the senior NCO. "The intent of this kind of technology is to provide a battlefield soldier or commando with the same kind of display a fighter pilot uses to gather maximum information visually, with as little effort as possible on the soldier's part. It's also covered in Kevlar armor as a nice little extra."

Pleased, Mathews turned to the Gunny. "What else?"

Still looking thoroughly dour at his relegation to the nonweapon part of the discussion, the Marine gestured to Mathews' uniform. "The uniforms and body armor you've been issued are coated with a special material to keep you from being seen on an enemy's infrared imaging gear. You'll wear standard infrared strobes for identification by friendly forces." The Gunny lifted the ballistic vest off the table and helped Mathews into it to ensure its fit, talking while he worked.

"The vest is the latest in ballistic protection. It's filled with a new material—Liquid Body Armor. Technically, it's known as magnetorheological fluid. It remains in a liquid state until a magnetic field is applied. When an enemy round or knife thrust begins to penetrate the vest, a small purpose-built microchip senses it and activates the armor. The magnetic field is applied, and the metal molecules suspended inside the liquid align with one another to stop penetration. The fluid weighs less than Kevlar, and the rigidity the armor takes can be adjusted based on the type of ballistic threat you expect to face."

After thanking the two NCOs and packing his old uniform into a green duffle they provided, Mathews hoisted his gear and headed back up the corridor to the door marked "Team Areas" and used his badge to gain access. He found Mallory underneath the standard-issue government desk under a sign that read "Team Three Leader" hanging from the ceiling. The team area was an open-office floor plan, executed in standard U.S. government–issue tans, aluminum trim, white walls, and desk cubicles for each team member. Team leaders and their NCOICs each shared a larger cubicle with a small, glass-enclosed, four-person conference area.

Mallory took Mathews down to Level 9, where he spent the next four hours on the weapons range getting more familiar with his M8. He even launched a couple of twenty-millimeter grenades with it.

He and Mallory took an hour or so to have dinner in the base's main cafeteria. Mathews didn't realize how hungry he was until he had started eating. He had skipped lunch as he worked on the weapons range. The helmet had altered his sight lines a little, so he practiced until he had gotten comfortable.

After dinner, Mallory suggested he take a trip down the unit's version of Hogan's Alley to hone his skills in a more practical environment and begin to get "qual'd-up," the SEALs' designation for becoming fully qualified in all the skills needed to go into the field with a SEAL platoon. If you weren't qualified, you stayed home, and Mathews did not intend to stay home. Ever. He wanted to be going after the bad guys, not sitting in the rear with the gear.

Bringing his thoughts back to the present, Mathews kept his eyes on the street. It was pitch black in the alley, but the light-amplification camera projected a view as bright as high noon onto the clear face of his helmet. He crouched alone near a car at one end of the street. Mallory had told him that this was a "Lone Wolf" Scenario. He would be pitted against an unknown number of hostiles, in the form of remotely operated mechanical targets, as he moved down the street.

Each of the targets had a laser illuminator attached to it, remotely directed by a human operator. The operator would need to be paid off in beer if he or she managed to hit him with the laser. If he were hit, his MILES gear would announce his simulated death by emitting a beeping sound that was as annoying as it was unmistakable. If he could get through this exercise without "dying," he would be considered competent enough to move to the next phase of his training.

The car he was crouching behind had seen better days. It was a burnt-out ruin and the rear bumper was hanging off. It smelled faintly like burnt charcoal, but it was decent cover—for the moment. The problem was that he needed to cross the next thirty feet of the street without being "shot," and there was no other available cover.

Mallory's voice sounded in his ear, "OK, Shane, this isn't as tough as it looks. I'm mission commander for this exercise, and I'm going to help you as much as I can. We're feeding you tactical data now."

Mathews' helmet projected red outlines on two of the buildings on the side of the street he crouched nearest, and Mallory's voice came through again, "OK. The buildings outlined in red are suspected to have bad guys in them. There is no other cover on the street but the car you're behind now, so the only practical way to get down the street is to clear the buildings first. Hug the left side of the street and move to the first building. As you reach it, look left, and you should see a stairwell leading down. It's the basement entrance from the street level. If you stay low enough and our bad-guy remote operators don't get a clear shot at you, they won't fire. If you do something tactically dumb, they'll zap you and we'll start over until you get it right. Go ahead and move when ready."

Taking a deep breath, Mathews broke cover and moved left from behind the car to the row of simulated brownstones lining the street. He hugged the walls of the houses as best he could, and moved toward the first building outlined in red. As he reached it, he saw the stairs Mallory had described and headed down them, his M8 pointing in the direction of his movement. As he reached the last step, he heard something move off to his right and turned to face it. Almost without thinking, his finger tightened on the trigger, and his M8 fired a three-round burst, right into the head of the paper target that had swiveled to face him.

"Good job," said Mallory in his ear, "but you were lucky. We almost killed you. Make sure you clear your corners at all times," he rebuked him.

"Copy," was Mathews' only reply as the adrenaline of the unexpected contact surged in his bloodstream. Taking a moment to examine the target, he noticed a small camera mounted at the top and the barrel-shaped extension from the target's "waist" that was probably the laser illuminator.

"We suspect there are three hostiles inside; probably no civilians present, but you need to be sure of your target before firing. We can't see through walls, this isn't Hollywood," Mallory's voice spoke in his helmet again. "Clear the building at your own pace."

Mathews tried the door and found it unlocked. He found cover against the wall on the hinge side of the door, turned the handle, and pushed the door open. Leaning around the opening, with his M8 pointing where he looked, he visually inspected the basement. It had unfinished walls, exposed electrical wiring, no furniture, a single stairwell heading up, and no targets present.

Mathews proceeded into the room and moved toward the stairwell. He was starting to sweat a little now, and noticed a cool feeling begin to trace itself from his right hip across his lower back and up his chest as the temperature-control garment went to work. Refocusing on the task, he kept his rifle trained on the door at the top of the stairs and slowly ascended the steps.

At the landing, he tried the door but it was locked. Reaching into his left cargo pocket, he withdrew a small charge and attached timer. He placed the charge on the door near the handle, set the timer to twenty seconds, and backed two steps down the stairs. He released his M8 to hang by its sling and pulled a flash-bang grenade from his combat webbing. He pulled the pin, discarded it, and then gripped his M8 as he descended two steps and crouched down.

The charge on the door exploded, separating the handle and causing the door to swing open from the force. Without hesitation, Mathews lobbed the grenade through the door on an angle that would carry it into the center of the first-floor room. He turned his head immediately away from the doorway and closed his eyes. The flash-bang detonated with the loud bang and blinding light he was familiar with and he immediately began moving up the stairs and left into the room looking for targets.

He saw two targets like the one near the basement entrance to the brownstone, currently facing the front door, raised his rifle, and fired three-round bursts into both on reflex as he moved into the center of the room. As he turned to complete his sweep of the room, his MILES gear began beeping horribly.

"You're dead," said the flat voice of Mallory in his ear. "More important, you killed one of the civilians in the house. Nice job." The sarcasm in his voice wasn't lost on Mathews.

Turning first to see what killed him, he noticed a third target at the top of the stairs leading from this room to the second floor. It had a clear sight line on him the moment he reached the center of the room near the two targets. As he turned back toward the ones he'd shot at, they turned to face him, likely on the orders of the remote operators. One had the picture of the typical bad guy—red sweater, unshaven chin, pistol pointed at him. The second was of a woman holding an infant wrapped in a blanket. Both targets had bullet holes tattooed neatly in the center of their chests.

Taking this in, Mathews responded to his failure the way most professionals do. "Shit, let's reset and try it again."

"We will," Mallory's voice said in his ear, "but first I want you to come back to the entry area for the alley. You can reload and re-equip while the operators reset the targets."

Shaking his head at the rookie mistake caused by his fascination with the new equipment and his adrenaline, Mathews headed out the front door and back down the street past the burned-out car, realizing it was time to get his game face on. Many people had died in Texas, and he would never get the chance to deal with the bastards who did it if he couldn't measure up to what this unit required. He was sure that being a SEAL would get him a little time to settle in, but not much. The look on Mallory's face as he approached the load-out area confirmed his expectation.

THE FORENSICS LAB IN QUANTICO was quiet. Every technician assigned to the lab had shown up no later than six this morning and with little water-cooler talk, got right to work.

All other cases were on temporary hold as the technicians began processing the evidence from San Antonio. The forensic techs donned rubber gloves and face shields, and then started the lab equipment. The lab's senior scientist quickly devised a plan of action. All items, no matter how small, were to be dusted for fingerprints by a technician prior to being submitted to other tests. Every print or partial print found would be sent through the Integrated Automated Fingerprint Identification System, or IAFIS.

Technicians scraped residue samples from objects like wires, blackened and burnt metal parts, and, in one case, a child's doll. The residue samples were loaded one at a time into the gas chromatograph for spectral analysis. Every result was scrutinized by a tech and logged, which the senior scientist then reviewed before countersigning. Each item was examined under microscopes for hair or blood remains. The techs would conduct DNA profiles whenever remains were found.

The team took extreme care in every case to ensure record accuracy. The animals responsible for this mass murder, they reasoned, would not be allowed to escape justice due to shoddy forensics. The FBI lab was a world-class facility, and today it would exceed its own exacting standards.

Several hours into their efforts, the technician that was examining one set of the gas chromatograph results from one of the wire scrapings sang out, "C-4! It was C-4, not an AMFO device." C-4 meant military grade explosives. AMFO, or Ammonium Nitrate and Fuel Oil, was usually the hallmark of a domestic criminal.

The senior scientist ordered additional tests on the wire and the technicians took more scrapings and other samples. By late morning, the chemical analysis identified the chemical tags within the traces of C-4. The chemical tags were compared to a catalog that the FBI kept for that purpose. They now knew which country had manufactured the C-4: *Russia*.

The next order came from the FBI agent who had sat for the entire morning sipping coffee and watching the lab techs and the senior scientist work. "I need that conclusion written up as quickly as possible. Be sure it's marked 'Law Enforcement – Sensitive.' I'll call CTS and tell them what to expect."

Prior to 9/11, the orders Agent Marks just gave probably would have gotten him fired immediately. The lab's conclusion might form the basis for a charge of mass murder when the FBI arrested the bombers. It was definitive proof in a courtroom that a deliberate and likely premeditated act to take human life had occurred, and it was about to be handed to the U.S. intelligence community. Agent Marks knew that some of the older hands in the Bureau had major problems with the intentional sharing of criminal investigative information with the intelligence community.

Fortunately, this twenty-five-year veteran agent knew better. He had spent time working with CIA case officers and NSA's specialists, and he knew what they could do with this kind of information. More important, he did not know who else in the intelligence community might be able to take that small nugget of information and, using their sources of foreign intelligence, turn it into the lead the FBI could use to catch these criminals. That was the reason the 9/11 Commission demanded that Congress break down the wall between law enforcement and the intelligence community, and one of the reasons CTS existed.

THE RINGING OF THE OUTSIDE phone line was insistent. Fred Simpson picked it up on its third ring, "2522, Simpson."

"Special Agent Simpson, this is Agent Marks. Go secure with me."

Simpson pressed a button on his STE phone and watched the display window change from "UNSECURE" to "GOING SECURE" to "SECRET" in four seconds.

"Agent Marks, I have you SECRET," was the ritual greeting from Simpson when the line was secure.

"Same here," replied Agents Marks. "Agent Simpson, I need your secure fax number. I have a preliminary report on the explosive used in San Antonio in at least one of the bombs. The short version is that it's C-4. *Russian* C-4."

"That was fast," replied Simpson, "I'm glad to see the boys in Quantico are still the best."

"You bet."

"Can't you e-mail it to me?"

"Sorry, I don't have an INTELINK connection here."

"OK, our secure fax is 202-555-9867; we'll need the hard copy ASAP to take action."

"I'll send it as soon as we hang up," Marks responded. "What will you do with it?"

"We'll share it with everyone first. That will have every agency checking their sources for stolen Russian shipments of explosives, possible Russian direct involvement, the works. More likely, the Defense Attaché in Moscow will ask his Russian friends to help us and provide the substantive findings from your fax. If they're smart, and they usually are, they'll give us everything they can so they will look helpful publicly."

"Thanks," Marks replied, "I'll send that fax immediately."

"Out here," responded Simpson, hanging up the phone.

Turning to look up at the CTS director sitting at his desk, he raised his voice, "David, preliminary read from the FBI lab at Quantico is that the explosive used in San Antonio was Russian-manufactured C-4."

Cain looked up from his desk with that "Oh, really?" look that professional intelligence officers managed to perfect during their careers: equal parts surprise at the new information, and curiosity, followed almost immediately by a "well, that would fit" realization as they quickly analyzed the implications of the new fact.

"Put it out to the community when you have a copy of their report,"

Cain said. Looking at his watch he added, "Give DIA a call and tell them to contact the Defense Attaché in Moscow and tell him his day is going to get extended. Pass DIA the relevant abstract from the lab report and ask them to pass it along."

Pleased that he had predicted accurately what would happen, Simpson turned back to his computer and started typing.

CHAPTER 10

· ·

THE EARLY MORNING OF THE day after the horrific bombings in San Antonio was dark and very cool, no different than anywhere in the Northeast in late autumn. Brightly colored leaves occasionally dropped from the trees, littering the bright green grass with splashes of red, orange, and yellow. Dawn was still a little less than three hours away and the roads and streets in the suburbs of New York City were silent and still. Cars parked on roadsides gathered dew, and then frost, as the temperature dropped to hover just below freezing for the first time that year. The air was fresh and clean, the result of a high-pressure system moving southeast across New England from Canada.

The houses on Main Street in Little Falls, New York, were mostly dark, with a porch light lit here and there. One of the houses was markedly different. All its first-floor lights were on. The small, brick house was built in the late 1950s and altered only by the addition of an enclosed white porch during the early 1980s by the previous owner. The new owners had bought the house a few years ago and kept to themselves— a man, his wife, and their two children. Quiet residents of Little Falls who had mixed well with the local Islamic community, they sent their children to the local Islamic school, called a madrasah, with the children of other Little Falls residents who shared their faith. They even allowed their children to play in the local soccer league.

Strangely enough, even though the lights were on, no one was on the first floor. The curtains were drawn across the windows on both floors. The wife and the two children were asleep in their beds, while their father, Ahmad, and his friend, whom the children were told to call Uncle Omar, were in the basement. Uncle Omar had arrived from France yesterday and had spent his first afternoon in America doting on Ahmad's children and staying a respectful distance from Ahmad's wife.

Unlike the rest of the house, which was clean and modestly furnished, the basement was bare concrete with unfinished wooden studs and exposed wiring. There was a makeshift table made from two sawhorses and a sheet of plywood at one end of the basement, illuminated by two bare bulbs on the ceiling. Both men had their backs to the stairwell as they hunched over their work, sitting on two chairs Ahmad had brought down from the dining room. He would have to replace them before his wife awoke. Ahmad was as rail thin as Omar was portly. Both men were cleanly shaven. Ahmad had been so since he had come to live in Satan's land, and Omar had removed his beard before driving to Charles de Gaulle International Airport. Omar was uncomfortable not wearing his beard as he felt his faith dictated; Ahmad less so since he had been without it so long.

The men moved with purpose, oiling, cleaning, and assembling their tools. Today they would do Allah's bidding—truly. Ahmad's wife would take the children to JFK International Airport in the afternoon and board a plane for Paris. When they arrived, they would catch a Syrian Airlines flight for Damascus, where his grandfather would allow them to live with him for as long as needed. If all went well, he would join them in a couple of weeks.

The assembly was complete. The two men loaded their tools into two black golf bags, already nearly full of clubs, and then placed the golf bags into black nylon traveling bags. Uncle Omar carried the two bags out to the man's Lincoln Town Car, and Ahmad took his wife's chairs back to the dining room. Ahmad resolved to have the table, chairs, and the rest of the household goods shipped to Damascus at some point. His wife would appreciate that; she loved the home she provided for her children. She understood the necessity of his purpose, and had been stoic about leaving her house behind if need be. It was his duty as her husband to replace it if he could. If he couldn't take it with him, he would take her shopping to replace as many of their belongings as possible.

Ahmad went up the stairs to the second floor and looked in on his sleeping children. They would sleep in a safer world after today. Their father would do his part to ensure that. He went into his bedroom, kissed his wife on her head as she slept, thinking fondly of her warmth, her chaste obedience to him and recognition of his duty to the faith. She would do as he ordered, as was proper, and, Allah willing, he would do what he must.

Returning to the first floor, the man turned out the lights, closed and locked the front door behind him, and headed to the curb, where Uncle Omar was waiting in the Lincoln, motor running.

IN CHICAGO, ATLANTA, MIAMI, AND Washington, D.C., other pairs of men also rose before dawn, prepared their tools, bade their families good-bye, and drove off into the early morning hours.

THE SECOND MAN WAS ALSO up early today. He awoke before the alarm had gone off and headed to the bathroom to urinate, shave, and shower. After dressing, he headed for the kitchen area and began to make eggs, Canadian bacon, and toast for breakfast. He would have preferred black bread, but the local stores only had white, wheat, or rye. The Americans had so much, but they still didn't stock black bread locally. Perhaps he could find some online and have it shipped to a post office box. He would investigate that while he monitored the news reports for what would happen today. He wanted to see how long it would take the newsies to figure it out.

His food was ready. He gathered his plate and morning coffee, the one thing the Americans really did well, and headed for the table, where he could watch the televisions while he ate.

AHMAD AND UNCLE OMAR HAD reached their destination. Parking the car properly had proved difficult. Omar had to move it twice to get it right. "The car is so big," he had said. Such cars were not common in Omar's country.

Ahmad climbed into the backseats as the sun was beginning to rise, its rays gradually streaming through the tinted windows of the Lincoln. Pulling the center portion of the rear seat down, he reached into the spacious trunk and pulled one of the golf bags toward him. Thanks to Allah, Omar remembered to put the zippered opening closest to the rear of the trunk. Unzipping the top, he pulled out the Remington Model 700 SPS rifle.

Omar handed him two of the six .223 caliber rounds they carried with them, and Ahmad pulled back the bolt and chambered the round before pushing the golf bag back into the trunk to the left so that it wouldn't be in the way. He slipped through the open portion of the rear seat toward the trunk lid in a low crawl, until he could reach the small latch built into the lid.

Cutting the small four-by-four-inch window in the trunk had taken a long time. He had hinged the cut-out metal to the inside of the lid and then placed the small retaining bar across the bottom of the metal flap to keep it in place. It rattled a little when the car was driven, but unless you looked closely, it easily blended into the car's black paint.

Sliding the latch aside so that the flap could move freely, he called to Omar in Arabic, "Clear?"

"*Insha' Allah*," was the reply from the driver's seat, after Omar had looked around.

Ahmad took a small dowel he had cut to fit and painted black, and used it to prop the small metal flap open. He could now see clearly to the commuter bus stop at the far end of the parking lot. The portion of the lot Omar had parked the car on was nearly half full and slightly elevated from the rest of the area. Cars streamed in at irregular intervals as the morning commute into New York City began.

Ahmad had decided to be merciful this day; surely, Allah would smile on that. Head or chest shots only. The short distance would make it easy; he wouldn't even need a scope. There was no need for the infidels to suffer. These were not Marines or soldiers, just misguided people who had not learned the true faith. Perhaps some would even be permitted into Paradise, if Allah judged their transgressions against him to be forgivable.

Raising the rifle to his shoulder and resting the barrel on the lip of the trunk, he looked down the sights and selected his first target. A man, of course. Ahmad would not kill a woman—warriors do not kill women. The target was perhaps thirty, blond hair, with white headphones in his ears, moving his head to the beat of music—probably rock and roll, Satan's music; so much the better.

Ahmad looked down the rifle's sights and placed them on the upper center of the man's chest. Flicking the safety off, he curled his finger around the trigger, took a deep breath, let half of it out, as he had been taught, and then slowly began to squeeze the trigger. The sound of the rifle firing surprised him, concentrated as he was on the sight picture.

Blinking from the surprise, and smelling cordite in the close confines of the trunk, Ahmad looked down the sights again to see the blond man had crumpled to the ground, with several people gathered around him. Pulling the bolt back, he ejected the spent .223 cartridge casing and loaded the second round.

"Hurry, brother," said Omar from the front as he prepared to start the car the moment he heard the second shot.

"Patience is Allah's gift," the man in the trunk breathed, choosing his next target, a dark-haired man about forty years old, who seemed to be doing the most to help the blond man. The man had stood up, speaking on his cellular phone, probably calling for help. The second shot was just as surprising as the first, and now the dark-haired man was on the ground, bleeding from a head wound no doctor could repair.

After hearing the second shot, Omar immediately started the car and slowly drove toward the parking lot's exit. Ahmad, still in the trunk, pulled the dowel out, latched the metal flap in place, and crawled into the backseat. As they reached the main road, the sound of sirens in the distance announced their success. Both men began saying *"Allahu Akbar"* in unison as they drove away to their next targets.

IN CHICAGO, ATLANTA, MIAMI, AND Washington, D.C., similar random shootings occurred, stunning the inhabitants. People died at bus stops, in their cars outside of their houses, and on above-ground commuter train station platforms. Local police immediately began investigating. Washington, D.C., had a contingency plan already in place from the sniper shootings late in 2002. Police stood post near all the major commuter bus and train stops and aggressively patrolled the city streets, subway, and mass transit system for suspicious vehicles or persons.

IN THE DHS SITUATION ROOM, direct feeds of all the major metropolitan-area news networks were monitored twenty-four hours a day. The local broadcasts began to cut to their "Special Report" graphics followed by the anchors reporting the sudden, near-simultaneous shootings in their broadcast areas. In each city, six people had been killed during the morning rush hour, all in public areas while on the way to work. The DHS situation room's senior officer immediately saw a potential pattern, and ordered his people to start talking to the local police forces. Then he lifted a phone and dialed the secretary's office.

PITTMAN HAD LEFT AGENT JOHNSON at what passed for the Visiting Officer's Quarters at Camp Delta. Johnson had spent the remaining part of his first afternoon in Guantanamo reviewing Ali's prisoner log. He had a light meal, and crawled in bed early in order to be fresh for his first encounter with Ali.

After showering and dressing the next morning, he walked across the Camp Delta compound toward the mess hall set up for the Marine guard force but stopped midway to return to his quarters for an unexpected call of nature. Heading back out a few minutes later, he noticed that the temperature had risen appreciably. *Damn, it got warm down here fast!* Maybe he would talk to the wife about changing their retirement plans to somewhere in the Northeast instead of Florida.

Entering the mess hall, he moved toward the serving line and picked up a tray. It was comfortably cool in the building and as he looked around, he was pleasantly surprised to notice that the guard force had it pretty good. The food was impressive.

There was a cold bar with six different kinds of fresh fruit, yogurt, and iced carafes of milk, along with kid-sized boxes of cereal stacked on one end. Normally he'd head for the cold bar and be satisfied, but he was hungry, and what his wife didn't know wouldn't hurt her, so he moved toward the grill.

The navy steward behind the grill greeted him with a cheery, "Good morning, sir," and Johnson ordered three eggs, ham, and two pancakes. A few minutes later, the steward passed him two plates, one with the eggs and ham, and one with the pancakes. Johnson placed them on his government-issued plastic tray with the triangle-shaped unit symbol of Camp Delta imprinted on it and headed off to the beverage machines at the end of the line for his daily dose of Vitamin C in orange juice form and a cup of coffee.

The furniture was cut-rate metal and plastic; even the tables were aluminum tubes with simulated wood-grain tops. Settling in at a table, he attacked his food as quickly as good manners would allow. While he ate, he watched the wall-mounted flat-screen TV that was showing a cable news feed from some satellite. Seemed like the usual: trouble in the Mid-East, the President vetoing a bill from Congress, and Hollywood stars doing silly and outrageous things. The "matched" pair of attractive morning anchors reported it all with perfect smiles and easy banter between stories—he in the dark, slim, and handsome mode most women preferred, and she in the blond, buxom, and beddable form most men preferred. Even their expensive suits matched. Johnson shook his head at what the crossing of entertainment and journalism had become and finished the last of his eggs.

As he was putting his tray and dishes on the motorized belt, the TV news broadcast on the flat-screen on the wall had just turned from the latest idiocy of the young star of the hour to a breaking news story about a multiple shooting at a bus stop in New York. Ordinarily, the peace officer he was would have stopped to watch the story, but he knew that not all the facts were available to the news yet, and he could catch the story later that night. Without looking back, he headed out the door and back across the Camp Delta Compound to the entrance to the prison.

The prison area consisted of the usual assortment of security devices with the added refinements that only the U.S. military could provide. Two twelve-foot chain-link fences, an inner and an outer one, surrounded the compound, with a twenty-foot no-man's-land between them. At four-foot intervals midway between the fences in the no-man's-land were steel I-beams sunk ten feet into the hard packed earth to prevent a vehicle from penetrating the perimeter. The interior fence was topped with coils of razor wire. Steel-frame guard towers equipped with .30 caliber machine guns and Remington .308 sniper rifles were spaced every hundred feet around the perimeter. The tower guards stood in areas sheathed in half-inch plate steel that was chest high. Only one road came into the camp, and vehicles entering were searched with a degree of thoroughness that stopped just short of disassembly.

Approaching the entry control point for pedestrians, Johnson extracted his FBI credentials and showed them to the Army sentry. The NCO told him to spread his arms and legs, and then passed a handheld metal detector over his body. Johnson had left his sidearm locked in his quarters. After the NCO had identified his room key and belt buckle following a beep and a red light from the metal detector, Johnson signed in, and was told to wait.

After a few moments, another Army NCO appeared and escorted him into the compound, into the main administration building, and up a flight of stairs to the second floor to see Colonel Mike Davis, Camp Delta's commander.

The colonel's office was regulation Army in every respect. There was not a paper out of place on his desk, and the colonel's sidearm hung in its holster from a hook on the coatrack standing behind the desk in the corner. The occupant matched its room: Colonel Davis wore camouflaged battle dress and a regulation Army haircut to go with his square jaw and trim physique from the mandatory company runs he led around the camp perimeter. After the usual pleasantries, the colonel came to the point.

"Procedures here are very strict, Agent Johnson. Medical officers will examine any prisoner you wish to interview before and after your interview. You will not touch a prisoner. You will not interview a prisoner without at least one person from a different service observing. You are not authorized to use any form of interrogation technique other than those authorized in Field Manual 34-52. If you violate these restrictions, I will put you on the plane home myself. These procedures are non-negotiable. Do we understand one another, Agent Johnson?"

"I understand you clearly, Colonel. The prisoner I'm here to talk to should be more than willing to talk to me, and I don't expect him to be evasive. Everything I've read so far tells me he'll be willing to talk."

"Good," said the colonel returning to his desk, clearly preparing to send the agent on his way.

"There is one more thing, Colonel," Johnson said expectantly.

The colonel turned back toward him, his eyebrows raised in a silent question.

"Does Ali have a lawyer?"

"Why do you ask?" said the colonel, his expression grim, his tone bordering on acidic.

"Well, if I'm to interrogate a prisoner, he'll need his attorney present."

"Actually, Agent Johnson, he doesn't. Ali is being detained as an enemy combatant, but the military commission authorized to try detainees did not determine that his case warrants trial."

"But, sir —"

Waiving a hand, the colonel cut him off. "Our expectation is to release him to the Afghan government in the next few months. We're waiting for the Afghanis to allow us to send him back. They may choose to try him based on what he's told us, but we won't be putting him in a court of any kind. You will be interviewing a man who is a petty criminal and will likely pay for those crimes under Islamic law in his home country in the not-too-distant future. Thanks for your time, Agent Johnson. Agent Pittman should be waiting for you."

The colonel returned to his desk, leaving Johnson feeling like a lowly private. Johnson turned and headed out of the office, nodding to Agent Pittman, who motioned toward the door and preceded him out and down the steps to the ground level.

When they were in the compound away from the administration building, Pittman asked, "Feeling a little unwelcome?"

"You bet." Johnson wiped his brow as they stood in the Caribbean sunshine.

Pittman regarded him for a moment, looked around to ensure they were out of earshot of anyone, and spoke softly, "The colonel is probably a good guy, but you need to remember, the Military Commissions Act and Detainee Treatment Act tied the hands of the military and the CIA in the way they handle these guys. You and I are reminders of the rule of law and proper procedure that some of the folks in the military believe is a little too 'soft' when dealing with these guys. In a way, I understand where they're coming from. I observed an interview with one guy who sat there and told us he wasn't going to cooperate, and that when he got out, he would go to all our homes, kill our children, rape our wives and sisters, and then kill them. He said Allah wanted him to do it because we're infidels."

Pittman, visibly embarrassed even to say such things, continued, "The CIA and military's attitude is a bit more *direct* about how we should deal with these kinds of people. You and I come from a world where even the worst criminal gets certain rights, an attorney to represent him, and a trial where somebody has to prove to a jury that a person committed a crime. In a civil society where laws are enforced and courts function, that works. Many of these folks were captured in a foreign country, usually with guns in their hands on a battlefield, right after they killed some of our soldiers, while shouting *Allahu Akbar.*"

Pittman wiped the sweat from his face with his hand now, and motioned Johnson over to the shade of one of the buildings before he continued, "I'm a God-fearing man, and I hold my faith very dear to me, but I don't use it as an excuse to start killing people. Some of these people believe they are on some holy quest to keep Islam from being wiped out. They justify any atrocity to accomplish that goal by claiming that you are either an unbeliever or you are a threat to the Islamic faith, and, as such, your life is worth less than a Muslim's. I think that the attitudes of some of the prisoners here, coupled with the deaths of the military's and CIA's friends on battlefields and the strong inherent desire to protect our nation drove the Army's and CIA's approach to the interrogations. After their techniques and methods became public knowledge and Congress began to investigate, it was determined that the military and CIA had gone over the line. Congress stepped in along with the courts and drew the line in brighter ink with the new rules. Our presence here reminds them of that pretty strongly."

Johnson nodded and said, "I see your point, but we can't run around torturing people. That's not who we are as a nation, and it's *not* what I swore to uphold as an agent. People have rights."

Pittman looked at the younger agent with a slightly sorrowful expression. "Let me ask you this. You know about the bombings in San Antonio, right?" Getting an affirmative nod from Johnson, he continued, "Let's say you raid a building in Alexandria and arrest a bombmaker who you know just finished building five car bombs destined for Washington, D.C., where your wife works, and your child goes to daycare. The guy you arrested knows where those cars are going. What do you do?"

Johnson began to speak, but Pittman silenced him with a questioning look and then said, "Think about it. Really think about it. Your wife and child may lose their lives to one of those bombs. Dozens or hundreds of other people are going to lose their lives if those bombs detonate. You swore to uphold the Constitution and protect our nation against all enemies foreign and domestic, just like I did. In doing so, you accepted an obligation to protect the lives of our nation's citizens from an imminent threat. So you look me in the eye and tell me that the guy with the information that will save the lives of your wife and child isn't going to get bounced around the room a little for 'resisting arrest' until he tells you what you need to know."

Johnson had started to stare into the middle distance between them while Pittman was talking, wondering just how far he would go to protect his family in that kind of situation. It was not something the instructors at the FBI Academy covered. He would not commit murder, but if his wife and child were in imminent danger? The mere thought of anyone harming his wife made his heart feel like an invisible hand was squeezing it hard enough to stop beating. He knew without a doubt the feeling would be worse if his child were threatened. Pittman was right. The guy's head *would* be bounced off a few solid objects until he told him where the cars were going. By the letter of the law, it would be wrong, but, then again, the people who didn't die that day probably wouldn't mind, if they ever found out, which they wouldn't.

Looking back up at Pittman, he replied, "I take your point."

Pittman, looking into Johnson's eyes, saw the rare sight of a new agent getting some of the green shaken off him, and entering the slightly grayer world of law enforcement. Pittman nodded, and motioned Johnson to follow him again.

The two men continued across the compound to one of the long white buildings near the rear of the camp. As they walked, Johnson saw prisoners, some dressed in orange jumpsuits, some in white ones, all with white knitted caps on, walking in the exercise areas. Some noticed the two men and stared at them with undisguised distaste.

Climbing the short flight of steps into the building, both men entered it and greeted the Army and navy NCOs on duty. The agents were scanned again with handheld metal detectors, and then signed in.

"Room 12, Agent Pittman," said the navy man.

Nodding his thanks, Pittman led Johnson past the desk and left down the corridor that spanned the center of the building. Stopping at a door marked 12-O, he opened it and walked in.

The room was simple, with bare walls and a couple of tables and chairs. One of the tables had three video cameras on it, and a computer sat on the other. An Army captain was sitting in front of the computer typing away, and rose when the two agents walked in. The wall in front of the video cameras held a six-foot-long by four-four-foot-high one-way mirror, which overlooked the adjoining room where a lone man in an orange jumpsuit sat on a wooden chair, smoking a thin cigar, while he stole occasional glances at the mirror between puffs. The cameras pointed into the adjoining room through the mirror.

"There's your man," said Pittman.

Johnson studied him briefly. Ali was of average height, and thin. His black beard was sparse, and he scratched absently under his cap before taking another puff on the cigar. Giving the mirror a half smile, he waved with his free hand, and then turned his gaze to the wall opposite his chair.

Pittman pulled a small box of cigars from his back pocket and handed them to Johnson.

"Your timing is pretty good. That's his last cigar. He's been hoarding it for a few days. Since he's smoking it now I'd say he's a little nervous. I haven't talked to him in almost a month. Don't give him the box unless he answers all your questions. He likes his comforts, such as they are in here, so use that as much as you can. Oh, and remember, first names only. We don't need these guys using our names as leverage or for survival with the Taliban or some other extremist group at some point in the future."

Johnson took the cigar box and thought for a moment. Then without another word, he removed one cigar, left the rest of the box on the table, and headed out of the room. Turning left, he headed for the next door down the corridor, marked 12-I, and opened it.

Ali turned as Johnson walked in, and he smiled. In heavily accented but understandable English, he said, "Ah, a new person to talk to." Ali leaned back in his chair and took another puff on his cigar, which was almost down to its last inch.

Johnson sat down in the chair opposite Ali and said, "Hello, Ali. I'm David." Making a show of putting the cigar in his shirt pocket, he continued, "Eric tells me you've been talking to him about your time working for the Taliban."

Ali's eyes lingered on the cigar for only a moment, before he replied wearily, "I've told Eric everything about my work for the Taliban. What is left to tell?"

Johnson leaned in a little and said, "I'm a historian, Ali. I like to learn about people, why decisions were made, that sort of thing. Eric is only interested in events, in actions. I want to know the *why* of things."

Not believing him at all, Ali appeared to be considering what the younger man really wanted, but the answer didn't seem readily available.

Ali dodged, "How would I know the why of anything? I was only a collector of money for the Taliban. Eric knows this. I planned nothing against your country, I killed no one."

"But even money collectors understand why they do what they do; they even understand why they are asked to do it."

"I wasn't asked to do it, I volunteered," Ali replied with a smug grin. "Collecting money was better than trying to run a shop. I prefer to enjoy Allah's world as much as I can." Taking a long drag on the cigar to emphasize his point, Ali exhaled the smoke toward the ceiling.

Johnson replied with a look of amused accusation, "That explains why you kept some of the money you collected."

Ali looked back at him and his smile faded somewhat. He had long ago come to terms with the man he was in this place, where all a man had was time to think. In here, a man thought mostly of himself, and Ali had long ago taken an unvarnished look at his life. In telling his captors about the beatings of shopkeepers he had ordered, and the women he had his men abuse so that their husbands would be more generous, he had unburdened himself in a way.

Ali had learned to look unflinchingly in the mirror at what he had done. He knew that the Americans would send him back to Afghanistan someday. He knew he would likely be tried and perhaps executed, because crimes against women in Islam were considered some of the vilest. He would pay that price someday, but, for now, he clung to the hope that he could be of use to the Americans. Perhaps they would free him or the Afghanis wouldn't take him back and then the Americans would put him on trial and be unable to make the case against him. That they had brought no charges yet didn't concern him. Being here with three meals a day, exercise, and free medical care was infinitely better than treatment in an Afghan prison, where the authorities might not be as enlightened about prisoner welfare as the Americans were.

"That is so," Ali replied.

Johnson saw the slight change in his subject's demeanor and used his next question to steer the conversation closer to what he wanted to know.

"Why didn't you give it all to Sadig al-Faisal? Surely he would have killed you if he had found out you were keeping money you weren't supposed to."

Ali laughed. "Sadig was doing the same thing. I once sent him 600,000 afghani, almost 15,000 of your dollars! Later that month at a meal in his home, he actually praised me before the other collectors in the district as the leading collector of money for Allah! Sadig said he had deposited the whole 400,000 afghanis in the Taliban war chest. He had forgotten how much I really gave him. We were all keeping a little."

Ali's cigar had reached the end, and he stubbed it out in an ashtray on the table, trying and failing to ignore the end of the new one sticking out of Johnson's pocket. Noticing his interest, Johnson asked, "What do you think Sadig did with all that money? Did he spend it on women, cars, maybe fine cigars?"

Ali smiled ruefully as he answered, "Sadig probably shipped it all out of the country to a safe bank in Europe or the Bahamas. He said as much to me as we traveled together before I was captured."

Bingo, thought Johnson. Looking at his watch, he said, "It's almost time for lunch. I wouldn't want you to miss that. Would you mind if we talked more tomorrow?"

"Not at all, David," Ali replied, his eyes on the cigar.

Johnson rose, headed toward the door, and then stopped short. Turning to Ali and removing the cigar from his shirt pocket, he said, "This is for you. Eric said you like them."

Eyes alight, Ali took the cigar. "Yes, I do."

Johnson opened the door, and just before he closed it behind him called out, "I'll see if I can find you more before we talk again tomorrow."

CHAPTER 11

· ·

"IS EVERYBODY ONLINE?" ASKED CAIN.

"Yes, David," answered Mike Goodman, Cain's deputy. Goodman was tall, lanky, and a little bleary eyed. He'd been up at 4 A.M. to get into CTS early enough to read the morning intelligence reports, get caught up on overnight developments, and check the slide package for this morning's briefing.

The CTS video teleconferencing room could hold forty people and it would be a packed house today. Goodman had posted a couple of his people at the doors with instructions to let no one in under the rank of full colonel or CTS-assigned personnel. The lights were already dimmed, with high-intensity spots shining down on the individual positions around the conference table. The light almond-colored room was furnished with a V-shaped dark mahogany table and slate-gray chairs that cost $400 each. An expensive luxury to be sure, but that was government purchasing. Cain suspected somebody probably had ten or twenty thousand dollars left over at the end of one fiscal year and rather than giving the money back, which was frowned upon, it was spent on $400 chairs. Granted, they were comfortable chairs.

The initial slide package was already loaded, and the receivers at the seventeen different intelligence and military agencies, linked together through secure fiber-optic cable sheathed in steel pipe, were seeing two images. One focused on the center two chairs of the table at CTS, and the second from the title slide of CTS's daily intelligence update.

The two view screens in the CTS room showed the conference participants on the left, each appearing in their own box on the screen, and the title slide on the right screen. As the participants talked, the teleconferencing system would automatically select the image corresponding to the speaker's location and enlarge it to cover the entire left-side screen. After that person finished speaking, the system would shrink the image back into its former position.

Goodman ran a hand through his dark hair for the umpteenth time in the last twenty minutes, and continued to riffle through the hard copy of the slide package, looking for spelling and format errors, and other stupid mistakes that might have slipped into the briefing as the tired minds on the midshift assembled it. Pulling a red pen from his pocket, he circled two format errors. He headed for the door to the CTS operations floor, his head bent down as he turned to the next page, and collided with General Holland coming into the room.

Looking up in surprise, he bounced back into the conference room and blurted out, "Sorry, sir! I didn't see you."

The director of NSA reached out to steady Goodman with his right hand and gave him a quick once-over. He knew Goodman was a good analyst, and he was doing a great job as Cain's deputy in CTS. The last thing he was going to do was chew him out when the man was obviously doing his job and not running into general officers for the sheer thrill of it.

Smiling, the DIRNSA told him, "Don't sweat it. I'm in the way here. You're trying to get your job done," and he moved aside to let him pass.

As Goodman headed out the door and walked past Cain's desk to his own to make the changes to the slides, he raised his voice and said, "DIRNSA is here."

Cain picked up his head, looked at the world time clock on the wall, and said, "Oh, shit. He's early." He rose from his desk and grabbed his tie. Tying the knot in record time, he headed to the conference room.

He greeted the DIRNSA with a "Good morning, sir," that had little enthusiasm in it.

DIRNSA replied in kind, "Good morning, David." Then, noticing the tie and knowing Cain's distaste for them, he commented with a smile,

"Nice tie." What good was a senior pay grade without twisting a subordinate's tail occasionally?

Knowing that the DIRNSA was yanking his chain a little, Cain just looked at him with a deadpan expression and replied, "Thanks," as he dropped into the chair beside him.

As the chief of the CTS, it was Cain's job to run these conferences each day, but with the DIRNSA attending, he would defer as required when the general had a comment to make. Cain knew the director would let him do the briefing without interruption, and then as the heads of the various agencies began to consult, Cain would be relegated to head observer and note taker as needed for the director. If the DIRNSA had any orders to give, Cain would pass them on to his executive officer to ensure the actions were tracked.

Looking at the clock, Cain said, "We're on in about five minutes, sir. Can I get you a cup of coffee or something?"

"No thanks, David. Your people have better things to do at the moment," and he smiled as he continued, "and I get my own coffee."

"Yes, sir," David smiled back. In spite of the occasional chain yanking, the director was an OK guy. It was a nice change from the previous DIRNSA, a pain-in-the-ass who expected his coffee to be ready at the table when he showed up, usually with an entourage in tow.

Goodman barreled back in through the conference room door, three fresh hard copies of the slides in his hands. "Sir, Mr. Cain, I've got copies of the slides if you would like a preview."

"Outstanding," replied the general, reaching out for a copy.

"Nice job, Mike," said Cain, taking his own after the general had collected his.

Goodman, holding his last copy of the slides, took his position at the teleconference control console, ready to flip slides for the briefing.

The room was starting to fill up. In twos and threes, the various division heads from within NSA were filing in. They were a roughly equal mix of senior-ranking civilian employees and uniformed officers, colonels, and generals from all branches of the service. Nearly all of them worked directly for General Holland. Those who didn't were senior liaison officers from other government agencies. The turnout was much bigger than usual. Cain could pick out nearly every head of every major

NSA division and most of their deputies. Most looked serious or down-right grim. Few smiles were exchanged over handshakes or other greetings. The overall mood was quiet and expectant.

"Thirty seconds, Mr. Cain," came the warning from Goodman at the control console, his eyes locked on the green LED readout counting toward 06:00.

Conversation in the room immediately halted as Cain and the director looked up toward the display screens on the far wall and the camera between them. The five-second warning tone beeped once per second until the clock reached 06:00 and sounded a steady three-second tone across the entire teleconference network. The seventeen miniscreens on the large display showed similar images of agency leaders looking up from their morning briefing books or taking last sips of their morning beverages, knowing CTS had the floor.

Cain cleared his throat and started, "Good morning. I see we have all agencies present this morning and given the current situation, I'll dispense with the roll call and ask all speakers to identify themselves if they are not an agency head. As usual, this is an open forum, but in this case I'll ask that questions pertaining to my brief be held until I complete it."

Glancing over to Goodman, Cain nodded, and the first slide came up.

"As you are all aware, five car bombs exploded in San Antonio two days ago. The FBI and ATF inform us that preliminary forensic investigations are complete. Each vehicle was loaded with an improvised explosive device made up of a shrapnel-enhancing shell of either nails or ball bearings. The explosive used was Composition Four and was manufactured in Russia. The U.S. Defense Attaché Officer in Moscow relayed this information to his contacts in the Russian Ministry of Defense, and was informed this morning Moscow time that the C-4 in question was sold to unidentified Middle Easterners by a supply sergeant to supplement his army pay."

There was a small amount of murmuring in the gallery of observers around the conference room behind Cain, which the director silenced with a look.

"The Russians informed the USDAO Moscow that the sale of the C-4 came to light during a theft investigation last year and that the supply sergeant in question was found guilty of selling nearly 300 pounds of C-4 from the depot he was assigned to manage."

Seeing some movement from the people on the miniscreen showing the FBI watch center and anticipating the question, Cain added, "Unfortunately, following his trial, the sergeant was shot for misappropriation of Russian state property, so we will be unable to question him further. The Russians will provide the results of their investigation to the USDAO Moscow, but he's already warned us that the information will not be substantive. After the attaché returned to our embassy, he was able to tell us that his Russian contact at the Ministry of Defense took him aside and explained that the sergeant's arrest, interrogation, and trial was dealt with swiftly. The intent was to avoid any international embarrassment and to assure the world community that Russia took such problems seriously. Unfortunately, this leaves us in the position of having that investigative avenue closed off."

Taking a quick sip of water from the bottle Goodman had placed on the table earlier, Cain gave them a moment to digest what he said and then plowed on.

"The only other item of significance CTS wants to bring to your attention is a series of shooting deaths yesterday morning. DHS took special notice of them yesterday and followed up with the local law enforcement agencies. Given the information DHS has supplied to CTS, it appears that these incidents are likely to be terrorism related."

There was a second murmur in the room and on the distant ends of the VTC; people at the distant ends were leaning over to talk to one another. The sole exception to this trend was the miniscreen showing the secretary of DHS, who aside from Cain and his on-duty team, already knew this.

Cain continued, "Twenty men were killed yesterday morning. Four in each of the following cities: Chicago, Los Angeles, Miami, New York, and Washington, D.C. With only two exceptions, each of the men was apparently killed by long-range rifle fire while waiting for a bus or a train. The remaining two men were killed in their cars while waiting at stoplights at major intersections by unidentified males who simply walked up to the driver's side window, pulled a large caliber handgun, and fired twice. The killings all took place within a two-hour window of time. The timings of the deaths were the first tip-off. The D.C. police force already considers the killings in their city to be the work of another beltway sniper-like criminal. Looking at these killings from a nationwide viewpoint, the deaths of these eighteen men under similar circumstances, by an apparent long-range rifle shot, within a two-hour time frame during the morning commute, looks very *wrong* to our analysts here at CTS and the folks over at DHS. I want to stress that the investigations are continuing, and that we will undoubtedly learn more over time, but that given the suspicious nature of these killings, occurring so close after the events in San Antonio, CTS is recommending that we consider this a terrorist-related event until we can determine concretely that it wasn't."

On the screen, the DHS window zoomed in to full screen, as the secretary of DHS chimed in, "DHS concurs with that recommendation. Based on the bombings in San Antonio, we've already moved the threat alert to Imminent, and certain precautions are taken automatically, but now we'll contact state and local police forces and recommend increased police presence at bus stops, rail stations, and other commuter parking facilities and as many intersections as the forces can handle. I'll also speak to the president this morning, and ask him to contact the governors and get them to have a quiet word with their National Guard commanders in case additional support in the form of military police units is needed. Does anyone think we should recommend to the president that we call the Guard out now?"

The silence on the link lasted long enough for the DHS picture to shrink back to its smaller size on the large display. After a moment, the DHS picture enlarged again as the secretary began again, "Very well. No one here thinks that should happen yet. I'll be making a statement to the media later today after I've spoken to the president. For now, we'll describe the recommendation for increased police presence as a protective measure beyond what we have already done to increase public area surveillance as a result of the bombings. If we develop any more concrete information about these shootings, I'll pass it along."

The briefing continued, with Cain covering the locations and current known information about other terrorist groups and their leaders throughout the world. As he finished and the agency and department heads began to talk, he kept his ears open for anything significant but let his mind drift back to the bombings in San Antonio and the unexplained shootings.

Were they connected? It was possible. If they were, there was a major problem. Most of the world's major terrorist organizations were really just independent actors, focusing on their little portion of the world, sometimes making noise about attacking the U.S., but not really capable of doing so without resources. Certainly the leadership of those organizations never rose to the level of a central unifying force as the core portion of al-Qaeda did in the 1990s. Based on everything he had seen to date, Cain was very confident that after the U.S. invasion of Afghanistan, the near destruction of the Taliban regime, and the liberation of Iraq from that lunatic Hussein, most terrorist actions had been relegated to overseas locations and were largely uncoordinated.

If these two events were related, or worse, executed by the same group, the U.S. had a new enemy, and it had just proven itself capable of striking inside the U.S. practically at will and, so far, with impunity. Granted, random shootings did not require a lot of effort or resources, but, if they were carried out by the same group that conducted the bombings, that group had shown itself to have considerable resources and a functional command-and-control network.

Because of the bombings in San Antonio and the increase in security at the nation's airports and seaports, every passenger was practically strip searched now, instead of just suffering through random checks. Liquids of any kind had become totally banned again for air travelers. Cargo about to be loaded on planes or ships was screened so slowly now that nothing departed on time. After DHS spoke to local law enforcement agencies in the various states, police officers would be standing post near public commuter areas and at intersections where the traffic lights had long wait times. They would look for any suspicious vehicles, people, or activity.

If anything, the country was becoming more secure, not less, so why would this unknown threat organization commit both sets of attacks? There were still too many questions and not enough answers. After this meeting, Cain would talk to his team and bring his shift leaders in for a skull session. CTS needed to search aggressively for the answers, more so than it was already doing.

AZIZ SAT BACK IN HIS chair after taking a sip of the coffee the young male secretary had provided and took a moment to admire the room. The coffee was bitter and slightly yellow tinged as was expected in the House of Saud. The luxurious room was almost entirely white, with an abundance of gold trim. The chairs in the waiting area around the low coffee table were dark cherry and matched the table. The chair's upholstery was light tan premium leather and Aziz had decided to ask where they were acquired. He would have to get some for his offices.

As he waited, he perused the local paper, *Al Riyadh*. The story about the car bombings in San Antonio was on page six, near an editorial that talked about the justice promised in the Qur'an for those who commit evil acts.

Aziz thought the closeness of the two articles in the paper was probably a not-too-subtle commentary by the paper's editor on America reaping some of what it had sown. He was disappointed that the shootings were not mentioned. His Russian hireling had told him that the coordinated intent behind them would likely go unnoticed by the media in the U.S. and certainly abroad, at least until the American government recognized it and determined who was behind them. The shootings were not intended to cause a major impact, just to keep police forces working longer hours, getting tired, and then getting frustrated with the extra duty and the disruption in their personal lives. That way when the real strike happened, their reactions would be dulled.

Aziz had to give it to Repin. He was worth the money he demanded when Aziz had sought him out. If Allah willed it, Repin's plans would continue to go well.

Aziz finished his paper and began to reach for his coffee cup to drain the last of the bitter beverage when the door at the far end of the room opened. The young man serving as the assistant to His Excellency had returned. He was wearing a thawb, the long white dresslike garment common to the Middle East, with the customary red-and-white-checked shemagh head covering held in place by a black agal. He addressed Aziz in Arabic.

"His Excellency will see you now, sir."

"*Shokran*," replied Aziz as he rose and headed through the open door.

A prince of Saudi Arabia, His Royal Highness Hassan bin Abdul-Aziz was dressed like his subordinate and rose to greet his guest. He was a tall man with a slight paunch that his thawb hid well. Like most male members of the House of Saud, he wore a neatly trimmed beard that framed an angular face and dark eyes. He and Aziz had spoken many times before and formalities were kept to a minimum.

After the men shook hands, Prince Hassan asked if he could offer him more coffee. Aziz agreed, pleased that the prince himself would inquire, knowing full well that Aziz had already been served coffee by the prince's assistant. It was a measure of the friendship the two men shared.

After brief pleasantries, Aziz came to the point. "Your Highness, I was disturbed to see that oil prices have fallen yet again. Does this drop in price concern the Kingdom at all?"

The prince smiled to hide his mild discomfort, "Not too much, my friend. We are examining the impact of the reduced price per barrel to be certain that all factors are taken into account, but it seems that the primary culprit is increased gasoline inventories in America. The larger mileage standards that are required of new cars went into effect this year and it seems that the Americans drove less during the summer months."

"And what of the recent car bombings in America?" asked Aziz.

"If the Americans react the same way they did after the attacks in 2001, the Kingdom's profits and our ability to provide for our citizens could suffer."

Aziz had to smirk inwardly at that. The Kingdom had been founded on oil wealth and its exclusive stranglehold on the money earned from that oil wealth. The various princes and other Saud family members mingled their wealth with the wealth of the provinces and ministries they ran. As such, the Kingdom's wealth was their wealth, and while they did provide certain services for their people, any allusion to the "Kingdom's profits" really meant their source of wealth and the power garnered and maintained through that wealth. It had become an accepted form of corruption everyone knew about and no one attempted to change. Aziz took it as more evidence of the Saud family being less than true to the faith they publicly professed to hold dear, and proving them poor custodians of the two Holy Mosques.

Aziz replied in a way he knew the Prince expected, "I am prepared to help the Kingdom in any way possible. Perhaps if I were to reduce production to help reduce the supply of oil, prices would stabilize." By stabilize, Aziz actually meant increase to offset present losses. "Certainly my efforts in this would not be enough to have a major impact, but as a friend to the Kingdom and the House of Saud, I am willing to help if His Highness would think it prudent."

The prince smiled knowingly. Aziz had offered the Kingdom, and more specifically, the House of Saud, a favor, knowing full well that the prince could repay that favor many fold. "The OPEC ministers are already meeting in Sharm Al-Sheikh, as you may know. They are likely already considering such a strategy. I will speak to our minister and tell him to advocate that position to the other ministers. Thus, the Kingdom and Allah's people will not suffer any adverse consequences."

"I'm sure that is most wise, Highness," replied Aziz, keeping his joy at this news well hidden. "I will order an immediate cutback of production after I leave; we will not wait for the formal OPEC decision."

"You are a good friend to the Kingdom, Aziz. The king appreciates your willingness to work with us."

With that, the men bade their farewells. Aziz was escorted back to his armored Land Rover by another of the prince's male underlings. The Land Rover was already waiting beneath the covered driveway of the prince's winter palace in Riyadh.

Ordering the driver back to the airport, he settled into the black leather seats and allowed himself the smile he had avoided in front of the prince. It was a virtual certainty that oil prices would rise at the announcement from the OPEC ministers' meeting later tomorrow. The rise in prices was important to his plan, but not the only item within it. His company, Arabco Oil, a medium-sized oil drilling company operating under a license from the state-owned Saudi Aramco, had already received its orders to curtail production.

On a good day, Arabco, the first privately owned oil producer in Saudi Arabia, pumped 150,000 barrels of oil from the Saudi sands. Licensing Arabco to drill for oil within the Kingdom was mostly a showpiece for the Western and European companies hoping to drill in one of the richest oil reserves in the world, and a talking point for the Saudi government to use against internal detractors of the state-owned oil production effort. The behind-the-scenes price for Arabco's license was that it operate in complete lockstep with Saudi Aramco's production goals, and that 20 percent of its profits be sent yearly to the oil ministry as the license fee.

Overall, nearly 14 percent of U.S. oil imports came from Saudi Arabia. The U.S. consumed more than 6.8 billion barrels of oil per year. A little more than 50 percent of that volume came from overseas suppliers, and nearly 40 percent of that overseas supply originated from OPEC nations. By curtailing production, oil and the products made from it—gasoline, heating oil, diesel fuel, jet fuel, propane, asphalt, petrochemical feedstock, synthetic rubber, and plastics—would all become more expensive soon. Aziz particularly enjoyed knowing that, even with Arabco's tiny percentage of the overall production, every time an American filled his gas tank, he was helping to fund his nation's eventual downfall.

Since its founding, Aziz remained in the shadows, allowing the Arabco board to manage the day-to-day affairs, knowing full well that when Aziz made a "request" they should carry it out. That understanding was recently reinforced when the last CEO balked at the early payment of dividends to Aziz. His sudden death from a drug overdose while in the company of two Thai women of "questionable character" in a Bahrain hotel room raised serious questions about the CEO's Islamic faith and disgraced his family.

In addition to his investment in Arabco generating millions of additional dollars to fund the jihad his mentor started, being the power behind Arabco gave him access to the Saudi leadership structure in a way that kept his face out of the papers. If all went well, he mused, that access would bear fruit soon.

The Land Rover had passed onto the airport grounds and stopped at the checkpoint to the airfield. The lone civilian guard, a uniformed Pakistani because no Saudi would stand at any checkpoint in this heat, waived the Land Rover through with barely a glance.

The driver pulled up near the extended boarding stairs of Aziz's G550, got out, and crossed behind the vehicle to open Aziz's door. Exiting the car, he walked briskly to the waiting jet, climbed the stairs, and ordered the pilot to take off immediately. The flight plan was already filed and air traffic was light at this hour. Fifteen minutes later, the G550 reached V$_r$, velocity rotation speed, as it hurtled down the runway at 140 knots, and the pilot pulled the nose up. A few minutes later, the pilot retracted the gear and turned left to a heading of 300 degrees as the G550 passed through 2,000 feet, climbing to its 32,000-foot cruising altitude.

REPIN SLAPPED THE SNOOZE BUTTON on the alarm clock and rolled over on his bed in his hidden command post. He could afford to sleep another hour or so. It was only eight in the morning, and nothing important would happen just yet. The shooting teams should be lying low and waiting for the events that would signal their next missions.

He'd stayed up late last night listening to police radio broadcasts while he surfed the web for some of his favorite porn sites. It was amazing what some of these women in America and other countries would film or photograph themselves doing. Of course, they were making a lot of money doing it. More important, he had not caught any signs of increased patrols from the police radio scanner he had for the local area. And no one was calling into dispatch complaining about standing post in commuter parking lots or bus stops. The cable news channels had no announcements from the government about increased police presence other than the stricter security screening at airports and train stations.

Repin would spend some time today walking the streets, doing some window-shopping here and there, and seeing if he could spot the changes he needed to see before starting the next phase of the operation. If the Americans did not put the police on those corners, he would have to order other shooting teams into action until the government officials acted the way he needed them to.

The last thought he had as he drifted back into sleep was of how reactionary the Americans were. They were always guarding the wrong thing, always looking in the wrong place, never looking at themselves the way an enemy would, determining what the exploitable weak points were, and then defending those weak points properly.

"AH, DAVID THE HISTORIAN IS back!" exclaimed Ali. Johnson could almost hear the quotation marks around the word historian in Ali's exclamation.

"Did you bring me more of those wonderful cigars?"

Johnson settled himself in the chair across from Ali again. Today they were in room 5-I. Ali and Johnson had been talking over the past couple of days and they had settled into a comfortable routine. Johnson would bring Ali a cigar or two and Ali would talk freely while he smoked.

Johnson had learned a great deal about the Taliban finance system from Ali. Johnson had known the Taliban were total bastards, but what he had learned from Ali had confirmed it. Ali and his men had roamed throughout their district administering beatings and selectively raping the more attractive wives of some of the shopkeepers to ensure they paid.

Couriers would transport the money collected by Ali and the men like him throughout Afghanistan to Kabul where it ended up in the hands of Sadig al-Faisal. Al-Faisal would then send some of it overseas to his personal bank account, and then used the rest to support the Taliban in *their* overseas bank accounts.

Of course, the Taliban was giving some of it to al-Qaeda so they could put it in their overseas accounts.

Johnson studied Ali for a moment and decided that he'd spent enough time building rapport and learning about the relationship between Ali and Sadig. It was time to focus on what happened to Sadig when they encountered Task Force Eagle's patrol.

"So what did your friend Sadig do when the Taliban realized we were going to attack you?" Johnson asked.

Ali smiled and shook his head. "In the beginning, right after 11 September, they thought all you Americans would do was fire more cruise missiles into the training camps, like your President Clinton did. They ordered all the camps evacuated and told the fighters to hide in the mountains in small groups. Then after a few days, Sadig had me come to his house in Kabul. When I got there, his staff was packing up everything that could be packed."

Ali paused to light the fresh cigar Johnson had brought him, and continued, "Sadig told me that the Pakistanis had sent a warning."

"The Pakistanis?" Johnson asked with his eyebrows arched.

"Oh, yes, certain elements of the Pakistani intelligence service were very friendly with the Taliban government." Ali arched his eyebrows in return, "They too were well paid by the Taliban. When the Pakistanis had been informed by your government that you actually would be invading Afghanistan, the Taliban leaders got scared. They never admitted it publicly, of course. They videotaped speeches and began sending their families out of the country, usually over land or by air into Iran or Pakistan. The money soon followed. Sadig told me he was transferring some of the Taliban's money into Swiss, Canadian, and U.S. accounts in the names of some of his distant relatives for safekeeping and asked if I wanted to have my money moved out as well."

"Did you take him up on the offer?"

Ali smiled again, "No. I wanted to keep my money. I didn't want it to end up in the hands of one of Sadig's 'cousins.' I told him it was already safe outside the country. But I did ask him if I could travel with him and his brother when he left Afghanistan."

"Is that how you ended up in the mountains?"

"Yes, where your soldiers found us that day."

Wanting to hear an eyewitness account, and verify that Sadig was killed during the attack on the group, Johnson probed, "How did Sadig die?"

"Die? Sadig didn't die. We came across another group of jihadis in the mountains. One of the men in the group was a Saudi whom Sadig knew. He decided to travel with him into Pakistan and then find his way out of the country."

Johnson was astonished but held it in check. Sadig didn't die in the mountains in Afghanistan. Somehow, he ended up in the government's files listed as missing-presumed dead in the same strike that killed most of the men in the group Ali was in. "So that was the last you saw of him?"

"Yes. He headed off with the other group and I haven't seen him since."

"But the reports we have say he was killed in the airstrike that hit your group just before you were captured."

"Why do you say that? I never told anyone Sadig was dead."

"Our records list him as dead." Johnson explained before continuing. He leaned forward, watching Ali intently as he asked the next question.

"If Sadig managed to get to Pakistan, where did he plan to go?"

Ali noted Johnson's interest, and held out hope that his answer would be enough to make the Americans delay returning him to Afghanistan.

"He didn't tell me where he was going to go, but he had his passport with him. I remember him waving it at me when he asked if I had mine."

"His Taliban-issued Afghani passport wouldn't get him far outside of Pakistan," Johnson opined.

Ali shook his head. These Americans always leapt to conclusions. "His passport was Saudi, not Afghani."

PITTMAN AND JOHNSON WERE IN Pittman's closet-sized office. Ali was back in his cell and the two agents had just finished reviewing all the transcripts from Johnson's sessions with Ali.

"What do you think?" asked Johnson.

Pittman looked thoughtful for a moment and threw the transcript he had been reviewing on the desk that took up most of the room in the office.

"If Sadig had a Saudi passport, fake or not, with some elements of Pakistani intelligence favorably disposed toward the Taliban, Sadig would have used their help to leave Pakistan the moment he made it to a city with an airport."

"You think there is any chance that the Pakistanis would have a record of his departure from the country?"

"Hell, no," Pittman replied. "Sadig was a senior member of the Taliban. Even if the Pakistanis kept a record, if the wrong guys in Pakistan get wind of an official request from us, you'll get a polite 'No Record' response and then you'll be stuck. You'll have better luck with the Saudis. They may not take too kindly to a member of the Taliban using false credentials to enter their country."

Johnson looked at Pittman with a wry smile on his face. "Do you think the director might spring for a plane ticket to Saudi Arabia?"

CHAPTER 12

. . . .

"WHISKEY ONE, THIS IS CHARLIE Five, how copy?" Technical Sergeant Thompson said into the headset microphone and then swore at herself silently as she realized she was still holding the transmit button down.

The CTS watch floor was bereft of people not assigned to CTS. Mr. Cain had put the place into lockdown for the duration of the exercise, which was now in its fourth hour. The lights were dimmed a little more than normal and all the liaisons were at their positions.

Mr. Cain . . . *David*, she corrected herself, had briefed them that they would be providing intelligence support to an assault element of the 152nd Joint Special Missions Unit. Called Whiskey Team for this exercise, they were going to practice an assault on a simulated terrorist camp near their base. The CTS would provide on-site intelligence during the assault. David would act as exercise controller and play the part of other national intelligence agencies as needed. The cameras and sensors on the two MQ-11 Avenger unmanned aerial vehicles, or UAVs, were already trained on the simulated camp, on station 45,000 feet over the target area. Emily had the video feeds from both available on her computer. They were also displayed on the large screens in the CTS.

Simulated man-shaped solid targets were already positioned throughout the camp, each coated with a chemical that would make them fluoresce when viewed through an infrared camera, just like a real person would.

"Charlie Five, this is Whiskey One, have you Lima Charlie," the radio links crackled back.

She had electronically connected her headset to the radio links with the click of a mouse a few minutes ago. The link was encrypted, and bounced through a satellite link, just as it would during a real operation. The half-second delay was noticeable but tolerable and the Lima Charlie—or Loud and Clear—response from the ground team assured Emily that they could hear her clearly.

"Whiskey One, Charlie Five, we have eyeballs on Objective Camel, advise when you reach the LZ." Emily received two clicks back in a positive response.

Looking at the imagery from the first UAV, Avenger 5, she selected the IR camera controls. Sliding her mouse left, she slewed the camera west toward the landing zone Whiskey Four's team was going to use.

"LZ clear," she announced to the room at large. Stealing a quick glance at David, she saw him smile and make a note. She got that right, at least.

On the infrared image from Avenger 5, she saw the bright white silhouettes of two Sikorsky S-76 helicopters against the cooler, dark background move in from farther off to the west. Their engine exhausts and the tips of the rotor blades glowed brighter than the other parts of the fuselage. The helicopters reached the LZ and began to hover. Emily saw the side doors slide open and ropes drop from both helicopters. Men slid quickly down the ropes, each wearing a miniature infrared beacon on their shoulders that blinked steadily, so that they could be distinguished from enemy forces on the battlefield the camp would soon become.

Emily watched the men fan out on her God's-eye view of the LZ and then stop.

"Charlie Five, this is Whiskey One. We're at the jump-off point for Objective Camel, anything to report?"

Emily slewed the camera back to the east with her mouse, following the path the ground team would take to the objective.

"Negative, Whiskey One, proceed when ready." Emily received two clicks in reply as she moved her camera back to the team, and then cursed silently at herself again. There were *two* UAVs. She selected the second one, Avenger 7, and pulled up its infrared camera and trained it on the simulated camp. Now she could watch the team's progress and the camp at the same time, which was the purpose of having both UAVs supporting the exercise. She shook her head for missing the obvious while not taking her eyes off the two images now side by side on her computer.

Unless she saw something important, or someone on the CTS floor received some kind of intelligence that indicated a threat to the team or the operation, there would be no more transmissions to the ground team. Whiskey Four would also maintain radio silence until the assault began.

MATHEWS WAS MOVING QUICKLY ACROSS the bare ground toward the objective 200 yards away. His team was spread in a line on either side of him, each member three yards apart. The night was crisp and clear. The moon hadn't risen yet, and the view from his helmet's sensors, superimposed on the clear faceplate, was as bright as day.

The camp was easy to see in the distance, and the map in the corner of his helmet display showed that he was now 160 yards away. At 100 yards, the team would stop for a final observation of the objective. The last transmission from Charlie Five told them the coast was clear, but it was prudent to look around. He'd have to ask who Charlie Five was when he got the chance. Her voice sounded very nice in his ear. Maybe on his next trip to Washington, he could have a drink with her.

The team reached the 100-yard point and, as one man, knelt on the ground, scanning the area ahead. Mathews looked carefully at the camp and saw no movement. The green night vision display showed the tents, the simulated firing ranges, and the obstacle course clearly with a couple of fires burning brightly. The fires caused his night vision display to flare whenever he looked directly at them, obscuring his view of segments of the camp. That was all right, he had planned for that. As soon as he heard from . . .

"Sierra on station," crackled into his helmet speakers.

That was what he wanted to hear. Rising to his feet, he moved forward. His men saw him get up, took that as the signal to continue, and followed suit.

At the 25-yard point, Mathews stopped and knelt, as did the two men on either side of him. They were the close-in overwatch team.

The remaining six men split into two-man teams and approached the closest three tents. As they stacked up by the entrances, Mathews whispered into his helmet-mounted microphone, "Weapons free."

At those words, three things happened simultaneously: the two-man teams entered the three tents, Mathews saw movement near the far end of the obstacle course, and his radio crackled, "Sierra One, targets near the firing range, engaging."

Three targets had popped up on the other side of the tents, where Mathews and his overwatch team couldn't see them. He thought about switching manually to thermal vision and engaging through the tents, but his team members were still clearing them. He had to trust the Sierra Team on the left flank.

IN CTS, EMILY KEYED HER MIKE and practically screamed, "Whiskey One, this is Charlie Five, armor on the far side of the obstacle course!" while she zoomed Avenger 5's camera in on the single armored vehicle moving toward the camp.

Mike Goodman, acting as the CTS director for this exercise, looked at the image on the large display on the left of the CTS wall and called out, "Confirmed, one M2 armored vehicle heading for the camp. Friendly troops are outside of the blast zone, weapons free." Goodman moved his mouse over the bright red "master arm" icon on the display, enabling the weapons on both Avengers for the CTS staff.

"Weapons free," confirmed Technical Sergeant Thompson as soon as she saw the indicator on her display turn red. Using her mouse, she zoomed out a little from the moving image of the M2 armored vehicle, centered her cursor on top of its flat roof, and clicked once. A small red box appeared around the vehicle as the Avenger's targeting system stored the infrared image of the vehicle in its memory and began tracking it. The Avenger's onboard computers then lit an invisible laser and pointed it right at the roof of the M2, directly underneath the center of the red box on Emily's display.

Emily called out into the radio link, "Charlie Five engaging a single M2 north of the firing range."

Moving her mouse down to the bottom of the screen, she clicked on the bright red box in the Avenger 5's control panel that said "FIRE." The screen blinked once as the laser-guided 500-pound GBU-12 Paveway II bomb dropped away from the fuselage.

Keying her microphone again, she said, "Whiskey One, shot out," in a slightly calmer voice than in her initial report.

ON THE SLIGHT RISE OFF to the left of the camp, Mathews could see the two snipers lying still on the ground, twenty yards apart. They had parachuted in two hours before the arrival of the main force, and had low-crawled to their observation point on the left flank to cover the assault.

Both fired simultaneously on the two closest targets of the three that had popped up on the far side of the firing range. "Sierra One, Tango down," said the lead sniper. "Sierra Two, Tango down," said his partner.

Both snipers shifted to the third target, by unspoken understanding trying to eliminate it before the other man could. Sierra Two fired first. "Sierra Two, Tango down." Turning his microphone off for a second, he called over to his partner, "Beer's on you."

"We may not be done yet, keep your eyes open," Sierra One called in return.

"Yes, sir," replied the junior man as he reactivated his radio.

THE BRIGHT OUTLINE OF THE M2 was bracketed in red on Mathews' helmet display, designating it hostile, courtesy of the data link from the UAV that was enabled when the CTS tagged the vehicle as a target. Mathews saw the flash in his display, followed immediately by the loud crash of the explosion. The hottest parts of the now-burning M2 and the small mushroom cloud from the pillar of fire burned bright on the display, flaring out that segment of his vision.

Following their radio calls of "Clear," his three close-quarter assault teams had exited the first set of tents just as the M2 had exploded and moved to covering positions on each side. Mathews and his two accompanying men moved forward to a new overwatch position in the same line as the close-quarter assault teams. When the overwatch team had knelt again, the close-quarter teams leapfrogged forward and stacked up at the entrances to the next set of tents.

Mathews called in to the sniper team, "Sierra, Charlie, confine your fire to a line north of the close-quarter assault teams." He was answered by two clicks on the radio from the sniper team, followed by a terse "Copy" by that nice voice of Charlie Five.

The close-quarter assault teams entered the next set of three tents, and Mathews could barely hear the sound of silenced gunfire as his people shot the dummies inside them.

Mathews' radio spoke to him again, "Whiskey Four, clear," followed quickly by "Whiskey Six, clear," then "Whiskey Eight, clear."

Mathews immediately replied, "Whiskey Four, Six, and Eight, fall back to the overwatch team."

Without hesitating, all six men came running back to Mathews' position, turned around, and filled in the spaces in the overwatch team's line.

"Sierra, this is Whiskey One, team falling back to LZ Green, cover as required."

"Copy Whiskey One, we've got your back."

"Charlie Five, Whiskey Team moving to LZ Green."

"Copy Whiskey One."

"Whiskey Team, this is One, move now."

The man at the far end of the line, closest to the sniper position, rose, turned to his left until the green triangle marking the LZ appeared in the center of his helmet's display, and began walking quickly toward the LZ. One by one, the other team members began following their point man.

EMILY PULLED AVENGER 5'S CAMERA back again with a mouse command to get a wider view as the team moved toward extraction. Suddenly she saw movement to the west near LZ Green and started counting.

"Whiskey Team, this is Charlie Five, movement in the trees near LZ Green. Looks like twenty men in the tree line."

"Whiskey Team, hold!" responded Mathews. All the white man-shaped silhouettes with blinking strobes on Emily's computer screen immediately stopped and knelt on the ground, scanning for targets.

"Charlie Five, Whiskey One, what do you advise?"

"Mr. Goodman," queried Emily, looking up from her computer to stare at him. Goodman was looking at the wide-angle video feed from Avenger 7 on the right-most main display. After a few seconds, he keyed his own microphone, "Whiskey One, Charlie One, LZ Red looks clear, recommend you proceed there for pickup. Sierra Team, recommend you orient to cover."

"Whiskey One copies, Charlie One. We are proceeding to LZ Red. Sierra Team, orient as needed to cover our movement."

"Sierra copies."

"Whiskey Team, this is Whiskey One, proceed to LZ Red. Move now."

EMILY WATCHED AS THE WRAITHS reoriented themselves along a line headed southwest and started moving away from the compromised LZ. "Mr. Goodman, do we engage the troops in LZ Green?"

"Negative. They're not a threat at this time and the Paveway bombs on the UAVs aren't the best weapon for the job. Keep an eye on them. If they move toward either team, we'll do what we can to take them out."

"Understood," she replied.

MATHEWS KEPT PACE WITH HIS MEN as the single file approached the clearing that was LZ Red. It was outlined with a green triangle on his map display in the upper-right corner of his helmet's faceplate. It was at 300 yards, reducing rapidly as the team moved.

When the distance read 200 yards, he called their ride, "Magnum, this is Whiskey One, we could use a lift."

"Whiskey One, Magnum copies, ETA, eight minutes."

"Copy Sierra Team, cleared to leave your observation point. We'll cover."

At that, the two Whiskey Team members at the rear of the line stopped, turned around, and then spread apart and knelt, keeping an eye out for the sniper team coming up from the rear.

The rest of the team continued until it was thirty yards from LZ Red and then fanned out to cover the approaches.

"Sierra Team, approaching rear guard," Mathews heard on his radio.

"Whiskey Ten copies, come ahead," was the immediate reply from the two men who had stayed back to wait for the sniper team.

Four minutes later, four men became clear on Mathews' helmet display, loping toward the LZ. "Rear Guard and Sierra approaching LZ."

"Copy," Mathews answered immediately. "Visual contact. Come ahead. Whiskey Team, weapons tight."

The sound of the two helicopters that were Magnum Flight began to grow louder near the LZ, and Mathews turned his head to look at their approach. The two S-76s were coming in low at about 80 knots, and began to nose up to slow the approach to the LZ, and then flare for landing, in a simulated combat recovery.

As soon as the helicopters touched down, the Whiskey Team members ran toward them in twos and threes and boarded. The moment each helicopter was loaded, the team member closest to the pilots slapped one of them on the shoulder and shouted, "Go, go, go!"

The pilots immediately increased collective and the helicopters practically exploded off the ground and then pivoted in opposite directions, and nosed down to increase speed and clear the area.

Mathews felt like his stomach had been left at the LZ. He swallowed once, and said on the radio link, "Whiskey Team is clear. Charlie Team, thanks for your support."

"Anytime, Whiskey Team. Charlie Five, out."

AS THE IMAGES OF THE two S-76 helicopters from the Avengers cleared the visual range of the cameras' two UAVs, Goodman called out, "Weapons, tight!" and clicked the icon disengaging the master arm on his console, rendering the remaining weapons on the two UAVs inactive.

Then Cain called out, "ENDEX. This exercise is concluded."

An audible exhalation of breath came from everyone in the CTS. Emily realized she'd had a death grip on the computer's mouse, and her eyes were dry. She blinked for the first time in several minutes and then looked around the CTS watch center to find everybody grinning.

"Nice job, everyone," said Cain. "Take a ten-minute break and we'll do the hot wash in the conference room."

As everyone got up, the day's swing-shift personnel moved to take their places and began to return the CTS to its normal watch state. The computer system in CTS automatically recorded the radio transmissions and the Avenger video streams for follow-on analysis and review. The new shift of watch standers manually stopped the recording and then contacted the UAV pilots, who were sitting in a secure bunker some 800 miles away, and told them to return the Avenger UAVs to base.

JOHNSON WAS RIGHT. THE DIRECTOR of the FBI had sprung for a ticket to Saudi Arabia, courtesy of SAIC French, but the trip wasn't quite what he had hoped for.

He had left Guantanamo the morning after his request at the ungodly hour of 5 A.M., flying on the same Marine KC-130F that had brought him there. He had expected that the aircraft would drop him off in Washington within a couple of hours, where he could catch a commercial flight from Dulles International to the Kingdom. When he had asked the pilot how long it would take to reach D.C., the pilot just started laughing and then told him that his orders were to complete his usual mission, which meant flying to Puerto Rico, then Bermuda, then to D.C.

Eighteen hours later, the KC-130F's flight crew headed off to the Visiting Officer's Quarters on Andrew's Air Force Base. Johnson got in the back of an FBI-owned dark blue Ford Crown Victoria for the ride across town to Dulles International, where he boarded the 11 P.M. British Airways flight to Jeddah, Saudi Arabia. After sixteen hours in the air, he landed in Jeddah and transferred to a Saudi Airlines flight to Riyadh. After he landed in Riyadh and picked up a rental car, he drove over to the Riyadh Hilton, checked in, took a long, hot shower, and collapsed on the bed completely exhausted.

The next morning, he asked the desk clerk for directions to the Ministry of the Interior. Under normal circumstances, the FBI Legal Attaché would have met him and escorted him around, but the man had returned to the States two days ago after his father had a stroke. Johnson managed to get lost twice in the unfamiliar city, but he finally found the building and a place to park the car.

The air was so dry that he had already drained his two-liter bottle of water from the hotel during the car ride. If he had done the same thing back in Virginia, he would have needed to pee by now. The climate was drying him out faster than he expected. He'd need to remember to drink water regularly. *At least this place is less humid than Cuba,* he thought.

The Ministry building was only six stories tall, and reflected the Middle Eastern culture in design. Its doorway arches were high and domed, and the floors were polished marble. The door handles were gold and a large gilt-framed portrait of the Saudi king gazed benevolently down upon the lobby, and he was greeted by the modern convenience he appreciated the most—air conditioning. While the building temperature was probably 80 degrees instead of the standard 72 in the States, it was still pleasantly cool.

As he neared the front desk, the young Saudi man in traditional garb looked up from the magazine he was reading and briefly appraised him.

"Agent Johnson?" his English was accented but clear.

"Yes."

"His Excellency, Minister Ali al-Saud, has instructed that you be taken to Mr. Akeem al-Haddad's office. He is special assistant to the Minister. May I offer you some refreshment?"

"Thanks, I'd love a bottle of water if you have it."

"Certainly, Agent Johnson," the receptionist said with a smile. "We stock it for our foreign guests."

He motioned for Johnson to follow him, led the way around the low wall behind the desk to the elevator alcove, and turned into a small snack area. He got a liter bottle of water from the refrigerator and handed it to Johnson.

"*Shokran,*" Johnson said, thanking him.

"*Al'afw. Hal tatakallamu alloghah alarabiah?*"

"I'm sorry. Please and thanks are the limits of my Arabic."

"It's quite all right, Agent Johnson. Many people would not even attempt to learn that. As long as you are visiting my country, continue to use what you know. Most people will appreciate your respect for our culture. Please follow me."

Johnson followed the receptionist back into the elevator alcove behind the front desk. The receptionist pressed the elevator call button, and Johnson took the chance to take a long pull from his water. As he replaced the cap, he noticed the lettering on the bottle was in English and Arabic, with the Arabic characters more prominent and the English printed below them in small letters. He was surprised to read that the water came from a desalination plant in Qatar.

Boarding the elevator, he and the receptionist rode to the fourth floor. When the doors opened, the man led him out and down the corridor to the right, knocked on the third door, and entered.

The room was a medium-sized office dominated by floor-to-ceiling glass windows that looked out on the city. Behind the desk attending to paperwork was another man in traditional dress. He was middle-aged, with silver streaks in his goatee, wearing a black-and-white checked shemagh. He looked up as they entered and spoke briefly to the receptionist in Arabic. All Johnson could catch was the *"Shokran"* at the end. The receptionist bowed slightly toward the older man and retreated from the room, closing the door behind him.

The man behind the desk rose and crossed the room to shake Johnson's hand.

"Agent Johnson, I am Akeem al-Haddad, special assistant to His Excellency the Minister. Your director spoke to His Excellency yesterday, and I have been instructed to give you whatever assistance you require. Please take a seat."

"Shokran, Mr. Akeem, if you'll forgive me, I would like to come to the point."

"Of course, I deal with many foreigners in my position; I will take no offense if we omit the usual pleasantries."

"I am seeking any information you can provide me about a man named Sadig al-Faisal. He was the Taliban's finance minister. We have information we believe to be reliable that Sadig escaped into Pakistan and had a Saudi passport. He may have used that passport to travel abroad. We are hoping your passport records will give us details of his travels."

"I can look into that for you, Agent Johnson. If you will wait here, I shall go to our passport section and see what I can find for you."

"Thanks very much. How do you say that in Arabic?"

"You say 'Shokran jazeelan.' I will return as soon as I can. Please be comfortable. If you would like more water, please dial 237 on the phone, and Sabir at the reception desk will bring it to you."

Akeem left and Johnson fished inside his sport coat for his cell phone. Checking the signal meter, he dialed.

"French."

"Mr. French, Agent Johnson."

"How are our Saudi friends treating you?"

"Well, sir. Mr. Akeem just left to check on the passport records. I hope that they'll be able to tell us something. Did we have any luck with the banks?" After the last session with Ali, Johnson had recommended to SAIC French that the FBI recontact all the banks known to have held money for the Taliban or Sadig, and ensure nothing was missed.

"Not what I would call luck. During the follow-up, the director of the Chilean Banco de Nacional told us that the Taliban accounts were emptied. We had recorded them as closed out, not emptied. The director swears on a stack that he reported the accounts emptied and closed out, and our agent from the legal attaché's office must have simply recorded them closed out."

"So what happened to the money?"

"According to the director, the cash was converted into bearer bonds and hand-carried out by a courier."

"Is there any chance of tracing the bonds or the courier, sir?"

"No. The bonds were issued across multiple corporations and banks, and the serial numbers were broken up in lots of threes and fives within each institution. There's no way for us to trace any of them. All the director remembers about the courier is that he was a well-dressed young man with a Middle Eastern accent. He had the proper letter of introduction and knew the numeric pass phrase the director and your buddy al-Faisal agreed to."

"How much money was in the account, sir?"

"$34 million."

"Holy shit."

"Yep. Your investigation just got a whole lot more horsepower. I briefed the director yesterday, that's why he called the Saudis and why you're getting personal attention from the minister's right-hand man. We've assigned this investigation the codename INHERITOR. You make requests for resources as you need them under that name and it will get routed to me and the director for immediate approval."

"Yes, sir. What do you need me to do?"

"Let's see what our Saudi friends can come up with. I've got a dozen agents working at this end to pick through the bank records to make sure we didn't miss anything else. Your buddy Ali has been put in seg-regation at Guantanamo and has two agents as permanent bodyguards. We're also having him sign affidavits for all his statements to you."

"I'd recommend not turning him over to the Pakistanis just yet, sir."

"Not a problem. He's going to be bumming smokes from us for a while longer."

"Is there anything else, sir?"

"Call me if you learn anything new."

"Will do," Johnson replied as the line went dead.

Putting the cell phone back into his inner jacket pocket, Johnson took a long pull from the water bottle again, then another. Somebody associated with the Taliban had managed to vanish with $34 million. *Damn.* That was nearly fifteen years ago. That was a lot of funding for somebody to play with.

Johnson's musing came to a halt as Akeem exploded through the door clutching a sheaf of paper.

"He is here, Agent Johnson. Sadig al-Faisal is in the Kingdom."

CHAPTER 13

. . . .

REPIN WAS STANDING AT THE bus stop, doing his best to stay out of the gusty winds the city was known for and away from the other waiting passengers. Two women and a man were huddled inside the metal and Plexiglas shelter, but Repin stood outside. From time to time, he would glance at the police officer in his cruiser parked on the corner across from the bus stop. The blue and white color combination reminded him of the police cars in Moscow, as did the chill in the wind. The officer appeared to be alternately talking on his cell phone and filling out forms on a tablet in the warmth of his car. The sun had tried to work its way through the clouds today but so far had not succeeded. The sky was a dirty gray and the temperature was in the mid-30s, but the wind chill made it feel 10 degrees colder. Repin could not blame the man for not wanting to expose himself to the cold, but he was a sentry who simply was not thinking like one now.

Finally, one of the blue and white transit authority buses arrived at the stop, and the three people in the bus shelter practically ran on board as soon as the driver opened the door. The driver looked expectantly at Repin, who shook his head back and forth. The driver shrugged within his heavy coat, closed the door, and drove off as soon as the traffic cleared.

Now that the people were gone, Repin moved quickly into the shelter and withdrew a black cell phone from his pocket. He had three of them. He bought them this morning for cash in one of what the Americans called a big-box store. Each was a disposable prepaid cell phone from a different manufacturer with one hour's worth of talk time.

He quickly dialed a number in the northeastern U.S. from memory. The phone began ringing.

"Yes?" The voice was male, one Repin recognized. His English was pronounced slowly, with a mild Middle Eastern accent.

"This is John. I need you and your friends to meet me at the gas station in twelve hours."

"Twelve hours?"

"Yes. Is that a problem? I told you it would be on short notice."

"No, no. It's no problem. It's just a surprise. We'll be there in twelve hours."

"Good." Repin disconnected the call, cast a quick glance at the policeman to see him still talking on his phone, and immediately dialed another number. This one rang in the southeastern U.S.

"Hello?" This voice was also male, but the Middle Eastern accent was thicker.

"This is John. I need you and your friends to meet me at the gas station in twelve hours."

"Twelve hours. I understand."

"Good." Repin could have sworn he heard the faintest *Allahu Akbar* from the other end of the phone line as he disconnected the call. He had warned them about that. Religious fanatics were the worst kind to work with. They had unquestionable loyalty to the cause, given that they perceived it as God's will, but they had some behavior patterns that made them easy to identify. He could do little about that now. Besides, the two men he just spoke to would very likely be dead in twelve hours.

The countdown had started. It was midafternoon and Repin had twelve hours to get back to his command post to do his part. That was plenty of time to work his way back on the bus line, making a few detours to ensure he was not being followed. With luck, he would just miss the bulk of the late afternoon commute. He took the cell phone apart, removed the battery, and discarded the phone in the trashcan near the bus stop. His timing was pretty good. Five minutes later, the bus he wanted pulled up, and he boarded it for the ride back.

UNNOTICED BY THE LOCAL AUTHORITIES, twelve men, equally split between two vans, approached Long-Term Parking Lot 5B at Bradley International Airport in Windsor Locks, Connecticut. The drivers guided their vans nonchalantly through the lot's gated barrier, taking a ticket from the unmanned podium for what would be a very short stay, and began cruising the lot.

By prearrangement, they cruised slowly and stopped whenever they were near one of two types of cars. In short order, six sedans and six minivans on the National Insurance Crime Bureau's most stolen list were quickly broken into, hot-wired, and driven out of the lot by the twelve well-practiced jihadis, the drivers paying cash at the automated kiosk. The van drivers, slipping their vehicles in amongst the sudden outflow of stolen cars, paid nothing at all, since their stay in the lot was less than the thirty-minute minimum.

The drivers of the stolen cars paid careful attention to the speed limits and left plenty of following distance as they split up, ensuring no more than two of the stolen vehicles—one car and one van—ended up in one of six different garages in the nearby towns of Southington, Wethersfield, Newington, New Britain, Bristol, and Waterbury.

Similarly well-orchestrated thefts by other jihadis took place at municipal parking lots in the towns of Orange, Pinehurst, and Bridge City, Texas. The lower population density of northeastern Texas denied them the option of spreading the vehicles out as their brothers in Connecticut had done. The four cars and the minivan were driven to an abandoned property on Coke Road outside of Groves, Texas, where the jihadis parked them all in a barn to avoid detection.

In both states, the thieves began by removing the license plates and emptying the glove compartments, and then the car interiors, of anything that might easily allow the vehicles to be traced. The men removed or severely defaced the vehicle identification numbers wherever possible. The minivan drivers loaded quarter-inch steel plates along the sidewalls and doors. Their hasty and sloppy installation was done with little regard for the intentions of the car's interior designers. They removed the rear seats, and one man even blowtorched free his seats that were more permanently affixed.

Next, they loaded guns and the explosives. They packed ten pounds of C-4 into each car trunk, and stacked AK-47 and AR-15 rifles in the back of the vans along with loaded magazines and the odd Remington Model 870 shotgun and spare shells.

The grenades were the last to be loaded. The men placed two boxes into each van, marking one with a large red "X" for easy identification. Each man would carry one rifle and four extra magazines or a shotgun and spare shells along with two grenades from each box.

When their work was completed, the thieves in Connecticut threw the scrap material in dumpsters at the rear of the garages, while the Texas jihadis sank theirs in a nearby pond off the road.

Each man then purified himself by washing his hands and feet with bottles of water and small basins and then sat in a communal circle with the others near their vehicles to enjoy a meal. The men in Texas dined on lamb shawarma with rice, yogurt, fruit, and coffee made and delivered by one of the men's wives. The men in Connecticut ate curried chicken, eggplant, olives, and tea.

During the meals, tales of victories over the infidel were told, and passages from the Qur'an were quoted. Some of the men took turns operating the video cameras that were now running, recording the meal, the vehicles and equipment, and the men. Some of the men made impassioned speeches to the camera, praising the greatness of Allah and promising death to America.

As the meals ended, the flash memory cards from the cameras were removed and sealed in prepaid FedEx shipping envelopes. One man from each group took the envelope and deposited it in the nearest drop box, while his comrades bedded down under blankets wherever they could. There would be time for prayer later. The envelope and the memory cards would find their way to a cutout to serve another purpose.

FOUR HOURS AND FIVE BUSES later, Repin took his coat off and hung it on the peg by the door inside his command post and locked the deadbolt. Then he put three steel security bars in place across the door. The door would need to be torched or blown out of its steel frame before anyone could get to him.

He rubbed his hands together to warm them and walked over to his work area, dropping the bag from his favorite American fast-food restaurant next to his computer on the desk. One of his weaknesses was the burgers and fries from the clown's restaurants. He had lost track of how many missions he had been on all over the world in the late hours of the evening and had still managed to pick up a cheeseburger, fries, and chocolate shake from that ubiquitous restaurant.

For the last thirty-six hours before his trip out to the bus stop, he had listened on his police scanner to the increasing complaints of police officers standing post at commuter bus lots. Over the last few days, he had ridden the city's bus system and kept his eyes open. Fewer officers were on the street at non-rush hour times, and the constant police presence was gone. There were no signs of the National Guard on the street yet. Using just one city as an indicator of a national trend was not the best measure he might have, but it had been nearly a week since what newspapers were still calling the "random shootings," and he had to work with the information at hand. The Internet helped, and he read every major paper from every major U.S. city and factored in what he read and what he did not see in print. This seemed to him to be the proper time to initiate the next phase of the plan.

The operational concept was based as much as possible on psychology. The operations up to now had been designed to ratchet up the level of tension in the country and tire the security services. The bombings in San Antonio had killed people but were not crippling. In order to cripple the country, something bigger needed to happen. People just could not die; the very idea of America needed to be attacked and shaken. Aziz understood this. The land of safety and complacency would soon be less so. It would be diminished in the eyes of the world.

To make the larger event as successful as possible, Repin needed to make the local police forces and security services work longer hours. This would cause their sleep patterns and normal personal lives to be interrupted. Then he could order the next strikes just as they started to relax again but before they got into a rhythm on their new schedules. It would give Aziz's followers an extra edge when they hit the more heavily defended targets in the next phase.

In any event, Repin had less than eight hours to get ready for his part in what was to come. He pulled off the sweater he had worn beneath his jacket for extra warmth and threw it on the bed. Moving to his work area, he turned the televisions back on and broke the screen lock on his computer. He brought up the websites of the major papers while he ate, going through one at a time while watching the cable news shows one last time. He saw nothing that might cause him to abort.

Next, he checked the Weather Channel's website for the forecast in the Northeast. The cold front that was sweeping through his part of the country was moving east quickly. It had originated in Canada as a cold high-pressure system and begun its trek south and east yesterday, gathering speed along the way. Daytime temperatures in the New England and the mid-Atlantic states were already in the low 30s. Once the front arrived, temperatures were forecast to drop into the low 20s during the day and then into the single digits at night for the next week as the front stalled out. That would be helpful—in fact, necessary—to ensure the impact of what would come next.

As he sipped the last of his melted shake, he checked his watch. Six hours left. It would be a long night.

"I STILL THINK WE SHOULD have had a second sniper team out there, sir." The senior NCO—Sierra One, the lead sniper during the exercise now officially called OCTOBER FROST—made a valid point, Mathews thought. He had argued for a second sniper team during the hot wash after the helicopters had returned the team to base that night, but this was the last formal review of the exercise. The exercise controllers had taken a few days to commit the final time line and recommendations to paper, and Mathews was taking one last chance to go over the write-up with his team.

A second sniper team positioned farther north of the first team would have provided additional over watch and support, and would have permitted the two teams to leapfrog and cover one another moving into and out of the objective. The problem was that Mathews didn't have a second set of qualified snipers on his team, nor did he have the manpower slots for them.

"I agree that having a second sniper team would be better, but we just don't have the qualified personnel, Sergeant. I'll endorse your recommendation to the colonel, but don't hold your breath."

"Understood, sir. In the meantime, could we cross-train some current Team Four members?"

Mathews mulled that over. The members of his new team were pretty well cross-trained now, and further specialized training with the dedicated sniper pair would only increase that level of preparedness.

"Yes, you can. Cull through the volunteers and pick the two you think are most qualified." The lead sniper smiled at the thought of the competition he would orchestrate to pick the two best.

"However," said Mathews, preparing to burst his bubble just a little, "The extra pair will only be available for sniper duty when I don't need them for their primary job as assaulters, and command concurs prior to our deployment. Understood?"

"Yes, sir," replied the SNCO, who was experienced enough to understand why his new team leader applied those constraints.

Getting everyone's attention back to the formal review of OCTOBER FROST, Mathews asked, "Does anyone have any more comments?"

The team looked around expectantly at one another, but no one had anything else to add.

"All right then, thanks again for some good work out there. Everyone is dismissed. I'll see you tomorrow morning at PT. Let's see if we can bring our run time down another ten seconds."

A chorus of halfhearted groans escaped at this announcement, but Mathews knew they would all try. Running five miles in thirty-nine minutes was great by anyone's standards, but he had learned that people tend to slack off if they weren't regularly challenged. Eventually he would get those ten seconds. Then he would tell them to knock off another ten seconds, and the cycle would repeat.

The same thing happened on the weapons ranges. His men shot daily, with both sidearms and their M8 rifles in different configurations. They held friendly competitions, usually paid off in beer. Mathews was learning to hold his own in weapons proficiency against his men, who'd had the advantage of almost daily practice he hadn't enjoyed with his SEAL team, budgets and other requirements being what they were. In spite of this, he trained hard with them on the range, earning their respect by demonstrating his work ethic and by getting up to speed quickly.

Things were different when he led them through close-quarters battle. He had practiced leading CQB as a SEAL, and had led his SEAL platoon through the kill house more times than he could count. Always entering in the second position as the team leader, he had proven his ability to clear his sector of the room quickly and efficiently. The last trip down Hogan's Alley with his team in an urban setting was the first perfect score ever recorded in the alley. He had led them through the kill house and cleared it in record time with not so much as a simulated civilian hostage getting scratched. The alley remote controllers were still paying up in the recreation areas of the base and picking up bar tabs for his team. The rest of the teams were spending much of their unscheduled duty time in the alley to try and beat Team Four's record.

OCTOBER FROST was a good way to underscore their training, and it had felt good to get out in the field to practice. Team Four would head out again tomorrow in another local exercise of a controlled withdrawal from a hard contact scenario in the mountains to the north. In the meantime, the duty day was over. Mathews was going to meet Captain Mallory and the other team leaders in the dining hall for dinner and a more informal discussion of OCTOBER FROST and the impact Team Four's participation had on the training budget for the year.

"AGENT JOHNSON, YOU MUST REMEMBER that you have to stay with me," Akeem insisted.

"I understand, Mr. Akeem. I will not interfere. I'm just as eager to get him as you are."

Akeem looked doubtfully at the younger man. The American kept reaching for his right hip as if he'd forgotten something, and Akeem suspected he would have preferred to have his FBI-issued sidearm drawn to accompany the Saudi Special Emergency Force into the building.

But Johnson couldn't carry his weapon for many reasons. Agent Johnson was a guest in Akeem's country, and Akeem could not expose any guests to danger. Also, the Special Emergency Force for the Riyadh area was not very pleased to have this American along. Some of the comments about him in Arabic had caused Akeem to remind the unit commander privately that this man was an honored guest in the Kingdom of Saudi Arabia and should be treated accordingly, as his command chain had ordered and as Islam required. The man had reluctantly agreed, but he flatly refused Akeem or Johnson permission to be any closer than one mile from the site. He also required they remain under the close escort of two of his men.

Naturally, the two elite Saudi commandos took little pleasure in nurse maiding an Interior Ministry observer and his American guest. They sat in the front of the armored Chevy Suburban with identical looks of disgust and were barely civil. Akeem had practically threatened them to get the tactical radio channel monitored so he could appraise Johnson as the team's assault progressed.

Johnson instinctively reached for his right hip again and cursed the rules that said he couldn't bring his sidearm into the Kingdom without permission. He was a trained law enforcement officer, and he had to sit still while others captured the man he was hunting. Akeem had explained the rules of courtesy the Saudis were required to extend to him, but he still got the distinct impression that the Emergency Force team leader did not like him being around at all. He wished he knew more Arabic. He even would have to rely on Akeem to translate the damned radio traffic.

The Suburban was parked underneath a palm tree on the side of the main road leading to Sadig's apartment. The complex was an understated set of dwellings that seemed to have sprung up from the desert alongside the two-lane road. The buildings were light tan with white tile roofing. Very little else was nearby. The complex was fenced and had a central playground for the children and a swimming pool.

According to the Saudis, Sadig's apartment was near the back of the compound, and, in order to guard against being compromised, the assault team members had actually rented apartments near Sadig's earlier that day and hired Pakistani and Philippine laborers to move furniture and boxes in during the afternoon. The team's uniforms, weapons, and assault gear were secreted inside the furniture and among the boxes of clothes.

Later in the early evening, other members of the assault unit, dressed in civilian clothes, arrived at one of the apartments bearing food and sweets as part of a faux housewarming. One of them actually even saw Sadig watering his plants on the third-floor balcony of his apartment.

It was now nearly 4 A.M., the scheduled time for the assault. Akeem had explained to Johnson that the assault would proceed one hour before the first call to prayer a little after 5 A.M., in order to ensure they were not compromised if Sadig was an early riser. The team should be getting ready to move about now.

The radio came to life, and Johnson heard a brief exchange in Arabic. He looked at Akeem expectantly.

"They are moving into position now."

A few minutes passed slowly. The only sound in the big four-wheel drive was the air conditioning running on low since the bulletproof windows couldn't be lowered. All four men unconsciously leaned toward the radio, willing it to come on again.

Their wish was quickly granted. The radio came alive again suddenly with a clipped word in Arabic, and both of the escorts looked at each other.

Akeem spoke up, "They were just ordered in."

There was silence for a few beats and then the sound of panicked voices as someone on the assault team keyed his mike and held it down, shouting. Johnson looked at Akeem, but he just shook his head. He couldn't make out anything in the din of voices.

Finally, there was silence, followed by a lengthy string of Arabic. Both men in the front seats visibly relaxed.

Akeem said, "They've got him. No one was hurt, praise be to Allah."

"Thank God," Johnson intoned.

"I just did," replied Akeem with a smile at the younger man.

IT WAS TIME. REPIN STOLE another glance at his watch to be sure. 2 A.M. He muted the movie he was watching just as Cary Grant threw himself to the ground as the biplane passed over him. He could get back to it in a few minutes.

He went into the adjoining room and headed down a short corridor, through two doors that were barred much the same as the main entrance, and then up a ladder to the small enclosed shed on the building's roof. He lifted the cover of the five-kilowatt generator and checked its status board to ensure it was in working order. It would not do for power to fail on him now. His computer equipment had backup battery power, but that would only last so long. If the power did fail, the generator would kick in automatically after a sixty-second delay to power his command post's equipment. The shed was insulated for sound and well-ventilated, so no one on the outside would notice the generator operating.

After resealing the doors and returning to his work area, he sat down at the computer and broke the screen lock. This was the first direct attack he would make on America, and, if all went well, no one would ever know he was responsible for it.

He opened up a program labeled SCADAKILL on his desktop. On the program menu, he double-clicked the icon labeled NORTHEAST GRID. The computer responded with the message CONNECTING, and he leaned back to wait while the hourglass spun.

If the program didn't work, the plan would end there. The programmer he had hired to create this software would be unable to fix any problems with it. Programming anything was very difficult with two 9mm bullets in your skull. The pimply faced young man had promised that this was his best hack ever and had really bought into Repin's story about wanting to prove a point about how dangerous America's nuclear power plants were. His naiveté reminded the Russian of his own youthful gullibility.

Repin had asked him how much money he wanted for the job, and the boy had asked for a quarter of a million dollars for the software. Repin had told Aziz, who had happily paid. After the software had been delivered, Repin tested it and then promised to meet the boy to pay him at the local landfill. Now the boy was a permanent resident there, and Repin was $250,000 richer. It was an unpleasant decision, but the young man had seen Repin's face. Leaving him alive was not conducive to Repin's survival.

The computer finally displayed the CONNECTED message and began drawing a schematic block diagram of the northeastern power grid. Repin could see everything: all the power plants feeding the Northeast grid, even the ones in Canada and in the western portion of the U.S., as well as the major substations and the long-haul transmission lines between them.

The way the boy had explained it, his software tapped into what was called the Supervisory Control and Data Acquisition network that ran over the Internet, managing and monitoring all electric power generation and distribution. Called the SCADA network among the professionals in the industry, it was more commonly referred to by politicians and utility companies as the Smart Grid. The SCADA network itself was nothing more than a large number of computerized sensors and controllers, he told Repin, attached to every piece of major electric power generation and transmission equipment throughout the nation, loosely managed by a conglomeration of the Department of Energy and the nation's power utilities. When the SCADAKILL software connected to the virtual paths in the network that the SCADA system relied on for communication, it gathered the status of any nodes in the selected grid.

As an added refinement, the boy had learned the electronic identities of the master control computers within the SCADA network, stored the identities in the program, and had his software assume the identity of one of them at random when it connected to the network. The SCADAKILL software would randomly change its logical identity every ten to fifteen minutes to masquerade as an available master control computer in order to stay hidden from anyone trying to search for it. As long as it appeared to be one of those master control computers, any orders the SCADAKILL program issued would be acted on by each of the nodes' computers on the network without question or confirmation.

The best part was that every power plant and every transformer substation had computerized controllers that were nodes on the SCADA network. These nodes normally reported simple things, like the position of a switch, or the current amount of voltage on a long-haul transmission line. The capability Repin was more interested in was that they could also remotely alter the configuration of switches, transformers, or generators at power plants when commanded.

This was something the boy had been enthusiastic about. Turn off enough of the switches routing power into the outbound or load portions of the major switching substations and all that power would have nowhere to go. In order to avoid having the power plants and their associated generators damaged when the load was removed, the control systems would automatically disconnect the generators at the power plants from the grid. He had said it would be temporary but attention getting. Repin planned to take it one step beyond attention getting.

AZIZ'S G550 WAS CRUISING AT an altitude of 42,000 feet at Mach .85 heading east south east over Armenia.

Aziz sat in a plush leather chair behind the custom rosewood desk he had installed in the right side of the aircraft when he ordered it. He sipped dark coffee—his preference—from his gold-lipped cup. The warmth of the coffee flooded into him as he replaced the cup on the matching saucer and then sat back and closed his eyes.

The deal he closed in Georgia with the infidel owners of that oil production company would add more wealth to Arabco, and then to Aziz. That money would then find its way through the false fronts, dummy corporations, and their associated bank accounts to the cutouts Repin had put in place.

The cutouts would withdraw the money and funnel it to his jihadis through the intricate web of familial ties so that the cash would end up deposited in hundreds of banks throughout the world. His—no, *Allah's*—soldiers would use this money to great effect.

Even today, men and women traveling the world ostensibly to see relatives in various countries carried a few thousand American dollars or its equivalent in euros, francs, or pounds sterling. After they arrived at their destinations, they would deposit the funds in specific accounts in certain banks. Then after a few days, they would return to Europe or the Middle East, sometimes with messages from some of the faithful working for the jihad, wait a few weeks, and then repeat the process.

These couriers never carried more than the amount the customs service in that country mandated declaring, usually 10,000 euros or 10,000 U.S. dollars. Amazingly enough, the seventy or so people that the cutouts employed as couriers had moved more than two million euros last year alone, in fewer than six trips each.

It was so simple it brought a smile to Aziz's face, his eyes still closed. The infidels were so stupid. To think that their Western banks could actually track the movement of the money needed to finance his jihad against the Americans and their corrupt and evil nation. He and his people had their faith and the unwavering support of Allah. They would not be found or captured. They were too far "under the radar," as the Americans say.

The discovery of the MV *Spring Tide* and its cargo was a setback. The best that Aziz could determine was that the shipping container holding the explosives and weapons had accidentally fallen to the dock during unloading, spilling its contents onto the dock.

Fortunately, Windmere Manufacturing was a dummy company, whose single office in Bern, Switzerland, was now empty, its bank accounts closed out, phone disconnected, and mail stopped. Its sole employee had relocated to Bahrain. The Americans would find nothing even if they kept looking, and soon they would have bigger problems to occupy their attention.

Aziz opened his eyes, rose, and then stretched. He looked at the coffee and decided against another sip and then motioned to the male cabin attendant to remove it.

He walked toward the rear of the plane and closed the master cabin's door behind him. The lights were muted in this room. He took a moment to brush his teeth, and then he disrobed and climbed into bed. The cabin attendant would wake him no more than one hour before touchdown. In eight or nine hours, he would be home. It would be good to watch the next round of chaos in America from the comfort of one of his favorite houses.

CHAPTER 14

· ·

THE MEN IN TEXAS KNELT on prayer rugs inside the barn, the scent of damp hay, gasoline, and cooked lamb in their nostrils. Prayer was required before such undertakings. To ensure victory, Allah's beneficent help must first be begged.

Thoughtfully, the group's leader had brought water for the partial ablution, the *Wudu,* performed before the *Salat* began. The men had taken pains to sweep the barn floor down to bare dirt beforehand. They had also brought fresh clothes to be properly clean and purified before speaking to Allah.

The *Salat* lasted nearly thirty minutes, and then another ten as each man made his personal prayers and then rose to greet his brothers nearest to him with the traditional "May Allah receive our prayers." The men finished by carefully gathering up the prayer rugs and placing them on one of the clean spots on the floor. They would need their rifles and Allah's help more than they would need the rugs. The four men who would certainly see Paradise tonight huddled together in a small circle, heads down, holding hands and chanting *"Allahu Akbar"* quietly and repeatedly.

When the other seven men were ready in the van, the leader, who would drive the van tonight, walked over to the huddled group, placed his hands gently on the shoulders of the two nearest men, and said, "It is time for you to see Allah with your own eyes, my brothers. Be strong, for surely He will reward you."

The men looked up as one, their eyes distant and wet with tears. Without another word they released one another's hands, embraced each other, and walked to their individual cars.

The leader returned to the van and as he slid into the driver's seat, he heard the engines of the four cars come to life.

Glancing over his shoulder at the seven men crouched in the back, he said in Arabic, "Set radios to Channel 2, and make sure you have your grenades."

The men checked the store-bought FRS radio clipped to their shirt pockets and ensured they were set to the proper channel, touched the four grenades they had affixed to each of their equipment harnesses they had donned before entering the van, and then rechecked their rifles for chambered rounds and activated safeties. The one man with the shotgun had already chambered one shell and double-checked that the safety was on.

The leader sounded the horn once, and the four cars led the way single file out of the barn and down Coke Road.

When the small convoy reached 39th Street, the first two cars turned left and headed north as the rest of the group stopped briefly. When the driver of the third car saw the lights of the first two cars turn right off 39th onto Locust Avenue to head east, he led the fourth car over to Redbud Avenue. All four cars paralleled each other as they headed east. The van moved toward 39th Street and stopped, focusing on the taillights of the third and fourth cars as they continued down Redbud toward the bloom of bright light surrounding the security checkpoint almost a half mile away.

The first two cars continued moving down Locust Avenue toward the other illuminated security checkpoint. Two hundred yards from the checkpoints, they mashed the accelerators to the floor.

The cars reached fifty miles per hour in seconds. Each driver had one target in mind: the guardhouse in the center of the pool of light at the north and south checkpoints, between the inbound and outbound roadways.

THE CIVILIAN GUARD FORCE AT the U.S. Strategic Petroleum Reserve was beyond bored. At 3 A.M. there was precious little to watch on television, and the guards in the main monitoring center were playing cards or "resting their eyes" with their feet up on desks or vacant chairs.

The shift leader sat at the card table with two men and one of the women on his shift. He pulled toward him the two cards the dealer pitched him, and with barely a glance at his fresh hand, threw his cards down in disgust to signal his fold. A pair of deuces wasn't going to get him anywhere.

Rising, he walked over to the window in the monitoring center that overlooked the vast expanse of the reserve. It wasn't the most exciting of jobs, but guarding the emergency storehouse of crude oil maintained by the U.S. Department of Energy was important. He stretched, thinking back on the mandatory orientation he had received when he was promoted to shift leader six weeks ago, still somewhat in awe of what the acres of piping, short steel platforms, and open ground before him represented. Created as a hedge against a sudden disruption of crude oil shipments from overseas, the massive underground cache of raw crude ensured that the nation's economy would not slowly stop by keeping industries that needed petroleum products functioning. Industries that made plastics; provided vital chemicals for pharmaceutical manufacturing; and grew, harvested, and delivered food, along with providing dozens of other necessity items, were a key component of daily life in America. He had also paid particular attention to the portion of the orientation that talked about the reserve not being meant to keep people's cars filled with gasoline. Aside from keeping the nation's manufacturing and agriculture bases functioning, the reserve was maintained to keep the Department of Defense's ships, tanks, trucks, and planes operating to win any war or manage any crisis that had disrupted the flow of crude oil from overseas in the first place.

Beneath his feet, the reserve held more than 600 million barrels of crude oil, stored in a series of salt domes 3,000 feet below the surface, enough to cover a total disruption in oil imports to the U.S. for nearly sixty days. Letting his eyes range over the bare ground dotted with stainless-steel clumps of pipes and pumping equipment, he could see most of the entire southern portion of the field, including the lights of the vehicle checkpoint in the distance.

THE TWO MEN AT THE southern checkpoint were the youngest on tonight's shift. As usual, they were discussing the ample charms of the blond waitress at the nearby watering hole when they noticed the approaching lights of a car.

Instinctively realizing something was up, they both pulled the Mossberg 590 shotguns free from the spring-loaded clips holding them against the guardhouse wall. Then, as they had been taught, both moved to cover behind the concrete jersey barriers on the far side of the roadways away from the guardhouse.

The guard on the far side of the inbound roadway was just reaching for his radio when the third car tore across 32nd Street, angled left down the inbound roadway, and slammed into the guardhouse. The driver shouted *"Allahu Akbar!"* and as the wheels left the pavement just before impact, he pressed the button on the controller.

The ten pounds of C-4 in the trunk detonated almost exactly in the middle of the guardhouse as the car smashed through it. The car and driver disintegrated instantly from the blast wave. Fragments of the car and driver carried by the pressure wave slammed into the walls and ceiling of the guardhouse, ripping them apart.

The two guards were blown farther from the explosion. Fragments from the car and guardhouse peppered their bodies, and their clothes smoldered. One struggled to rise, blood streaming from his ears and nose, but the pain from broken ribs and a fractured tibia overwhelmed him and he mercifully sank into unconsciousness. The other guard struck the side of a parked car forty feet from his cover position, suffering a cracked skull and the accompanying concussion.

A similar explosion rocked the northern checkpoint when the first car slammed into it, but its two guards were not as lucky as those at the southern checkpoint. Their bodies immediately joined the suicidal driver's in the expanding blast wave as it flattened the guardhouse.

As soon as the drivers of the second and fourth cars saw the small fireball and smoke begin to recede, they raced their cars through the obliterated checkpoints and drove quickly down the roadways in the SPR toward the next target.

The guards playing cards in the main monitoring center looked up when they heard the crash of the two blasts and then looked at each other incredulously. The guards who were sleeping didn't even stir. The man dealing the game of seven-card stud asked rhetorically, "What was that?"

The group of men around the table began to get up when the two cars smashed into the building from opposite sides. At the moment of impact, the drivers pressed the buttons on their detonators. The flash and the hammer impact of the two near-simultaneous detonations ripped the already damaged cinder-block-and-wood building apart. The guards' bodies were crushed by the pressure waves and then immolated by the heat of the two blasts.

The driver of the van waited until he heard the distant sound of the explosion at the main monitoring center and drove quickly through the remaining fires and debris of the southern checkpoint into the massive complex of tanks, pipes, and pumping equipment that lay beyond the security perimeter.

The leader knew that at least one of the nearby residents was calling the local police force, and his team had limited time to accomplish its mission. As he reached one of the main pumping stations, he slowed the van to a crawl. The man closest to the side door pulled it open, and two of the men jumped out. They immediately began climbing the metal stairs to reach the small metal control shack where the pump controls were.

The leader sped the van up a little and stopped at the next pumping station. Two more men jumped out.

At the first pump station, the two men had reached the control shack and wasted no time, putting a three-round burst from an AK-47 into the lock and tearing the door open. The man who shot out the lock turned and stood in the doorway to cover the second man, who began activating the pumps that served one of the main oil storage caverns.

When he was finished, he turned his AK-47 on the pump controls and shot up the panel. Then both men ran down the steps, located the valves that controlled the connections that large rail-carried tanker cars would on-load from, and opened them. The raw crude shot out of the pipes onto the ground and began to pool rapidly. Both men ran toward the van and passed the other two groups of men at similar pump stations. They had also turned on the pumps, damaged the controls, and were waiting for them to pass before opening the loading valves. Then they too ran off to the van that was waiting to take them to the next set of pumps.

The man who had activated and then shot up the controls at the first pump station stopped before entering the van, turned, and pulled one of the grenades from his belt. Checking to see that it was the proper type, he pulled the pin and threw the thermite grenade as hard as he could back in the direction of the large pool of crude oil growing at 2,000 barrels a minute from the combined output of the three pumping stations. It landed near the second pumping station and ignited seconds later, its thermite payload burning at more than 2,500 degrees centigrade.

The resulting fireball blew the man off his feet and singed his eyebrows off. His face instantly sunburned from the flash. Two of his fellows leaped from the van and dragged him back into it as he shook off the stunning effect of the concussion.

As the driver pulled away toward the next set of pumps, he decided he would park farther away after they had opened the next set of valves.

He dropped off the men at the next set of three pumps almost a half mile from the first set, where the fire was now raging in the distance. Even in the darkness, the light from the huge conflagration illuminated the massive pall of black smoke rising into the air. So long as the wind stayed calm and steady, his men would not suffer from the poisoning gases emitted from a crude oil fire, but they needed to hurry.

The jihadis assigned to the second set of pumps found two technicians huddling behind the thick pipes feeding the pumps, and dealt with them swiftly. They left their victims' bullet-riddled bodies laying in the dirt at the base of the pumping station, their souls no doubt being burnt in Satan's fires as the jihadis worked to release the crude from its underground storage. The van's driver smiled grimly at the fate of the two Americans, certain that Allah would be pleased with this night's work.

In the distance, he could hear the wail of sirens coming closer. Putting his head out the driver's side window to listen, he thought the sounds were moving from the left to the right. The infidels were probably going to come in from the northern checkpoint to try to fight the fire.

"In the name of the Prophet, hurry!" he screamed into the FRS radio.

Heeding his admonition, the men ran back toward the van and huddled inside. The last man threw his thermite grenade back toward the newest pool of crude forming around the pumps and the two bodies, and immediately entered the van. He had no wish to suffer the same injuries his brother had.

As soon as he was aboard, the driver tore away from the scene and saw the new fireball rising into the sky in his rearview mirror. The van reached the area of the northern checkpoint before the American first responders did.

The van crunched to a halt on the gravel surface a hundred feet from the now-smoking remains of the guardhouse at the checkpoint. The flattened and burnt rear end of the first car protruded from what had been the corner of the structure.

"Now, my brothers!" the driver shouted. "Praise Allah and find cover. We must hold them off as long as possible."

The eight men leapt from the van and split into two four-man teams on either side of the roadways leading into and out of the SPR. They sought cover inside small-parts warehouses and behind the concrete jersey barriers along the sides of the roadway and prepared themselves.

The leading elements of the Port Arthur police and fire departments approached the scene. The lieutenant aboard the lead fire engine had just called in a third and fourth alarm to the dispatcher after seeing the second explosion inside the SPR complex. He knew he and his company would need help from surrounding counties and parishes in Louisiana to extinguish this blaze.

A Port Arthur police cruiser driven by a rookie officer led the two fire engines to the scene. As he approached the guardhouse, he saw the wreckage of the car and the checkpoint. "What the hell?" he wondered as he pulled off to examine the guardhouse area and allow the fire engines into the SPR. He exited the cruiser and moved to examine the charred and nearly unrecognizable pieces of the first car's driver that littered the ground. The engines slowed to pass the officer. As he turned toward the entrance to wave the fire engines on, two 5.57mm rounds from a jihadi's AK-47 slammed into the rear plates of the body armor he was wearing, one of them penetrating and burying itself in his left lung.

As soon as the young policeman collapsed, the leader shouted "Fire!" into his FRS radio. His small force opened fire on both engines. They aimed for the glass-enclosed front cabin, instantly killing the drivers of both of the fire engines, the lieutenant, and the rescue squad leader in the passenger side of the second engine.

Both engines immediately careened out of control. The lead engine slammed into a maze of piping and came to a halt. The second one made a sudden turn to the left as the dead driver's hands slipped off the wheel. The engine immediately rolled over onto its right side before sliding forty feet and stopping.

As the stunned survivors climbed out of the now-wrecked engines, the jihadis mercilessly gunned them down. Then two of their number raced over to the engines and shot out the pumping controls and tires. To add insult to injury, two of the jihadis pulled fragmentation grenades off their harnesses and wedged them beneath the fallen bodies of the firemen. Then they pulled the pins, allowing the weight of the dead bodies to hold the spoons of the grenades in place. When the bodies were moved, the spoons would be released, and the grenades would perform as designed.

More sirens sounded in the distance as the two men raced back to their brothers in the van. As soon as they climbed in, the leader, back in the driver's seat, gunned the engine and sped off through the northern checkpoint back up Locust Avenue. Looking left as he crossed 32nd Street, he could not yet see the lights of more police or fire services approaching. Good, he thought mercilessly.

He turned left onto Terrell Street and then after a mile or so, right onto Route 366 North, which would take the men to Beaumont, Texas, where a safe house was waiting. He held to the speed limit and kept checking his mirrors. In the back, his men began to chant, *"Allahu Akbar!"* After they had been on Route 366 for ten minutes and repeated glances in his mirrors assured him that they were not being chased by the police, he joined their chanting.

IN CONNECTICUT, THE MEN HAD also completed their Salat and drove off to finish their missions. The six sedans and six minivans joined up into prearranged pairs and headed off to individual targets. One pair headed to Perth Amboy, New Jersey, one pair to New Haven, Connecticut, and the last to Groton, Connecticut.

The first pair of vehicles struck the New Haven facility of the Northeast Home Heating Oil Reserve at a few minutes past 3 A.M., just as the lead car slammed into the southern checkpoint at the SPR in Texas. The lead car raced down Bridge Street, rammed the guard checkpoint, and exploded when the driver detonated the C-4 in the car, clearing the way for the van and its team of two men to drive into the facility and race past the heating oil storage tanks.

As the van drove deeper into the storage area, the man in the back pulled open the side door and was greeted by a blast of cold air. He then pulled a medium-sized wooden box of canvas bags toward him. The driver continued until he reached the back row of tanks. Then he yelled over his shoulder, "Now!" and began slowly driving alongside the tanks again, weaving a path back toward the entrance and passing as many tanks as possible.

The man in the back pulled a cord hanging from one of the canvas bags and threw it out the door at the base of the tank. He repeated the process for every tank they passed.

When he had thrown the last of the twelve canvas sacks, he slammed the side door shut.

"In Allah's name, hurry!" he shouted to the driver.

The driver sped toward the demolished entry point and back out down Bridge Street, where he turned left onto Ives Place and then headed up the on-ramp to I-91 Northbound. When he was on the interstate he slowed down. The second man looked out the rear windows, waiting.

He did not have to wait long. One by one, the timers in the satchel charges reached zero, detonating the C-4 inside them. The compression wave punched into the thin sidewalls of the tanks, instantly rupturing them. The heating oil inside immediately gushed out, weakening the tanks so that nearly half of them collapsed outright.

Miraculously, none of the oil ignited, but 750,000 barrels of heating oil was now forming a giant pool around the shattered remains of the storage tanks, seeping into the ground and finding its way into storm drains and toward Long Island Sound.

The second pair of vehicles did not reach the storage facility in Groton until nearly 4 A.M. After the lead car's driver had gone to Paradise when he eliminated the small guard shack at the entrance, and the van began its destructive rounds, the second man in the van found he could not open the side door. After three panicked minutes, he finally pried the door open and started tossing his satchel charges at the base of the containers. Then fate caught up to him again when he tossed a charge but neglected to pull the cord to arm it first.

He armed the next one, screamed at the driver to stop, threw the last charge at the nearest tank, leapt out of the van, and ran back toward the charge he had failed to arm. Once he reached it he had to crawl halfway under the steel stairs it had slid under, grab it, pull the cord, and then crawl out again.

He ran back to the van, hearing the charges he had thrown earlier beginning to explode. He was just about to climb in when he realized that he was an utter fool. He looked up into the eyes of the van's driver, who clearly had just realized the same thing, when the last charge he had thrown, the one laying nearest to the parked van, detonated.

The blast threw the van and both men into an adjacent tank, crushing them to messy pulp against its steel skin and flattening the van. The remaining charges still did their work, wrecking the steel walls of the storage containers and spilling heating oil into an ever-increasing puddle in the area. A spark from the van's electrical system soon started a fire that spread over the area, and the better part of 200,000 barrels of heating oil began its conversion into heat, light, and smoke.

The last pair of vehicles had drawn the toughest of the targets. The heating oil storage tanks in Perth Amboy were the largest grouping, and they had split the satchel charges between the car and the van, with two men in each vehicle. In this case, there would be no suicidal charge into the front gate. The cars would have to get in and out again using only rifle fire.

As they approached the main gate at the Hess Company storage site on Smith Street around 4:30 A.M., both vehicles slowed and stopped. The two men on duty at the gate noticed their approach but didn't seem overly alarmed. One of them rose, slid open the gatehouse's door, and said, "ID, please." He had only a moment to register the size of the barrel of the pistol the van's driver used to shoot him in the head.

The second guard was still fumbling for his sidearm when the van's driver calmly put four rounds into him through the still-open door.

"*Allahu Akbar,*" he said. He knew Allah would be pleased with him for dispatching two infidels.

The van's driver led the way into the complex. When they reached the area of the storage tanks, the car turned left and the van right, each heading for the most distant row of tanks to begin planting the charges.

Less than ten minutes later it was done. As the two cars headed back to the entry point, they noticed the flashing lights of one of the complex's security vehicles parked at the entrance. They could see two men inside the checkpoint through the wraparound glass windows. One was shouting into his radio, and the other man appeared to be giving the second guard CPR in the vain hope of saving his life.

So much the better, thought the driver of the van as he led the way toward the outbound lanes of the checkpoint. His brother crouched ready behind him on the left, the window in the rear opened fully.

The man shouting into his radio saw the van and car approaching, and knowing what had just happened to his two friends, immediately drew his sidearm and moved across the checkpoint's floor to the outgoing side to stop the vehicles. The second jihadi in the van opened fire and cut him down instantly. He was shifting fire to the other man giving CPR when the van's driver accelerated hard, back out onto Smith Street, and fouled his shot, the rounds going wide and high.

The explosions and fires were already starting in the distance when the two-vehicle convoy reached the Garden State Parkway and headed north to their safe house in Rahway. Behind them, nearly 900,000 barrels of heating oil burned in the chill morning air.

CAIN PLOWED THROUGH THE DOOR to the CTS and immediately headed to the night-shift supervisor. He'd just made record time from his house in Pasadena, Maryland, after the emergency text message hit his cell phone.

"What the hell is going on, Eddie?"

Eddie Falco looked at Cain as he took the stairs two at a time up to the director's area. Falco was an eighteen-year veteran of the intelligence community, and his expression was as grim as Cain had ever seen in the time they had worked together.

"We're being hit again. The cable news channels are talking about explosions and fires occurring at the SPR in Texas, and at least three home heating oil storage facilities in the Northeast."

"What do you mean 'at least three'?" Cain asked as he scanned the large displays.

"We haven't heard about any more yet, but I wouldn't be surprised if we get hit again."

"What makes you think this is hostile action?"

"We're getting some information from Homeland Security now. The locals on scene at the SPR are reporting vehicles crashed into guard-posts, one police officer shot, and two fire engines shot up and their crews killed on scene as they responded. Oh, and this is the real killer, no pun intended: booby-trapped bodies."

"What?"

"Apparently, whoever shot up the fire engines and killed the crews used hand grenades to booby-trap the bodies. Two paramedics are dead after they rolled one of the firemen over to check him and the grenade rolled free. The local cops checked the other bodies and found one more body with a grenade under it."

"Did they call in the bomb squad?"

"They couldn't. The fire at the facility is raging out of control and everybody had to pull back. The image is in the center on the right display."

Looking at the footage being broadcast from a news helicopter, he could understand why. The flames were a mass of reddish orange and covered much of the facility. The massive pall of thick black smoke rising over it had caused the helicopter's pilot to pull back from the area, and the wide-angle shots showed the revolving lights of fire engines and police cruisers well outside of the SPR perimeter.

"Just before you got here, the newsie anchoring the night desk said that the local fire chief thinks the pumps were turned on and are feeding the flames. He's asked for assistance from every firehouse within a hundred miles to contain it. The local cops are evacuating everyone in a twenty-five-mile radius and are warning people about the toxic fumes that are produced by this kind of fire. What a mess."

"Jesus," said Cain as he sat in his chair, still staring at the images on the screen. "What about the other three fires?"

"We just confirmed this with Homeland: all three are at facilities that make up the Northeast Home Heating Oil Strategic Reserve. It provides a ten-day reserve of heating oil in case of a supply disruption. More than five million people are going to have problems heating their homes from now on."

"Oh, shit. I think you're right, Eddie. We have been hit." Cain paused for a moment to absorb this, and then the professional in him took over.

"I want my day shift in here now. Recall them all. Tell them to get in as soon as they can and to expect a long day. Your people stay here an extra two hours to ensure we get a good pass-down from your team to the day's crew."

Eddie nodded and then grabbed a pad and pen, taking notes as Cain continued.

"Contact Homeland and the Department of Energy—we need to know what the storage capacities of those facilities were, and what the preliminary estimates of the losses are. Ask them for a read on the impact of the loss of a major part of the SPR, too. Wake up whoever you have to. Get estimates of how long it will take to repair and replenish the reserves. Then check all our available information on terrorist activities. I want to know if we had any inkling of this and missed it, and if so, I want to know why. DIRNSA is going to want as many answers as we can provide for the morning briefing."

"Anything else, David?"

"Yeah. Pull up the National Weather Service website and get the forecast for the northeastern U.S. for the next two weeks. Call somebody for a guesstimate for the next thirty days. Winter is about to come to New England and the mid-Atlantic states, and nearly fifty million of our fellow citizens just had their immediate source of heating oil destroyed."

IT WAS MIDAFTERNOON IN SAUDI ARABIA, and Johnson was sweating in spite of the air-conditioned comfort of the observation room. The Saudis were interrogating Sadig al-Faisal, and they were not being very gentle about it.

Sadig's face was a bloody mess. His nose had been broken, both eyes were black and blue, and his lip was split open in two places. He sat naked in a chair, sweating from the pain and trying to breathe in spite of the two cracked ribs the "interrogators" had inflicted on him before this beating began.

Johnson looked over at Akeem and began to object again, but, before he could, Akeem said something in Arabic to the man recording the session and led him outside the observation room.

When they were alone, Akeem looked at him with a pitying expression and said, "Speak, my friend."

"What's going on in there is wrong."

Akeem looked at him quizzically for a moment and then asked, "Don't you want to know what he can tell us?"

"Yes, but . . ."

"This is the quickest way to the answers you seek. You must remember, Agent Johnson, this is Saudi Arabia, not America, and the rights your constitution gives to your citizens do not apply in this country. Sadig is in this country illegally, is a former member of the Taliban, and is likely helping to finance terrorist acts in various places in the world, to include the U.S. and the Kingdom. He also claims to be a Muslim, yet the alcohol and drugs we found in his home that he has been polluting himself with prove that he is far from a pious one."

"Yes, but . . ."

"Agent Johnson, I have spoken to you as a friend, but you must understand if you continue to object or complain, you will be returned to your hotel and I will provide the results of our questioning to you before you leave the Kingdom." Akeem's voice hardened, "This is not America. It is our nation, and here you are our guest. Respect our methods as we would respect yours, or you may go."

Johnson looked at the floor in frustration, and Akeem placed his hands on the younger man's shoulders.

"You must remember that our desert heritage is sometimes a harsh one, and we do what is needed to survive. Like you, we have little respect or kindness for those who would wish our people harmed; we simply do not try to pretend that these criminals deserve kind treatment and the special privileges of lawyers and their day in court where they might be released because of procedural error or jury ignorance. Islamic law is harsh, but our murder, rape, and robbery rates are mere fractions of those in your country."

Akeem headed back into the observation room, leaving the door open behind him. After a few moments' contemplation, cut short by a grunt of pain coming from the audio system that recorded everything in the cell next door, Johnson followed Akeem inside and shut the door.

CHAPTER 15

· ·

REPIN COULD NOT HAVE BEEN more pleased. It had been a long night, but the smile on his face helped erase the weariness. He had just finished a late breakfast of eggs and fruit and now was sitting at his computer, a cup of black coffee steaming on the desk, watching the news coverage on his multiple television screens.

The teams in New England and Texas had done well. The live news footage of the fires and damage at the Strategic Petroleum Reserve alone had been impressive. The news anchors were already talking about the expected rise in crude oil prices—possibly well beyond $190 per barrel—that was likely to occur as soon as the markets opened. Crude oil had been hovering at around $92 per barrel since OPEC had announced a production cut a couple of weeks ago. The secretary of energy had already been on the morning talk shows trying to reassure the public about the availability of crude oil, but he had not performed well in front of the cameras. The man was obviously worried, and when he was pressed for specifics about the exact size of the losses, his bland reassurances and total omission of any hard numbers only made him appear to be anything but in control of the situation. It got worse when he was asked about the fires at the three heating oil storage facilities.

One of the anchors, or, more likely her brighter-than-average producer, had discovered that those storage locations were part of the Strategic Home Heating Oil Reserve for the Northeast. When the anchor asked the secretary what the impact would be on the five million households that used oil to heat with, his stammering reply imparted no confidence. The commodity traders interviewed after the secretary's comments were speculating that home heating oil futures contracts would be bid well over $15 a gallon, up from $2.67 the day before.

No one in the government was calling it an attack yet, but that would not last long. The president's press secretary had made a brief statement that the president was monitoring the situation and meeting with his cabinet secretaries. He would address the media at noon. Repin was sure what he had to announce would not be good.

Repin's eyes wandered from the television screens and came to rest on his cup of coffee. As he reached for it, his eyes strayed to the unframed photo propped against the computer monitor. The photo was of an eight-year-old girl, the carefree smile only a child wears on her face as she poses for a camera. He had taken that picture the last time he had seen her. It had been almost nine years now. His thoughts drifted back to her birth, and the too-few years he had spent watching her grow and learn. The arguments with his wife, and then long years away from his beautiful Tatiana. She would be almost seventeen years old now. He wished he could see her again. He sent money to her mother and presents for Tatiana every Christmas and on her birthday. Her mother would not speak to him anymore; she knew what he had done, and what he had chosen to do. Repin hoped she used the money to make a better life for herself and Tatiana, and hoped she gave Tatiana the presents.

He wiped his eyes and then looked at his watch. It was almost noon. Time to get back to the job at hand.

THE PRESIDENT'S MORNING HAD NOT been a good one so far. His bedside phone had rung at 4 A.M. when the senior watch officer in the White House Communications Office told him about the attack on the Strategic Petroleum Reserve. After a moment to remind himself why he had wanted this job so badly given the frequency of these early morning calls, he had gotten out of bed. The calls usually heralded a long, difficult day. He had showered and dressed quickly, giving his wife a quick kiss on the forehead as she slept, and headed out of the third-floor residence's bedroom.

As usual, the Secret Service agents standing post in the center hallway on the Executive Residence floor were waiting for him. The agents seemed even more alert than normal. The Secret Service watch officer had probably been informed by the WHCO that they had roused the president early. The president looked at them briefly. "Situation Room," he said. Today was not a day for a cheery "Good morning!"

As he rode with the agents in the small elevator down to the sub level containing the Situation Room, the president let his mind wander a little.

He hoped it was the WHCO calling the watch officer. He had never really bothered to ask about the microphones, but he was sure the Secret Service had installed them. Just after he had been sworn in, he had been tempted to scream, "Don't shoot!" in one of the empty rooms of the third-floor residence just to see what the reaction would be. After some internal debate, he had decided he didn't really want to know just how closely the Service monitored his activities on the residence level.

The elevator doors slid open, breaking his chain of thought and bringing him back to the weight of the oath he had taken. He could already see the people gathered in the Situation Room through the thick glass separating it from the surrounding hallway.

The staff in the White House Situation Room briefed the president on the night's events before he chaired the cabinet meeting via secure video teleconference. Then he placed a call to the governors of Connecticut, New Jersey, New York, and Texas before a quick conference with his chief of staff and press secretary. Now that he had a handle on the situation, he took his notes and headed back to the elevator with his aides and Secret Service agents in tow. A few minutes later, he rounded the corner heading for the Briefing Room to speak to the press corps and the nation.

The president had always appreciated the White House briefing room as a marvel of technology, but it was not the biggest room in the White House. In spite of the refurbishment it had undergone during the George W. Bush presidency, it was still cramped, to say the least. The simple fact of the matter was that the West Wing of the White House had limited floor space and without an addition to the complex, there was only so much that could be done inside its walls. Building the addition would have given the Secret Service nightmares, anyway.

The electronics in the room had been upgraded, better displays were installed for the slide shows that sometimes accompanied press secretary or presidential briefings, and the flooring was reinforced and replaced. The White House Press Corps had not gotten any smaller over the years. In fact, with the explosion of the Internet and the status of the United States as the only remaining superpower, the White House was where news was made, and every news organization on the planet wanted to have an accredited journalist there to record it.

The president walked to the podium, now adorned with the presidential seal, since he, not his press secretary, would be speaking. The networks and the cable news channels hurriedly cut to the White House as he reached the podium. The press corps rose as he entered.

"Good morning, ladies and gentlemen," he nodded to the assembled journalists. "Please sit."

Pausing for a beat to clear his throat, he looked up into the glare of the klieg lights and began. "My fellow Americans, as I'm sure most are aware by now, there have been a number of incidents at some of our crude and heating oil storage facilities. We are still receiving information from the investigators on scene, and I can share some details with you. I'll start with the fire in Texas." The president straightened his notes before continuing.

"At least fourteen people are dead at the Strategic Petroleum Reserve site in Texas. As you know from the live coverage, the fire continues to spread but for the moment remains within the facility itself. State and local fire officials have established a fire perimeter around the facility and have no choice but to let the fire burn itself out. I have spoken to the governor of Texas, Christine Samuels, this morning, and at her request, declared the county of Jefferson, Texas, to be a federal disaster area. I have further directed the Federal Emergency Management Agency to begin deploying personnel and equipment into the area as needed, in coordination with the state and local authorities. Director Hendricks informed me that his available emergency assessment and command team departed Andrews Air Force Base by military aircraft an hour ago."

The president paused to sip some water. "Unfortunately, the most disquieting news from the fire at the reserve is that most of the fourteen people who died were shot to death by an unknown number of assailants."

A ripple of shock went through the assembled press corps at this announcement. The president continued, "We are working to confirm these initial reports and will report more to you as we learn it. Moving to the fires in New Jersey and Connecticut: there are at least three dead from the fire in New Jersey, and two each at the two facilities in Connecticut. All are confirmed to have died from gunshot wounds in an apparent attack on the sites. I've spoken to the governors in both these states, and they assure me that their fire departments have the fires contained although they will burn for some time. I want to reassure our citizens in all three states that your fellow citizens stand with you in this time of crisis and tragedy and that our thoughts and prayers go out to the families of those who have lost loved ones."

One of the journalists thought the president's remarks had ended and shot his hand into the air. The president shook his head no, and then went on, "I have had a long conversation with the secretary of energy, the secretary of homeland security, and the director of national intelligence. The secretary of energy, based on advice from his experts, believes that the losses of heating oil at the three facilities will be extremely high. He also believes that a significant portion of the Strategic Petroleum Reserve has been lost. Until the fires are extinguished, and a complete assessment by the Department of Energy can be made, we will not know the complete scope of the losses of crude oil or heating oil. The secretary of energy will have more information for you later today, and will be recommending some heating oil conservation measures for our citizens in the Northeast as well as working to replenish our heating oil supplies in that area."

The president paused again to sip more water and then started the last section of his remarks.

"Based on the limited facts as we know them and the apparent commonality of the shootings that took place at each location, I have directed the Department of Homeland Security to leave the nation's threat level at 'Imminent' for the immediate future, with particular emphasis on protecting our nation's oil and gas infrastructure. The Director of National Intelligence has no information on any planned or expected terrorist or foreign nation involvement in these attacks, but I cannot do less than take prudent action until we can determine what exactly has happened.

I have contacted the leaders of both houses of Congress and advised them of the situation and the actions I am taking. That is the end of my prepared statement, so I'm ready to take a few questions."

Every hand in the press pool immediately shot into the air.

"Karen," said the president, giving the first question to the most senior correspondent in the room.

Karen Adams from Associated Press stood, "Mr. President, it seems hard to believe that this is not the work of some organization or nation; why have you not characterized this as an attack on our nation, and have you ordered the military to a higher alert level?"

"I'll take the second question first. I have spoken to the secretary of defense, and he reports that no unexpected or aggressive action appears to be underway against U.S. interests, forces, or facilities anywhere in the world, outside of the United States. He has not advised me to increase our alert level, and I am not inclined to do so without sufficient reason. To answer your first question, this administration does not flail about in the middle of a crisis or a national disaster. The American people expect good decisions to come out of this government, and you need good information to make them. While these events may be a terrorist attack, the information we have at the moment is preliminary, and, until those reports are confirmed, I believe raising the terror alert to 'Imminent' provides the needed level of emphasis for our nation's law enforcement and security apparatus to act on. The alerts we'll send out later today will give local, state, and federal law enforcement and security agencies the information they need to institute necessary security precautions. An alert to the public will also be issued."

He paused a moment and the reporters shot their hands in the air again to get the next question. Rather than call on someone, he raised his hand to gesture for them to wait. The reporters lowered their hands while he added, his expression set and grim, "But it should be clearly understood, that if these events are a concerted attack upon the United States of America, those who are behind it will be identified and brought to justice, one way or another."

ALL OF THE WRAITH TEAMS were watching the president's press conference on the televisions mounted on the walls around the team area, nicknamed the Bullpen. Mathews and the rest of Team Four were also glued to what their commander in chief was saying. After the president's response to the old biddy's first question, his team NCOIC muttered under his breath, "Fuckin' A, Mr. President."

Mathews agreed with him but didn't say so out loud. He figured the Wraiths would not get orders until the Pentagon had a better idea of what was going on and whether or not it was a foreign power. The Wraiths could provide technical support to law enforcement, including weapons and communications gear, but the Posse Comitatus Act prohibited more than that. Anything that needed to be done domestically was the FBI's problem to deal with.

Colonel Simon's entry into the Bullpen proved Mathews wrong. He came through the cipher-locked door quickly, with Zeus hot on his heels. Captain Mallory called the room to attention, and everyone stood and braced. Zeus sat at his master's left side watching the team members and alternatively looking at Simon.

After a moment's observation, the colonel said, "Stand easy, Wraiths."

Each man relaxed and some fell into a more formal parade rest stance, with their hands clasped behind their backs. One soldier muted the president's press conference.

"You've all been watching TV, you know what's happened. I just spoke to General Crane and he wants us prepositioned for a rapid response overseas if the intel-pukes determine that a less-than-friendly country or organization is behind what's happened. He's cleared it with the Pentagon, so, deployment orders."

The colonel looked at each team leader in turn and then started running down deployment locations and departure times. Mathews tuned out a little, reminding himself that this would be his first deployment as a Wraith Team leader. He started to smile until he remembered that, if he led his men into a real operation, he was supposed to bring them all home again alive.

Colonel Simon had reached Team Three's assignment by the time Mathews refocused. "Royal Air Force Base, Lakenheath, in the UK."

"Yes, sir," responded Captain James, Team Three's leader.

Turning to Mathews, the Colonel barked out, "Andrews Air Force Base outside of D.C."

Startled, Mathews responded, "Yes, sir."

The unspoken question mixed with disappointment was not lost on the colonel, especially because Mathews' face displayed it for everyone to see.

"You're our newest team lead, Mathews. This gives you a chance to get your feet wet helping the FBI if needed. The general wants more veteran team leaders at the overseas locations. Got it?"

"I understand, sir."

The colonel continued the assignments, posting the seven teams from Guam in the Pacific to RAFB Lakenheath in the UK, to Panama in Central America, along with Mathews and the other relatively new team leader in the U.S.

His NCOIC, MSgt Harris, looked at him and said, "At least we didn't get Offutt, sir. The nightlife out there sucks. There's nothing but cornfields for miles out there, and this time of year, it's freaking freezing. At least in D.C. we might be able to hit a few clubs."

His lead NCO's attempt at humor wasn't totally lost on him, and there was truth to what he said. It was cold in Nebraska this time of year, but he was still disappointed.

The colonel was not through giving orders just yet. "OK, people. Team leaders, get your people and their gear loaded. The transports are fueling topside now. Assume a thirty-to-sixty day deployment at the overseas locations, and a thirty-day deployment to the stateside ones. Pack accordingly. Take full weapons and explosive load-outs from the prepackaged stores. I expect the first transport to be starting its takeoff run in less than an hour and a half."

Simon slowly looked around the room at each man and then said, "Let's hope we aren't needed. But if we are, good luck to all of you, and I'll see you when you get back. Get moving. Dismissed."

The room emptied quickly as the men headed for the equipment lockers and the main armory to grab the prepackaged supplies they would need. They loaded them onto the large cargo elevator and then returned to their quarters in small groups of five and six to retrieve their personal gear for the deployment.

The deployment plan was straightforward enough. The teams for Lakenheath and Guam would each deploy on board one of the unit's own C-17 Globemaster III cargo planes, refueling in the air en route. This provided the added benefit of forward deploying two of the AH-64D Apache attack helicopters and one of the OH-58D Kiowa Warrior scout helicopters as well as one of the Avenger drones. Coming along with them would be the necessary support and maintenance teams for the aircraft and a limited supply of munitions for the Apaches and the Avengers. Everything and everyone fit in the massive belly of the C-17 with room to spare. The aircraft could carry more than 170,000 pounds of cargo, and this load of helicopters, drone, gear, extra fuel, weapons, and people was barely more than 95,000 pounds.

The pre-palletized gear, maintenance equipment, fuel, and weapons made loading the people and their personal and mission gear the most time consuming part. The C-17 flying Team Three east to the UK would also carry Team Seven deploying to Offutt, and Team Four, being deployed to Andrews. That aircraft would make two stops to unload them and their limited amount of gear prior to the long hop across the pond with Team Three, the helicopters, and the Avenger drone.

The C-17 flying west would also make two extra stops: dropping Team Five and their equipment at Edwards Air Force Base in California, and Team Two and their gear at Elmendorf Air Force Base in Alaska, before proceeding to Guam with Team One and their supporting aircraft. Team Six would be the last to leave, heading to Panama on one of the 747-400s sans supporting aircraft, which they could call upon from the States if needed.

Colonel Simon was only mildly displeased that the actual departure of all the teams took fifteen minutes longer than he had expected. An hour and forty-five minutes after he issued his orders to the teams, he stood in the airfield's control tower to watch as the giant hangar doors rolled open and the massive C-17s and a single 747-400 rolled out into the midday sun, then down Taxiways Delta and Bravo to the end of Runway 28.

Ten minutes later, first one, then the other of the aircraft lumbered down Runway 28 and lifted off into the clear blue sky. The first aircraft made a wide sweeping turn to the right as it climbed out, and the second held the runway heading as it climbed to altitude. Both were lost from sight in less than five minutes.

WHAT REPIN SAW PLEASED HIM. It was better than theater in some ways. The press, in their urge to get the story, covered the attacks so completely that they barely broke for commercials. Each network's talking heads had said that the U.S. had suffered major losses in crude and heating oil, which, in typical news fashion, they repeated and then added some "profound" statement while sounding grave. So much the better to attempt to win an Emmy or even a Pulitzer in broadcast journalism.

Interviews with heating oil distributors in the New England region had revealed that Americans were calling to have their heating oil tanks filled immediately, and were even wanting to prepay for their next shipment before the prices went up. A few stories had even circulated about some of the more profit-minded distributors charging exorbitant prices for their current stock, often $25 to $30 per gallon. That demonstrated the signs of panic and concern in the population that Repin and Aziz were aiming for.

The stock and commodities markets were also reacting as they had predicted. The Dow Jones Industrial Average had dropped more than 100 points at the open and was down more than 575 points with more than an hour left in the trading day. Crude oil prices had shot up to $225 a barrel in the first hour and were now holding at around $230 per barrel, and heating oil futures contracts were being bid at $25 a gallon when he had last checked. All the major oil company stocks were trading down by an average of forty points.

His actions over the last day had just made life much more expensive and uncomfortable for a large number of Americans. In a few more hours, he would make it more so.

JOHNSON HAD TO STEP OUT in the hallway and go to the men's room. He washed his hands and face, and then washed them again in a vain attempt to remove the images from his memory. Sadig had curled up into a ball on the floor in a corner of his own personal hell. He was a puddle of pained flesh, sweat, vomit, and urine.

The Saudis had started beating him after he refused to answer their questions. After an hour, he answered everything by swearing in Arabic through split lips, two broken teeth, and in between ragged breaths drawn in shallow gasps due to his cracked ribs.

His face had become hideously deformed from multiple bruises, two black eyes, and blood from his lacerated forehead and lips. He looked like the victim of a car crash that no one chose to help. In addition to cracking his ribs, they had broken his right shin with a steel pipe. Sadig had screamed, and almost broke. But in the end, he refused to talk.

They finally affixed electrodes to his body, gave him a low-amperage sample of the new agony, and although he screamed again, he did not speak the answers. After a time, they attached two more electrodes, none too gently, to the most sensitive part of a man imaginable, and began again. From that point forward, every time the current was applied, Sadig's screaming literally caused the walls to shake in sympathy with his pain. His leg was grossly swollen now around the area of the break, and the repeated electrical jolts were going to induce a compound fracture from his body's spasms.

Halfway through the controlled electrocution, Sadig had lost control of his bladder and bowels. Still he would not speak. Scream Allah's name, swear at his tormentors—but not talk.

The Saudis had brought in a fire hose and used it to clean the room and, as an afterthought, Sadig. As they did so, the chief interrogator maliciously reminded Sadig that the water would improve the electrical contact. That wasn't strictly true, but Sadig didn't know that, nor was he capable of calm, rational thought at that point.

Five minutes after they started using the electricity on him again, Sadig had screamed for them to stop. They continued, and in fact, increased the duration of jolts. A few minutes later, he had begged in Allah's name for them to stop, tears mixed with blood streaking his face. The chief interrogator, a thin Saudi with a well-trimmed beard and dispassionate manner, had told him that he would stop only if he was willing to answer their questions. Sadig's only reply was an affirmative nod, as he lay gasping for air from the last jolt of electricity.

After a few minutes to catch his breath, he told them everything. How he got into Saudi Arabia, who helped him, how many al-Qaeda cells he had helped create in the Kingdom and who their leaders were, but not what Johnson needed to know. Sadig had passed out about an hour after he started talking, probably from a combination of shock and exhaustion. The Saudis had sedated him and turned him over to a military doctor for treatment in a prisoner wing of the Royal Saudi Military Hospital in Riyadh. He would answer more questions later.

Johnson looked long and hard at the dripping wet face in the mirror, and then looked away to reach for a brown paper towel. He dried his face and hands while he considered what he had witnessed, and what his role was in it. How was this right? To abuse a human being like this was not something the FBI tolerated. If this were American soil, he would arrest them all for assault, human rights abuses, and probably attempted murder. But he was not standing in America. How did he reconcile this with what Pittman had told him in Guantanamo? Would he go that far to get the information he needed from Sadig if his wife or future child were in danger? Would he be able to live with himself afterward? Had he just been an accomplice to everything he abhorred?

He tried to imagine Sadig knowing something that would keep his wife alive. Would he torture Sadig to get that information? Inflict as much pain as he could until he talked? How far would he go to preserve his wife's life? Would he take Sadig to the edge of death if he wouldn't talk? That thought frightened him. Once that door was open, would he forever be nothing but an animal that he despised every time he looked in a mirror? If his wife ever found out, would her love for him be diminished or would he be a man who had done what was necessary so that he could protect her?

The door to the men's room opened, and Akeem walked in. Johnson didn't notice him; his eyes were lost in some middle distance between the world of men and the world inside himself.

Akeem touched his arm gently. "My friend, are you all right?"

Johnson blinked his eyes and started slightly, surprised to see Akeem in the men's room.

"I'm sorry, Mr. Akeem. I didn't hear what you said."

Akeem examined him with concerned eyes. "Are you all right?"

"Yes. Yes, I'm fine. *Shokran.*" Johnson visibly pulled himself back to the present, wadded up the paper towel, and tossed it in the trashcan.

"Let me take you back to your hotel."

"*Shokran.* I could use a good meal and a nap." He would be returning tomorrow morning to interview Sadig under the watchful and no doubt menacing eye of the skinny chief interrogator.

CHAPTER 16

· ·

CAIN AND HIS PEOPLE HAD gathered for their second roundtable briefing of the day. The swing shift had come in early and was stacked up near their stations, which were now occupied by Cain's dayshift team. The FBI liaison, Fred Simpson, was going over what the investigators at each of the fires had discovered so far. It wasn't a lot, and it was frustrating.

"The firemen and the security guards killed in Texas were murdered, shot to death, specifically. Before the firefighters pulled back, they were able to recover the bodies of all the firemen, save the one with the unexploded grenade under him, along with the body of one police officer. The initial results of the forensic exams and autopsies confirm that all of them were shot with high-powered rifles, using 5.56mm ammo. Striations on the rounds recovered from the bodies are consistent with AK-47s, but we don't have any weapons from the scene to gather exemplars from for comparison."

Everyone in CTS was having trouble meeting one another's eyes. Partly it was the strain of a long day sifting through the current intelligence and watching the never-ending press coverage of the fires. It was also from the institutional shame that, yet again, the intelligence community was unable to predict a strike on U.S. soil by terrorists, and innocent people had died. Their people. Americans.

"Is there any video footage from the area?" asked Emily.

"No," replied Fred as he ran a hand through his short dark hair in frustration. "The video feeds went into the main monitoring center, which is now in the middle of the fire. We do have video from the New Jersey and Connecticut fires. The lab in Quantico is trying to pull faces and license plate numbers off the DVDs, but they aren't very hopeful. They've even reached out to NSA for supercomputer time, but you can only push the image enhancement algorithms so far before the pixels become distorted and useless."

"Look," chimed in one of the swing-shift folks, "there has to be something we can do." The exasperation in his voice was clear. Specialist Graham was one of the younger ones, an Army intelligence specialist, known as a 98 Charlie. He was only an E-4, not even an NCO yet. He had been in the Army all of two years and assigned to CTS, working for the last three months in the NSA liaison position. He was not the smartest member of the team, but Cain was willing to give him a chance in spite of his inexperience. He had also decided to ignore how sloppy Specialist Graham usually looked in his uniform, and his frequent lack of attention to detail. Cain had hoped that he could be mentored and would grow into the increased responsibility, but he hadn't done so yet.

Cain answered him from the chair he had pulled over into the watch area. "For now, we've done what we can." To the entire team he said, "Keep monitoring the available intelligence from your agencies and make sure everything gets shared. Also, be aware that the teams from the 152nd Joint Special Missions Unit are deploying forward in case they're needed. When they reach their deployed locations, they'll hook into INTELINK and contact us for an intelligence update, so let's get the standard briefings set up for each of the areas they're deploying to, and have them ready to e-mail out when they are online."

Cain stood and the meeting broke up, as each of the analysts headed back to their positions.

Lieutenant Osborne, the day-shift NSA liaison, waited until he and Specialist Graham got back to the NSA desk before mentioning, *sotto voce*, as he grabbed a fishing magazine out of the bottom drawer, "I've got to go to the head, keep an eye on things."

"The head, sir?" the young specialist asked.

"That's the latrine to you."

"Oh. Sorry, sir."

Shaking his head at how green this kid still was, Osborne headed out the door.

Graham sat in the chair at the desk and started rereading some of the same SIGINT reports he had already read twice that day. They covered so much. The silly, the mundane, and the routine. Graham knew the bastards responsible for this were probably still in the country. If NSA could capture some of their communications, then maybe the FBI could locate and arrest them. *Why didn't we ask NSA to do that yet?* he pondered.

Turning to look over at Mr. Cain, Graham noticed his superior had leaned back in his chair and had put his feet up on the NGA liaison desk, a couple of desks away from his NSA liaison position. His eyes were closed and he looked to be on the edge of drifting off. He must be beat.

The thoughts raced through Graham's head: *They must have forgotten. Holy shit, they forgot!* This was his chance to make sergeant eighteen months early. He could put in the request, NSA would intercept their phone calls or whatever, and then the FBI could swoop in and make the arrests. He would get decorated and then promoted in short order. Now *that* would impress his girlfriend. Well, she wasn't really his girlfriend yet. She danced at the Fuzzy Rabbit downtown and talked to him a lot when he was there. She had said her name was Kelly and even had a couple of drinks with him once. In spite of how much he had to pay for the drinks, she seemed interested in him. When he became a sergeant he would be able to take her to a really nice place for dinner, and maybe he could start seeing her more often.

Trying to keep his thoughts off Kelly dancing in that red outfit and already feeling the extra weight of the stripes on his sleeves, he started typing up the tasking message.

THE PHONE STARTLED CAIN OUT of the light sleep he had drifted into for the third time after moving back up to his desk. "Mr. Cain, this is Marty Brown, NSA Oversight & Compliance." Oversight & Compliance was NSA's in-house watchdog that had total access to all of NSA's SIGINT operations. They ensured that NSA's activities were carried out consistent with U.S. law and that the attorney general and Congress were informed of any potential violations.

"How can I help you, Marty?"

"One of your people requested SIGINT targeting of all communications within a 250-mile radius of the Strategic Petroleum Reserve and the Home Heating Oil Strategic Reserve storage sites."

Cain's blood pressure immediately soared and he gripped the phone hard enough to turn his knuckles white. Taking a deep breath and then letting it out, he said, "I want to know who issued the request, and, more important, who approved it, because I sure as hell didn't."

"There was no approval on it, but the request was issued by a Terry Graham, currently assigned to CTS."

Cain's eyes scanned the desks until he found Specialist Graham talking to Lieutenant Osborn and Fred Simpson at the FBI desk.

"What is the proper procedure in this case?" inquired Cain.

"We have an official request from someone on your staff to conduct SIGINT against three geographic areas of the United States that would without question capture the communications of U.S. citizens as defined by the Foreign Intelligence Surveillance Act of 1978. The request will not, under any circumstances, be acted on. It is illegal. If your shop has sufficient information for a FISA Court warrant for a specific person's communications, we can route the request through to the FBI where it belongs. Do you have such information?"

"Absolutely not. That tasking request should not have been issued. What about Specialist Graham? Has he broken the law?"

"No. Merely making the request does not violate the law, but he will attend a mandatory four-hour training session on FISA. We have one scheduled next week he can attend. After he attends that remedial class, if he makes another mistake like that, we'll take his clearance away, which will immediately bar him from the NSA campus. Any other disciplinary action is up to you or his supervisory chain."

"All right," replied Cain, his tone glacial. "How did you find out about this?"

"The tasking message was put through the standard review process by our office after he sent it. As soon as we saw it, we put an immediate hold on it. The tasking will not be executed, and this incident will become part of our quarterly report to the NSA Inspector General and the Attorney General. I'll need an e-mail from you stating what action will be taken with regard to Mr. Graham."

"He's Specialist Graham, an Army-enlisted man assigned to me. Thanks for catching this. I'll get back to you on the e-mail."

"No problem, Mr. Cain, that's what we're here for."

Cain replaced the grey phone in its cradle and sat back for a moment to think. Up to this point, Graham's mistakes were not malicious, and he was not a bad man, but at the minimum, he had just proven himself an ignorant one. No—he had just proven himself a *stupid* man. He had undergone the same oversight training every person in the intelligence business was required to undergo every year. Protecting the rights of American citizens was drilled into everyone from day one. He would need some help with this one from his parent command.

Reaching for the black phone on his desk, he called the 91st Military Intelligence Battalion and asked for the first sergeant.

TWO HOURS LATER, STANDING IN the doorway of the conference room, Cain called out, "Specialist Graham!"

"Yes, sir."

"Join me in the conference room, please."

Graham ascended the steps with the certain knowledge that he was going to be thanked privately for remembering to task NSA when everybody else had forgotten. He was sure Cain wouldn't want to thank him publicly until after NSA had developed some good information from his tasking.

When he passed through the conference room door, he was mildly surprised to see his platoon leader, Staff Sergeant Kimke, and his first sergeant, Master Sergeant Sullivan. Sergeant Kimke was OK, but he didn't like First Sergeant Sullivan much. He was way too gung-ho Army for Graham. He had a haircut more fit for a Marine, and Graham was sure he had put the Fuzzy Rabbit on the prohibited list just to keep him from spending time with Kelly.

"Take a seat, Specialist Graham," said Cain.

The First Sergeant shook his head. "I'm sorry, Mr. Cain, but this is a matter of military discipline as much as anything else."

Turning to Graham, he issued an order, "Stand at attention."

Graham looked confused for a second or two and then braced to attention, figuring that the First Sergeant was being his usual pain-in-the-ass self.

"Go ahead, Mr. Cain," said First Sergeant Sullivan.

"Specialist Graham, you submitted a tasking message to NSA asking them to collect all communications in an area 250 miles around the Strategic Petroleum Reserve and the Home Heating Oil Strategic Reserve sites in New Jersey and Connecticut. Is that correct?"

Looking pleased with himself Graham replied, "Yes, sir. I did."

"Do you understand that in doing so you also were requesting that NSA collect the communications of every U.S. citizen within that 250-mile radius?"

"So what, sir? We need to get these guys."

Cain shook his head. "Do you remember anything you were taught in the classes run by Oversight and Compliance on the FISA law and what your responsibilities are under that law to protect the rights of U.S. citizens?"

"They won't mind, sir. We've got to get these guys!"

Cain closed his eyes and his head sagged. This kid just could not wrap his mind around one of the most basic rules that permeated every facet of U.S. intelligence operations. He looked over to the two NCOs.

"I can't have him on my team anymore."

The First Sergeant stood, crossed to Specialist Graham, and removed his access badge.

"Staff Sergeant, escort your platoon member from the NSA complex. I'll keep his access badge. You and I will meet with the battalion commander in the morning to discuss Specialist Graham's future with the Army."

Graham began to protest, but Sergeant Kimke cut him off, "Terry, you're in enough hot water as it is. Right now, you need to just do as you're told."

Graham stopped talking and just looked at the floor in bewilderment. He did what he was supposed to do, and now he was in trouble? He didn't get it. Cain was getting rid of him because his actions made Cain look bad. *How the hell was that right?* Cain was asleep at the switch when he figured out what needed to be done to protect people. Now he was being *kicked out? What was wrong with these people?*

Kimke took the young specialist by the arm and led him from the conference room. Graham left the room with the bewildered look still on his face.

"What's going to happen to him?" Cain inquired.

"We'll tell the battalion commander about this tomorrow. As his platoon leader, Staff Sergeant Kimke will represent Specialist Graham during that discussion. Then we'll have Graham report to the battalion CO formally to give his side of things, again with Sergeant Kimke present. Then the CO will need to decide what to do with him. He might give him nonjudicial punishment—dock his pay, maybe a letter of reprimand—so we get his attention but not kill his career. Then we'll send him back for intelligence oversight refresher training and assign him somewhere else. Unless you want him back?"

Cain shook his head, looking at the floor, professionally disappointed that he hadn't been able to mentor the young specialist in spite of his obvious lack of ability. "No. I can't take him back, not after this. His experience level isn't where I would prefer it, and he obviously is not demonstrating good judgment. Maybe in another couple of years, if he matures and his judgment improves . . ."

Cain met the First Sergeant's eye. Both men knew Specialist Graham would never see the inside of CTS again.

IT WAS ALMOST 4 P.M. ON the East Coast and nearly time for him to act. Repin brought the SCADAKILL program up from the system toolbar. He had left the program running but had disconnected it from the SCADA network.

Selecting the Northeast grid again, he waited while the clock spun and the program regained access to the grid and refreshed the map of the electric power network. The software quickly filled in the icons and lines placed on the country's geographic map as it masqueraded as a master control computer within the SCADA network, interrogating every node on the network and requesting each one's status. Each node responded in milliseconds, and the software added an icon representing that particular node to the map. The program then drew logical lines between them to represent the path of the electrical power lines.

Each node was color coded to represent its current status: gray for unknown, meaning the program couldn't get its current status; green for up and operating; yellow for partially operating; and red for nonoperational. The lines connecting the little icons were similarly colored. After a minute or two, the computer had finished covering the map with green nodes and lines.

Repin left clicked to select the global delay option and when the computer requested a value, he entered 4:45 P.M. EST. Every command he entered would execute at exactly the same time unless he overrode the system.

Selecting the nuclear power plant icon labeled "Calvert Cliffs," he opened the option menu and chose "Generators 110%" and then "Reactor SCRAM." Then he picked the icon "Susquehanna" and selected the same options. He kept working steadily until all eighteen nuclear power plants in Nuclear Regulatory Commission Region One were set to SCRAM their reactors and run their electric generators up to 110 percent of rated capacity. It was now 3:10 P.M. local time.

Then he started selecting as many of the dozens of oil- and gas-fired power plants as he could and ordered their generators to run up to 110 percent of capacity. He kept an eye on the clock in the lower right-hand corner of his computer screen as he worked. At 3:30 P.M., he stopped.

Locating the major transformer stations, he began ordering them to open the connections to the "load" portion of the network, where the customers were, and then overrode the automatic disconnects on the supply side of the network. To facilitate this, the software raised the value of the voltage threshold the SCADA computer at the transformer station used to determine when to break the supply side circuit. The new value was high enough to ensure that the computers would never decide there was a problem.

These automated disconnects were designed to isolate transformers at the station from the electrical grid if there was ever a power spike that went beyond the design limits of the units. This would save repair time by preventing severe damage to a vital part of the energy infrastructure.

It was 3:38 P.M. when he finished with all the major transformer stations routing power for the large statewide areas. Next, he started working on each of the two or three medium-sized transformer stations serving major cities. He had made his way to the stations in Richmond, Virginia, from Bangor, Maine, when the clock on his computer reached 3:45 P.M.

THE COMPUTERS WITHIN THE NORTHEAST SCADA network issued the orders they had received earlier from Repin's SCADAKILL program. Repin's computer had changed its electronic identity three times while he worked, so some of the SCADA nodes in the network had orders from what they believed to be the master control computer in Boston; others had orders from what they thought was the master control computer in Richmond. The rest believed they had gotten their orders from the one in Dallas.

The SCADA computers controlling the turbines in the nuclear and oil-fired power plants issued orders and the turbines obeyed, running their paired generators at 110 percent of their rated capacity. In control rooms throughout the Northeast, technicians saw the spike on their monitors and leaned forward, curious, but not concerned.

Simultaneously, the computers at the electrical substations disconnected the service load from their group of transformers and locked the supply side connections open. Suddenly, thousands of megawatts of electricity had nowhere to go but across the transformers at the stations and substations.

The electric overload immediately blew out the transformers in the medium-sized and smaller electrical substations in spectacular fashion throughout the Northeast. The oil-filled transformers in the smaller stations heated up and exploded violently, damaging several nearby power lines. In the larger stations, high-capacity transformers heated up and because of their sturdier construction, began melting. Connections fused, internal wiring shorted and began to melt. Fires ignited and spread.

Immediately after the blowouts, every nuclear reactor in the Northeast began to SCRAM. Control rods automatically slammed into the reactor cores under orders from the automatic control systems, absorbing the neutrons active in the cores and stopping the nuclear reaction. The lack of heat from the nuclear pile immediately reduced the amount of available steam in the loop, and the lack of steam caused the turbines to slow and stop. When the turbines stopped, the electrical generators stopped.

When orders reached the oil and coal-fired power plants, steam loops driving turbines opened their emergency valves, venting superheated steam into the atmosphere. Oil feed lines and coal conveyer belts automatically stopped. The furnaces began to cool and then shut down. Technicians scrambled to restart them but found the automated controls unresponsive.

The only power plants unaffected were the small ones in hydroelectric dams that relied only on falling water to generate electricity. In spite of that, the SCADA systems at the hydroelectric plants noted the massive power spike on the electric grid and automatically disconnected the plants from the grid, fulfilling Repin's goal even though he didn't get to them before 4:45.

The northeastern U.S. was now completely dark. Electric power to houses was out. Streetlights were dead. Car accidents occurred immediately and then increased geometrically in the middle of the East Coast rush, causing huge traffic jams at major intersections. Hospitals automatically switched to standby generators, as did police and fire stations. The telephone system went to battery power. Subways and other mass transit systems relying on electricity failed, trapping thousands.

Backup generators at major airports automatically activated, keeping radars, landing systems, and air traffic control towers powered. But the terminals did not fare so well. Power was out everywhere. Movement through security checkpoints came to a screeching halt as metal detectors and X-ray equipment shut off. Reservation computers died and tens of thousands of passengers groaned aloud in unison.

People began to grope their way out of subways and off of trains stopped in the middle of intersections and at their stations. They flooded the streets of cities from Boston to Richmond, further snarling traffic as they tried to make their way home in the fading sunlight. Many were poorly dressed for the cold temperatures, expecting a warmer and more comfortable ride home on mass transit systems. The frigid evening air bit into them as the mercury dipped below 30 degrees Fahrenheit. The forecast low in New York for the night was 23 degrees.

After they reached home, they comforted family members by candle-light, flashlight, and propane and hurricane lantern in homes growing colder by the minute. Gas grills and ovens allowed for hot meals. Those fortunate enough to have fireplaces had some source of heat. Fires broke out here and there. Prepared homeowners extinguished most of them, but several hundred people were forced to watch their houses burn to the ground while waiting for the fire engines to grope their way through gridlocked traffic.

Hundreds of thousands of citizens made phone calls to utility pro-viders, whose automated response systems were overwhelmed. People turned battery-operated radios to AM news and talk stations, now serving their largest audiences in years, to monitor events. There was little information to report, other than the fact that a large portion of America had just returned to nineteenth-century conditions for an unknown reason.

Parents and caregivers tucked heavily clothed children into bed under many blankets before returning to their radios to listen to the news and to talk in hushed tones about what was going on and just what might be done to fix it. Hours after the event, the radio newsmen and newswomen still couldn't report why the power had gone out. Eventually, the adults turned off the radios, turned out the gas lamps and candles, bundled up, and went to bed wondering if but ultimately believing that the utility companies would fix the problem before morning. Their expectations would prove to be overly optimistic.

DAVE RYAN KNEW EXACTLY WHAT was wrong with the Northeast electrical grid. He also knew it would be weeks, maybe months, before it could be restored. Ryan was an electrical engineer working for the Department of Energy who spent his workday, usually on the swing shift, in the basement of the Department's headquarters building at 1000 Independence Avenue Southwest in Washington, D.C.

Ryan had seen the massive surge in electrical output from the power plants and then the load removal from the transformer stations. That was followed by the immediate and not unexpected—at least to him— failure of the transformer stations themselves. Commanding his computer to rerun the events of the last twenty minutes, he watched for any anomaly that would help him pinpoint the root cause of the events he had just witnessed. Fortunately, the backup generators running on hot standby in the department's subbasement came online instantly when power to the D.C. area failed.

Ryan knew that all over the Northeast, utility company executives, senior managers, and repair and plant maintenance crews were being called back to work. He also knew that the men and women in the utility company monitoring centers were doing just what he was doing: trying to figure out why this happened. Without that knowledge, restarting the grid would be risky, if not outright dangerous.

The thing that concerned him the most was his complete inability to get a status report from the major and most of the minor transformer substations throughout the Northeast grid. He repeatedly tried to query them through the SCADA network, which maintained its own backup power, good for nearly forty-eight hours, but was unable to get a response. Much of this was probably because the Internet in the Northeast was inoperative from the power outage. The major substations were equipped with satellite transmitters running off battery backup power, and he couldn't even access those.

That inability kept drawing him back to the replay of the event on his computer. After watching it for the twelfth time, he finally came to the inescapable conclusion that the substations had utterly failed. It would take manual inspection of every substation to determine the level of damage and repair them. The real problem would be getting the needed replacement equipment to the sites, which was expensive, plus spares were not exactly commonplace. Depending on the damage, it could be weeks before the power was restored.

Before he picked up the phone, he asked the computer to make a hard-copy printout of the last twenty minutes of orders issued across the SCADA network and then list the orders to the power plants and electrical substations in the Northeast grid for his analysis.

Holding the handset, he punched the first speed-dial button. When the ringing stopped, he said, "Mr. Secretary. I need you in the watch center now. We have a major problem in the Northeast grid."

THE CABLE NETWORKS WERE COVERING the outage, albeit from locations outside of New York and Washington, D.C. CNN led the pack from its broadcast center in Atlanta, which was unaffected, and Aziz was enjoying the show from his home outside of Tehran, Iran. He could not have been more pleased. He was reclining on the pillows on the floor of the great room in the rear of his house, watching the large plasma-screen television on the wall. It was showing him CNN's European feed captured by the satellite dish on the roof. The network even had footage from the International Space Station as it passed over the eastern U.S.

The northeastern part of the country was pleasingly dark, while the normal, somewhat dimmer strings of lights along major highways interspersed with the brighter globs of the major cities against the blackness spread across the rest of the nation.

Aziz knew he must give thanks to Allah soon for his success. First, though, he wanted to revel in this. *America, the Great Satan, has been humbled again. Its people, cold and in the dark, reduced to living as much of the Middle East did, with rolling blackouts and no heat in their homes in the chill of winter. Let them suffer. Allah's justice would humble them and eventually force them to withdraw their military forces from their bases in the region of the Caliphate.* He would help that withdrawal along with the next major phase of his plan. When their political and military influence had diminished in the Middle East, he could begin to rebuild it as Allah had intended. There would be a return to glory for the Arabic peoples. Great scholars and poets would once again thrive in the rebirth of the cultural achievements not seen since the fifteenth century. All of this would be driven by the people's return to the true faith and Allah's word.

There would be no more tolerance for the dogmas of other so-called religions. The Caliphate would stretch from the western Mediterranean to the Philippine Sea. Islam, in its proper form, would govern and guide all. Women would be properly chaste and know their place in the home. Being properly dutiful to their husbands, they would bear many children for the glory of Allah.

Aziz had not chosen a wife yet, although some of his friends within the Iranian government had offered their daughters. He had even spoken to a few of these young women under the supervision of their parents, as was proper. All were virgins, but none of them had truly captured his interest, despite their obvious piety and reverence for Allah. He had not felt the need to ask to see their faces, which had disappointed their fathers; but he had explained to the men that he could ask only if he truly felt love for the woman. They had understood. He did not know what he sought, but he was certain that when the time was right, Allah would provide him a suitable wife, and she would bear him many sons. Humbling the Americans was what Allah wanted him to do now, and the first major step of that process was complete.

JOHNSON'S FIRST INTERVIEW WITH SADIG in his room in the military hospital was a study in contrasts. The white tile walls, white sheets, and cleanliness of the room were soiled by the presence of the skinny, bearded lead interrogator, who sat quietly in the corner smoking. He had not spoken a word since Johnson began talking to Aziz, but he remained a visual reminder of what would happen if the captive did not cooperate. *Answer the American's questions, or you will suffer anew.* Sadig was talking freely now. The analgesics in his bloodstream dulled the pain, but not his memories.

Johnson had struck a friendly tone in hopes of setting the man more at ease, but in reality, he seemed more the good cop to the lead interrogator's bad cop. Sadig's English was quite good, which made things easier. If he ran into trouble, Akeem sat behind him, ready to translate.

"I am told you handled all of the Taliban's money. Tell me what happened to it."

Looking nervously at the lead interrogator, Sadig replied, "What do you mean?"

"The Taliban no longer exists, yet the money used to finance their government in Afghanistan has not been completely recovered or identified. What happened to it?"

"Much was frozen by the international community, you know."

"Yes," Johnson leaned forward with a smile on his face, "but we both know that they didn't get everything. Tell me about that."

"Oh, yes, of course," Sadig chuckled nervously and looked down at his hands and winced as he scratched an itch under the upper portion of the white cast on his leg.

"Many of the . . . ah . . . private accounts of the Taliban leaders were not touched."

Johnson nodded encouragingly, "What did you do with them?"

"I . . . ah . . . added them together, then moved the money into accounts I created."

Sadig's smile seemed to indicate that he hoped the men would find his embezzlement clever. When no one said anything, he went on quickly, "I spent much—"

"As you hope to see Allah in Paradise, you will give us all the account numbers and the bank names, along with any access pass phrases or codes you know," the lead interrogator interjected. His tone left no room for discussion.

"Yes, yes," replied Sadig hastily, his hands beginning to shake a little. He had also begun to sweat even though the room was pleasantly cool.

"Did any of these accounts belong to al-Qaeda?" Johnson asked him, leaning forward a little to study Sadig's face.

"No . . . no . . . no al-Qaeda accounts," Sadig said with a nervous glance at the interrogator, who took that opportunity to rise from his chair in the corner and step forward, a disbelieving look in his eyes.

"Wait . . . wait," Sadig blurted out. "I think that a couple may have been . . . were, yes, were accounts that belonged to Osama Bin Laden himself. We didn't have any al-Qaeda accounts, only accounts for Bin Laden and Ayman al-Zawahiri, that's what I meant."

"I want those account numbers and access methods, too," said Johnson, his heart pounding at the thought of being the agent who identified the money of the two former al-Qaeda leaders and enabling its seizure.

"I can't give them to you."

"What?" both Johnson and the interrogator asked simultaneously.

Sadig shook his head and held his hands up pleadingly, "Please, you don't understand. I could give you the numbers, but the accounts are empty, they were emptied before I could conduct the transfers. I didn't have the access codes to move the money, but as Finance Minister I was allowed to query the account balances, so I knew that the accounts were emptied."

"Who emptied them?" demanded Johnson.

"I don't know for sure. I was called one day by a man who called himself Aziz. He wanted to know why I kept checking the balances. I explained to him that I was appointed the guardian of the money, and he told me that if I was, then I should understand that the man who owned the money had given it to Aziz to use. He, this Aziz, also said that the 'Great Man' had trusted him with the access codes to move it and use it as needed, and that I should forget this matter."

"Did Aziz tell you where he was calling from?" asked Akeem.

"No. But I had the caller name function on my phone. I don't remember the number entirely, but he was calling from Iran."

"Do you remember any of the number at all?" Johnson asked, leaning far enough forward now that he might as well have sat on the bed.

Sadig looked as if he was going to say no, and then caught the eyes of the interrogator as he took one step closer to the bed. Hastily raising his hands, he pleaded, "Wait . . . let me think . . . "

Sadig closed his eyes and tried to concentrate. He was sweating profusely now. After a minute or so, and two more puffs on the cigarette the interrogator held, his eyes snapped open.

"I can remember only the first few numbers, 98 21 333. I can't remember the last four digits."

"Are you sure?" asked the interrogator, a hard look in his eyes.

"As Allah is my judge and witness, that's all I can remember—98 21 333," his voice was becoming panicked, "I swear upon the Holy Qur'an, that's all!"

JOHNSON QUESTIONED SADIG FOR ANOTHER twenty minutes, but Sadig could remember no more. The skinny interrogator even went so far as to order two men to take Sadig back downstairs. Sadig had started weeping and begging them in Allah's name to believe him. The interrogator ordered Sadig returned to his bed and he, Johnson, and Akeem huddled briefly in one of the empty offices in the military wing. All agreed that Sadig appeared to be telling the truth. Johnson decided the information should go up chain fast and called SAIC French on his cell phone.

"Well done, Agent Johnson. This is a solid lead. I'll get it passed out to the rest of the intelligence community."

"Yes, sir." Mindful of the presence of his Saudi hosts, Johnson held back on discussing how the information was obtained. "Any further orders?"

"Sit tight for now. We've had a major power outage in the Northeast. It looks like most of the grid is down."

"Is the power out in Virginia, sir?"

"From what little I know at the moment, yes. Virginia, Maryland, Pennsylvania, New York, Connecticut, New Hampshire, Vermont, Massachusetts, and Maine are all dark."

"What the hell happened?"

"No idea yet. I'll call you after I figure out what you need to do next. For now, sit tight, and enjoy Saudi Arabia."

Before he could protest, the phone clicked off. He took a few minutes to call his wife and see if she was all right. She had a slow commute home on the highway but had gotten a fire going in the living room and would sleep there to stay warm. He would have preferred to be there, but she was an outdoors girl who loved camping and hiking, so he wasn't too worried. After the requisite "I love you," he hung up.

"So what will you do now, my friend?" inquired Akeem.

"Go back to my hotel and wait for orders."

"I have a better idea. Join me for dinner in my home and meet my family. Then my driver can take you back to your hotel. You are our guest and it is the least I should do for you."

Johnson hesitated a little, "Thanks, but I should . . . "

"No, no. I insist. You should see what our people are like while you are here. Please come."

Johnson reluctantly allowed Akeem to lead him out into the night. It was late and the temperature had dropped significantly. During the ride to Akeem's house, his thoughts kept drifting back to his wife, alone in their home in the dark.

CHAPTER 17

· ·

"IS IT WORKING YET?" The frustration in Goodman's voice was hard
to miss. The technicians were still trying to get the briefing room computer to work. When the power went out, it had taken only a minute
or two for the emergency generators to kick in and provide power for
the NSA complex, but the computer refused to boot up. The two Army
NCOs had it in pieces on the floor now and did not look very optimistic.

"Forget it, guys. The briefing will start in a few minutes and it's too
late now. Unplug it and take it to the scrap heap. You can replace it after
the briefing."

As the two men began removing the failed computer, Goodman
headed back into the CTS watch area to find Cain on the phone. He was
asking questions and taking notes furiously.

Goodman went back into the conference room and let the two technicians pass him with the cart the recalcitrant computer was sitting on.
The video teleconference was already established, but the video from
CTS was blanked and the audio muted from when the technicians had
been working. Mike walked over to the control console and tapped two
buttons on the touch screen, and the video feeds came back up. A few
still showed the organizational seals of the government agencies that
had not dialed in yet, but on most, senior leaders and their small reti-
nues sat in place waiting. Some were sipping what was no doubt very
strong coffee.

The major difference with this daily conference was that the seal of the White House Communications Agency was on one of the small screens this time. The DIRNSA should have been here by now. They had only a few minutes before the national security advisor came on.

Goodman was reaching for the grey phone to call the director's executive officer and find out where the DIRNSA was when General Holland came through the conference room door. He was followed by a small group of his division chiefs and Cain.

Cain dropped into the seat next to the general and they exchanged a few words. Cain did most of the talking while the general listened. When Cain stopped, Holland turned to one of his senior civilians and issued an order. He in turn stepped over to one of the grey phones on the conference table and made a call.

A moment later, the WHCA seal was replaced by a view of the Situation Room in the White House basement. The president's national security advisor, Dr. Jessica Owens, sat at the head of the table, her well-tailored blue suit and silver-frosted black hair contrasting with the brown leather chairs and dark mahogany conference table. Her bearing and economical movements bespoke a highly intelligent and organized person. She held a sterling silver pen at the ready and an open portfolio before her.

"Let's begin, people, and make it brief. I need to bring the president up to speed in about fifteen minutes."

"Yes, ma'am," said DIRNSA. "I'll let Mr. Cain, my head of CTS, tell you what we know and ask the other agency heads to chime in as needed."

Dr. Owens nodded. Cain did not waste time on pleasantries.

"Homeland Security also has this information, so I'll ask them to step in if I miss anything. I spoke to Mr. Dave Ryan, a watch officer over at the Department of Energy, a few minutes ago. He explained to me that it appears that orders were issued through the SCADA system managing electric power generation and distribution to create a power surge on the Northeast grid, and simultaneously remove the commercial and civil load from the network. At the same time, the safety systems protecting the major transformer stations were disabled in order to permit the power surge to cause significant damage to the substation equipment."

Cain paused for a moment to let that sink in and then continued,

"Mr. Ryan also went on to say that pending a complete on-site assessment of the damage, his initial read is that power will be out in the majority of the northeastern U.S. for three to four weeks."

On all the screens, heads that had been reading reports abruptly came up.

Dr. Owens stopped writing notes and asked, "Homeland, anything to add?"

"Only that Mr. Ryan has been analyzing the computer logs of the orders issued through the SCADA system and so far it appears that at least some of the orders that precipitated this event were issued by three of the SCADA system's own master control computers."

Owens took two more notes and then asked the most obvious question, "Does anyone think that the attacks on our strategic petroleum reserve, home heating oil reserve, and then the sudden failure of our electric power infrastructure are *not* related?"

Silence greeted her question as every head of the agencies just stared back at her on the link. She then asked the next most obvious question, "All right, then who is behind these attacks?"

The silence that followed this time was more uncomfortable. The men and women at each intelligence agency were charged with identifying, understanding, and keeping track of America's enemies. They did not like being unable to answer that question. On the screen, Cain could see heads look down at notes or at colleagues, not at the camera. In the CTS conference room, he heard the stone silence of nervous bureaucrats.

Holland spoke up. If nothing else, he needed to reassure Dr. Owens and therefore the president that they were trying. "Every available asset of this agency is being used to discover that, but at the present time, we have nothing to indicate who is behind this or how they are communicating."

"CIA is in the same boat as NSA, Dr. Owens," added the Deputy Director of CIA, attending for his boss, who was stuck behind a multiple-car accident on the Dulles parkway. "Our assets overseas have not provided us any indication that any kind of assault on the U.S. like this was planned or being planned. We will make this an immediate priority, but, at the moment, we have nothing."

The secretary of homeland security chimed in, "We have no indication of any internal threat beyond the events that have already occurred. We are working closely with the FBI, and they have interviewed a number of what can be best described as people with serious axes to grind against the U.S. government, no matter who is sitting in the White House or Congress, with no leads so far."

"Anyone else?" inquired Dr. Owens, her tone acidic.

After a beat or two of additional silence, she continued, "I'll tell the president what we know, and what we *don't* know. Find us some information, ladies and gentlemen, find it fast."

Slamming her portfolio of limited notes closed, she added, "The president will be mobilizing the National Guard in the affected states immediately. He'll also be declaring all the states federal disaster areas after he consults with the governors later tonight. I suggest you people get back to work."

With that, Dr. Owens rose and exited the Situation Room. Immediately afterwards, the screen blanked as the WHCA closed their end of the connection.

THE NATIONAL EDITOR OF *The New York Times* was pissed. A huge story about a power outage affecting most of the northeastern U.S. and he could not report it. After all, the power was out. Computers needed power to format the story for print or web publication. Flashlights were the order of the day. Journalists in New York and other cities in the Northeast were calling into the CBS stations outside of the affected area, rather than writing copy to submit their stories. They could not produce hard copies unless they wrote it by hand. As a result, most of the married news staff had gone home to look after their families, but many of the younger, single staffers had decided to hang out in the pressroom. They were sitting in small groups, eating junk food from the snack machines they had broken into in lieu of a better dinner.

With nothing better to do, the editor opened the bottom right-hand drawer, withdrew a bottle of Jack Daniels and a glass, and put his feet up. He was on his third glass when one of the interns tapped on his open door.

"Excuse me, sir."

"What is it?" was his somewhat guff reply. How dare she interrupt his mildly buzzed self-pity?

"I'm sorry to bother you, sir. But I came across a letter postmarked from Chicago that seems a little weird given what's happened with the power out and the fires and all."

"Weird, how?" was the bored response.

"See for yourself, sir," she said, crossing to his desk and handing him the letter.

He reluctantly put down his drink and took his feet off the desk. Taking the letter from her hands, he tore it from the envelope, unfolded it, and tilted it so the light from the flashlight on his desk illuminated the writing. He read it, stopped, and then read it again. He checked the postmark on the envelope, and then he grabbed the bottle of Jack Daniels and threw it against the wall.

The girl stepped back two steps and stammered, "I'm sorry, sir."

He turned to look at her and held his hand out to her. "It's not your fault, honey. You see if you can find me the number for the Department of Homeland Security. Real quick now."

The editor shook his head, cursing his luck. The biggest story in the last five years and he could not report it to anyone as an exclusive. At least he could break it through one of the CBS television affiliates before he talked to Homeland Security or the FBI. He was after all, a reporter first.

THE CBS TV STATION THAT the national editor at the *Times* called was in Atlanta. WUPA, known locally as CW Atlanta, broadcast both the national CBS and CW networks' programming. The backup generators at the CBS news studios in New York were not working, and the CBS news desk had no idea when they would be back on the air. But the network's nightly news anchor would not be telling this story, anyway.

The WUPA producer was going to put him on air via phone in about three minutes and had even cued her fellow producer at CNN in Atlanta about this one. CNN would broadcast WUPA's interview of him live. It had been about an hour since he'd read the letter, and he had managed to swallow two cups of cold coffee purely in an attempt to make him feel more sober. He hoped the phone lines held up. He knew the phone system worked off batteries during a major power outage, but he didn't know how long the battery power would last.

He heard the producer on the phone in his ear say "Thirty seconds" and reflexively touched his tie to straighten it but stopped, silently cursing himself as he remembered he would not actually be on camera. Then he heard the audio feed of the female half of the late-night news anchors doing the intro, "Now we have what we believe to be a Channel 69 exclusive. On the phone with us is the national editor for *The New York Times*, Mr. Harold Spade, who believes he knows who or what is behind the massive power outage in the northeastern United States tonight. Mr. Spade, can you hear me?"

"I can hear you just fine. Can you hear me all right?"

"Yes, sir, I can. What can you tell us?"

"Well, first I want to be clear that the *Times* does not have any definitive proof of who did this. What we do have is a letter postmarked several days prior to the fires in Texas, New Jersey, and Connecticut, as well as tonight's power outage, and I want to read the text of that letter to your viewers now, so that they can draw their own conclusions from it."

"Go ahead," prompted the woman, staring at the camera feed with a suitably grave expression.

"OK. The letter begins, quote, 'In the name of Allah, the merciful, the compassionate, from Allah's most righteous warrior, the successor to Osama Bin Laden, to the people of the United States and the crusader U.S. government: May Allah's blessings be upon those who abide by his word and Sharia. The incidents that will take place in your states of Texas, New Jersey, Connecticut, and the whole of the Northeast of your evil country are Allah's will. These actions will be carried out by the faithful sons of Islam in defense of their religion and in order to protect Muslims throughout the world, as decreed by Allah and his prophet, may Allah's peace and blessings be upon him.'"

Spade stopped reading for a moment and added, "I have to tell you that when I first read this, it struck me as remarkably similar to the letters that Osama Bin Laden and his deputy would issue from time to time. Experts will need to review it, but from a journalistic standpoint, this alone seems to lend some credibility to it."

The male anchor in Atlanta chimed in, "What else does it say?"

Spade held the letter a little closer to the flashlight. The light was getting dimmer. *Damn.* He should have gotten fresh batteries for the light before making the call.

"The letter continues, 'What the U.S. president, the pharaoh of all infidels, was doing by killing our sons in Iraq and Afghanistan in the early years of the twenty-first century, and how he encouraged Israel, his close ally, to rape and murder the innocents of Palestine with U.S.-made aircraft, helicopters, and bombs, were sufficient for any reasonable ruler to distance themselves from the Great Satan of the West. Our brothers and sisters in Palestine have suffered death and unspeakable tortures under unlawful occupation. If we defend our brothers and sisters in Palestine and throughout the world, the world stands against all Muslims, under the falsehood created by the Great Satan called the "War on Terror." If your governments choose to ally yourselves with the criminals of the Great Satan, what do you believe you shall gain? Gold? A more prominent seat at the table laid by the pharaoh of all infidels? Living in fear, destroyed homes, dead fathers, mothers, sons, and daughters should not be the lot of the Muslim nation, the cherished people of Allah's Caliphate, while the decadent subjects of the world's infidel nations live in happiness, ignoring the Muslim plight. This inequity will be addressed. You will be killed in kind for the murders your leaders have ordered, and you will be bombed just as your leaders order the bombings of innocents. You shall feel cold in your homes. You shall fear Allah's reprisals in the dark. The industries of the Great Satan will grind to a halt and its economy will be destroyed. And expect more that will humble you before all nations and in the sight of Almighty Allah. The beloved sons of the Islamic nation, pledged to Allah to continue jihad, will bring death to your homes and ruin to your nation and expose the truth of your actions against all Muslims. In conclusion, I ask Allah to help us champion this jihad for His sake until we meet Him in Paradise. Praise be to Almighty Allah.' The letter is signed, 'The Rightful Successor to the Warrior Bin Laden and the Ruler of the Returned Caliphate.'"

There was a stunned silence on the other end of the phone as the two anchors shuffled their notes and tried to form a cogent question or two. Spade took the opportunity to remind everyone whose exclusive this really was.

"To be very clear again, the *Times* doesn't have any definitive proof of who did this. What we do have is a letter postmarked several days prior to the fires in Texas, New Jersey, and Connecticut, as well as tonight's power outage; that refers very clearly to events yet to come in those states. The *Times* feels that this demonstrated foreknowledge, coupled with the style and format of the letter, leads to only one conclusion. Someone has taken over for Osama Bin Laden since his death at the hands of the U.S. military in Pakistan and is again leading al-Qaeda in attacks against the United States."

CAIN SAID, "DID WE RECORD THAT?"

One of the swing-shift people operating the DVD recorder in the corner waived affirmatively to him. Cain thought fast. "Two of you get into the conference room with that recording and start making a transcript by hand. I want that sent to every agency immediately. Alert the FBI. Recommend that they get somebody in New York to get that letter fast for a forensic examination and have those agents send us a copy to check our transcription."

Goodman asked, "What about the information the FBI gave us about that Aziz guy who got his hands on al-Qaeda's money? That and the phone number is a solid lead."

"Yes, it is." Thinking for a moment, Cain turned and looked down into the watch area at the NSA desk.

"Lieutenant Osborn," he commanded.

"Yes, sir."

"That phone number we got from the FBI. What can you tell me about it?"

"I checked on the Internet, and NSA confirms—which means they looked there too—that the number is a partial phone number located in Tehran. NSA has nothing else on it."

"Did you put that information out there yet?" Cain asked.

"No, sir. I'll do it now." Turning to his keyboard, Osborn started typing up an information tipper, providing the partial telephone number that the FBI's INHERITOR investigation had turned up and including the geographic location of the number. It was scant information, but sometimes that's all that existed, distributed in the hopes that others in the intelligence community could add more to it.

Cain spoke to Goodman again. "Mike, I want you to get Emily and some of the other folks together and start doing a more formal written assessment on what we have so far. Don't try and put a bow on it, just pull the information together and make it available on INTELINK for consumption. Be sure to include whatever Ryan over at Energy has been able to come up with."

"You got it, David."

GOODMAN AND HIS IMPROMPTU ANALYSIS team quickly put together what they knew. They posted it to the web page established by the INTELINK central management for the current crisis, which had been given the project name AUTUMN FIRE. Analysts at every intelligence agency in the government were accessing the AUTUMN FIRE page at a rate of more than one hundred times an hour.

SECRET
AUTUMN FIRE Situation Update # 01-18
FM: CTS WATCH
DTG: 0200Z 02 NOV 18

1. Information from the U.S. Supervisory Control and Data Acquisition (SCADA) network acquired by the DoE indicates that an unidentified hacker accessed the SCADA network at approximately 0900Z 15 NOV and masqueraded as three master control computers on the SCADA network. While doing so, the U/I hacker issued multiple commands, ordering increased power output from nuclear, coal, and oil-fired power plants, while simultaneously disabling safeties on transformer equipment at major substations, likely resulting in extensive equipment damage. Further analysis of SCADA network traffic has traced the source of the commands, issued

via Internet Protocol version 4, to an Internet Service Provider (ISP) in the Chicago metropolitan area. The name of the ISP and the IP addresses used to issue the commands have been forwarded directly to the FBI for follow-up.

2. Recent information from the FBI, obtained via Saudi Arabian Internal Security Forces, has identified seven bank accounts that held, according to bank records, more than $200,000,000. These accounts are believed to have belonged to Osama Bin Laden. The money was transferred out of these accounts early in 2012 to unknown locations/accounts. A person named "Aziz" (Not Further Identified – NFI) is probably associated with the transfer of these moneys. The partial phone number 98 21 333 is associated with Aziz (NFI). Open source information confirms that the phone number can be geographically located in the Tehran, Iran, area. No information is available from any intelligence agency about the user of the number, because the number is incomplete.

3. Recent open source reporting has revealed the existence of a letter, apparently claiming responsibility for the attacks and subsequent fires at the Strategic Petroleum Reserve in Texas, and three separate components of the Northeastern U.S. Home Heating Oil Reserve in New Jersey and Connecticut. The letter also alludes to "incidents that will take place in . . . the whole of the Northeast. . . . " Based on preliminary review by the CIA of the form and content of the letter, the letter is adjudged to be very similar to those issued by the terrorist group al-Qaeda. The signature at the bottom identifies the writer as "The Rightful Successor to the Warrior Bin Laden and the Ruler of the Returned Caliphate." CIA assesses this to indicate that the drafter is claiming to be Bin Laden's successor and intends to continue to pursue al-Qaeda's previously stated goal of establishing a Caliphate spanning Eastern Europe to Southeast Asia. The letter's

postmark is from a Chicago metropolitan area zip code seven days prior to the attacks in Texas, New Jersey, and Connecticut.

4. CURRENT ANALYSIS/RECOMMENDATIONS: CIA, DIA, and CTS all concur in believing the letter to be authentic. The date on the postmark is seven days prior to the events in Texas, New Jersey, and Connecticut, and eight days prior to the widespread power outage in the Northeast. If the information from the Saudi Arabian Internal Security Forces is accurate, it is possible that Aziz (NFI) is a member of "core al-Qaeda" or is running a revived major branch of al-Qaeda that has considerable financial resources to use in enabling the recent attacks. Informal discussions with FBI investigators and Homeland Security personnel reveal that fewer than 60 people have likely been required to carry out the recent actions. The Chicago postmark on the letter and the identification of the ISP's location in the Chicago area point to this city as a nexus and a potential base of al-Qaeda operations within the United States.

S E C R E T
//EOT//

"It looks good, Mike. Nice job." Cain was staring at the final report on his computer screen.

"Thanks, David. I think we need to start getting our people some rest. We've got our first leads. Things will snowball from here."

"Yep. Get the teams organized. Have them nap in the conference room for now. See if you can get some blankets or something from somewhere."

"I'll ask everybody to call home and see if they can donate to the cause," Goodman said over his shoulder as he headed down onto the watch floor to talk to the analysts and liaisons.

COLONEL SIMON COULD NOT ADD anything to the information tipper he received from the CTS folks at NSA, but he had heard the letter read about ten times now. CNN kept rerunning the tape of the Atlanta station's broadcast. No matter how nice the female anchor was to look at, Colonel Simon cared more about the text of the letter, which harkened back to the days before Bin Laden died.

While it had taken the world awhile to accept that Bin Laden was just a bad memory, Colonel Simon needed no convincing. He had been the joint operations planner for the SEAL assault that killed Bin Laden in his bedroom in his Abbottabad compound. He had flown into Pakistan with the SEAL assault force because he had faith in the intelligence he had collated and the operational plan he had put together.

The SEALs performed a picture-perfect assault on the compound, located Bin Laden in the third-floor quarters of the main house, and shot him "resisting capture." After securing the noncombatants in the house and evacuating them to a safe part of the compound, they placed Bin Laden in a body bag, checked his house for useful intelligence, and jumped back on the helicopters for the flight back to Afghanistan, clearing Pakistani airspace before their Air Force could respond.

He left the decision of whether to tell the world Bin Laden was dead to the politicians, accepted his promotion to lieutenant colonel and received the Silver Star, and offered his opinions regarding the creation of a permanent joint special operations unit. A unit that was not just a cobbled-together command from various service components of the special operations community—but a real, full-time joint element with the most advanced equipment and the best people drawn permanently from every branch of the service.

After convincing the general and meeting with the president and SECDEF to discuss the idea, he was able to mitigate the individual service chief's complaints and begin serious work on building the joint team. Two years later, Congress authorized the funding, and the 152nd Joint Special Missions Unit was established.

Glancing at the map on the wall in the operations room, he decided to pad his hand a little just in case something unexpected happened in the Middle East. Looking at the captain in charge of the operations center on Level 8, he issued an order, "Order Dumbo-25 to ferry Team Three, their equipment, and their support aircraft to Riyadh. I want them closer to Iran than they are now."

IT WAS JUST AFTER DAWN at Lakenheath Royal Air Force Base in England when the order from Colonel Simon reached them. Team Three relayed the order to the flight crew, and the support team started prepping the mammoth C-17 for flight. The flight crew headed for the tower, filed the necessary flight plans with the British airmen on duty, and checked the weather along their predicted flight path.

An hour later, the C-17's engines spun up to idle, and the ground crew pulled the chocks away from the seven-foot-diameter wheels. Dumbo-25 lumbered down Taxiway Alpha toward Runway 24.

The tower gave Dumbo-25 takeoff clearance, and the pilot turned the aircraft left onto the runway and began to accelerate. The copilot called out "V-One" and put his hand on top of the pilot's on the throttles. A few seconds later he called out "Rotate" as the aircraft passed velocity rotation, or V_r. The pilot pulled back on the yoke and the aircraft's nose came up. "V-Two," the copilot called out as the aircraft's speed passed 145 knots and the mighty C-17 lifted off the runway and began to gain altitude.

It was not quite a hundred feet in the air when a flock of snow geese already flying south, their gray-white feathers blending in with the background clouds, flew straight into the transport's flight path.

Four of them were sucked into the right outboard engine, causing it to flame out instantly, triggering the automatic fire-suppression system. Five other unlucky geese were pulled into the hungry maw of the right inboard engine, snuffing it out just as effectively as its outboard twin.

The aircraft immediately rolled right as the pilots fought to control it and regain level flight. Then Murphy's Law sneaked up on them. The cargo tie-down straps holding the helicopters in place snapped, causing the two Apaches and the Kiowa helicopters to tip over onto their sides and smash into the right wall of the cargo bay. The loadmaster, who was not strapped in for takeoff, was slammed against one of the cargo pallets and immediately broke three ribs. The passengers gripped the hand rests of their seats and could do little more than scream or pray, knowing whatever happened next was out of their control.

The aircraft's center of balance was now severely impaired, and the right roll became worse. The aircraft was no longer gaining altitude and in fact was beginning to "slide" downhill at nearly a 90-degree right bank. A few seconds later, the right wingtip struck the ground, and the forward momentum of the C-17 caused the tail to flip up over the nose, as the now-doomed C-17 started to cartwheel.

The cartwheel ripped the left wing off at the wing root, and the tail slammed into the ground, causing the cargo hold to collapse as the aircraft buried the left side of its fuselage fifteen feet into the earth.

The men of Team Three and the support crews for the helicopters and UAV were crushed by either the collapsing right wall of the cargo hold or the aircraft and cargo pallets in the bay. The pilots were still strapped into their seats, mercifully unconscious from the impact when the nearly 35,000 gallons of aviation fuel spilling from the Globemaster's ruptured tanks caught fire and exploded.

THE DEPARTMENT OF ENERGY'S DAVE Ryan had sent along not only the name of the ISP that the commands to the SCADA network came from but also the times and IP addresses used to the FBI. The FBI was nothing, if not quick, when it came to following up a lead on a terrorist. Two agents in the Chicago office had the information in their hands thirty minutes after the CTS bulletin was posted.

The two agents left their office on West Roosevelt Road and headed straight to the home of senior U.S. District Judge Marvin Plunkett and explained the situation as they knew it. They even had a copy of the classified CTS bulletin and gave it to the judge to back up their warrant application. Showing the judge classified material was not a problem in this case because he was a U.S. citizen with thirty-two years on the bench, and they needed the warrant signed with a minimum of fuss.

After taking three minutes to read CTS's summary of the situation, Judge Plunkett brought both men into his study, recorded their credentials by photocopying their identification, and then asked them to raise their right hands and swear to the truthfulness of the warrant application they had placed before him.

Five minutes later, they were back in their black Chevy sedan, lights flashing, heading to the offices of WestNet downtown. They had already called the company's president and asked to meet him there.

After a brief conversation with the president, who made a copy of the warrant, the two agents were introduced to the lead network administrator. Ten minutes after telling the administrator what they needed and handing him the list of IP addresses and times, they had an address. They headed back to their car.

Forty minutes later, they pulled up into a dark parking lot near the corner of West Grand Lake Boulevard and Freemont Street in western Chicago and killed the car's lights. The senior agent called the FBI watch center in the Hoover Building.

"DAVID," SIMPSON SAID, "I'M GETTING a request from the FBI for technical and intelligence support for a Hostage Rescue Team operation against a suspected al-Qaeda safe house in western Chicago. HRT is heading for Andrews now."

"Tell them they've got it," replied David, knowing the FBI's elite SWAT unit was a regular customer for CTS support, and then adding to the room in general, "Heads up, everyone! Let's get set up to provide technical and intelligence support to the HRT action. Mike, wake up the folks in the conference room, we'll need the extra bodies."

"Got it," Goodman said as he headed for the closed conference room door.

Behind him on the floor, liaisons, not already set up, donned their headsets and plugged into the internal communications system.

"Got an address yet, Fred?" Emily asked.

"16072 West Grand Lake Boulevard."

"Got it. I'll volunteer to work open source on this one, since CIA isn't likely to have anything to add."

"Do that after you check to be *sure* CIA doesn't have anything," Cain ordered.

"Yes, Mr. Cain," she replied, the impish grin on her face telling him she had intended to check anyway.

AT ANDREWS AIR FORCE BASE, Team Four was roughing it inside one of the hangars on the base. The base's backup generators were supplying electrical power to all essential facilities, including the hangars. The base commander had turned over the hangar to them and assigned a small Air Force security contingent to keep the curious away. The plan was for Team Three's personnel to make daily trips in two- or three-man relays to the base gym for showers and to the base dining hall for meals, but other than that, they would stay close to the hangar.

They had converted the hangar into a temporary team headquarters and had partially unpacked some of their gear. They had also set up a Very Small Aperture Terminal for secure communications with Colonel Simon back at the 152nd JSMU, and to connect to INTELINK. The VSAT was a suitcase-sized satellite antenna and modem combination ruggedized for military use. It included a heavy-duty battery for emergency power and a small, highly sophisticated encryption device. The VSAT allowed mobile units to rapidly establish secure, two-way communications via phone or computer, no matter where they were in the world.

Shane Mathews was reading the CTS bulletin for the third time when the VSAT's attached secure phone rang. Mathews grabbed it. "Team Four."

"Orders," said the voice of Colonel Simon.

"Ready to copy."

"The FBI Hostage Rescue Team will deploy from Andrews to western Chicago to search and clear a suspected al-Qaeda safe house. Your team is ordered to accompany them and to relay tactical intelligence as well as provide tactical backup if required. The HRT leader is aware of your participation. Authentication is Zulu Tango 34."

Mathews looked at his watch. The first two characters of the authentication phrase were meaningless; as long as there were two letters used and the two numbers matched the minutes after the hour, plus or minus one minute, it was a valid order.

"Team Four copies all. Executing now."

"Out," said Simon. Then the line went dead.

Mathews hung up and headed over to the telephone in the hangar office to call base operations.

"Major Turner."

"Major, this is Mathews in Hangar 262."

"Yes."

"You have an FBI team coming in to catch a plane to Chicago. My people and I are traveling with them."

"How the hell do you know that? I was just told about that movement half an hour ago and to keep it quiet. I just got done briefing the flight crew."

"Sir, I'm not permitted to tell you that. My orders are to tag along. The FBI guys should tell you that when they show up."

"All right," said the disbelieving voice of the major, "for now we'll say they will. Head over to the C-5 Galaxy two hangars down from you in Hangar 266. If the FBI guys say you can come along, you can go. If not, you'll have some explaining to do."

"Thanks, Major," Mathews said, and hung up.

"Grab your gear, people!" he yelled to the members of Team Four, "we've got a plane to catch."

THE CTS WAS A HIVE OF controlled action. Homeland Security had arranged through the local police to have the video feeds from the traffic cameras near the target routed to CTS for monitoring. The FBI agents on scene had given strict instructions to the Commander of the Western District of the Chicago Police Department and, so far, they had been followed.

The commander had ordered some of the districts' patrols to a diner nearby and told them in person what was happening rather than over the radio, as the suspects in the building might be monitoring the police frequencies. The patrol officers would create a perimeter around the target building when the time came.

The commander then headed back to the Western District station and informed the officers that were part of the district's SWAT team what was happening and that they would back up the FBI team when it arrived. His officers immediately protested on the grounds that this was their jurisdiction and the FBI had no business handling this when they were perfectly capable of doing the job.

The commander explained that they would follow orders, just as he had been doing since he'd spoken to the governor and the mayor. Both the governor and mayor had consulted with the director of the FBI and the secretary of homeland security ten minutes before calling the commander. The Chicago Police Department would act in a support role this time. As a precaution, and to help mollify his men, he told them that they would accompany him back to the area to set up a command post and meet the FBI team when it arrived.

Emily had checked and then rechecked with CIA to ensure that they had no information regarding the establishment of a safe house of any kind within the Chicago suburbs. Her contacts in the CIA watch center had assured her, twice, that they had no such information.

Now that she had satisfied Cain's instructions and her own personal decision, undertaken long before Cain reminded her, she put the target address into an Internet search engine to see what she could get. She scanned some of the resulting hyperlinks, and one of them caught her eye.

"David," she raised her voice enough for him to hear, as Cain wasn't on a headset.

"Yes," he said as he came down the steps into the liaison area.

"I found the floor plans for the building," she said with a smile. "The county has an online database of commercial structure floor plans. I'll bet the FBI guys would like them."

"Sure enough," he said, returning her grin. "Send them off to Team Four after they set up the VSAT link. Nice job."

Fred picked his head up from his terminal. "David, FBI informs us that the warrant was delivered to the Chicago AT&T office. The phone lines that terminate at that address are now tapped. Agents are monitoring them in real time at the local switch. The FBI command post will keep us informed."

"Great. Will they be sending the information to the HRT guys directly or will they want us to relay?"

"They're asking for the relay. Their people at the switch only have cell phones. They've set up a three-way call among themselves, the FBI command post in the Hoover Building, and here."

"All right, keep me informed."

IT HAD BEEN FOUR HOURS since Team Four had boarded the C-5 with the FBI's Hostage Rescue Team at Andrews. The HRT moved fast when they and Team Four reached the command post the Chicago PD had set up at the corner of West Washington Street and Tye Court in an empty parking lot about three blocks from the target building.

Team Four had set up its VSAT and had received the floor plans via e-mail. Mathews passed the plans on to John Sampson, the HRT leader, who immediately huddled with his people for a few minutes to devise an assault plan.

When they were ready, the HRT members and the Chicago SWAT team formed opposing lines of men as Sampson, a twenty-six-year veteran of the FBI, went over the current situation.

"The warehouse is a suspected al-Qaeda safe house here in Chicago. We have evidence that the orders that shut down the Northeast power grid came from the Internet connections that flow into this building. My team and I will attempt a stealth entry from the available door on side two, level one, and sweep through level one."

"What about my SWAT unit?" the Western District Commander asked.

"We need you to back us up on the entry. My expectation is that when we enter the warehouse, we're going to have too much ground to cover with one unit. After we have the initial beachhead, we'll call for your team to enter behind us and split up. You'll sweep level two."

The Chicago SWAT unit looked a little mollified at this announcement. The Western District Commander's look said it all. *So the Feds were going to let them work in their own jurisdiction, how nice of them.*

Sampson saw the looks on the faces of the District Commander and the Chicago SWAT unit and knew he needed to try and smooth over the unspoken federal versus local jurisdiction issue. "We're going in first because we've trained for this kind of thing. We learned the hard way in Iraq and Afghanistan that terrorists love booby traps, so we will clear an entry point and then call you in. Even so, keep your eyes open for wires, lasers, and cell phones. If you come across a device and feel you can disarm it, call out first and then do so. If not, and you need a hand, I'll send one of my guys along to help. If you hear a phone ring nearby, run."

Some of the Chicago officers traded, "Don't worry, we can handle it" looks. Sampson's voice hardened.

"This is no time for ego, gentlemen. You'd better believe that if we find something we can't handle, we're calling for help and backing off. You need to do the same. The goal here is that we and the suspects go home at the end of the day alive, if possible."

Mathews, standing on the periphery of the impromptu briefing with his team, did not agree with that sentiment but held his tongue. Only the good guys should go home at the end of the day alive as far as he was concerned. *Then again,* he thought, *I'm a soldier, not a cop.*

The HRT veteran continued, "Other than that, the usual rules apply. Deadly force is authorized if your life or the life of a teammate is in imminent danger from a suspect. Let's gear up, take a last look at the floor plans our friends in CTS sent, and get to our jump-off points. It'll be getting light in another hour and I want to take maximum advantage of the darkness."

CHAPTER 18

"HOTEL LEAD, COMM CHECK," SAID the voice of Sampson, the HRT leader, over Mathews' headset. He keyed his microphone and replied, "Whiskey One has you five by five."

"Forty David has you same," chimed in the leader of the Chicago SWAT team.

The HRT unit was stacked up on the northern side of one of the wood-shingled houses to the east of the warehouse. They had chosen that house because it was close to the warehouse and the only home nearby that did not have a fence around it to obstruct the HRT unit's approach. The Chicago SWAT team was ten feet behind them, with half the team wrapped around to the front of the house.

Unmarked cruisers had just finished evacuating the nearby residents as quietly as possible. When the team made entry, the marked cruisers were ready to barricade the area.

The warehouse was actually two buildings built closely together and sharing a common wall. The eastern building, the larger of the two, was closest to the HRT unit. It also had a second story. The plans retrieved by the folks at CTS had shown a relatively open interior, except for the area nearest the western building on the first floor. They also showed a small office space of eight rooms, roughly in the center of the warehouse. Eight feet west of the office space was the common wall between the two warehouses.

From the outside, the buildings were almond-colored metal, rusted in places, with dark brown steel roofs. No lights were visible in the few grime-streaked windows, but the perimeter was well lit by the orange-white glow of sodium vapor lights, except for two that had gone out. Fortunately, one of the malfunctioning lights was over the door the HRT and SWAT teams were going to use. The warehouse had a small concrete parking area wrapped around it, which was barren except for six unoccupied cars parked at the outer edges of the lot.

Taking a deep breath, and saying a brief prayer to God for the safety of his men as he always did, Sampson whispered, "Moving now," and tapped his point man on the shoulder.

Mathews called in to CTS, "HRT commencing entry now."

"Copy Whiskey One," was the reply from Goodman, now watching the large monitors showing the view from the three traffic cameras near the warehouse.

As one man, the HRT unit moved quickly in single file across the backyard of the house and then onto the open concrete parking area toward the inviting circle of darkness near the door they had chosen for entry. The team passed between two cars parked nearly twenty-five yards apart in the lot, training weapons briefly on each car, alert for an ambush. Twenty yards later, they stacked up on the door.

Inside the warehouse, Repin heard a single electronic beeping from the infrared motion detectors hidden in the parked cars. He exploded out of bed. Running to the bank of monitors in his underwear, he checked the security camera feed and saw a group of eight men stacked up by the ground-floor door on the east side.

"Ahueyet!" he exclaimed in his native tongue as he looked at the image. The Americans had found him. As he watched the monitor, the assault team's point man reached for the door handle and tried turning it.

Knowing that the door was locked, Repin ran back into his bedroom, opened his closet door to grab a bag of clothes, and then slipped his feet into a pair of shoes without tying the laces. If the Americans chose to execute a rapid entry, he was already out of time. He ran back to the monitor and checked their progress. The lead man was now picking the lock while his teammates covered him.

They were still taking the stealthy route, and Repin knew time was running out. He dropped the bag of clothes on his desk chair, leaned over it, and with two hands simultaneously pressed four keys on the keyboard for two seconds. The computer's monitor blanked, and he knew the computer was now deleting all the data on the hard drives in the machine.

He grabbed the bag of clothes and raced toward the door on the far side of the room, away from the Americans' point of entry. He hadn't taken six steps before he stopped and returned to the desk to retrieve his daughter's picture, and then ran for the door again, putting her picture between his lips to hold it. Opening the door, he went through and then slammed it closed behind him, ramming the dead bolt home.

He raced down the small hallway, turned right, and headed down a flight of stairs into the basement. At the bottom of the stairs was a heavy steel door that he swung open easily. He shut it behind him and dropped a hardened steel bar across it and then grabbed a flashlight stored in a clip on the back of the door. He shined the light on two switches just to the right of the doorframe, tucked the bag of clothes under his arm, and used his now-free hand to flip both of them.

Turning, he raced down a narrow dirt passageway that was seven feet high and little more than three feet wide. Shifting the bag of clothes back to his left hand and gripping the flashlight in his right, he headed down the passage as quickly as he could, doing his best to keep holding his daughter's picture carefully between his lips.

Back at the door on the east side, the HRT point man finished defeating the lock and then ran the thin reed of a fiber-optic camera under the door to view the interior. The small LCD display showed only an empty hallway with one door on the left. He withdrew the slender reed of the cable and signaled to the leader, who keyed his microphone again, "Commencing stealth entry now. Forty David, hold position."

One click on his earpiece from the Chicago SWAT leader confirmed receipt of his message, and he tapped the point man on the shoulder again.

The point man opened the door and then proceeded inside, followed immediately by the rest of the team. The black-suited HRT members flooded into the small dark hallway, their H&K MP5 submachine guns with attached SureFire tactical flashlights pointed toward the end of the hallway.

After scanning the far end hallway for trip wires or similar devices, the leader signaled his left hand toward the sole door on the left side, and the HRT unit stacked up on its left side. The point man withdrew his fiber-optic camera again, slid it under the door, and turned it to look up. Sampson watched the screen intently with him as he checked the interior portion of the door for trip wires or other traps and saw only the three bars securing the door. The point man then turned the camera back toward the interior of the room. He leaned toward Sampson, making sure the HRT leader had a clear view of the screen and the look of grim surprise on his face.

Sampson saw the point man's look and studied the screen, realizing something was very wrong. The door was heavily barred and the plans they had for the building were not right. The camera's screen showed a miniature apartment beyond with office furniture, a kitchen, and a small sleeping area, not an open warehouse floor. Worse, there were no suspects visible. Years of experience and training screamed danger, and so he made an instant decision. Keying his microphone to be permanently open he yelled, "Compromised! Breach, bang, and clear!"

Immediately the point man threw the fiber camera down the hallway and pulled a prepared sheet charge of C-4 explosive from his tactical webbing. Slamming it onto the center of the door, he physically backed up a pace, shoving his teammates backward. Then he drew the radio detonator with his left hand while grabbing his own H&K MP5 submachine gun's pistol grip with his right. Silently counting to two, he depressed the trigger on the detonator, and the door exploded into the room with a crash.

Sampson tossed a flash-bang grenade around his point man's shoulder into the room, shouting, "Flash out!" to warn the team before turning his face away from the door. As soon as he saw the flash of light through his closed eyes and felt the skull-shaking bang move through his body, he opened his eyes and followed his point man into the room, weapon up, looking for suspects.

The entire HRT was in the room now, each member calling out, "Clear!" as they confirmed to each other that the room was devoid of suspects. "The floor plans are wrong. Repeat, the floor plans are wrong," the leader said over the open radio link so the Chicago SWAT team would have some idea of what was going on.

The Chicago PD SWAT team heard the compromise call and immediately did what all brothers-in-arms do when their comrades are believed to be in danger: they rushed out in single file toward the warehouse and the now-open door to support their fellow team members.

Two of the SWAT officers split off from the team and took up cover positions behind two cars on the concrete lot, scanning for threats. The rest of their unit advanced, just as the HRT leader made his radio transmission about the floor plans. Little did the two officers know that Repin and Aziz had been thorough in their planning for this eventuality.

Eight inches under the floor in the center of the command-post apartment, the timer Repin activated when he had flipped the first switch by the heavy steel door reached zero. As fate would have it, the point man of the Chicago SWAT team had also just passed between the two cars his men had taken cover behind, breaking the infrared beam activated when Repin had flipped the second switch.

The three near-simultaneous explosions lit the predawn sky like rocket launches at Cape Canaveral. The two cars the Chicago SWAT officers had taken cover behind blew apart spectacularly, ripping the two men into pieces and scattering them across the parking lot in smoking chunks of torn flesh and equipment.

The main explosive charge in the center of the floor shot the main warehouse's roof one hundred feet in the air, ripping it into five separate sheets before it began its return to earth. The walls of both buildings shattered into thousands of pieces as the charges embedded in them every few feet detonated simultaneously. The shrapnel and incinerated remains of the HRT tore through the Chicago SWAT unit over a 400-foot area and slammed into the surrounding empty houses. A small mushroom cloud of super-heated air and flame bloomed skyward from the center of the warehouse.

Mathews stared in open-mouthed horror at the cloud of heat and flame almost three blocks distant. Tearing his headset off, he led his men in a race across the three-block distance toward the fiery remains of the warehouse as police cruisers, lights flashing, sped down the roads into the area.

Behind him, Goodman's voice on the discarded headset screamed, "Hotel Lead, Forty David, come in! Respond immediately! Hotel Lead, Forty David, come in!"

In the CTS, Goodman's radio calls stopped after a few minutes. The entire watch floor sat in stunned silence as they watched the remaining pieces of the warehouse burn. They could see from the traffic cameras the burning, fragmented bodies of three Chicago SWAT officers littering the parking lot. No one else could be seen through the smoke and fire.

As they continued to watch, Chicago police cruisers entered the picture, followed by the men of Team Four running toward the site in their battle dress uniforms. The policemen and soldiers ran toward the blaze that had been the warehouse and dragged the fallen SWAT officers away from danger, and then began checking their burnt bodies for pulses and breathing. Two men began CPR on a fallen officer in the backyard of the house from which both teams had approached, sixty feet away from where he had stood prior to the blasts.

As everyone sat mute in horrified fascination before the images, Emily put her head in her hands and began to cry silently. The only sound in her head was Sampson's voice saying over and over, *"The floor plans are wrong. Repeat, the floor plans are wrong."* Focused on their own feelings in the face of the instant death of sixteen men they were charged to help, no one else in CTS noticed her agony.

ACROSS THE STREET FROM THE warehouse, in the garage of the three-bedroom house, Repin removed a shirt and pair of pants from the bag. He had one leg in the pants when the warehouse and cars exploded. He cringed at the sound of the explosions and reflexively ducked behind the passenger side of the car. The fragments from the explosions bounced off the left side of the house and the attached garage before littering the lawn with debris. Some of the larger chunks were on fire and burned as individual torches in the grass.

The house was the same uniform tan and brown of the others in the neighborhood, with a dark chocolate shingle roof, but the interior of the garage and the side of the house facing the warehouse across the street was reinforced by thick plywood and brick on the inside as insurance against the penetration of fragments from the explosions. The work had been accomplished shortly after Aziz had acquired it, along with the then-empty plot of land the warehouses once stood on, through a dummy corporation.

Aziz had liquidated the dummy corporation immediately after the sales had been finalized. Its only assets, the house and two adjoining warehouses, were marked condemned and were rumored to be up for auction in a few months. The house had even been modified by the same construction firm that had built the warehouse. The tunnel between them had been dug by hand over six months by four of Aziz's jihadis before Repin had taken up residence in the warehouse. They had dumped the spoil from the tunnel in the large empty pit left in the center of the second warehouse. Shortly after the tunnel had been completed, Aziz had sent the four men to Paradise himself, and had buried their bodies in the pit as well.

At the time, Repin had thought the tunnel was overdoing things a bit, but surprisingly, the Americans had proven themselves more than capable in locating him, and he was now glad Aziz had chosen to prepare for this contingency. As he pulled his oxford shirt on and then the heavy blue sweater and leather coat, he resolved to think long and hard about how they might have found him. For now, it was time to leave. He took his daughter's picture off the trunk of the car where he had set it down to dress and tucked it into his coat pocket.

Opening the trunk, he tossed the empty clothes bag into it. Then he opened a large, dark-blue travel bag resting in the trunk and withdrew a wallet that contained an Illinois driver's license, several credit cards with $10,000 limits, and $500 in cash. Putting the wallet in his right rear pants pocket, he rummaged around a little in the travel bag and extracted a tan zippered case containing another $2,000 in $20, $50, and $100 bills. It also contained a fresh U.S. passport.

He removed $400 worth of cash in $20s and $50s, put it in his front left pants pocket, and then slipped the blue U.S. passport into his leather jacket. He replaced the tan case, closed the travel bag, shut the trunk, and got in the driver's seat.

Starting the car and keeping the vehicle's lights off, he pushed the remote-control button for the garage door opener. The door rolled up quietly, and he eased the car out of the garage and into the driveway as he looked around. The bushes planted on the left side of the driveway were tall and full enough to hide the car from view until he rolled out onto the side street that served as the rear access to the houses on this row.

His heart was pounding and his palms began to sweat a little as he turned right to head up the access street. If he was going to be discovered, this was the time. He glanced in the rearview mirror and saw nothing but the flashing lights of police cruisers and men milling about amid the wreckage. He reached up again and touched the garage remote control again, hoping he was still in range. He certainly was not going back to check.

He continued down the side street, heading north, until he came to West Elmwood Avenue. He turned right onto it and glanced around. Seeing no one, he flipped on the headlights and headed east down the street.

He followed West Elmwood to Illinois Route 59 and then turned south. Route 59 led him to I-88, where he headed east and then south toward Midway Airport.

Thirty minutes later, he purchased a round-trip ticket to Los Angeles with one of his credit cards and bought a breakfast sandwich, hash browns, and coffee from the McDonald's in Terminal One. They wouldn't make him a cheeseburger and fries this early in the morning, so he resigned himself to the more pedestrian breakfast fare. Heading deeper into Terminal One, he sat in one of the blue vinyl chairs at Gate 4 and ate while he waited to board the 767 with the rest of the passengers.

"CHARLIE, THIS IS WHISKEY ONE. No survivors. Do you copy? No survivors." The edge in Mathews' voice was tough to miss, even across the radio link.

Goodman keyed the microphone and said wearily, "Copy Whiskey One. We were watching."

The people in CTS tried to go back to work, so the watch center was silent except for the sounds of fingers tapping on keyboards and the occasional ringing phone. The analysts would not look at each other, and most spent more time just looking at their desks but not actually seeing the reports on them or the e-mail open on their computer screens.

Cain saw his people's sorrow and tension, and he let them grieve for a few minutes. Then he cleared his throat and raised his voice, "Give me your attention, people."

Everyone stopped what they were doing and looked up at him. Cain stood next to his desk and when he had everyone's attention, he leaned forward and put both hands on the guardrail surrounding the platform.

"We lost people this morning. We don't know why yet. Until the investigation of what happened is complete, we cannot blame ourselves. All our radio traffic, a current snapshot of our INTELINK website, and copies of all our e-mails will be saved off into secure storage and will be provided to the FBI and the NSA Inspector General to aide in their review and investigation." Cain paused, took a deep breath, and continued.

"Until that review is complete, we have to continue doing our jobs and not spending time blaming ourselves for what happened. If any of you want to be relieved, all you have to do is ask; we have plenty of people available and on standby. There is no shame in that, and it will not be held against you. If you think you need time, even if it's just to head to the gym and run for a while, or go spend time with your family and hug your spouse or kids, say so." Cain paused again and looked each team member in the eyes, one by one. He tried to project confidence, sympathy, and understanding all at once. He was not quite sure if he succeeded.

No one volunteered immediately—not that he expected anyone to do so publicly—so he continued, "All right. If anyone wants to speak to me or Mike privately, please feel free to do so. Otherwise, please do what you can to keep your minds on what you need to do here and now. Our nation has been attacked, and we've just witnessed what is probably just the first battle. I need your best now and for the foreseeable future. Enough said."

The CTS team seemed to let out a collective breath. Then they returned to work, many of them obviously still distracted. Cain noted that his brief speech had not helped much. He and Mike would make the rounds and encourage the more distracted people to take a break. It was all they could do for now.

COLONEL SIMON HUNG HIS HEAD. The base commander at RAFB Lakenheath had just sent a FLASH priority message about the crash of Dumbo-25 to the Pentagon, and the Pentagon sent a copy of it to him.

Team Three and their support team, the flight crews of the transport and the helicopters, and the maintenance team, all dead. Nearly sixty members of the Wraith family were gone. *Fucking birds.* He would have to mourn later. "Raise Team Four in Chicago," he ordered.

THE VSAT PHONE WAS RINGING again. Mathews and his team had returned to the command post the Chicago PD had set up. After they had helped pull the bodies of the Chicago SWAT team away from the fires, they tried to revive them. But all the battlefield lifesaving techniques that his people were trained in were of no use. The combination of crushed or damaged organs, internal bleeding, and head trauma had rendered Team Four's meager skills impotent. The responding paramedics, who could do little but cover the few bodies left with sheets until the coroner could arrive and authorize their removal, relieved them a few minutes ago.

For the most part, Mathews' men sat on the ground or on the bumpers of nearby vehicles, hating their own powerlessness. The phone had rung seven times before Mathews answered it.

"Team Four."

"Simon here, status report."

Mathews swallowed hard once before replying. "The HRT and the Chicago PD SWAT team are dead. The building they were entering was wired. Local FBI, ATF, and emergency services are on scene now."

"Was your team involved at all?"

"Negs, we were providing comm and intel support from the local CP when it happened. We rendered what first aid we could before the locals took over."

"Shit," said the colonel from 1,500 miles away. "I'm sorry, but I need you to pull your team together and head for the airport. We lost Team Three in England. I need you to pinch-hit for them."

Mathews shook his head in disbelief. "What happened, sir?"

"Their C-17 crashed after takeoff. The team and all aboard were killed."

"Damn, Colonel. Today's just not our day, is it?"

"No, it isn't, son, but I still need your team in Saudi Arabia. That's where Team Three was headed before the crash."

"Copy that, sir."

"I have a C-17 with a support load-out heading for Midway International now. Two Apaches, one Kiowa, and an Avenger drone are on board along with their flight and support crews. You'll stop at Andrews to recover your gear there and to refuel before hopping the pond. We're also setting up aerial refueling points over the Azores and Mediterranean for you so you can make it nonstop."

"Understood, sir. What's the ETA on the C-17 at Midway?"

"Touchdown is in two hours."

"We'll be ready."

"I know you will, Lieutenant. Out here."

Before the colonel could hang up, Mathews said, "Sir, you didn't authenticate the orders."

"Do I need to after what's just happened today?"

"No, sir, you don't. Team Four is moving."

JOHNSON'S CELL PHONE WAS RINGING. He pulled it from his pocket on the third try—it had been caught in the fabric the first two times. On top of that minor annoyance, room service had just delivered the cheeseburger he was craving for lunch, and he had yet to take a bite. Worrying about his wife was not improving his mood either.

"What?" he almost yelled frustratingly into the phone.

"Special Agent Johnson?" inquired the voice on the distant end of the call.

Uh, oh. "Yes," he said in a more civil tone.

"Hold one for SAIC French."

He headed over to the bed and grabbed the pen and pad the hotel had left on the nightstand. Then he returned to the desk where his cheeseburger was cooling and sat down.

"David?" asked the voice of SAIC French.

"Yes, sir."

"A special military unit is being forward deployed to Saudi Arabia. They'll land in Riyadh in about eighteen hours. Arrange with the Saudis a secure hangar at the airport in Riyadh and hotel rooms for at least fifty people."

"I'll call Akeem and ask him to help me out."

"Good. Provide the team whatever help they require after they arrive. Also, ask the Saudis to share whatever information their intelligence services have about this Aziz with you. Dr. Owens, the national security advisor, will be calling her Saudi counterpart just after 2 P.M. your time and formally requesting Saudi assistance to locate this man."

"Got it, sir," he said, holding the phone between his head and shoulder while he scribbled furiously on the notepad.

"One more thing: when the unit arrives, you want to speak to a navy lieutenant named Mathews; he's in charge. Ask him to show you AUTUMN FIRE Situation Update 01-22. That will bring you up to speed. You are authorized to share it with the Saudis if you believe circumstances warrant it."

"01-22, got it, sir."

"One other thing: do you know anyone on our HRT?"

"No, sir. A couple of academy classmates wanted to try out for the team, but they haven't served enough time in the field yet."

"Well, they might get their chance sooner than they expected. The entire team was killed in Chicago earlier today."

Johnson was dumbfounded. After a moment he asked, "What the hell happened?"

"They executed a stealth entry on a suspected al-Qaeda safe house around dawn this morning. The building was wired with explosives. Our team and the Chicago PD's SWAT team were both killed in the explosion."

"Both of them?"

"Yeah. All sixteen men. Read the update when Mathews and his team get there. If you have any other questions, ask him. He and his unit were on site in a support role when it happened."

"Yes, sir," Johnson intoned as the call disconnected.

AKEEM HUNG UP THE PHONE and looked at the ceiling. Johnson seemed to be a good young man, and he was trying to understand Arab culture, but Americans always wanted things *now*. They were always in such a hurry. In the Arab world, *Insha'Allah*, or "if it is Allah's will" in English, was how everyone always prefaced what they wanted to have happen. This way Allah would invoke his blessing on what you tried to do, especially if it was difficult. If you failed, then what you wanted to do was not what Allah wanted. If it did happen, then Allah had desired that outcome as well as blessed its occurrence. Either way, you could rest well at night knowing that Allah's will had been done.

Insha'Allah, our intelligence services knew something about Aziz, or could find out about him, Akeem hoped. Because Aziz was last known to be in Iran, perhaps the intelligence services had Iranian friends who could be of help.

Reaching for the phone again, he called the Director of the Saudi Intelligence Service and posed Johnson's question to him. The conversation that followed was polite but spirited. The Director or Saudi Intelligence said that he would do what he could, *Insha'Allah*, and hung up. Obtaining the fifty hotel rooms, *Insha'Allah*, would probably be easier.

CHAPTER 19

THE SAUDI AMBASSADOR TO IRAN read the morning's *Iran Javan* with mild satisfaction. *So, the Americans were having a few problems. Good. Perhaps, Insha'Allah, they would finally become less arrogant and a little more respectful of the people in the world who had less. Let them freeze in their homes for a few weeks. Allah has undoubtedly decided to teach them a lesson.*

The ambassador thought back over how many times he had seen the Americans deciding unilaterally what was right and proper for others, especially in the Arab world, yet they never seemed to apply the same restrictions to themselves. No, they considered themselves "civilized" and above reproach. *It is perhaps far overdue that the Americans be humbled, praise be to Allah.*

This nonsense about an Arab living in Iran being behind it all? More American bullying, rather than accepting the blame for their own ignorance and self-righteousness in their diplomatic and military blunders in the Middle East. It was likely all an excuse to lash out at a preferred Middle Eastern enemy than it was the truth. He had told the king that opinion almost two hours ago when he called from the Winter Palace in Riyadh. The king had reminded him, in a polite way, of the debt of friendship the Kingdom owed the Americans and, more important, what the ambassador owed the king for his current position within the Saudi diplomatic corps. The ambassador did not think the first reason was true, but the second certainly was.

Because of that, the lean, autocratic man now suffered through the indignity of a thirty-minute ride over to the Iranian Ministry of Intelligence and Security building to speak to his old friend Nader Maadani, the current head of the MOIS. It was sunny and only 65 degrees in Tehran today, a bit cool for a man raised in the arid heat of Riyadh, where 105-degree days were commonplace, especially in the summer. His driver had thoughtfully turned the climate-control system off to keep the temperature in the cabin closer to 80 degrees in the black Land Rover. The thick, polycarbonate windows in the heavily armored SUV, coupled with the black leather seating, held in the warmth nicely.

The trip to the MOIS headquarters building lasted ten minutes longer than it should have because they had to stop for every light in the busy downtown area. His driver pulled the car up in front of the nine-story main building constructed in the typical fashion of Iranian government facilities. The obligatory pillars of Persian architecture framed the entrance. The large blocky building was desert-colored brownstone and meant to provide the image of imposing power and grandeur that the Iranian regime believed it had.

After pulling into the small traffic circle in front of the building, the driver got out and held the door for his ambassador. Closing it, he began to follow his principal into the building, when the ambassador motioned him to stop.

"Wait here, Jalil. I will say hello to my old friend Nader, and he will no doubt confirm the American's idiocy in short order. I will be back soon."

Jalil nodded his thanks to the ambassador and watched as he ascended the steps from the courtyard. He was met by one of Nader's aides just outside the heavy, four-meter wooden doors leading to the Ministry.

As soon as the ambassador was out of sight, Jalil moved the car down the road toward the corner of the MOIS building. He parked and retrieved the Ambassador's newspaper from the backseat. He had just leaned back against the car to read. And to wait. What he was waiting for took only a couple of minutes.

"Hey! You can't park here." The young man was in his late twenties and wore the precise mustache and crisp uniform of an Iranian army captain. He was speaking Farsi and waiving Jalil away as he approached the car. He had exited the building shortly after seeing the car stop at the far corner of the building.

Jalil feigned annoyance and replied in the same language, "I'm the driver for the Saudi Arabian Ambassador to Iran. He just went in to meet the head of your Ministry. I stay here until he comes back out."

The young man walked closer to Jalil with a similarly feigned stern look and said, "Show me your embassy credentials."

Jalil reached into his suit coat, withdrew his diplomatic passport and his embassy identification, and handed them to the young officer. He was good, Jalil thought. The folded piece of paper tucked into his passport vanished almost as quickly as the captain noticed it.

"These documents are in order," the captain said, "but you should have been told to park back there while you waited." Gesturing back toward the area where Jalil had dropped off the ambassador, the captain handed the passport and identification back to Jalil.

"Please move your car to the proper area."

"Gladly, Captain," said Jalil, and got back in his car.

TRUE TO HIS WORD, THE ambassador did not spend very long with his friend Nader. Forty minutes later, he had left the building and walked toward the car where Jalil was waiting, smoking a cigarette, with the well-read newspaper under his arm. He discarded the cigarette and opened the rear door for the ambassador, who quickly entered the car and motioned imperiously for Jalil to get them going.

As Jalil pulled away from the building, the ambassador started bemoaning the waste of time he had just endured.

"I told you! The Iranians know nothing of this man Aziz. The Americans are so full of themselves. They probably made up this man so they wouldn't have to look themselves in the mirror and realize their own folly. What a waste of time and energy, may Allah forgive it."

The ambassador lapsed into silence for the rest of the ride and looked sullenly out the car window. Jalil hoped his source would find more useful information. Unlike the ambassador, his driver had a more moderate and eye-opening education, conducted at the battle of Ras Al Khafji during the 1991 war. The Americans were not quite the bumbling fools the ambassador believed them to be, and he was far too easily swayed by his prejudices.

Jalil could not be too hard on the man though. He had been very close and protective of the ambassador's younger brother, a new lieutenant in the Saudi National Guard when that maniac in Iraq had chosen to invade Kuwait. The boy had survived the 1991 war only to be killed by a land mine while on patrol at the Kuwait-Iraq border after formal hostilities had ended. The investigation had shown that the land mine was of American manufacture. Jalil knew the Americans were not mining the border area; the Iraqis had bought American-manufactured land mines from their suppliers in the Philippines and buried them all along that area before the invasion. Even the Americans had lost men and vehicles to them.

The ambassador was still staring out the window, his face now slack and sorrowful. He was probably thinking about his young brother. Knowing that this resentment and loss might color his judgment and reports wherever the Americans were concerned, the king had requested that his intelligence services place one or two men in the ambassador's employ to get a more balanced viewpoint of ongoing events in Iran.

THE CTS MORNING BRIEFING GOT off to a late start. The technicians had set the replacement computer up with only minutes to spare. The CTS day-shift team was working on only a few hours of sleep and was still suffering from the emotional effects of watching the two teams get killed yesterday morning. To make matters worse, those events would by necessity be the focus of the day. Eventually, they would grow numb to it, but for now it was still an open wound.

"All right, David," said DIRNSA, grabbing his coffee mug. He had been drinking green tea in the mornings from the Starbucks in the OPS 2 cafeteria, but, since the shit had hit the fan, he had gone back to coffee. Black and strong was the order of the day now. He also had not gone home in three days. He would need to get the sheets on the camp bed in his office changed soon and ask his wife to drop off some fresh clothes at the visitor's gatehouse. His executive officer could run down for them when he had a minute.

Cain was not looking any more rested than his staff, but he had gone home to hug his wife and catch about four hours of sleep before getting back in at five that morning.

"I'll cover what we have and then I'll ask the agency heads to chime in," he said in the direction of the video link. The major telecommunications companies had managed to transport some of their emergency generator vehicles to the major telephone switches in the D.C. and Baltimore areas. They also brought the fuel needed to run them for a few days, so there was no immediate danger of local and long-distance communication going out.

"The search for this Aziz, believed to be responsible for the recent attacks on our power, oil, and heating fuel infrastructure, has not yielded any useful information. We requested support from the Saudi Intelligence Services because they developed the initial information about Aziz and his possible whereabouts. For more information, see CTS messages 01-22 and 02-22. We recovered two hard drives from the destroyed warehouse in Chicago. The FBI lab in Quantico is performing a forensic analysis on them and is receiving technical assistance from the DoD, the computer science laboratories at Carnegie Mellon, and MIT. ATF and FBI investigators on site in Chicago believe the building was wired to explode, possibly as a means to avoid capture, certainly to destroy the facility to limit forensic recovery of evidence. Two bodies were also recovered from the collapsed area of the second, smaller warehouse. Both bodies are badly decomposed, and autopsies are being rushed." Cain paused and looked up into the camera before continuing.

"The last item I have is that the National Guard deployment in the affected mid-Atlantic and northeastern states continues. I'll leave the details to the Pentagon and ask the other agencies to add to the discussion as they feel necessary."

The FBI director chimed in immediately, "The two bodies Mr. Cain mentioned are not related to the assault last night and the subsequent explosions. The decomposition is too advanced, and my agents on the scene tell me they probably died from gunshot wounds to the back of the head. The autopsy will tell us for sure." As he paused, DIRNSA took a moment to comment.

"Terry, I want you and all your people to know that you have the deepest sympathies of my agency and my entire workforce for the losses you suffered last night."

The mood of the meeting immediately became even more somber, resulting in an unplanned moment of silence from all connected on the video link. At the FBI's command center, the director wiped his eyes and nodded his thanks. Having known Sampson for more than twenty years, he had gone to his house to tell his wife and children that he would not be coming home.

The J2, the Chief of Intelligence, currently a three-star Army general at the Pentagon, broke the silence first. "Mr. Director, if you or the Chicago PD need anything from us—transport, technical help, people—just ask."

"Thanks, Mike, Charlie, and everyone. We lost too many good people last night." The director shook his head, and added, "We have nothing more at the moment."

The Secretary of the Department of Homeland Security spoke up next, "We're working to coordinate the movement of utility crews and assist the major power companies in their restoration efforts. Initial estimates from the Department of Energy are placing the outage times at a minimum of three weeks for the major metropolitan areas, and six to eight weeks for the outlying suburbs."

Heads came up on the separate video screens as the enormity of what they had just heard sank in. On the subscreen showing the CIA's conference room, the CIA director pressed the mute button, reactivating their audio feed.

"Can't you just reroute what you need from the western U.S. or Canada?"

The secretary shook his head. "No. The entire western U.S. doesn't have enough capacity to power the eastern half of the country, as well as themselves. Even if they did, it's a moot point. The *infrastructure* that moves electricity around is crippled. That's the key vulnerability. The energy security people in my department and the Department of Energy have been warning about this for years. If you take out enough of the critical infrastructure that moves electricity, gas, coal, fuel around, you can seriously cripple us. That is what has happened. Fortunately, it's only the Northeast and Mid-Atlantic. The real problem is how long it will take to move the replacement equipment in and install it."

He could see from the incredulous looks that most of the audience still didn't get it.

"Look, folks, we are talking about 34,500- and 25,000-volt transformers the size of large cars or vans and their associated substation equipment. This stuff isn't just laying around waiting to be installed. There are a certain number of spares, but not enough for a major outage like this. The equipment will need to be built by companies overseas and in the central and western U.S., since they still have power, and then trucked east and installed. It's going to take time."

The DHS secretary shook his head in frustration. For years, Congress and the government agencies had focused on trying to secure power plants, particularly nuclear reactors, with considerably less attention paid to the equally critical component of the nation's energy infrastructure—the transport and supply portion. The sad part was that even if those were focused on, securing the critical points from a physical security standpoint would require the equivalent of the National Guard's permanent deployment in every state in the Union. That kind of physical security mechanism just was not something Congress was willing to fund, let alone the costs of the security needed for the cyberspace portion like the SCADA systems. Granted, the opinions of the senators and congressional representatives in the affected states were likely to change on that subject, now that they were sitting in the dark.

The navy admiral, currently the Pentagon J-3, Director of Operations, added to the conversation. "We're moving a team from the 152nd Joint Special Missions Unit to Saudi Arabia. Our intent is to pre-position them in case this Aziz can be located by our intelligence services." In reaction to this, the admiral cast a slightly derisive look at the J-2. Certain institutional prejudices, like those between intelligence and operations, would never completely go away.

At this, the CIA director spoke up again, "Any news on that front yet?" His frosty tone betrayed the CIA's general distaste of the FBI being the source for a foreign country's information.

If the FBI director was affected at all by the CIA's concerns, he didn't show it. "Not yet," he replied, and then took the chance to twist the knife a little, "we've asked our Saudi source to see what he can get out of Iran." Just a few of the people on the link winced on the CIA's behalf.

THE YOUNG IRANIAN CAPTAIN WAS risking his life, and he knew it. He was a moderate Shi'a who looked with great distaste upon the Khamenei regime's attitude toward the West. He had attended Tehran University and had the opportunity to have coffee in friends' houses with a number of French and German professors visiting Iran to lecture on literature and the arts.

At first, he disbelieved everything they said about America, its policies, and its actions. He had spent his whole life believing what the great imams in Tehran told the people: America was the Great Satan, bent on destroying the Islamic religion throughout the world. Then, as time went by and he debated these issues with his friends and the visiting professors, he slowly began to change his opinion.

The real turning point had come a few years later when he had gained access to the Internet. As a trusted member of the Ministry of Intelligence and Security, he had been a part of the unit that instituted the firewall controls prohibiting public access to certain parts of the Internet that the government had decided would "improperly influence and expose the Iranian people to Western lies and immoral behavior."

As he worked to help cut off the Iranian people from the insidious websites, he had asked and was given the responsibility for the compilation of the list of those websites. Then he proposed that the MOIS strictly monitor Western news and government websites in order to ensure that the government-controlled Iranian media could filter world news on behalf of the Iranians. MOIS would select the stories, redact any offensive material where needed, and occasionally add the proper "context" for later broadcast or publication by the media in Iran. Approval came rapidly from the MOIS director.

After the initial stages of the project were complete, he had requested and been granted permission to run the unit as it continually monitored the Internet for new offensive material. This position required an Internet connection that bypassed the government firewall. His e-mail was not monitored, and he could surf any website he wanted. Reading all the Western news services every day eventually led him to an inescapable conclusion. It simply wasn't possible for every Western news source to be publishing the same lies, every day. He had even cross-checked some of the stories with similar ones published under different bylines in English-language Pakistani, Indian, and Italian papers. Not only was it informative, but it also gave him a chance to practice his English.

Sitting in his office in the middle of the day, the captain logged on to his MOIS secure computer terminal and leaned back in his wooden desk chair to think. His superiors valued his work, but not his comfort. His office was little larger than the cells where his counterparts in the ministry put prisoners into, and just as sparse. Desk, chair, and one bookshelf, all made of inexpensive wood. An ancient safe that probably dated to the time of the Shah sat on the bare tile floor, and a photo of his parents were the only other objects in the room. The books on the shelves were bound editions of Iranian legal codes, ministry regulations, and a copy of the Qur'an he read during his brief lunch breaks.

All his Saudi contact had given him was a partial name and a partial Tehran area phone number. Fortunately, the MOIS internal computer network could access passport control records, telephone records, and government records for the various social programs. The Captain snorted at the memory of how naïve he had been once. When he was a young boy, he remembered how overjoyed he had been to learn that the government had promised pensions and medical care to the entire nation, in the name of proper Islamic charity. But, as a captain in the MOIS, he understood that the personal information collected for these programs was used to monitor Iranian citizens, because it provided a huge database of names, addresses, phone numbers, and travel records. It was a long shot, but he decided to query the social programs database first. In order to cover his tracks, he would order the computers to search for all the names, addresses, and other pertinent information for anyone in the Tehran area whose phone number began with 98 21 333. As he pressed the graphic symbol to start the search, he breathed, "Insha'Allah."

A few minutes later, the computer provided him a list of some 20,000 people. He groaned inwardly and then leaned back, thinking. He could input the first name and rerun the query, but that would leave a trace in the logs that might point back to him. Instead, he asked the software to provide the list in spreadsheet format.

A few moments later, he had the spreadsheet open before him and used the sort function to list the names alphabetically by first name. There were four people named Aziz on the list, thanks be to Allah. As he reviewed them, his eyes were drawn to one record with a flag on it. The flag denoted a special relationship with the government of Iran. It was a warning to all MOIS personnel that if this man were arrested, he was to be released at once. If his name had come up in an investigation, the ministry officer should seek his superior's guidance quickly. In short, it meant, "hands off." Only the Director of the MOIS could put this kind of flag on a person's record. This had to be the Aziz his Saudi friend wanted to know about.

He had a name, an address, and a phone number. It would be better, though, if he could get a face—the note had said, "Full details needed." The easiest way would be to search the passport database for the name, which would get him a passport photo. The drawback was that searches in the passport database were also logged and would lead back to him.

It took a few minutes and a trip to the men's room before he hit on a way to get the photo. Choosing three names off the list at random, he called the passport control office and requested travel habits and copies of the passports for the three random names and for Aziz Abdul Muhammad. He stated his reason as a check of international travel and activities related to suspect Internet activity. Many such requests were made every day, and his request would very likely be lost among all the others.

Two hours later, he had the electronic images of the passports for all four men.

THIRTY MILES AWAY IN HIS embassy office, Jalil's e-mail software set off an electronic *ping* on his computer as a new e-mail was downloaded from the embassy's public Internet server. He walked over to his laptop, sat down behind his lacquered wooden desk, and opened the e-mail. While he waited for the virus scanner and then the commercial decryption software to finish their work, he began worrying about the young captain's safety.

During their last clandestine meeting in a quiet park, Jalil offered to establish a more secure dead drop somewhere in the city, but the captain had assured Jalil that his access to the web-based e-mail services was not monitored. Moreover, his access to the encryption program was easily explained. After all, as an MOIS officer, he needed to understand how Iranian citizens might try to hide things from the Iranian regime. Jalil had told him to be careful and had worked out a duress phrase for the e-mail communications between them. If the captain were compromised, the duress phrase wouldn't appear in the first line of the e-mail. If Jalil saw that, the best he could do was pray for the young man's soul. Helping him get out of Iran would be impossible at that point.

When the decryption program finished, Jalil took a few minutes to read the e-mail, breathing a sigh of relief when he saw the quote from the Qur'an in the first line. Then he cut and pasted the relevant text and image into a fresh e-mail, ran it through the separate encryption program he used to communicate with Saudi intelligence, and forwarded it to an e-mail address in the headquarters of the Saudi Diplomatic Corps. The email left Jalil's computer on the internal embassy network connection and then headed out of Tehran via an encrypted satellite link on the embassy roof.

In the Saudi Diplomatic Corps headquarters, the satellite antenna received the signal from Arabsat's BADR-6 satellite in geosynchronous orbit and sent it to the main e-mail server. The server recognized the inbound e-mail from the Tehran embassy, evaluated its destination address, and automatically routed it via secure landline to the headquarters of Saudi Intelligence, where the Iranian desk officer opened it immediately.

He spent ten minutes typing up a formal report listing the full name, address, telephone number, and photograph of the Iranian citizen that he had been told was most urgent by his section head. When he was finished, he proofread it and transmitted the report directly to the Chief of Saudi Intelligence, the Foreign Minister, and the Chief of the Interior Ministry. Ten minutes after that, Akeem was called to his minister's office.

JOHNSON HAD MANAGED TO FIND a couple of Chevy Suburbans in white, which seemed to be the only color of rental cars in the Kingdom, and asked the OIC of the Marine guard force if he could borrow one of his men for a few hours. The major agreed, but only after Johnson told him he would be helping a military unit that was landing that afternoon.

He had also managed to borrow a couple of coolers full of ice from the embassy mess and buy about two dozen one-liter bottles of water from a nearby store. Making the purchase had given him a chance to practice his Arabic; luckily the store owner spoke good English. The Arabic lettering on the bottles still fascinated him. He took a moment to admire it before stuffing the last of the bottles into the coolers and heading off to the Riyadh airport.

He sat in the lead Suburban, which he had parked near the corner of a huge hangar to the east of Runway 01, the air conditioning running on medium. The airport's operations manager assured him that the C-17 would park there and use that hangar for its stay in the Kingdom.

It took about thirty minutes of checking his watch and squinting into the low afternoon sun before he saw the massive four-engine aircraft in the distance. He could see that its landing gear was down and its landing lights shimmered in the heat rising off the Saudi landscape as it made its approach.

The C-17 touched down in the middle of the second set of white stripes on Runway 01 and rolled out the next 2,900 feet to Taxiway Charlie, where it turned right and then right again onto Taxiway Alpha to go back the way it came. When it was precisely parallel to its touchdown point, it turned left and pulled into the parking spot the Saudi Air Force ground crew indicated.

When its wheels were chocked, the engines began to cease their steady whine. The plane's side door slid inward and then upward, and the aircraft's loadmaster immediately jumped to the concrete tarmac. He quickly checked the chocks, the power cart, air-conditioning hookups, and finally the electrical grounding before signaling the pilot, who cut the last engine and turned off the auxiliary power unit in the base of the three-story tail. Johnson turned off the Suburban's engine and got out of the vehicle.

By now, men in black fatigues wearing sidearms were exiting the aircraft, stretching, squinting into the sun, and donning sunglasses. A few of them noticed Johnson approaching.

"Lieutenant Mathews?" Johnson called out.

As the young officer walked over to him, Johnson thought he noticed two of the men behind Mathews shift their positions to the left, their hands drifting near, but not quite touching, their pistols. Covering their officer perhaps?

Mathews slowly withdrew his credentials from the pocket of his shirt, glad he remembered to take them out of his suit coat, which he had left in the Suburban.

"I'm Special Agent Dave Johnson. I'm leading the INHERITOR investigation for the Bureau. My SAIC, Steven French, told me to meet you and provide all the help I can."

"That's news to me, Agent Johnson." Mathews was giving Johnson's credentials a good long look.

"Maybe this will help. I was told to ask you to show me AUTUMN FIRE Situation Update 01-22. If that doesn't help, you can call home and check on me, I suppose."

At the mention of this piece of classified information, Mathews' eyebrows raised in surprise. "It adds to the confusion actually, but I'll accept that you are genuine for now and verify that as soon as our comms are set up."

"You do that. In the meantime, I've arranged permission from the Saudi government for you to park here and use the hangar behind us as a base of operations. I've also got fifty hotel rooms reserved in the Hilton downtown and two Suburbans for your use."

Mathews nodded as he looked over the SUVs and the hangar. The Saudi Air Force guys were rolling the doors open now. The hangar was empty and fairly large, but it wouldn't hold the C-17. This guy was probably legit, but he wanted to hear it from Colonel Simon, just to be sure, especially before he handed the man any classified information.

"All right, Agent Johnson, what else do you have for us?"

Grinning, Johnson answered, "How about some cold water?"

At that, Mathews smiled and finally held out his hand, which Johnson shook immediately. The agent was passing out the bottled water to Mathews and his men when Akeem called his cell phone.

CHAPTER 20

· ·

CAIN STOOD AT THE TOP of the steps leading down to the operations floor in the CTS, the center of a maelstrom of activity. His people were talking to the watch standers in the command centers of the agencies they liaised for via the ring-down phones, coordinating last-minute notifications and requesting any information that might be pertinent to the impending operation. A high-resolution digital map of Tehran and its surrounding suburbs was visible on the left display, with a thick red circle electronically drawn around a small portion of it. On the right screen was an enlarged area within the circle that covered a single half mile to the west-southwest of Tehran, between the towns of Ba Ba Salman and Deh Maviz.

The street address provided by the Saudis by way of the FBI's Agent Johnson had reached them through the Wraith team sitting on the airfield at Riyadh. Almost immediately, the CIA liaison, Roger Jones, had typed the address into Google Earth to obtain a set of geo-coordinates for Aziz's probable address. A few minutes after CTS had issued AUTUMN FIRE message 03-18 with the address and geo-coords, CIA had confirmed them, which meant that they had probably typed them into Google Earth too.

Cain's deputy had just gotten off the phone with the people at the National Photographic Intelligence Center and was sitting at his computer waiting to pounce on the e-mail they had promised would contain the hi-res digital photos of the area. The NPIC folks had promised rapid action on the CTS request. When they had arrived, Goodman would send them out as part of AUTUMN FIRE message 04-18, already typed up on his computer.

The other intelligence agencies had nothing to add just yet. Cain hoped that would change soon. They would be briefing National Security Advisor Owens in a little less than three hours.

HALFWAY AROUND THE WORLD, THE Avenger support team was busy too. They had just finished showing the Saudi airmen how to fuel the drone and had politely, but firmly, ushered the Saudis away when the tanks had been filled. After the refueling crew had left the immediate area, the support team began rolling a dayglow-orange-colored cart with two olive green GBU-12 Paveway bombs on it under the right wing of the drone.

After they jockeyed it into position under the wing's hard points, two of the support crew's experts screwed long metal pipes into the threaded openings in the nose and tail. When fully seated, the pipes gave the three men and two woman of the crew the lift points they needed to pick the 500-pound bomb up off the cart and hold it steady on their shoulders, while one of them completed the attachment of the bomb to the hard point. After it was securely attached, they removed the metal pipes and began fitting the guidance fins to the rear and the laser homing package to the nose of the weapon in the same threaded holes. When they were finished, they returned the cart with the lone Paveway missile to the cargo plane's interior and returned with another orange cart holding eight midnight-black AGM-114 Hellfire missiles.

Each Hellfire weighed only a hundred pounds. Two team members lifted two of the AGM-114 missiles into place simultaneously under the left wing, while another completed the attachment to the two available hard points. After the two Hellfire missiles were in place, the support crew began the Avenger's preflight checkout.

Behind them, the Wraiths clustered around a laptop with a seventeen-inch display showing the digital imagery of Aziz Abdul Muhammad's home.

"This is the latest imagery available?" inquired Mathews.

"Yes, sir," replied the team NCOIC. "It came in a few minutes ago from CTS as part of AUTUMN FIRE message 04-22. They got the hi-res shots from NPIC. The dates on the shots are fewer than three weeks old. The real question is: is Mr. Aziz at home to greet us if we get asked to pay him a visit?"

"We don't know yet. Assuming we can sneak it through the Iranian air defense system, the Avenger will give us some nice real-time imagery before the assault, but it can't tell us if he's in the building. A thermal blob of a human doesn't come with a name tag attached on the display." Frowning, Mathews turned to Johnson, who was standing among his team members.

"Think your Saudi friends can find out for us?"

Johnson had no idea, but he replied in the only way he could when a member of his country's military asked for help. "I'll ask," he said, reaching for his cell phone. Speed-dial number three was now assigned to Akeem's home phone.

THE REQUEST MOVED QUICKLY FROM Akeem to his minister to the Saudi intelligence director and then the diplomatic e-mail channels to Jalil. He'd been playing solitaire on his computer when the e-mail came in. Putting the game in the background, he opened the e-mail and uttered a series of curses in Arabic that he would have been very ashamed of had his mother been present. These immediate action requests were never good. It would place the young Iranian captain in great danger to have him act on this now, but orders were orders, so Jalil took a few moments to add some cautionary language to the request before encrypting it and sending it to the public account his source used.

THE CAPTAIN HAD JUST REACHED for his monitor to shut it off for the night when he saw the little tan envelope icon in the system tray appear, indicating that he had a new e-mail in his public account. Wondering if it might be a note from that girl in Kuwait he'd seen on the Islamic personals site, he brought up the account and was sur-

prised to see that it was from his Saudi friend. His eyes grew wide after
he read it.

He wants me to do what? How in Allah's name do I do that without
knocking on the door and asking for him? The young officer was stunned.
Going to the house was out of the question. He had no plausible reason
for doing so. He would be discovered, most certainly. He frowned and
began to wonder if he had made a mistake in choosing to provide his
Saudi friend information. He had no wish to be killed by the government he had come to despise.

He could ignore the message and cut off all contact with the Saudi.
That would be the safer course of action. Carrying out his latest instructions would invite discovery and a quick death. Thinking carefully, he
decided to wait a few hours and then send his Saudi friend a carefully
worded e-mail before he left for the day.

JALIL HAD DECIDED TO PLAY chess instead of solitaire while he
waited and almost had the computer checkmated when the response
came in. Glancing at it, he nodded appreciatively at the contents, mildly
surprised that the young man had managed to find out so quickly. He
must have done something very risky. He uttered a silent prayer for the
young captain's safety before re-encrypting it and sending it to Saudi
Arabia through the diplomatic channel.

JOHNSON'S PHONE RANG. HE GLANCED at it quickly and saw
Akeem's number.

"Yes, my friend," he answered in his best Arabic.

"You are getting better," was Akeem's response in English. The agent's
pronunciation was something children would laugh at, but he didn't
want to dampen the man's enthusiasm by telling him.

"*Shokran,*" Johnson said, switching back to English, "that's still about
my limit. What's up?"

"Our source tells us that your friend Aziz is at home."

"Really? That's great. I have some friends who want to meet him.
Will you mind if I give them directions from your house to his?"

There was a pause as Akeem considered the implication of the request. A request for U.S. forces to launch a military operation from Saudi Arabia would normally come from the U.S. military liaison in the embassy. But in this case, his new American friend seemed to be applying an Arab approach to the issue. Asking as one friend to another ensured that an informal "no" would not become an official diplomatic embarrassment. *This young man learns quickly.*

"I'll ask the head of my family and get back to you soon."

"*Shokran,* my friend."

"YOU DID WHAT?" SAIC FRENCH practically screamed at him.

Johnson winced at the tone and managed not to take the phone away from his ear. In spite of that, he could tell from the look on Mathews' face that, even standing six feet away from him, he'd heard the question.

He started to explain "Sir, that's how . . . "

SAIC French cut him off, his voice still strident and now about ten decibels louder in Johnson's ear. "Special Agent Johnson, who do you think you are? Last time I checked, you weren't elected president, or appointed SECDEF or SECSTATE, so what in God's name possessed you to make you *think* you could make that kind of request?"

Johnson swallowed hard and began his explanation, his voice cracking a little as he started, "Sir, I've learned a little about Saudi culture since I've been here. Out here, friends help one another out. Friends can ask *informally* the things that can't be asked formally because they might cause embarrassment if there is a formal refusal. I asked my friend if his government would mind. He'll ask quietly, informally, and if he tells me no, then the SECSTATE or the president won't be embarrassed when they ask formally for Saudi help and get a refusal."

The exhalation of breath on the other end of the line while SAIC French absorbed this made Johnson wonder if he had killed his career. After a moment or two of consideration, SAIC French spoke.

"Special Agent Johnson, for the moment, I'll accept your explanation. I do know enough about Saudi culture to understand what you're saying, but if this blows up, you will pay for it. You're sure Mr. Akeem considers you a personal friend?"

"He invited me into his home, sir."

"Hmm, well that is at least a sign of more than just a passing acquaintance. Did you meet his family?"

"Yes. I met his children and very briefly his wife—only to thank her for the meal, and then she left us alone."

"Well, let's hope you're right. You call me back the moment you hear from him. Depending on the response, you may want to work for the Department of State instead of the Bureau." French broke the connection.

Johnson closed his cell phone and stood there for a moment. His boss's implication was clear: if he wanted to keep working for the Bureau, next time he would check in first before making any more informal requests of a nation's government on behalf of his country.

THE PRESIDENT'S NATIONAL SECURITY ADVISOR would be on the video link in a few minutes. Everyone was ready and in place. Cain had copies of all the AUTUMN FIRE messages in front of him, and Goodman had provided copies to the DIRNSA when he had walked in. Goodman then seated himself in the back row of the conference room, pad and pen in hand ready to take notes. All the other agencies had dialed in to the conference and had been waiting for the White House side of the link to become active.

A male voice came through the speakers in the room, "This is White House Communications. We'll be up in sixty seconds. We are resetting our crypto."

Cain cleared his throat and clasped his hands together. *The comm guys at the White House must be having trouble with their encryption gear.* Thirty seconds later, he realized it was more than that.

The White House video feed appeared from the Situation Room in the basement. Cain could see the president seated at the head of the conference table, his national security advisor seated to his left, and the vice president seated to his right. Other members of the president's inner circle filled the remaining leather chairs. The president and the others in the room were not wearing jackets. A few of the men had their shirt sleeves rolled up. Everyone looked as haggard as Cain felt. He also noticed on all the other video displays the principals of the other agencies sitting up a little straighter. Some tried to adjust their ties or put down cups of coffee.

Naturally, the president started the conversation. "People, I'm told you can clue me in as to who is behind the attacks on our country. Start talking." His brusque manner bespoke little sleep and patience for the usual formalities as loudly as the thirty-six hours of stubble on his face did.

Cain looked at DIRNSA, who just nodded his head.

"Mr. President, I'm David Cain, Director of the CTS hosted at NSA. It's our responsibility to coordinate the information we have available, so I'll give you a summary of what we know."

The president nodded. "Keep it a short summary, Mr. Cain. Several million of our citizens are cold and in the dark and I don't want to keep them waiting for answers."

"Yes, sir. The Saudis have developed information, provided via the FBI, which leads us to believe a man named Aziz Abdul Muhammad Al-Zahiri is probably behind the assaults on the strategic petroleum reserve, the national home heating oil reserve in the Northeast, and the cyber attack on our power grid. He may also be responsible for the random shootings in several of our cities and the bombings in San Antonio. We believe, based on the information from the Saudis, that Aziz is the inheritor of al-Qaeda's monetary wealth, and he may have reconstituted the al-Qaeda organization to carry out these attacks."

The president looked slowly at his inner circle around the table, a look of undisguised distain in his eyes, and then back at the camera in the Situation Room. "That is an interesting statement, Mr. Cain. Tell me why a terrorist organization believed to be predominantly destroyed, and that none of my advisors has told me was a resurgent threat, is behind these events." On his left, Dr. Owens winced as she made notes in her portfolio. She would be getting chewed out immediately after this meeting. Of course, she would return the favor for the directors of CIA, DIA, and NSA and the Director of National Intelligence as soon as the president had finished with her.

"Yes, sir. This information has only recently become known, Mr. President. The FBI was conducting a routine review of the al-Qaeda organization to ensure that nothing had been missed. That review led their lead investigator, a Special Agent Dave Johnson, to Guantanamo, where he interviewed a man who extorted shopkeepers and other Afghanis on behalf of the Taliban Finance Minister. The results of these interviews led him to Saudi Arabia, where he provided the Saudi government with information that led to the capture of the former Taliban finance minister, one Sadig al-Faisal. The Saudi interrogation of al-Faisal revealed that a man named 'Aziz' had obtained access to the money that Bin Laden and his second-in-command, Ayman al-Zawahiri, had squirreled away. This al-Faisal also revealed a partial telephone number for Aziz."

The president leaned forward. "Was NSA able to do anything with the phone number?"

Before General Holland could answer, the FBI director chimed in. "No, sir. The Saudis managed to track this Aziz with a HUMINT source they have in Iran."

Cain stole a quick glance at the DIRNSA and saw a very grim face. Trying to move the conversation past this quickly to save his host some embarrassment, he continued. "The Saudi HUMINT source in Iran has been able to positively identify Aziz as Aziz Abdul Muhammad Al-Zahiri and has located his house outside of Tehran. He's there now."

The president leaned back in his chair and looked at his advisors. "Opinions? Recommendations?"

The people around the conference table began to talk while Dr. Owens leaned toward the camera and said, "Stand by." She then pressed a button on the console in front of her to mute the sound from the White House.

Cain touched a similar control in front of him, muting the CTS side of the link, and then turned to General Holland. "Sorry about that, General."

"No sweat, David. It's not your fault. I'll be having a few words with my division chiefs after this, though."

Cain went back to sorting through his notes, occasionally glancing up at the screen for the White House to return to the conference. Some of the president's advisors were gesturing animatedly and obviously going back and forth over something. After nearly ten minutes of discussion, Dr. Owens touched the control again. Cain did the same in CTS.

Again, the president started the conversation. "All right, I need a confidence level from each of the agency heads. Question: Based on what we know now, how confident are you that this Aziz is responsible for the apparent attacks on our nation? CIA?"

The director of the CIA looked around his conference table and got several affirmative nods. "Mr. President, CIA believes the information to be reasonably reliable, but not conclusive yet."

Cain thought that was nicely phrased. CIA agreed but had left itself wiggle room if it came to a congressional hearing. The president's chagrined expression seemed to indicate that he noted the same thing. "DIA?"

The DIA director didn't even hesitate. "We've discussed this information at some length, sir. We believe the information is reliable. We don't think it rises to the level required in a courtroom, sir, but we don't render legal opinions." Cain lowered his head to hide a small smile. The director wasn't a lawyer, but he sure as hell knew the president better get some legal advice before he did whatever he was thinking about—he just couldn't come right out and say it.

"NSA?"

DIRNSA was equally quick to respond. "The information does seem to be accurate, and it would certainly take considerable monetary and logistical resources to carry out these attacks."

"DNI?"

The National Intelligence director took a moment before looking toward the camera. He was listening to a subordinate finish a point in his ear. "Mr. President, I will not disagree with the heads of our intelligence agencies. What I will do is point out in the strongest possible terms that there is no information yet confirming that this man Aziz is behind these attacks. Any assertion that he is behind them is an analytic leap with no supporting information. At the present time, we have no conclusive proof what organization, if any, is behind the attacks on our nation. Not one person involved in these events has been arrested, or interrogated. No intelligence source has provided anything other than the fact that this Aziz is probably an al-Qaeda operative, and is likely in possession of the funds of a previously known terrorist organization. Even that is from only one source. You need to take that into account before you issue any orders."

The president nodded as the DNI spoke and paused to consider all of the departments' words before speaking. "Ladies and gentlemen, our nation has been attacked. We have nothing other than this to go on. The repair and reconstitution of our electric power infrastructure will continue. I will be speaking directly with Homeland Security and FEMA immediately after this session. While it is clear that this Aziz is associated with al-Qaeda, it is not positive proof of his involvement. I believe it likely, however, based on what I have heard here."

The president paused again, gathering his thoughts. "Because we do not have positive proof, I will not order an air or missile strike on this man. Capturing him seems to be the best course of action considering he is a known al-Qaeda member, and we need to know what he's done with the money he received from Bin Laden. If we develop information that he is behind these recent attacks on our nation during his interrogation, so much the better. As it is unlikely that Iran will hand him over to us if we ask, we will have to go in and get him."

GENERAL CRANE RAN UP THE stairs nestled against the 747-400ER and entered the forward passenger door on the left side of the aircraft, just behind where the first-class cabin would normally be. The flight crew was already turning over the engines on the 910,000-pound aircraft when Crane headed up the interior spiral stairs to the nerve center of the flying command post and medical facility.

The Airman First Class handling cargo master duties for the forward section secured the passenger door and called up to the flight deck to inform the command pilot that the general was aboard. The pilots completed their taxi checklist, and the pilot called into the base tower. "SAM 2, ready to roll." A few moments later, the giant doors of the hangar began to open.

The massive 747-400ER had been pulled from its parking slot on the left side of the hangar and positioned in front of the massive hangar doors. It was liveried in gleaming white paint and bore the recently applied black "Air Cargo Ltd" ten feet high on both sides of the fuselage.

As soon as the hangar doors cleared the Boeing's 211-foot span, the pilot moved the throttles forward to the midway point, and the thrust of the four General Electric CF6-80 high bypass turbofans began to move the aircraft out of the hangar. When the aircraft was rolling at five miles per hour, the pilot reduced the throttles to near idle to maintain momentum and looked left and right to check the clearance of both wingtips. The copilot checked the right side, called out "Clear" so the pilot knew he was good on the right side, and then resumed setting IFF codes and presetting radio frequencies.

When clear of the hangar, the pilot guided the aircraft slightly to the right, heading across the large, open concrete pad for nearly a mile before reaching Taxiway Echo. He centered the 747 on Echo and headed south on it and then turned right onto Taxiway Bravo, heading west. After a half mile, the pilot turned left to approach Runway 90. Normally, the colonel driving the 747 would be calling into the tower for departure clearance about now, but this was not a normal airfield.

As the aircraft reached the yellow markings on the edge of the runway that indicated the hold short area, the tower called out, "SAM 2, winds light and variable from the north, clear for takeoff." The colonel immediately turned left onto the runway, pressed the button on his microphone for the cabin speakers, and announced, "We're clear for takeoff, everyone strap in." As he straightened the 747 out on the runway heading, he pressed the button for the radio and said, "SAM 2, rolling." Advancing the throttles to the stops and then pulling them back to above idle, he listened for the telltale signs of engine failure and looked at the engine gauges. Hearing and seeing nothing amiss, he called out, "Checklist complete?"

"Checklist complete," responded the copilot.

Advancing the throttles to 40 percent rated power, and leaving the brakes locked, he watched the engine gauges as the numbers slowly spun toward the 40 percent mark. Trying to get a loaded 747 from zero to takeoff speeds without bringing it to 40 percent first guaranteed an aborted takeoff or crash.

When the numbers on the four turbofans hit the 40 percent point, he released the brakes and pushed the throttles to the stops. The 747's four engines immediately began pouring more of their combined 260,000 pounds of thrust into accelerating the jet down the runway to takeoff speed. A minute later, the flight crew was retracting the landing gear and the flaps. As the aircraft climbed through 5,000 feet into the clear afternoon sky, the copilot activated the IFF transponder and nodded to the pilot. The pilot keyed his radio and checked in with air traffic control before keying the cabin microphone.

"General Crane, approximately thirteen hours to our mission orbit."

In the rear of the 747, General Crane sat strapped into his chair next to his mission-planning table on the upper deck, immediately behind the pilots. His communications team worked along the rear wall with their gear setting up secure video, data, and voice links with their home base, the Pentagon's watch center, and CTS at NSA.

Down on the first deck, occupying the midsection and rear of the aircraft, the onboard medical team prepped their area. Doctors and nurses worked together, securing whole blood in built-in refrigerators, checking stores of medications, surgical instruments, and prepackaged supplies, and sterilizing the two surgical suites.

In the forward area, two of the loadmasters began dropping pillows and blankets on bunks built into the walls. These would be places for weary crew members to sleep or for the wounded to rest after treatment from the medical staff.

The phone in front of the general rang and he pounced on it. "Yes."

"Sir," said the technician thirty feet away, "I have Wraith Team Four on the line."

"Wraith One, this is Apollo. How copy?"

More than 7,000 miles away in Riyadh, Mathews replied, "Wraith One copies you five by five, Apollo. Go ahead."

"Wraith One, I have orders for you and your friend from the Bureau."

NINE HOURS LATER, IN KUWAIT, two other flight crews received orders as well. Both had been looking forward to a night off duty, traveling the streets of Kuwait City in search of inexpensive gold in the souks, or having a few near beers in the club, when their squadron commanders and first sergeants had tracked them down.

After a very short and very pointed briefing, they donned their flight gear and headed out to their aircraft to find the ground crews topping off the tanks.

The CV-22B Osprey Tilt Rotor aircraft was a giant—it had to be. Operated by the Air Force's 650th Special Operations Squadron, its job was to take American Special Forces behind enemy lines, even in the middle of a hurricane or typhoon, if necessary. Each could carry thirty-two fully armed commandos, plus its four-person flight crew of pilots, engineers, and gunners, 390 miles without refueling. With the help of an MC-130P Combat Shadow for in-flight refueling, its range was limited only by the flight crew's endurance. The Osprey was unique because it looked like a normal turboprop airplane, but with props nearly twice the normal diameter. The size of the props and the ability of each engine nacelle to rotate 90 degrees vertically allowed it to be both a fixed-wing aircraft and helicopter.

Ten minutes after the crews had boarded, each of the aircraft's two Rolls-Royce Allison turboshaft engines were running at takeoff power settings. The 33,000-pound tilt rotors smoothly lifted off the concrete landing pads into the deepening Kuwaiti night and turned west to clear the airfield. When they were five miles away, at a cruising altitude of 10,000 feet, they turned northwest and began to run flat out at nearly 250 knots. Their first midair refueling point was four hours away, just east of Kirkuk, in northern Iraq.

CHAPTER 21

. . . .

"WHERE'S EMILY?" CAIN WAS LOOKING around the CTS watch floor, directing his question at Goodman.

Mike looked up from the AUTUMN FIRE messages he was reviewing. "No idea. Everybody's tried to catch some sleep over the last ten hours, but we're all pretty wrung out. She probably stepped out for some fresh air or to the ladies' room before we lock down."

Cain frowned, but not for long. He wanted to lock down the CTS now, but considering the circumstances, it could wait. Mike was right, he had been pushing his people hard since the disaster in Chicago, and last-minute bathroom breaks were an expected part of the routine, especially when knowing that certain events were going to take place at particular times. His primary team had been working long hours, and most of them were sleeping in the conference room when it was not in use. The married ones had headed home, when they could, except for Emily. It seemed she wanted to be there for everything; and since Chicago, she had been helping in any way she could. She had run errands for Mr. Goodman to other NSA offices when she wasn't officially on duty, even helped make some of the chow runs to the NSA cafeteria for pizza and Mountain Dew. The pile of pizza boxes out in the hallway near the door had become a monument to the long hours of his people.

After a few minutes, Emily came back in and headed for her position. She would be handling the Avenger's sensors and weapons for the first time in a live environment, and Cain decided that he would keep a weather eye on her during the operation, just in case.

Emily sat in front of her computer and got ready. She would *not* make a mistake again. She triple-checked the settings on her computer and saw that she had an hour before she would take control of the Avenger's systems.

As long as she stayed busy, the voice in her head stayed quiet. She wanted to see how this would play out; right now, she could not go home and look at her son or into her husband's eyes. They would see the guilt in her eyes. She did when she looked in the mirror.

The accusing voice was starting again: *"The floor plans were wrong."* She didn't notice how hard she was squeezing the mouse until she heard the case crack. The sound pulled her back into the present, and with effort, she focused on her work, calling up the latest images from NPIC that Mr. Goodman had sent out. She needed to be very familiar with the area around the target.

THE PILOT OF THE 747-400ER fought to hold the huge airliner steady against the buffeting generated by the wake turbulence from the KC-45 air refueling tanker. Both aircraft were at 30,000 feet over Iraq, just west of Baghdad heading northeast toward Kirkuk. They were connected in flight by the KC-45A's long aerial refueling probe, which was firmly seated in the receptacle on the centerline of the 747's roof, ten feet behind the pilots on the upper deck. This was their third refueling in more than eleven hours. Fortunately, both men had caught catnaps during the flight.

The copilot was watching the fuel gauges along with the engineer, seated directly behind him staring at his instrument set along the right wall of the flight deck. The 747 had taken on nearly 50,000 pounds of JP-8 from the KC-45A, and it was almost time to disconnect. The copilot looked at the pilot and said, "On-load complete." Then he leaned forward and blinked a small flashlight at the boom operator's window in the belly of the KC-45A. Its beam was easily visible to the enlisted man in the KC-45A. Seeing the flashes, he turned off the fuel flow and then retracted the boom's probe from the 747's receptacle.

The pilot of the 747 nudged the aircraft's nose down a little, and the giant aircraft began to lose altitude in relation to the KC-45A, which held its altitude. It was dangerous enough refueling midair in the near dark, especially without radio communications. If the Iranians, or anybody else for that matter, heard the 747 talking to a U.S. Air Force airborne tanker, the mission's Operational Security, or OPSEC, would be compromised. For that reason, the KC-45A maintained radio silence as they approached, and the copilot made contact via flashlight with the boom operator. The operator had kept the KC-45A's pilots aware of what was going on behind and below them. Soon, the 747 would disappear entirely.

WRAITH TEAM FOUR WAS ALSO airborne. They had slept for several hours and then stood by to watch the Avenger launch a couple of hours before they took off. This time they observed from the passenger compartment of a Saudi Airlines Airbus 320 that was on a regularly scheduled flight from Riyadh to Baku, Azerbaijan, on the Caspian Sea. The Wraith team members were the only ones onboard, which had come as a bit of a surprise to the flight crew. Rather than loading passengers at Riyadh International's terminal, the airline's terminal supervisor ordered the cabin attendants off the aircraft, and then ordered the crew to taxi over to the military side of the airfield.

When they reached the other side of the airfield, the pilot and copilot took a personal phone call from the king. Thirty minutes later, the plane was airborne, flying its usual route to Baku.

The Wraiths sat all the way in the rear of the jet, the cabin lights dimmed. They were passing around the photograph the Saudis had given Agent Johnson. Studying it would help them tell the wolf from the sheep when they reached Aziz's house. They sipped sodas and checked weapons and other equipment while the A320 flew north over Al Basrah, in southern Iraq, where it turned northeast on the air route to Esfahan, Iran.

THE 747 WAS JUST FINISHING its descent into the military airbase at

Kirkuk as one of the techs at the comm gear near the back wall of the upper deck gave General Crane a thumbs-up.

Crane adjusted the headset he was wearing and took another sip of the coffee he'd grabbed from the galley before heading to the upper deck. He had slept restlessly for ten hours on the way across the Atlantic and Mediterranean, extremely concerned about Team Four. Mathews was a new team leader, and he should have had more seasoning before leading his team into this situation.

"Charlie One, this is Apollo. How copy?"

The encrypted signal left the satellite dish in the aerodynamic fairing on the base of the plane's tail and passed up to the military satellite, down to the Pentagon, and then across an encrypted fiber-optic link to CTS, where it was decrypted in less than two seconds. Cain depressed the switch on his microphone, "Apollo, Charlie One copies you five by five. Are we still on schedule?"

"Affirmative. We should hear from Whiskey One in three hours or so. Apollo will be on orbit in an hour."

Crane heard, "Charlie One copies, standing by," as the 747's main gear touched down on Kirkuk's military airfield with the expected solid thump that shook the airframe and passengers.

Rather than decelerating, the pilot let the plane roll at zero throttle for 1,000 feet while his copilot reset the flaps to a takeoff configuration and then firewalled the engines. The 747 raced down the remaining length of the runway and took off again with 3,000 feet of concrete to spare.

On the flight deck, the copilot adjusted the IFF code and nodded at the pilot. The pilot called in, "Kirkuk Departure, this is Mobile-61, with you."

"Mobile-61," replied the U.S. Air Force controller, who had just been briefed by his major, "this is Kirkuk Departure, fly runway heading, climb at your discretion to flight level 390. Resume own navigation to Orbit Racetrack above 10,000."

"Fly runway heading, climb to flight level 390, resume own navigation to Orbit Racetrack above 10,000, Mobile-61," replied the pilot. Barring warnings about other aircraft in their airspace, he would not make another radio transmission until they departed the empty airspace near the Iranian border known as Orbit Racetrack.

On the ground, the flight controller's major had just left the air traffic control center. This ATC in Iraq was one of the few that the U.S. Air Force still held for its own use under the military assistance agreement worked out between the U.S. and Iraqi governments. It allowed the U.S. to watch the airspace of both Iran and Syria from a safe observation point, and for U.S. military aircraft to transit Iraqi airspace with a minimum of questions or red tape.

As the major departed, the flight controller remembered a line uttered by a naval officer on a destroyer in an old movie about a submarine being hijacked by its officers as a gift for the U.S. government. *"I was never here."*

He shook his head with a rueful smile and went back to watching the radar screen and waiting for radio calls from new aircraft as they entered his airspace. The blip that was now identifying itself as Mobile-61, a call sign known to the Iranians as an RC-135, continued east toward the Iranian border. The controller knew that when the blip reached Orbit Racetrack, it would drill holes in the sky in an endless circle before it came home, mimicking the habits of an RC-135 stationed at Kirkuk, just as if it had actually taken off tonight as scheduled.

THE AVENGER'S FLIGHT TEAM ON the ground in Riyadh sat alone in the hangar the Saudi government had loaned them. Their dark green mil-spec containers laid open on their ends, with two long orange extension cords running to the nearest wall sockets.

One thick black cable snaked out from one of the cases through the hangar door to a VSAT, which was pointed up to a military communications satellite. The two-man flight team sat on metal folding chairs in front of the containers. The first man, an Air Force major, worked a joystick and throttle arrangement while watching one of the computer screens sheltered in protective foam padding within the cases. The second one, an Air Force staff sergeant, monitored the onboard weapons and sensor systems and handled communications with CTS and the airborne command post.

The pilot's computer screen was divided into several small windows. One in the upper left showed the view from a forward-looking minicam; the longer rectangular one at the bottom displayed all the engine temperature and indicator lights; and the two in the center and right, respectively, showed the artificial horizon, airspeed gauge, flap indicator, and fuel state.

The major, who had loved flying the F-16D, had been transferred by the Air Force to the Avenger. The Avenger was not as much fun—he hadn't been able to fire the weapons at all. The enlisted man to his left controlled the weapons and sensors, if they weren't working with the Wraiths. When they were, Wraith command relied on CTS for that, using their ability to combine current intelligence with weapons release authority to shorten the kill chain. In an emergency or data link failure, the enlisted guy would shoot from here, and all the major could do was watch.

The Air Force was phasing out the F-16, focusing now more on drones for missions. Risking a human life to hit a heavily defended target in the initial stages of a war or crisis was not considered wise anymore by the Air Force. If the major could not shoot at bad guys, or transfer back to a fighter squadron flying the newer F-35A, he might as well work for United. It was just as limiting, and the pay was better. For now though, he had a job to do, and he would do it to the best of his ability.

The major had guided the Avenger nearly 650 miles since it launched five hours ago. He had put it on automatic over a flat portion of Iraq for a bathroom break an hour ago, knowing it would be his last until the mission was over. The Avenger was inside Iran now, and he held it at 100 feet and 190 knots, the combination of low-altitude, airspeed and built-in stealth features keeping it off Iranian radar. He was approaching the last ridge he had to climb before reaching his intended orbit point to support the ingressing Wraith team. He also needed to let the sensor operator and CTS people look at a valley near Hajiabad before then. The Nightstalkers would appreciate some advance knowledge of whatever they might find.

THE SAUDI AIRBUS A320 WAS passing to the east of Qom, about thirty minutes' flight time from Tehran. The Wraith team had donned their gear and had huddled together near the rear passenger door on the left side of the aircraft.

Mathews was tense, and he could see in the camouflaged faces of his men their determination to accomplish the mission. They were dressed in their thermal control suits, black BDUs, and ballistic vests and were loaded out with grenades, flash bangs, M8 rifles, and M9 pistols, the sound suppressors already attached to the weapons. They had put on their helmets and checked their night and infrared vision systems, as well as radios. And each member wore a parachute and IR strobes for easy identification. They were ready.

The Airbus pilots activated the cabin chimes, which rang four times. They began to depressurize the passenger cabin and slow the aircraft to near-stall speed. Each team member checked the lightweight oxygen mask worn under his helmet and started the flow of oxygen from the tank strapped to his thigh. Five minutes before the drop, Mathews went over the mission plan in his mind for the hundredth time before addressing his team.

"All right, men," he said over the encrypted radio link, "this is a covert snatch and grab. Maintain light and noise discipline after we are on the ground. The target's house is in a relatively rural area, so we shouldn't run into much trouble. When we hit the house, use the force needed to protect yourselves and your teammates, but avoid lethal fire against the civilians inside unless absolutely necessary. One of them is the guy we want. We believe Aziz is behind a series of attacks back home, and we need him alive. The men with the specials are on point when we enter the house. Everyone knows what to do if we are compromised. Any questions?"

The men looked at each other and then back at Mathews. The lieutenant was a good officer. He had just proven it by giving a short mission review before deployment. They would willingly follow this man into combat, trusting that he would look out for them first. Naturally, there were no questions.

The air pressure in the cabin matched the airplane's altitude now. The men moved close together and formed a long line from the rear passenger door back toward the forward portion of the cabin. Each man wrapped his arms around the waist of the man in front of him, forming a human chain. The linked mass of body weight would help them withstand the buffet from the airflow when the door was open, and would ensure they exited the aircraft as a team.

The lone Saudi Air Force officer assigned to watch the flight crew had exited the flight deck wearing an emergency oxygen mask, the green cylinder's carrying strap across his body, an improvised safety line the Americans had made him gripped in one hand. He shut the flight deck door behind him and stood at the last first-class row, gripping the safety handles on either side of the bulkhead and facing the team in the dim cabin lighting. The group of dark-clothed Americans, with their weapons and armor, looked frightening, and knowing what they were about to do, in the dark, at this altitude, made him fear them even more.

The pilots turned out the cabin lights. Only sixty seconds left until the drop. Mathews was closest to the door and began unlatching it. Then he pulled the door into the cabin, and the icy wind at 30,000 feet blasted in. A few unrestrained pillows and blankets flew around and toward the front of the cabin. The men tightened their grip on one another against the blast, their eyes on Mathews as he stood in the lead in the doorway. "Go, go, go!" he called out over the radio link and then led the group out into the night. The linked chain of men moved as one out the door behind him and into the darkness.

Alone now in the cabin, the Saudi officer moved carefully toward the rear door, wrapped the safety line around the bare metal of one of the passenger seat arms, clipping the steel carabineer to the line to secure it. He struggled to shut the door against the airflow but was able to get it closed a minute later. Unlatching himself and thanking Allah silently for preserving his life, he returned to the first-class cabin's galley, chilled to the bone and in need of some hot coffee. After calling the pilots to repressurize the cabin, he poured himself a cup, wrapped his hands around it, and pondered the courage of the men who had just jumped out of the plane into a country where they would likely be shot on sight.

THE AVENGER HAD JUST COME ON station in Iran, and the crew left behind in Riyadh at the hangar turned control of the weapons and sensors over to CTS. CTS would acknowledge the handoff any second now. The pilot in Riyadh would hold it in a long orbit over a nearby ridge to the west of the target house, hoping it would stay hidden in the radar clutter generated by the height of the ridge.

The voice was back again. *"The floor plans were wrong."* Every time her mind drifted away from her work, all she heard in her head was the last transmission of the HRT leader, condemning her for giving him the wrong information. Then her mind would replay the explosion, tormenting her with the memory of killing those men with her mistake.

She had found in the press reporting the names of the men who had died so she could remember her failure. What kind of a person was she to have allowed them to die? As she continued to berate herself, a light began to blink on the screen in front of her. Her eyes were unfocused, so it took a minute before she noticed it.

When she finally broke away from her guilty thoughts, she saw that the command data link indicator had turned green. She cursed herself for being distracted. Clicking the Command Data Accept icon on the screen, she called out, "Avenger on Station. CTS has sensor and weapons control."

"Copy. Begin area surveillance of the target building."

Emily uploaded the coordinates of Aziz's home to the Avenger's onboard computer and then with a mouse click, ordered both of the cameras to lock onto the house. Her display showed rapid motion for a moment, and then a house centered on it. It was just what she saw on the images from NPIC earlier.

The house sat in the middle of a large wooded lot, and none of the surrounding houses was very close. It looked like this Aziz liked having space between himself and his neighbors. Zooming in the camera with the scroll wheel on the mouse, she took a closer look. The camera was set to infrared mode, so the washed-out white-and-black image made small details tough to see. But some things were clearly visible, like the L-shape of the house. Its typical Persian architecture contained a lot of tan-colored stone, which she'd seen in the NPIC shots. The exterior walls featured the requisite arches and even a small minaret in one corner. It even had what looked like an Olympic-sized swimming pool in the rear yard.

The house was set on the property so that the driveway curved from the road into the interior of the L. The main portion of the house occupied the long edge of the L, with the pool area hidden from the drive and road by the house's main portion, conforming to the privacy standards of a practicing Muslim. Strangely, there was no fence around the perimeter, just the long arching semicircle driveway from the road with a car parked in front of the main entry. Given Islamic standards of modesty, Aziz must have thought his distance from his neighbors was enough to ensure they wouldn't be offended by any use of the pool by people "obscenely clothed" in swimwear. There were also three different sized satellite dishes on the roof. The edges of the house and the sparse stands of trees to the east and north were black or shades of black on her display because they were cooler than the ground, which showed up as white on her display. The guards walking outside were white too, their rifles clearly visible.

Emily counted quickly and called out, "I've got six perimeter guards with rifles visible near the target house, no one else in sight."

Cain looked at his deputy. "Mike, does the car look like a BMW to you?"

Goodman was CTS's resident gear head and was a serious BMW fan. After a moment's consideration to be certain, he said, "Sure as hell. Looks like a 7 Series. Mid-2010s I'd guess. Between the guards and the car, I think somebody politically important or wealthy lives there. Most Iranians would never even dream of owning a 7 Series. They cost more than the average Iranian would make in twenty years."

"Concur," said Cain, pressing the transmit button as he continued. "Apollo, this is Charlie One, are you getting a video feed from the Avenger?"

The reply was immediate. "Affirm Charlie One. Apollo has the picture from the Avenger. No contact with Whiskey One yet, but our encrypted data feeds are broadcasting."

"Copy Apollo. Charlie Team assesses the house to be the proper target. It matches with the NPIC imagery. Also, the make and model of the car in the driveway indicate it's not what your average Iranian would own."

"Apollo copies and concurs. Standing by."

THE WRAITHS HAD COMPLETED THE high-altitude, low-opening parachute drop and had gathered in the field east of the objective.

Mathews was surveying the landscape through the helmet's night vision and could clearly see the objective house in the distance, outlined in red in the helmet display.

A few moments after landing, the ruggedized mini-computer on his harness had begun picking up the secure data feed from the orbiting 747-400ER relayed via satellite. The mini-computer decrypted and translated the data feed and then had immediately outlined the target house with a thin red line, put a heading marker in his compass at the bottom of the display, and a few minutes later put the area map in the upper right corner. The area map even showed the little green plane icon representing the Avenger orbiting to the west.

His sightline to the house was broken up only intermittently by the sparse stand of trees in the intervening half mile of ground. The ground was relatively level here, and there were a few bushes, but no solid cover if the team made hard contact before reaching the house. The grass was long but not dry, so it wouldn't crunch under their feet and give away their approach. Mathews was not worried about running into the Iranian Army out here. CTS had told them as part of the mission prebrief that the nearest Army base was fifty miles to the east. The local police force and any guard force at the house were his biggest worries. If it came down to a firefight, the local cops would find themselves massively outgunned, so long as their extraction plan went off as expected.

As Mathews kept watch on the surrounding countryside, his team gathered around him in a circle, each man kneeling in the grass. Mathews' executive officer and NCOIC moved to the center of the circle and knelt next to their lieutenant. Tapping the side of his helmet, he switched over to the infrared camera. The image went from shades of light and dark green to black and white. His men's faces practically glowed white through their helmets from their body heat at this distance, but the rest of their bodies remained lighter shades of grayish white or black because their clothing and equipment were not as warm. More important, each man's infrared strobes were active, blinking away at the top of their shoulders. The strobes would make them easy to identify from the air, allowing the Avenger's infrared imaging systems to tell the good guys from the bad guys for the people at CTS and on board the airborne command post.

As Mathews checked each man's IR strobes, he counted them. No one had been lost in the drop. Next to him, his NCOIC, Air Force Master Sergeant Harris, made a circle in the air with his left hand and gave him a thumbs-up. Mathews switched the helmet display back to night vision mode, and the blinking strobes vanished as the pale-green display replaced the black-and-white image.

Activating his radio, he whispered, "Apollo, Whiskey One, ingress complete, proceeding to objective." Overhead, the Avenger picked up his encrypted signal and relayed it via satellite.

"Apollo copies," was the reply from 300 miles west and 39,000 feet up.

Mathews tapped his XO, Army Lieutenant Cochrane, on the right shoulder and pointed ahead. Then he reached across to tap Harris on his left shoulder and pointed ahead.

Both men moved off immediately, Cochrane out and to the left and then Harris out and to the right. As they passed through the circle of men, three rose and followed each of them, forming an inverted V-shape with five yards between each man. The two fire teams angled away from each other until they covered a hundred-yard front, and then they moved west toward the objective. Mathews gave both of his lead fire teams a minute head start and then moved off, straight at the objective, the remaining three men forming their own inverted V-shape behind him. Each team moved forward in unison, standing straight with their suppressed M8 rifles at the ready, scanning the terrain ahead as they approached the house.

"FRIENDLIES IN SIGHT," EMILY CALLED out inside CTS. "I have twelve friendlies in sight." She counted the white images of the men with the blinking strobes again to be sure. She saw three groups of four men moving in inverted-V formations toward the house. That was the Wraith team, all right. She had heard the radio call from the team leader and Apollo's reply from the airborne command post. Keying her microphone, she said, "Whiskey One, be advised, Avenger has eyes on six Tangos near the objective."

From behind her, Cain tapped her on the shoulder firmly, "Emily, that didn't go out. You're still on the CTS internal channel." She looked up at him in surprise and saw the reproving look on his face.

Emily's face flushed red, and the voice came back again. *"The floor plans were wrong."* Anger silenced the voice as she thought, *Great, now I'm fucking up in front of the boss.* She checked her radio settings and selected the one for the broadcast tactical channel that the 747, the Wraith ground team, and the CTS were on. "Whiskey One, be advised, Avenger has eyes on six Tangos near the objective."

"Copy Avenger, Whiskey hold," came back to her over the radio net. On the screen, the Wraith team stopped in its tracks.

"Avenger, Whiskey One is 150 yards from the objective. No joy on Tangos. Say locations on the hostiles."

Emily unconsciously leaned closer to her computer screen, as if it would help her see them better. "Whiskey One, Avenger has eyes on three Tangos on the east side of the house and three Tangos on the west side. I'm marking them for you now." Emily used her mouse to select the Designate Moving Target function and then with the cursor drew small boxes around the white images of the six guards. The computer software committed them to memory and began streaming data about their positions out into the common data link.

On the helmet displays of the Wraiths, small red diamonds appeared in their sightlines, seeming to float in the air in the distance. They overlaid on the red outline surrounding the house. Mathews knew the diamonds would grow larger as they got closer to the targets. They now knew the precise location of a guard force they could not see with their own eyes yet.

"Avenger, Whiskey One. How is the guard force armed?"

"Whiskey One, Avenger. Wait one." Emily zoomed in the camera tightly on each guard for a few seconds. Most of them were standing still, apparently bored with their duties. The two who were moving in the front of the house were only pacing a few steps occasionally.

"A little help here, I'm not a firearms expert," she called out to the CTS in general.

One of the Army Warrant Officers assigned to maintain the crypto gear and computers spoke up. "Those are AK-74s, looks like they have grenade launchers too."

"Are you sure?" Cain asked the warrant.

His predictable response was laced with sarcasm. "Of course I'm sure, I'm in the Army and people in foreign lands might shoot at me with them."

"Fair, enough. Emily, tell 'em."

"Whiskey One, Avenger. They appear to be armed with AK-74s equipped with grenade launchers."

Six thousand miles away, Mathews paused. *Grenade launchers? These guys were serious about guarding that house.*

"Apollo, Whiskey One. Recommend a change to the Romeo Oscar Echo. Please advise."

Onboard the 747, General Crane considered the options. The orders from the president were to bring Aziz back alive and limit civilian casualties. To that end, the Rules of Engagement, or RoE as Mathews had phonetically spelled it, required the team to use lethal force only after they were engaged. If one of the guards launched a grenade first, things would get very messy. "Whiskey One, Apollo, Romeo Oscar Echo change approved. Guard force expendable, repeat expendable. Weapons free."

"One copies. Whiskey Team, guard force is expendable. Sierra Team, are you in position?"

"Whiskey One, Sierra Team is in position. Three Tangos in sight." The two-man sniper team had guided their parafoils to the north and west of the house during their drop from the Airbus and had found a small knoll to hunker down behind 200 yards from the house. They wore Ghillie suits that disguised them as formless patches of local grass as they lay prone on the ground, so no one could see them even from only three feet away. As an added refinement, the Ghillie suits were lined with thick cloth to hide their IR signature, making them invisible to the Avenger's sensors. They had maintained radio silence until contacted, as ordered before the drop.

"Copy Sierra Team, guard force is expendable. Copy?"

"Affirmative, One. Say when," Sierra One replied. Cutting off his microphone, he said to his observer, "Get on your rifle and take the one farthest from us first. I'll get the guy at the front door, then we'll get the last guy closest to us near the garage."

"Copy," replied his partner. He immediately put away the small spotting scope he'd been using to observe the house and picked up his suppressed M8. Because of their close range, they had not brought their specially built long guns and were relying instead on their M8s, now configured for sniper work. The longer twenty-inch barrels and sniper bipods made them more unwieldy when moving, but they would do just fine at this distance, especially with 20x night vision scopes attached. The only downside was that to use them, they had to turn off their integrated helmet optics, but those would only take a second or two to reactivate.

"One to all elements, stand by to engage. Sierra Team, take your cue from Team Two."

"Sierra copies."

"Team Two copies," replied Cochran.

"Apollo, Whiskey One. Are we go-mission?"

On the 747, Crane took one more look at the wide-angle display from the Avenger. He couldn't think of anything else that needed to be done before risking the lives of Team Four, so he clicked his microphone open and set things in motion.

"Nightstalker-1, Apollo. How copy?"

"Apollo, Nightstalker, have you Lima Charlie." The Osprey was sitting in a steep valley thirty miles west of the house, just east of Hajiabad, its props turning at near-takeoff speed. The two 25mm minigunners kept watch on the landscape through their sights. The second Osprey, Nightstalker-2, was on orbit just outside of Iranian airspace, occasionally sipping fuel from the refueling probe of an MC-130P Combat Shadow tanker in case something went wrong.

"Nightstalker-1, start your countdown."

"Nightstalker-1 copies." The flight crew was set to take off in ten minutes, and fly a course and speed at low altitude to reach the house exactly ten minutes later to retrieve the Wraith team.

"Whiskey One, Apollo, you are go-mission. I repeat, you are go-mission. Twenty minutes."

"Whiskey One copies. Team Two, lead off!" Mathews started the stopwatch function on his watch to gauge how much mission time was left, if needed. As he looked up, he saw Team Two followed closely by Team Three, heading for the east side of the house at a light jog, both in the inverted-V formation. Time had become as much the enemy now as the guard force on the house was.

Mathews stood and led his three-man element southwest at a jog. They turned west after sixty-five yards and jogged another sixty before slowing for the final approach to their overwatch position. They walked the last fifteen yards slowly and then up a position on the southeast corner of the house. They would cover the south side to ensure no one escaped out a window. When they were kneeling in the grass, Mathews called to the other teams, "Team One in position."

A few moments later, Team Two reached the edge of the tree line east of the house's lawn. Every man on Team Two could see the three guards on the east side, visible through their helmet displays and overlaid with vertical red diamonds.

Cochran called in, "Team Two is in position."

Team Three slowly walked the thirty yards to Team Two at the edge of the tree line. Harris called in, "Team Three is in position."

It was up to Cochran now. He quickly issued his orders over the radio link. "Team Three, take the southern Tango. Team Two, take the Tango immediately west of us; I've got the northern one." The northern one was deep in the crook of the L-shape of the house and was the tougher shot. He waited a moment for his men to set up on the targets as he flicked his fire selector to single shot, centered the sights of his rifle on the northern guard's torso, and then issued two orders.

"Sierra Team, weapons free. Teams Two and Three, fire!"

The eight men fired simultaneously, the light-loaded rounds exiting the rifle barrels well under supersonic speed. With the silencers attached to their M8s, the loudest noise came from the high-speed metallic movement of the rifle bolts.

Three rounds from Team Three tore into the southernmost guard's head, and nine more ripped open his torso as if he had exploded from within. The guard immediately west of Team Two caught all nine rounds in the chest, shredding his heart and lungs. The northernmost guard took Cochran's single round to the head, which entered behind his right eye and ricocheted around in his skull. All three men crumpled with only the metallic clacking of their AK-74s hitting the ground to mark their passage into death.

The guard at the far end of the house turned to call out to his friend near the door. He had just enough time to see his fellow guard's body fall before the single round from Sierra Two found its mark above his right cheek, killing him instantly. The man by the front door didn't notice anything—he closed his eyes to blink when Sierra One's bullet shot behind his right ear and entered his skull.

Alerted by the sound of the guards' rifles hitting the ground, the man closest to the Sierra Team's perch at the northwest corner turned and saw the two bodies on the ground. He immediately ducked behind the northern wall of the garage and began moving east toward the pool to evade the snipers he thought were in front of him. Sierra Two shot at him but missed, the bullet embedding itself in the garage wall instead. The sniper switched over to three-round burst and kneeled to counteract the sudden surge of adrenalin in his veins, and this time led his target properly. The three rounds ripped into the last guard's chest and he sprawled face first into the ground, dead like his comrades.

"Team Two, clear."

"Team Three, clear."

"Sierra Team, clear."

Mathews called in, "Teams Two and Three, clear to proceed. Sierra Team, continue over watch."

Teams Two and Three moved at once out of the tree line and along the south edge of the pool. They set up on the two doors on the short leg of the L. One man from each team hung explosive charges on the door handles and then lined up with his fellows along the exterior wall. Two men on each team slung their M8s and pulled shotguns off their backs and readied them. Each shotgun was loaded with nonlethal bean-bag rounds. They would engage any targets in the house first, hoping to avoid injuring any civilians and capture Aziz alive.

Two seconds later, the doors were blown off their frames. Cochrane called out, "Breaching! Breaching!" and the eight men flooded into the house. Team Two cleared the kitchen and maids' quarters, while Team Three cleared the main dining room. So far, there was no sign of anyone.

After clearing the kitchen, Cochran's Team Two split into pairs, one shotgun and one M8 each. One pair entered the servants' quarters and found nothing but empty beds and dimly lit rooms. The remaining two crossed the kitchen and burst through the doors at the far end into a small office. The office was also dimly lit and empty. Both men moved quickly into the south door and entered a two-story great room with a single stairwell against the west wall. "Stairwell," they called out and then knelt, covering the area.

In the dining room, the four men of Harris's Team Three headed through the south door into an L-shaped hallway. Splitting up in the same manner as Team Two, two men opened the western hallway door and quickly cleared the foyer, laundry room, and garage, while the last two held the hallway. Harris called in, "Team Three, clear."

Back in the great room, the pair of Team Two men who cleared the maids' quarters caught up with their fellows who were kneeling and tapped them from behind. The four men moved as one unit up the stairs and halted on the second-floor landing. They paused and Cochran called out, "Team Two on the second floor. First floor is clear."

Harris heard the clear call and called in, "First floor is clear. Team Three holding in front west hallway; all units watch your fire."

"Copy Team Three," Cochran responded. "We're clearing the second floor now."

"Lead copies all," Mathews called in next and then said to the CTS, "Avenger, this is Whiskey One, how are we looking?"

Emily replied, "Whiskey One, Avenger. No sign of hostile activity."

"Whiskey One copies." Mathews looked at his watch. Eight minutes gone.

Team Two was moving through the second floor quickly. The rooms were silent and, for the most part, dark. A couple of lights were on in two of the bedrooms, but there was not a soul to be found. "Second floor clear—nobody's home. Lead, please advise."

Mathews thought fast. Either somebody warned him they were coming or the intel was wrong and this wasn't the right house. In either case, it was time to go. "Team Three, exit the rear of the house, get the three bodies in the rear, and move north to LZ One. Team Two, sweep the house for documents or other intel and withdraw through the front entrance."

"Team Two copies."

"Team Three copies."

"Nightstalker-1, Whiskey One, say ETA."

The CV-22B was running flat out at 240 knots. The pilot was guiding the Osprey over the Iranian countryside at a hundred feet and did not take his eyes off the terrain he saw through his night vision gear. The copilot glanced down at the GPS and called in, "Six minutes."

"Whiskey One copies six minutes." Then he said to his men, "Let's get the bodies out front," and ran for the front of the house with his three-man Team One.

Team Two was tearing the place apart, ripping open drawers in the bedrooms and throwing books off the shelves in the great room. Finding nothing, the men returned to the small office where they found Cochran stuffing his pockets with papers and trying to unplug the cables from the back of the desktop computer. "Grab the laptop on that shelf."

Out front, Mathews covered his three men while they dragged the bodies of the dead guards into the woods. Then he fell back with them. Team Three was already using fireman carries to move the guards from the rear of the house to the north. They angled left and passed the Sierra Team.

Mathews plopped down into the grass next to the Sierra Team and called over his radio, "Teams One and Three, fall back to LZ One. Take the bodies with you. Team Two, exit the house *now* and double-time to LZ One." Mathews heard acknowledgments from Teams One and Three overlap on the radio, and that was good enough.

"Team Two copies. Coming out now." Abandoning the desktop, Team Two raced for the doors, their pockets stuffed with loose papers, one man holding the laptop tightly to his chest.

Crane was sitting on the 747, fuming. He was watching the video from the Avenger showing one of units dragging dead men to their LZ. "Whiskey One, Apollo. Why are you wasting time with the bodies?"

Mathews ignored the general and watched Team Two struggle past him and the prone Sierra Team. Looking down at the Snipers, he ordered them out, "Get moving. Head for the LZ."

Crane called in again, "Whiskey One, Apollo. Why are you wasting time with the bodies?"

Turning to run toward the LZ, Mathews said in a rush, "Apollo, I'm not leaving them any evidence."

Mathews sprinted through the trees, dodging small brush and ensuring that the yellow waypoint caret in his display stayed centered in the compass heading. With thirty-five yards to go to the small clearing, he could distinctly see the outlines of his men becoming more clearly defined as he approached. Breathing heavily, he heard the Osprey's engines and he called out to it, "Nightstalker-1, Whiskey One, where are you?"

Nightstalker-1's copilot handled the radio call again. "Sixty seconds."

Mathews tapped the side of his helmet to switch to infrared. He looked up and scanned the sky. *There.* He could see the blinking infrared strobes of the blacked-out aircraft approaching. "Nightstalker-1, Whiskey One has you in sight. LZ One is clear for pickup."

"Copy, coming in." The copilot passed the word to the gunners that the LZ was clear and their fingers lightened on the triggers of the rotary cannon.

"Roger. Apollo, Whiskey One, we are extracting."

On the 747, Crane was staring at the image of the Wraith team around LZ One and thinking seriously about changing its CO soon. His reply was terse. "Copy."

The pilot brought the Osprey down onto the LZ fast, its engine nacelles already completely vertical, and the huge turboprops pounding the air to slow the aircraft. His night vision systems clearly showed the Special Forces unit kneeling in a semicircle around the LZ, facing in what he presumed was a likely threat direction. Twenty feet from touchdown, he pivoted the massive airframe left 120 degrees so the starboard and rear minigunners could cover the threat vector, the rear ramp already lowered.

Mathews tapped the side of his helmet again and the display went back to green. The spectral image of the Osprey landing was crystal clear. The violent downdraft of its two turboprops was powerful enough to cause the men to brace themselves against its buffeting.

"Team Two, hold position. Teams One, Three, and Sierra, extract now, take the bodies on board."

The nine men rose as one. Six of them lifted the dead guards and headed for the helicopter's rear ramp while the last three men scanned for threats. The downdraft made carrying the dead weight even tougher. Loading the all the bodies took two trips. When they were all in, Cochran walked to the end of the ramp and called on the radio, "One, get aboard."

Mathews looked back at the helicopter and saw the XO waiving at him. "Team Two, extract now!"

The four remaining men rose and ran for the helicopter. Mathews gave them a head start and then followed at a dead run, looking left and right quickly to ensure no one was being left behind. When he reached the ramp, he waived the XO aboard and then ran behind him up the ramp into the Osprey's fuselage. Looking toward the front of the aircraft, he saw one of the pilots glancing back into the open cargo area. Mathews gave him a thumbs-up and jerked it upwards a couple of times. "Nightstalker, Whiskey Team is on board, go, go, go!"

The pilot didn't hesitate. The 35,000-pound aircraft rose quickly off the ground and dipped its nose slightly, while the engine nacelles rotated forward 90 degrees to accelerate away from the LZ. The pilot held the altitude to less than 200 feet, made a wide, sweeping left turn to head west, and then descended to 150 feet when the airspeed was above 130 knots.

After thirty minutes, he began to hedge-hop through the mountainous terrain of western Iran toward the Iraqi border. The constant roller-coaster ride was something he enjoyed and had practiced plenty of times. The Special Forces teams he ferried around were not quite as accustomed to it. About fifteen minutes into the flight through the mountains, he could smell the vomit. *Another hour to go.*

CRANE WATCHED THE OSPREY CLEAR the area on the Avenger's wide-angle video feed. When it was gone, he ordered the UAV off station. It was heading southwest now, and CTS had surrendered its control of the sensors and weapons to the control team in Riyadh. They would land the Avenger at Kirkuk for refueling, and then they would fly it back to Riyadh late tomorrow after some sleep.

Nightstalker-1 had called in twenty minutes ago, just after it had crossed the border into Iraq. It was heading for a midair refueling with the Combat Shadow before proceeding to Kirkuk.

After the UAV exited Iranian airspace, Crane would order the 747 to land at Kirkuk. Team Four would be brought aboard and debriefed during the flight back to Riyadh. The spare flight crew had just taken over in the cockpit, and the plane had plenty of fuel on board.

Crane rubbed his eyes and tried to curb his impatience. He wanted to hear Mathews' explanation for risking his team members' lives to bring out dead bodies. And he wanted to talk to the CTS folks about their shitty intel.

MATHEWS AND HIS TEAM JOINED General Crane aboard the 747-400ER airborne command post at Kirkuk airbase. His initial debriefing with General Crane was a very unpleasant one so far.

"You will explain yourself, Lieutenant." The look on his face should have burned through the navy man and then the bulkhead of the 747. Crane had cleared the upper deck of personnel while the plane refueled at Kirkuk. The smell of jet fuel was heavy in the air, and the cabin was growing warmer in the morning sunshine.

"Sir?"

"Why did you take the bodies of those guards with you? You endangered your men's lives! What would have happened if you had run into a hostile force, or had been compromised on the way to the LZ? Your men would have had to take time to unsling those bodies before defending themselves and would have probably been shot or killed!"

Mathews stood ramrod straight and made his case in as even of a voice as he could.

"Sir, Avenger did not report any threats in the area and I understood our orders to be that we were to leave no residual presence. To me, that meant that any civilians we encountered would be restrained and blindfolded, and the target, if we found him, forced to leave with us. After we changed the RoE, we fired very distinctive rounds at six men and killed them. If nothing else, taking the bodies removes any potential ballistic evidence from Iranian hands. This leaves them with no physical evidence to point to U.S. involvement."

Crane pondered this while the young SEAL remained at attention. As circumstances would have it, the Kirkuk airbase had an Air Force chaplain who was a Muslim. He had taken custody of the dead guards' bodies and would arrange a proper burial consistent with the Islamic faith. Sadly, the fate of those men would always be a mystery to their families. Crane didn't like the thought of parents, wives, sons, and daughters being left in the lurch like that, but this mission needed to be covert and, in the end, the lives of the Wraiths were his responsibility, not those of the Iranian guards.

The young lieutenant also had a point. If he had left the bodies behind, the rounds would be recovered and examined. They would eventually be identified as coming from the M8 rifle, and the only nation in the world thinking about buying the M8 in bulk was the U.S. In addition to that, the laptop computer and papers the team had recovered might prove valuable, if, in fact, this man Aziz actually lived at the house. The papers had already been run through the fax machine on the 747-400ER to the base, where they would be faxed again, under suitable cover to DIA, for translation and analysis. The laptop would be carried by hand to the experts at NSA for forensic analysis after they got back.

As his thoughts progressed, the general's temper cooled.

"All right, Lieutenant, I can't say I liked it when you did it, but I understand and agree with your reasoning."

Mathews knew that was as close as a general officer was ever likely to come to apologizing to a junior officer, so he answered it in the only way possible.

"Yes, sir."

"You and your men will remain aboard for a more thorough mission debriefing. We'll ferry you back to Riyadh and you will rejoin the C-17. After the UAV lands in Riyadh and is loaded on the C-17, your unit will likely return to Andrews. Clear?"

"Yes, sir."

Team Four was called to the upper deck after the 747-400ER took off again, and they walked through every step of the mission, starting from the time they boarded the Airbus in Riyadh until the moment they stepped out of the vomit-slicked Osprey at Kirkuk. Then they ran through it again while the general asked questions. The whole session was recorded on video and would be electronically linked back to CTS and the Wraith home base. By the time they were finished, the command post had landed in Riyadh and was taxiing over to where the C-17 had parked.

Mathews and his men deplaned from the 747 and walked straight onto the C-17. By the time they had stowed their gear on board and taken showers at the gymnasium on the Saudi Air Force side of the air-field, the Avenger was landing. An hour later, the UAV's weapons were secured and the drone reloaded into the C-17. Two hours later, they were airborne again.

Dumbo-76 was heading west into the setting sun and climbing through 22,000 feet when Mathews fell asleep, sprawled across three seats in the cavernous cargo hold, yellow earplugs stuffed firmly in his ears.

CHAPTER 22

IT HAD BEEN A WEEK since the power outages in the northeastern and mid-Atlantic states had left twenty million Americans cold and in the dark, and three days since the assault on Aziz's house in Iran. Cain sat behind his desk in the CTS, sleeves rolled up and feet propped on an open drawer. It was a few minutes after 8 P.M., and the lights in CTS dimmed for the midshift.

He had sent his prime team home an hour ago with orders not to return for at least seventy-two hours. Strangely, Emily had protested strongly. She had insisted on staying and had only left when Cain told her that he too would be leaving in another hour and not returning. He was bone tired from the constant long shifts, and mentally exhausted. Cain knew that this kind of pace would drain his people emotionally, physically, and mentally, and they had begun to show signs of that drain after the assault on Aziz's house had failed to capture him. Goodman had screamed at an NCO about an e-mail he had sent to thirty people that should have included one more addressee. Cain had caught Emily crying in the conference room. He'd put his hands on her shoulders and reassured her that they would get the people who had done this. She'd wiped away the tears, gave him a wan smile, and fled to the ladies' room to compose herself. A few people had even tripped over doorsills from exhaustion. The final straw came when Cain, while working at his desk, reached for the computer mouse and knocked over his cup of coffee.

Before he knew what he was doing, he had thrown the cup across the room, swearing. His entire staff was staring at him and, after he regained his composure, he decided that enough was enough.

"I'm sorry," he sighed in remorse. "We've all been working some long hours and I got too emotional about a stupid cup of coffee. As of now, the prime team, and anyone else who has worked more than 160 hours in the last 14 days, is dismissed. Report back to duty in 72 hours. No sooner."

Shaking his head because he fell into the very trap he had been warning others to avoid, he got up from his desk and nodded to the midshift supervisor. He and the swing-team leader would be working twelve-hour shifts for the next three days with reduced staffs. Cain gave them orders to rest everyone on their watch teams that they could. Having all the watch standers burnt out was not going to help anyone.

"Keep an eye on things. Call me if you need me."

The team leader of the midshift looked at him and smiled as he shook his head. He would not call unless the building fell down around his ears. Probably not even then.

Taking one last look around the CTS watch floor, Cain headed out to his car. It was already pitch black outside. No streetlights, no traffic signals were lit, no moonlight. The stiff breeze from the north enhanced the chill in the air and he zipped his heavy coat up to his throat. His car's external thermometer read eighteen degrees. After a long drive in the dark, he arrived home and gave his wife a long hug. She had fireplaces lit in the living room and their bedroom, holding the temperature in the house at a chilly forty-five degrees. He took a lukewarm shower by candlelight, and burrowed under three blankets on his bed for what would be sixteen hours of sleep.

BALTIMORE GAS AND ELECTRIC'S MAJOR Substation 6, just south of Baltimore near the Harbor Tunnel Throughway, was not nearly as dark as the surrounding countryside and the nearby city. A battery of portable generators and flood lights lit up the large transformer pad and its massive transformers, as well as the maze of scaffolding and equipment around it.

BGE work crews had been on site for three days, removing the damaged transformers and preparing the eight-inch-diameter stranded cables for the new ones. They were working around the clock to restore power to the cold, dark region.

The crew of nine men and four women had dressed for the cold with heavy work suits over their regular work clothes and stocking caps under their hard hats. Clustered around the sole kerosene heater in the equipment yard, they chatted and sipped on hot coffee and soup from their thermoses. It was their first break of the night. One of the men fought the glare of the floodlights as he steered the conversation back to business.

"How much longer till the substation control gear gets here, Steve?" They had been waiting to get the gear since they had arrived on site. Without it, the whole substation was a worthless collection of steel, insulators, and transformer oil.

The supervisor of the work crew looked at his watch. "Another forty minutes or so, it's being trucked in from Atlanta."

"Why did it take so long?" asked one of the women.

"According to Mary at inventory dispatch, they had trouble . . . " Steve trailed off, a look of curious surprise appearing on his face. After a few seconds, he dropped to his knees and pitched forward onto his face.

"Steve!" exclaimed one of the men.

They all clustered around him. Two of the men turned him over and felt for a pulse. Steve's eyes were open and vacant.

One of them said, "I think he's dead!"

"Heart attack?" someone offered.

"I don't know," replied another as he took out his cell phone to summon help. Just as he raised it to his ear, the phone shattered. The man who was holding it fell onto his side instantly.

The remaining eleven people stared in shock. One of them was a former National Guardsman who had served in Iraq during the U.S. invasion in 2003. He looked at the man who had just collapsed. The left side of his face had a small, blackened, round hole over his left cheek. There was a small trickle of blood and the man's eyes were open. He recognized it instantly.

"Sniper! Everyone find cover. Get behind something solid!"

They all stared at him, frozen in place. The former Army PFC grabbed one of the women nearest him and propelled her behind the barrel-shaped steel cylinder of one of the medium-sized transformers. As he did, another man took a hit in the chest and dropped to the ground. That motivated the remaining eight people to run for the nearest solid object.

The former PFC got behind one of the larger transformers, pulled out his phone, and dialed 911.

"911 Emergency. What is the nature of the emergency?"

"Ma'am, this is Robert Mason. I'm a long lines repairman working for BGE. Our repair team at BGE's Major Substation 6 is under sniper attack. The substation is off Annapolis Road. We need help now!"

The operator was sure she hadn't heard him correctly. "Sir, did you say you were under sniper attack?"

"Ma'am, we have three people down and dead. Get me some fucking help!"

The stress and fear in his voice convinced her. "Help is on the way, sir. Stay on the line with me."

Twenty minutes later, three white and blue Anne Arundel County Sheriffs' cars and two olive and brown Maryland State Trooper cruisers were on the scene. Ten minutes after that, two ambulances pulled up. The troopers and county officers searched the immediate area until dawn, while the forensic experts went to work on the bodies and the crime scene. No one found a thing.

SPECIAL AGENT JOHNSON STEPPED OFF the plane at Dulles and headed out of the gate area. The commercial flight from Riyadh had been long, and he needed to go to work in the morning. But after the Special Forces guys had made it out of Iraq, he'd been called by SAIC French and was told to interview Sadig until he was sure the FBI knew everything Sadig could provide. That had taken a few days, and then he spent two more days to compare notes with the Saudis on the interrogation results and take a quick side trip to meet the Minister of the Interior, who thanked him for his service to the Kingdom.

His new Saudi friend Akeem had managed to pull some strings and get him on an Emirates Air flight back to the U.S., in first class no less. The private little cabin had made the trip an easy one. He slept in a seat that reclined completely into a flat bed. The male cabin attendant woke him two hours from landing and then brought hot coffee and breakfast after Johnson had shaved in the lavatory.

After he was through the security checkpoint, he was crushed by his wife's hug. She had promised to meet him after he called to tell her he was coming back. He wrapped his arms around her and squeezed as hard as he could. The feel of her curves against him eased the ache in his chest he'd had since he headed to Guantanamo. Her smile made him vow silently never to leave her again. It was a silly thought, because he knew he would have to be away from her, or she from him at some point. But he vowed it anyway, and he knew he would do nearly anything to protect her, sworn FBI agent or not.

"I missed you," she whispered in his ear.

"I missed you too. Have you been managing all right without power?"

"Sure. There's plenty of firewood, and I've been catching up on my reading by candlelight. The cold shower in the morning is a real pain, though. I rigged up a potholder in the fireplace and I've been heating water over the fire in the afternoons after work so I can take a sponge bath and wash my hair."

"That's very ingenious, sweetheart." He kissed her on the lips.

"I've also had some other things to think about while you've been away," she coyly added.

"What other things have you been thinking about?"

Her smile was even brighter now. "Names."

It took only a moment for the young investigator to figure that out.

"YOU CAN HEAR ME CLEARLY?" the head of the Ministry asked.

"Yes, my friend." The G550 was airborne again, heading north this time.

"I'm sorry we didn't contact you last week about this. We still don't know what happened. Your guards are gone, and the rear doors near your pool were broken open. The locks were blasted open, and the doors were heavily damaged, probably by gunfire. I regret to say your house also appears to have been ransacked, by thieves most likely."

"Thieves? Are you sure?" Aziz leaned forward in his seat.

"It seems so. Since your guards are missing, and your house ransacked, it was likely them. What kind of weapons did they carry?"

"They had AK-74s." *This man is a fool,* Aziz thought. *No wonder he works for the government.*

"Ah, yes. Then it is likely these men chose to break into your home and steal what they could. I have placed men from the Ministry at your house to guard it until your return. When you do, you can tell us what was taken. If you will give me a description of these men, I will ensure the local police and military forces apprehend them if they are found."

"I will see to it that you receive it. When I return I will tell you what was stolen. Thank you, my friend." He broke the connection.

The man from the Iranian MOIS was a fool, but a useful one. He kept Aziz informed of events within the Iranian government, but he was an appointee of a government run by those who *claimed* to believe in Allah, and was not to be trusted. They were such charlatans, using the faith to bind the people rather than to free them. They were also weak, because they did not carry the fight to the primary enemy. One day, they too would pay for their apostasy.

As far as his guards were concerned, they were well paid. He doubted they stole from him as that fool believed. Dialing a number he had committed to memory, it only took two rings before Repin answered.

"Yes."

"How are things going?"

"Generally very well, but my home was burglarized several days ago."

Aziz considered this news. It was wise to be cautious now. "Really? Was anything stolen? What happened to the thieves?"

"*Nyet,* I activated the security system. The burglars were shown the error of their ways."

"What about you?"

"I've relocated to another of my homes."

"Good. You will continue as before. Bring them to their knees." Aziz terminated the call.

The Americans had raided Repin's hidden command post in Chicago, and the guards at his house had vanished. The Americans were such wizards sometimes. Did they know? Probably. If they had found Repin's control center and taken his guard force at his house in Iran, they already knew much more than he thought they would at this stage. Something would have to be done about that. At least Repin had managed to destroy his data and kill some of the assault force sent to capture him. Repin was continuing to prove his worth.

To be safe, however, he would never return to that house in Iran.

REPIN CLOSED THE CELL PHONE he used only for calls to Aziz and placed it back in his pocket. The top floor of the new building wasn't quite as inconspicuous as the old warehouse, but it would do. Aziz had had the floor renovated, as part of the larger plan, consistent with Repin's needs. New walls, carpeting, utilities, and furnishings were installed. The downside was that he was now limited to a single TV and satellite television signal, complemented by an Internet connection. After living in it for almost two weeks, he had gotten accustomed to it.

He had been spending this day reading newspapers online and watching the cable news shows. There were many stories about Americans in the Northeast working with their neighbors to get through the current crisis. People were sharing supplies of food, water, and even heating fuel. Families with wood-burning stoves or fireplaces opened their homes to people without alternative sources of heat. Shelters had been opened by the government, and the National Guard escorted tanker trucks of heating oil into the northeastern and mid-Atlantic states, where there would be no relief from the cold weather until the following week.

These Americans were amazingly resilient. The majority of them were going to their workplaces anyway, despite the massive burden of the total lack of power and heat. People dressed warmly, and their companies promised their pay would continue during the crisis. Many of the employees, appreciative of their company's show of understanding, went in to their offices anyway, and, where possible, worked the phones.

Some enterprising people actually used their own laptops to draft documents, create presentations, and, when the battery power on their cell phones held out, transfer the work across the still-functioning telephone network to their corporate offices in other parts of the country. They would charge laptops and cell phones nightly at a shelter where a generator was available and bring them into work the next day until the battery power died. It wasn't efficient or extremely productive, but they were making do.

Repin knew that the men who had wrecked the heating oil storage facilities would have moved on to the next phase. Their orders were to begin randomly killing the power company's restoration crews as opportunities presented themselves. The sniper units in the major cities had the same orders. It would cause more chaos, and, more important, delay the restoration of power. He had not heard anything on the news about that yet, but it was sure to come.

The news stories were now heavily speculating al-Qaeda's involvement in the events. Ever since the *Times* broke the story of the threatening letter to that television station, the congressmen and congresswomen who could get on radio and TV stations that still had power were screaming for the president to do something about it. The administration kept telling everyone that the primary concern was the restoration of power to the affected areas and the movement of heating oil to the Northeast. Some members of Congress did not like that answer, especially those in the minority party. They criticized the president about it every time they came near a news camera or microphone.

Other news reports said that cellular telephone usage in the Northeast had dropped off, likely because large numbers of people throughout the blacked-out area, especially in the major cities where the population was denser, had trouble recharging their phones.

The Canadians had offered help to their neighbor and ally to the south. They sent 200 power crews into the northeastern U.S. to help make repairs, along with whatever spare equipment they could. The southern and midwestern states were sending crews north to assist. The Department of Energy was working with FEMA and the local power companies to coordinate power restoration and to get emergency generators and heaters to warming centers and shelters throughout the affected areas.

All of this caused by some firearms, high explosives, fewer than one hundred men, and one man at a computer, Repin thought with a satisfied smirk. One thing was certain. There would be more to come, and he would do everything he could to ensure those events were decidedly unpleasant for the Americans.

AVAILABLE FALL 2014
FROM TOM WITHER

AUTUMN FIRE

THE WHITE GULFSTREAM G550 GLIDED through the warm, dry air rising from the desert south of the city of Jeddah, toward King Abdulaziz International Airport's Runway 34 Right. The plane was one of the largest private aircraft types with transoceanic range and a cruising speed near Mach 1.

As the jet continued its descent over the southern portion of Jeddah, it passed over the small homes and apartment houses in the less wealthy portion of the city at nine hundred feet.

Still holding the plane's control yoke to maintain the slightly nose-high descent angle, the pilot, a former Saudi Air Force Colonel named Hamzah, reduced the throttle another 15 percent to increase the descent rate by 100 feet per minute to ensure he'd place the main gear on the runway at the optimum landing point.

Hamzah, whose name meant "Lion" in Arabic, prided himself on the technical proficiency of his flying—and knew almost instantly he had made a mistake. The sun had risen nearly nine hours ago and had heated the more than two miles of bare ground between the housing developments and the runway threshold, creating a strong updraft from the desert floor. The effect of the increased descent rate and the powerful updraft caused the jet to bounce as it entered the more turbulent air. The former 767 cargo jet pilot winced at the impact. As the senior pilot of his employer's small fleet of aircraft, he knew all too well that he did not like turbulence.

During the last mile of the approach, the G550 violently rattled twice more in the turbulent air before Hamzah placed the main gear down on the runway precisely between the thick pair of painted white lines marking the ideal touchdown point. Hamzah pushed forward on the yoke while simultaneously pulling the throttle back to idle to trip the spoilers and engage the thrust reversers. The nose of the aircraft rotated down to place the nose wheel on the asphalt, and the G550 began to slow to a speed more fit for driving.

After retracting the spoilers and flaps, Hamzah turned the aircraft left, off the runway, allowing the last of the landing speed to carry the jet onto Taxiway A. He set the throttle just above idle and "drove" the G550 west for half a mile, and then turned north onto Taxiway B, heading toward what first appeared in the distance as a large group of tall, off-white tents. As the G550 got closer to the north terminal, the "tents" resolved themselves to be the roofline of one of the largest airport terminals in the world.

Known as the Hajj Terminal, it was designed to accommodate 80,000 pilgrims at once during the annual hajj to the holy city of Mecca. Its largely open-air architecture of large tentlike canopies were supported by huge concrete-and-steel-reinforced central poles that covered nearly 210,000 square meters of floor space. The canopies provided a shaded place to wait for the buses that took the thousands of pilgrims passing through during a typical day from Jeddah to Mecca. Large international airports would naturally not be built in the holy city.

Hamzah guided the G550 to its assigned parking slot on the ramp near the Hajj Terminal and then locked the brakes.

Casting a knowing look at his copilot, Zaki, he said, "Complete the post-landing checklist. I'll speak to him about the landing."

Zaki, another Saudi Air Force veteran, gave him a look of sincere sympathy, reached down for the computer display in the center console between their seats, and began bringing up the engine shutdown and post-landing checklists on the flight computer's screen.

Hamzah unbuckled his seat belt and rose to unlock the flight deck door and then proceeded aft. His employer had already lifted his six-foot-tall frame from the plush leather seat and was not happy.

"Have your skills fled?" Aziz asked hotly, his bearded face stony.

Hamzah froze. The look in his employer's dark eyes was not a pleasant one.

"My apologies for your discomfort, Sayyid. The updraft from the desert today was stronger than predicted by the local weather forecasts. Such is the will of Allah."

Aziz continued to stare at him as the male cabin attendant opened the G550's cabin door, and hot, dry air spilled into the cabin. After a long moment, he spoke again.

"This is true. Allah's will is always present. Come with me. I have another task for you."

"Yes, Sayyid." Hamzah breathed a quick sigh of relief as he stood aside to allow Aziz to pass him and exit the G550 first. Hamzah was usually permitted to call him by name but had instead used the Arabic honorific of *Sayyid* to convey his understanding of Aziz's displeasure and his continued respect. It seemed to help calm Aziz, Hamzah thought.

Aziz led the way down the jet's steps, Hamzah in tow. Naturally, there was a small group of men awaiting Aziz's arrival. Two of them stood in the unrelenting sun in well-tailored, dark, lightweight suits and wore dark sunglasses. The remaining four wore the more traditional long white thawb and keffiyeh head covering and remained in the shade of the terminal canopy. Aziz motioned to Hamzah to wait near the jet and proceeded forward to speak to the two men in the dark suits. Both men inclined their heads briefly toward Aziz and listened intently. After a few minutes, Aziz beckoned Hamzah forward.

"Yes, Sayyid?" Hamzah inquired.

Gesturing to the men, Aziz explained, "These are my assistants, M'an and Saqr. Saqr will help you get through customs and immigration and then drive you to the southern terminal to a jet I intend to purchase. I need you to assess the aircraft, check the flight logs, and make note of anything you feel is deficient. I do not wish to pay for shoddy goods."

"I will be happy to, Sayyid. Let me get my bags from the plane."

"No need. Saqr will get them for you."

Aziz looked at Saqr and nodded his head in the direction of the G550. Saqr immediately walked over and headed up the stairs.

"I did not know you had assistants, Sayyid."

Aziz smiled. "I have assistants in many parts of the world, my friend.

Up until now, I have not had a need to have them close to me. Recent business events have necessitated a change."

"Is that why you are buying the new aircraft?" Hamzah asked. "Does it have better midair communications than this one?"

Aziz's smile did not change, but if Hamzah had looked closely, he would have seen his eyes harden a little.

"Among other reasons, yes. Ah, Saqr has your bags."

Turning, Hamzah saw that Saqr had descended the steps of the G550 carrying his black flight case with his air charts, logbooks, and manual navigation tools, as well as his two-suit garment bag. Passing Hamzah, Saqr led the way into the Hajj Terminal. Hamzah threw his copilot a wave, which he saw returned through the G550's cockpit window, and then followed Saqr under the broad canopies into the terminal.

Saqr obviously knew where he was going, and his employer's wealth apparently greased the wheels at customs and immigration. His bags were not inspected, and the Saudi customs official gave his Saudi passport only a brief look before stamping it and waving him on his way.

Exiting the terminal, Hamzah was not too surprised to see a car and driver waiting. The driver opened the trunk for Saqr to deposit the bags and then held the rear door open for him. Hamzah settled himself in the backseat, the air conditioning blowing cool air into his face. Saqr and the driver exchanged a few words that were muffled by the air conditioning before they both got in and sat in the front, as was proper. After all, they were only assistants, and Hamzah was Aziz's personal pilot.

The driver put the car in gear and pulled away from the curb, passing a few Saudi National Guardsmen on foot patrol as they headed north away from the main terminal.

"Why are we heading north?" Hamzah asked the driver. "Aziz said the plane I was to look at is at the south terminal."

The driver glanced into his rearview mirror to make eye contact with Hamzah.

"Do not be concerned. The Hajj Terminal roads do not connect directly with the south terminal. We must loop around the Hajj Terminal, and then we can head south."

"I see. *Shokran*."

"Think nothing of it."

Saqr spoke up next, "Aziz tells me you were called 'Lion' in the Air Force."

"Yes. My name means Lion and my fellow pilots chose that as my call sign after I completed initial training, may Allah bless them."

"Now I understand."

"Understand what?"

"Why he said I should tell you, 'Even the strongest Lion starves when he cannot make a kill.'"

Hamzah belatedly understood the depth of his former employer's viciousness as he saw Saqr raise the unusually long muzzle of a silenced H&K P2000 SK pistol up over the edge of the front seat in one smooth motion. Two quick, muffled shots later, Hamzah was able to speak to Allah more directly.

"AH, I SEE SAQR HAS returned," Aziz said, seeing his other bodyguard walking through the terminal. "I told you his errand would not take long."

While he waited, Aziz had been chatting amiably with the four other men in the shade of the Hajj Terminal, while M'an stood at his shoulder, alternately watching the four men and the people passing by in the terminal. The four men managed business interests for Aziz in Jeddah, and it would have been very impolite for them not to welcome Aziz after he had arrived.

Aziz addressed the four men again, dismissing them, "*Shokran,* my friends. It was very kind of you to meet me before I begin the Umrah. I will see you all again soon."

Walking back toward his G550, with Saqr and M'an in tow, he waved to the copilot to join them on the tarmac. The copilot hurriedly left the jet and stood warily before Aziz, having a much better sense of the man he was than Hamzah had.

Aziz looked at him carefully. "Zaki, you have flown as copilot for many years. Today is the day Allah has willed you to be promoted."

"Promoted, Sayyid?" A puzzled look crossed Zaki's face.

"Yes, promoted," Aziz smiled. "Hamzah has decided to retire from my service and he has been given a just reward for the quality of his skill. I have chosen you to succeed him."

Zaki was stunned by this because Hamzah had said nothing to him about it, and then he realized Aziz was looking at him expectantly. He quickly decided to save his speculation and curiosity for another time and put his thoughts on the present.

"Thank you, Sayyid. You are most generous. But who will fly with me as copilot? The aircraft is not certified to be flown with only one pilot."

"That is your first job as my new chief pilot. I will be spending a few days on the Umrah, so you will have time to identify candidates. Until you choose a competent one, I will trust you to fly me anywhere, no matter what the certifications may require. Am I understood?"

The menace in the question was certainly apparent to Zaki. Pick a good copilot, and until you do, fly me where I tell you to whether you have someone in the second seat or not.

"Yes, Sayyid. It shall be as you wish, Sayyid."

"Good. Naturally, your salary will increase with your responsibilities. I will leave you to them."

Aziz turned on his heel and strode back toward the terminal, Saqr hurrying ahead a little, anticipating his next destination, with M'an keeping pace on his left side. Reaching into his thawb, Aziz grasped his special cell phone and slid his finger across the screen to unlock it. Dialing the number from memory, he waited as the call went through and the ringing began.

"Yes?" The voice spoke English with a Pakistani accent that Aziz knew from his time in Peshawar, a believer in his old mentor's cause who was trusted with sensitive transportation needs.

"How are things going?"

"As expected. We are about two days away from our destination. If everything goes well with the people we hired, then we should pick them up when we arrive and leave shortly thereafter. The weather seems favorable."

"You are prepared to pay them as we discussed?" inquired Aziz.

"Absolutely. They will be paid in full, as we discussed."

"Excellent. I will be out of communication for a few days. If anything goes wrong, leave me a voicemail at this number and I will make other arrangements."

"I hope that will not be necessary, but it shall be as Allah wills."

Aziz smiled. "Yes, it shall," he replied and broke the connection. Save for one more thing, he could clear his mind of other concerns and prepare for the Umrah.

REPIN THOUGHT THAT FALL IN the Mid-Atlantic was very pleasant. The late autumn sunshine filtering through the branches of leafless trees, the crunch of dried multicolored leaves under foot, the sound of the wind moving through the evergreens, and brisk, cold air in his face—what could be better?

It was not completely like fall in Novosibirsk where he grew up—there was usually snow on the ground this late in the year there—but it would have to do. He had parked his rented sedan in the park's paved lot about thirty minutes ago, donned his pack, locked the car, and started hiking the well-marked trail east. He had followed the red blazes on the trees since he left the car behind, and as long as he'd chosen the correct trail from the painted map of the state park, he would be there after another ten minutes of hiking.

Before flying out he had looked at the overhead imagery of his targets on Google Earth as the first stage of this reconnaissance trip. He took a commercial flight from his new home city to Columbus, Ohio, and then a small twin-engine plane to the municipal airport in West Virginia. Landing there necessitated a long road trip in the rental car from the municipal airport in West Virginia, but that was preferable. The airports in the mid-Atlantic states were running at severely reduced passenger capacities, and he did not want to risk any additional scrutiny from the Transportation Security Agency screeners with less than their normal workload to occupy them.

The imagery had shown him the overall view, but he still wanted some handheld imagery and firsthand observations to complete the final intelligence package for the assault teams he would send against these targets. Besides, it had given him a chance to drive past the nearby plant's main entrance a few times to assess the perimeter security. The plant was the first of the three targets he was interested in on this trip.

The uniformed guard force and the cameras at the main entrance were the most visible security presence, but the barrier on the roadway was a simple steel-pole design, and no concrete "flowerpots" or other vehicle barriers had been erected beyond the perimeter fence.

Given the direction he wanted the assault force to penetrate the plant from, the guards and cameras wouldn't be a problem, but he'd needed a good idea of the level of security the assault group would be dealing with. The guards certainly wore their uniforms well, which spoke of their professionalism, or at least of the receipt of decent paychecks, but they carried no shoulder arms like rifles or shotguns, just revolvers in holsters.

Taking a small risk, Repin had pulled to the side of the road across from the plant entry road and pretended to check his tire pressure while watching the entry point. He was fortunate enough to witness a vehicle approach it while he was playacting a search of his trunk for a pressure gauge. The on-duty guard had actually propped open the door to the guardpost and approached the car without a hand on his holstered sidearm. The guards were obviously in a more relaxed routine, at least during daylight hours, in spite of recent events. They would pay for that casualness in a few days.

The sounds of children ahead brought his thoughts back to the present.

"Catch me, catch me!"

"I can, I can!"

The two boys—he assumed they were brothers judging from their similar features—were probably about four and five, both dressed in jeans and warm winter jackets. The older brother was running away from his younger brother right down the trail toward Repin. The older boy was looking over his shoulder to be sure his brother couldn't catch him, oblivious to the nearly six-foot-tall man right in front of him.

"Watch out, son!" Repin called in a friendly tone, affecting a midwestern accent, and amused to see the boy pull up short in surprise as he turned back to the trail in front of him.

"Oh! Sorry," the boy said sheepishly.

Repin was about to tell him it was all right when his younger brother practically tackled him from behind.

"I caught you!" the younger boy cried.

"No fair, I stopped!"

Repin noticed a woman in her early thirties hurrying up the trail in the boys' wake and knew this was a situation best left to their mother to referee. He stepped around the two boys, who were now accusing each other of cheating in increasingly loud voices.

As he passed her, she said, "Sorry about that."

Repin smiled and replied, "No problem. Good luck keeping up with them."

She smiled in return as she started to jog past him, calling over her shoulder, "Better this than having them cooped up in a cold house with no electricity!"

Repin could still hear the woman trying to distract the boys, and the older boy still claiming his brother had cheated, when he reached the small strip of beach at the end of the trail.

The stiff wind off the water of the Chesapeake Bay was cold, roiling the water into white crested waves before blowing toward shore and cutting into Repin. Two powerboats and a sailboat were on the bay in spite of the chill, and Repin watched them move across the bay. After a few minutes of tolerating the cold air, mainly to assuage his male ego, he zipped his heavy coat up and donned his gloves.

Before he got to work, he took a moment to enjoy the view. In spite of the cold wind, the bright blue sky and the white wave tops stretching east out into the infinity of the bay was beautiful. After a few minutes, it was time for the trained intelligence officer to take over.

The sounds of the two boys and their mother had faded down the trail, and he looked back toward the trailhead briefly to make sure no one else was heading toward the beach. He was alone for now, so he had to work quickly.

Repin examined the beach first. The pale brown sand was well compacted by the tidal flows, and he walked the length of the relatively short beach area, looking at the sand. The only footprints he saw were the smaller ones of the two boys and a larger pair he assumed were their mother's. That was good, and about what he expected. It was too cold at this time of year for this isolated piece of beach to attract too much attention, and because the park closed at sundown according to the sign at the entryway, it should be empty during the expected time frame of the operation.

Three-story-tall crumbling cliffs of clay, topped by small stands of thick trees, reached out from the land at each end of the fifty-meter stretch of beach. There were signs at both ends of the beach warning that the cliffs were not to be climbed. The evidence of multiple collapses was plain to see, and anyone who ignored the posted warnings and tried to climb them deserved to die in the resulting avalanche. Repin judged that the cliffs would provide good line-of-sight blockage to the north and south, and they would limit any approach to the beach to either the park trail he'd just come down or the waters of the bay.

Taking the pack off his back, he set it down on the packed sand above the current tide line and took a few sips of water from the integrated CamelBak water bladder's plastic tube, then pulled the expensive digital SLR camera from the pack. The target he came to see was more than a mile away from him, and he attached a 70–300mm zoom lens to compensate.

Checking that the settings on the camera were correct, he turned it on and began shooting. For the benefit of anyone who might be watching from the boats or the target, he started taking pictures of pleasure boats and ships on the bay, and then the target.

The target was more than 400 meters long and nearly 100 meters high, standing nearly a quarter mile offshore, so he photographed it in segments at maximum magnification and then took some overall pictures at the lowest magnification. When he was done four minutes later, he had taken more than 200 pictures in total, bookending the photos of the target with pictures of the boats and ships on the bay.

Three minutes later, the camera was in the backpack on his back, a blank digital memory card in it, and the memory card with the target images rested in a protective plastic case in his jeans pocket. Taking one last look at the bay, Repin turned and hiked back into woods on the trail he had come down on, back to the parking lot.

DARKNESS HAD FALLEN NEARLY TWO hours ago, the light as always vanishing from the sky quickly behind the rocky hills and dormant volcanoes surrounding the city of Petropavlovsk-Kamchatsky. The major population center of the Kamchatsky Peninsula in the Russian Far East, it was home to more than 180,000 people of Russian and Ukrainian descent. Most of the population worked serving the port, the Russian naval base on Avacha Bay, or the tourists who came to explore the volcanic ranges on foot or who traveled via ATV to hunt elk and bear or to fish.

Sergey Prebin looked out over the bay, breathing in the damp chill deeply and then slowly exhaling into the slight breeze that caressed his pale skin and moved through his thinning silver hair. The temperature would dip below freezing tonight as was usual in the fall, and the cold, clear air did not bode well for the plans he and his five friends had made. Nearly ten miles away, the faint lights of the once-secret base of the Russian Far East Fleet glimmered, outshone in the darkness by the much closer lights of the city shining in a circle around the shore.

The tourists hunting bear were mostly gone now or asleep in the hotels that in Western Europe would be considered no better than two-star establishments. But out here they were the best available, commanding 200 euros a night. Prebin's gray eyes shifted toward the port. He could see the ship from the doorway of the small warehouse nestled against the pier.

A sharp noise from behind him made Prebin look back into the warehouse. Two of his fellows had dropped one of the larger cases. Prebin almost walked back in to investigate, but his colleagues, all senior academicians from Khabarovsk's Lenin Institute, would certainly manage without his help. Each man had, at the very least, a graduate degree in his common field, and most had held doctorates for several years and split their time between lecturing classes and conducting research. As the Lomonosov chair of the department, he knew them very well. In fact, Prebin had handpicked each man for this effort, knowing that each shared his views and understood that while some lives might be lost in the next day or two, the benefit to humanity would be worth it. In any case, the State he grew up in did not teach him to believe in God, only the Party. That lie was exposed when the Berlin Wall finally fell, but he still did not choose to believe in a god.

Prebin believed in science, and the science told him that what was going on was wrong, no matter the government propaganda, and it had to be stopped. He had spoken out in public rallies, lobbied the local and national government, and written opinion pieces and given interviews to what seemed like every news outlet at every opportunity. He stopped giving interviews when the two men in the dark suits came to his small office one morning. They explained, in some detail, how his academic career would be ending in the near future, and then how his body would be found in his small apartment a few days after his very public firing, forgotten, not even a footnote in the science texts he had found the truth in. In the new Russia, they said that the KGB, now known as the SVR, was no longer something to fear. They were wrong.

A few months later, he had taken a trip to Ottawa to attend the annual worldwide conference, where a man whose Russian accent spoke of the Baltic coast approached him at one of the evening cocktail parties. Initially, Prebin was afraid the SVR had followed him to Canada to kill him. Instead, it was a man named Repin who told him that his employer, a very wealthy man, was concerned about the same danger Prebin was. The wealthy, unnamed man was also willing to help Prebin show the world that danger in a way that would leave no doubts in the minds of the politicians. He would even ensure Prebin and his friends escaped Russia in the process.

It had taken some time to arrange, but the day had finally come. Prebin and his colleagues had "borrowed" some of the equipment they would need and had come to the warehouse to load the trucks for the trip to the ship.

The sound of footsteps behind him broke into his thoughts.

"Comrade Akademician Prebin."

"*Da.*" He had to look up slightly into the face of his younger colleague. He envied the fifty-year-old with his fuller head of hair.

"We are ready. Everything is loaded."

"Excellent, Arkady. Let us go and meet our new friends."

Both men walked toward the two medium-duty Ural trucks and clambered aboard. The Ural's engines coughed to life after a couple of failed attempts, and they drove out of the warehouse toward the brightly lit port of Petropavlovsk.

TOM WITHER
served his country for more than 25 years as a member of the Air
Force's Intelligence, Surveillance, and Reconnaissance Agency and its
predecessor organizations. He served on active duty as an intelligence
analyst at various overseas locations and is a veteran of the Persian Gulf
War. He has been awarded the Meritorious Service Medal, three Air
Force Commendation Medals, and three Air Force Achievement
Medals. In addition to his graduate-level IT/Computer Security
education, Tom holds professional certifications from the NSA as an
Intelligence Analyst, and the Director of National Intelligence as an
Intelligence Community Officer. He lives near Baltimore.